Praise fo

'*Send Flowers* is so much ~~~~~~~~~~
concept: a climate activist's ~~dead bo~~~~
houseplant. Equal parts funny and furious, it's a book that blooms
as you read it' – **Bobby Palmer, author of *Isaac and the Egg***

'A prescient love letter to activism and the natural world that
serves as a timely call to arms for people and planet'
– **Henry Fry, author of *First Time for Everything***

'Original and aching with feeling, *Send Flowers* is the prescient
story of a lapsed, grieving activist, who must fall back in love with
her mission, her values and with herself. Buchanan has made a
powerful contribution to the new body of climate fiction, both
illuminating the curse of caring too much and warning us of
the dire consequences of caring too little. A novel for our times'
– **Seth Insua, author of *Human, Animal***

'A warm, witty take on grief – both for lost loved ones and for
our ailing planet – *Send Flowers* captures the beauty of found
family, the power of community and the challenge of finding, and
embracing, our true purpose in life. Buchanan's spirited message
will renew your appreciation for nature and leave your inner
activist inspired' – **Mikki Brammer, author of**
The Collected Regrets of Clover

'Radical, hopeful stories are exactly what the world needs right
now and through her characters, Buchanan gets to the heart of
what drives activism now and throughout history: the simple hope
that a better world is possible' – **Will McCallum,**
Executive Director, Greenpeace UK

SEND FLOWERS

EMILY BUCHANAN

VERVE BOOKS

First published in the UK in 2025
by VERVE Books Ltd., Harpenden, UK

vervebooks.co.uk
@VERVE_Books

Excerpt from *The Optimism of Uncertainty* by Howard Zinn, from *A Power Governments Cannot Suppress* (City Lights Books, 2006), reproduced with permission of Roam Agency. www.roamagency.com

A CIP catalogue record for this book is available from the British Library.

This is a work of fiction. Names, characters, places, and incidents either are the product of the author's imagination or are used fictitiously, and any resemblance to actual persons, living or dead, businesses, companies, events or locales is entirely coincidental.

ISBN
978-0-85730-893-1 (Paperback)
978-0-85730-894-8 (eBook)

2 4 6 8 10 9 7 5 3 1

Typeset in 11.15 on 13.4pt Adobe Garamond Pro
by Avocet Typeset, Bideford, Devon, EX39 2BP
Printed and bound in Great Britain by Clays Ltd, Elcograf S.p.A.

The manufacturer's authorised representative in the EU for product safety is Easy Access System Europe, Mustamäe tee 50, 10621 Tallinn, Estonia
gpsr.requests@easproject.com

'The future is an infinite succession of presents, and to live now as we think human beings should live, in defiance of all that is bad around us, is itself a marvelous victory'

Howard Zinn

1

The sound of the tinfoil peeling off the window reminds me of rainfall. If I had the wherewithal to enjoy irony, I might muster a smile. I scrunch the foil into a ball and sink my nails in. There is warmth trapped in the metal. I open the window. A wall of hot air stings my eyes. I stagger back and cover my face with my hands, peeking through my fingers. There is a dazzling mirage on the other side of the street, a kind of metallic patchwork quilt. But it's not a quilt. It's a block of flats. Every window is foiled over like mine, rectangular strips of silver kicking heat between the high-rises.

From the kitchen window of my fourth-floor flat, I can see up and down Stamford Hill. The street is quiet. I check for horses, my heart in my throat. There are none. I don't know what I was expecting. Some kind of disorder, something to qualify the horrors I've just seen on my phone. Normally I scroll away before the video has a chance to auto-play, but today I couldn't resist the promise of despair. It was a livestream of protesters gathered outside the gates to Number 10. They were from a new group, one that promises to stop climate change 'by any means necessary' and consists of a bunch of bright young things in matching T-shirts. But the bright young things barely had a chance to unfurl their *ACT OR DIE* banner before the police brought out the pepper spray. In the scrabble to escape, the person filming fell over. That's when I saw hooves. That's when I heard horses. They were charging. They were charging right outside my window.

Only, they weren't.

I listen again. Given the abandoned streets, the sound might have travelled north of the river. But all I can hear now is the distant whirr of a helicopter and the pulse of the heat on the concrete below. I look at Egg Stores Ltd., a kosher supermarket nearby. It shoulders three stories of tinfoil-clad flats and features a dated shop sign. A piece of paper has been stuck to the front door with a handwritten message: *Closed Until Further Notice.*

The quiet is almost as harrowing as the state violence I've just witnessed. Without traffic, the city feels unfinished. I inhale deeply, hoping for a hint of freshness in the absence of exhaust fumes, but melted tarmac and raw sewage replies. I crane my neck towards Abney Park, searching instead for the reassurance of trees. They are trapped in a state that Ed called *false autumn*, their leaves brown and crisp like the singed edges of a tea-stained pirate map. It is August. He would be horrified.

I go to shut the window, craving a return to darkness. Then I see something that makes me hesitate. There's a man on the other side of the street pushing a wheelbarrow uphill. His white face is boiled red. From up here, I can see the sweat blooming in dark patches across his T-shirt and dripping on the pavement in his wake. The wheelbarrow is full of bottled water. I draw my lips inside my mouth as my heart flutters against my rib cage. I know it's only a matter of time before restrictions, but the sight of this man struggling to preserve his access to water is jarring.

Boil your tea, cup by cup, to keep the water level up!

That's the slogan the government has been reciting like a nursery rhyme. They're blaming *tea*. Of course they are. It's the British proclivity for a cuppa that's causing water shortages, not the acres of pristine golf courses which remain miraculously green despite every other scrap of grass in the country being baked to a crisp. Injustice flares in my gut, then recedes like a poorly lit match. If I still believed it would make a difference, I might start a petition. Something that would reach right into the heart of middle England – Ban Golf Course Sprinklers, Not Our British Brew! Then I'd go to bed knowing that I'd *done something*. Because *doing something* made me a good person and being good made life under late-stage capitalism bearable. Because what else is there aside from the knowledge that I am morally superior to everyone else?

At least I've stopped doing anything, good, bad or otherwise. At least I know that nothing I do – nothing I did or ever will do – is, or ever was, or ever will be enough. I'll leave those baby activists, those bright young things, to figure that one out for themselves.

I close the window and reach for the tape, casting a quick glance at the flat in daylight. I guess I can add our home to the list of things that would horrify Ed. I tape down a new strip of tinfoil and smooth out the creases. With the room in shadow, my heartbeat finally slows. I go into the kitchen to wash my face at the sink. The blue dot on the faucet should be changed to yellow because the water is lukewarm at best. I open the freezer and take out a tray of ice cubes and a stack of frozen flannels. My brief foray out the window has left me feeling dizzy. I can't risk heatstroke, not when I live alone. I begin a familiar routine, angling the standing fan at my spot on the living room floor and taking off my clothes. I lie down on a towel. With a cushion wedged underneath my head, I put the frozen flannels over my naked body and dot ice cubes on top like glacier cherries. I close my eyes. Only then, when the fan hits the ice and cools my skin, does my body release the tension it's been holding all morning.

Pepper spray is a chemical weapon that's banned in warfare!

The sound bite erases my slither of peace. I shake my head to rid myself of the reflex to *do something*, even if that something is just composing a pithy caption. I see flashes of bloodshot eyes pleading with me to *act*.

I stare at the ceiling. *Just focus on the coolness of the flannels, Fifi. Picture a mountaintop. A walk-in freezer. A snowstorm.*

But swollen, weeping, red eyes refuse to let me be. A flash of guilt makes me sit up, the hammering of hooves threatening to return. The flannels flop off my pale breasts like warm slices of ham. Bruce starts licking melted water off my shin, and the sensation startles me. I look at him for the first time in ages. He seems a little worse for wear. He's thirsty. Everything evaporates so quickly now. It's why all the houseplants died. That and the lack of natural light – it turns out not everything is suited to life in the dark.

I fill a saucepan with water and put it on the floor. Bruce drinks for a long time. He usually only drinks from the tap. It's one of his quirks. It's one of the things Ed loved most about him.

'Fi, quick, come look!' he'd shout from the kitchen, where I'd find Ed filming the eight-hundredth video of Bruce crouched over the sink, lapping up running water with his little pink tongue. I used to call the tap Bruce's girlfriend. Ed would scold me for assuming the cat was straight, and then we'd laugh and prance around the kitchen and be so utterly delighted with ourselves.

How can something as innocuous as a tap remind me of him?

But it's not just the tap. It's the mug. The one that stores the last few sips of his final coffee, the bacteria from his mouth. It's the bedsheet. The one he carefully folded and tucked away in the cupboard. It's the poster. The one he blue-tacked to the front door to remind me to bring a linen bag to the shop. It's the earbuds. The ones in the case on his bedside table that he needed to fall asleep. It's the plants. All two hundred of them. It's the remorse, it's the heartache, it's the god-awful heat – things which have merged and multiplied like the mould in the bottom of that coffee cup, sending their spores up all around me until the only thing I know how to do is count the days I've been without him.

Ninety today.

The big 9-0.

That's almost as long as we've been without rain. I have my suspicions that the two are related. It was Ed, after all, who founded the group that inspired those baby activists to get pepper-sprayed in the face. With him gone, I think the earth has given up the ghost.

Just then, my phone vibrates. I stifle a scream. Prolonged isolation turns phone calls into fire alarms. I check the screen to see that it's Travis. I put the phone facedown on the floor. He's been trying to get hold of me for days. He wants to talk about my *obligations*, about my *contractually binding commitments*, my *highly paid, much-sought-after job* as a professional content farm. I can't face him. Ed hated Travis. He called him the leader of the 'ring light mafia' and blamed him and his 'ilk' for monetising narcissism. I clench my jaw and consider switching off my phone. Then the doorbell rings. A wave of panic careers up from my guts and reaches the very tips of my teeth. It's not like Travis to want to talk in person. Even phone calls are a stretch.

It rings again. I put my hands over my ears and groan. I associate that sound with journalists now. Hordes of them used to linger on the street outside, desperate for an interview or a money shot of me looking deranged. After months of stubborn reclusiveness, they gave up, but I still get their badgering emails.

What if it's the police? I think with an audible whimper. My followers have been rallying for a so-called wellness check since the funeral. Little do they know that I'm more likely to open the door for a convicted criminal than I am law enforcement. I try to ignore it, but the buzzing grows frantic – repetitive short bursts of sound followed by long, drawn-out trills as the intruder holds their finger down on the buzzer. Whoever it is, I have to get rid of them, even if that means going down four flights of stairs.

'Leave me alone,' I croak through the letter box, pulling the drawstring of Ed's dressing gown around my waist and clearing my throat.

'Hello, Fiona,' a familiar voice says. I open the door a crack. The sun bleaches my eyes, and it takes a second to focus. I smell her cheap pharmacy perfume before I see her.

'Mum?'

'I've called. I've texted. I've emailed. And nothing!'

'You drove down without telling me?'

'I *tried*, Fiona. What do you expect me to do?' Tracy raises her voice, apparently prepared to fight in the street. Normally, this pantomime of public emotion would concern me – an online frenzy is only ever a phone-wielding troll away – but with London in hiding, she can rave on all she likes. She's not coming in.

'I'm busy.' I widen the crack in the door to show her my assertive body language. 'You'll have to come back another day. Sorry.'

'I haven't driven all the way from Scotland to stand on the

doorstep. I'm coming in.' She puts her foot through the door and pushes against it with her knee. I stagger back. She makes a celebratory *hmph* sound, pleased to have won our first battle of the day. I try to block her from climbing the stairs, my hands on my hips in the hallway, but she uses her handbag like a riot shield to force me back. My dressing gown falls open and, in the second it takes to cover myself, she charges past me. I run up the first flight of stairs after her, but the heat drags me down like a riptide. By the time I reach the summit of the fourth floor, I am wheezing and sweating just as profusely as Wheelbarrow Man. I find Tracy standing at the open door of my flat with the top light on.

'Oh my god, Fiona. What have you done?'

'You can't just barge in,' I say, switching off the light and ignoring the question.

'It's been three months. Look at you. You're a *stick*!' She flings a disapproving hand in my direction. 'Your father and I have been beside ourselves with worry.'

'Stepfather,' I correct her, choosing to ignore her assessment of my body.

'That's hardly the point. This is disgraceful.' Tracy bats away imaginary flies and switches the light back on. I move to switch it off.

'Don't you dare,' she says through gritted teeth, jabbing her index finger in my face. Her acrylic fingernails are painted a shade of neon green that was fashionable five years ago. I grit my teeth right back and consider flicking the switch. I am a thirty-two-year-old woman. This is my home. She has no right to just show up and start calling the shots like it's 1994. But I drop my shoulders and step aside, lacking any means to stop her.

As Tracy stands there with her mouth agog, I notice that she's had lip fillers done since the funeral. With her glossy new pout, blond blow-dry and slight sneer, she looks like a discount Jennifer Coolidge. I can't help but roll my eyes. She turns into the kitchen, countering my disapproval with a gasp. It's been a while since I took out the bin or did the dishes or emptied Bruce's litter tray.

'Ed did a lot of the cleaning,' I say in a feeble attempt at self-defence.

'That's not good enough,' she replies, returning to the living room. Her trademark dangly cat earrings swing against her neck with every jerk of the head, her quest for youth extending to girlish accessories. 'Oh, Fiona. He'd be gutted to see what you've done to the plants.'

The scrutiny of the top light exposes the decay. Our flat used to rival the Palm House at Kew Gardens. Now it's like a botanical catacomb, with dead plants wilting from every surface and smothering the furniture in a blanket of leaves. It might have a Miss Havisham-esque charm, if it weren't for the heaps of dirty clothes, half-eaten takeaways and assortment of anonymous junk. I sink my teeth into my bottom lip and take a laboured breath, desperate to switch off the light. Tracy's hands are pinned to her forehead, her eyes bulging.

I did try. At first, my days revolved around plant care. I'd run back and forth with the watering can, I'd fertilise, I'd deadhead. I'd do everything we used to do together. But grief was an invasive species that took root in my heart. It curled around each organ, sent tendrils up my throat and crawled out of my mouth. After that, I was powerless to stop it. Grief pried open the brickwork. It got inside the plug sockets. It choked the entire building of light. When it came for the plants, I just lay on the floor and watched.

'It's boiling in here,' Tracy hisses, every bit the drama queen of my childhood. 'It's like a compost heap in *hell*!' She wipes her hand across a shelf that used to display Ed's collection of orchids. Dried petals cascade to the floor like wedding confetti. 'Now I see why you've gone quiet on social media.'

'That's not why,' I say, averting my eyes.

'You can hardly call yourself a houseplant *guru* if you've killed the whole lot, can you?' She spits the word *guru* like it repulses her.

'*I can't do it without him!*' I snap back, the words turning to ashes in my mouth. My eyes prickle with tears, and my chin crumbles. Despair ricochets between my heart and my brain, making both vibrate.

Plants were our love language. Plants were how we found our feet in the city, how we built our home, and then – quite by accident –

how I built a name for myself. When we moved from Edinburgh to London, the city felt so dystopian, like the ever-imposing skyline was a promise of bad things to come. So we sought out green spaces. First there was Irie's garden, East Peace, where we started RIOT 1.5. Then there was Kew Gardens, where we turned our backs on the city and roamed hothouse jungles. Then there was Columbia Road, where we bought calatheas and fig trees and maidenhair ferns, and Ed told me that he finally felt like a Londoner because people there knew his name. Before long, our flat was a pocket paradise, and I was sharing it with the world. *That's* when people started calling me a *guru*. It was never a self-appointed title.

'Well, that's your job down the drain, then,' she says. If this is Tracy's idea of being cruel to be kind, she's only getting one part right. She continues her health inspection, touching a spiky plant that looks like a crayon drawing of floppy blond hair. It's impossible to tell most of them apart now. I can identify the Columbia Road fig tree, the cheese plant and the banana palm, but the rest look like mulch and smell like the bottom of a compost bin.

'How can you live like this?' she mutters, her voice dripping with judgement.

'I... I don't know,' I admit, mortified by the question. What am I supposed to say? Ed held my seams together. He, with his meticulous attention to detail and enormous convictions, balanced out the scattier parts of me. The selfish parts, too, like the parts that forget to fill Bruce's water bowl and kill houseplants and ignore pepper-spray atrocities because I'm yet to figure out if misery and integrity can coexist. But Tracy wouldn't understand that. How could she? How could anyone?

'Have you been to the garden?' Tracy asks. 'Have you seen that lady, Irene?'

'Irie,' I correct her.

Saying Irie's name makes me feel sick. Somewhere among the gloom of this blighted place, there are packets of runner beans and poppy seeds and leaflets about RIOT 1.5 – tokens to the gardening community we found at East Peace, to the movement we built there.

'And no,' I say forcefully, shaking my head. 'It's too soon.'

'Busy burning bridges, I see.'

It is a statement, not a question: a statement that I will take to the mental graveyard where I abandon the things that bring me shame. I shrug, unable to justify any of it. Then, as if to dial up the heat on my mortification, Bruce comes out of hiding.

'There you are,' Tracy says, bending down to pick him up. Her neon claws curl around his belly. She gasps again, sounding like a wheezing set of bagpipes. 'He's skin and bones!'

'He's not interested in food,' I explain. 'He misses Ed.'

'Nonsense,' she says, running her hands over his grey fur. 'Why haven't you been brushing him? He's matted.'

It's true. He's not just a little worse for wear – he's a lot. His long fur is dishevelled, his sparkling green eyes downturned and dull. But looking at Bruce turns my already-shredded heart into a pulled muscle. He's a constant reminder of what life was like before – rich with possibility. It's easier to look away.

'I don't know what to say,' I whisper, scrunching my eyes shut. The tears that have been threatening to undo me since she got here break free and tumble down my cheeks. 'I've been struggling.'

'I can see that.' Tracy cradles Bruce like a baby – like a naked, abandoned newborn she's found on the doorstep of a church, his tail the severed umbilical cord. 'But this is neglect.' She takes a step away from me, her cat-saviour complex kicking into gear. Growing up, she worked for Cats Protection and spent more time fostering abandoned pets than she did helping me with homework. When her collection of crusty-eyed cats turned into a veritable colony, Dad had tried putting his foot down, insisting we only take in one at a time. But that didn't stop her. By the time I left home, by the time *he* did, there were at least five felines making a scratching post of the sofa. It's one of the few contradictions I enjoy about Tracy. She's a woman dedicated to glamour, and yet the scragglier the cat, the better.

'Don't be ridic–'

'This is neglect!' she interjects. 'I, of all people, know it when I see it.'

I tut loudly, keen to expose the melodrama. This is Tracy all over. When we first got Bruce, I thought she'd be happy for us. I thought we'd bond over it. Instead, she commented an eye-roll emoji on my first post about him and shared an *Adopt, Don't Shop* infographic with her one hundred and twenty seven followers. She, the great cat whisperer of rural shitholes everywhere, has been chomping at the bit to spoil things with Bruce since day one. I reach for him, determined now to get rid of her, but he sinks his claws into her top.

'He's terrified of you. What have you been doing to him?'

'Nothing! He's got a whole bowl of water. Look.' I point to the freshly filled saucepan on the floor and reroute more shame to the graveyard.

'Where's his carrier?' Tracy barks.

'Why?'

'I'm taking him with me.'

'No, you're not!' I try to pull Bruce away, to hold him close, to prove that I'll do whatever it takes to make amends – but he flips his body upside down and leaps forward, wrapping his claws around Tracy's neck.

'His carrier!' Tracy yelps, lifting a hand to her scratched up collarbone.

'You can't *take my cat*, Mum,' I say, squaring up to her, but my voice cracks down the middle, and my willpower is lost to full-blown sobs.

'It's not fair to keep a cat in this mess. I won't allow it, not after everything I've been through,' she says without a hint of self-awareness. 'You can have him back when you're better.'

'I'm not sick,' I splutter.

'Then prove it. Get a grip, Fiona. I know you're hurting, but you can't take it out on a defenceless animal. Now, if you're not going to offer me a cup of tea, I'll go. I don't want to stay in this city any longer than I have to. It's a whole *ten degrees* hotter here than in Strathyre. I don't know how you do it.' She eyes the wet towel on the floor and the moist flannels, then the tinfoil on the windows. 'Shutting yourself away like this isn't doing anyone any good, either.'

'Please don't take him, Mum,' I whimper, tears dripping off my chin as I hand the carrier over. 'He's all I've got left.'

'One day you'll thank me,' Tracy says, coaxing Bruce inside and locking it. Then she puts her hands on my shoulders – her version of a hug – and purses her mouth. Up close, I can see that her lips are slick with gloss and dotted with pinprick bruises. I blink away the tears to get a closer look.

'Did you get that done today?'

'Yes. This morning.' She covers her mouth with her hand, as if she hasn't been desperate for me to acknowledge it since her arrival.

'In London?'

'Yes, with my usual clinician on Harley Street. I don't trust anyone else.' She gathers her things, picks up Bruce's carrier and heads for the door.

'So you *didn't* come down to see me?'

'Two birds, one stone, darling.' She laughs, her bleached teeth like white war memorials. I see Bruce's green eyes through the grid, his grey fluff poking out the side, his unhappy, swinging tail.

I don't know how to say goodbye. So I don't.

2

In the video, my hair is loosely pinned with paintbrushes and falls in spirals around my face. When I wore it down, people said I looked like Lorde circa 'Royals,' but I was going for a young Helena Bonham Carter meets season one Phoebe Buffay. I wore striped tights, vintage dresses and an excessive amount of silver jewellery, creating an eclectic aesthetic that I deemed entirely unique.

But it was a long time ago. Now, I squat half-naked and sweaty and swallow tepid white wine as the video loads. I've scrolled to the bottom of RIOT 1.5's account, to one of our earliest posts. In it, the rosy idealism of youth sparkles in my eyes, and I am reminded of all those bright young things outside Number 10. Except back then, we could make our voices heard without the threat of police brutality. I'm wearing silver-framed full-moon glasses perched on a greasy button nose, and my cheeks are flush with pencilled-on freckles.

We're in Irie's conservatory at East Peace – a greenhouse turned events space that she offered to the community in exchange for gardening volunteers. The conservatory was host to friendship circles, needle-felting workshops and pumpkin-carving classes, but Ed's climate group was the first of its kind there. The video was shot in the winter, when the handful of people who showed up were dwarfed by Irie's collection of dormant geraniums. Come summer, we'd turned that half a dozen into fifty and spilled out onto the grass where we tried in earnest to be the change we wanted to see in the world. But for now, there were six of us. The camera pans around a well-worn farmhouse table.

'Tell us what's happening, Ed,' the person behind the camera says.

'We're making placards for the climate march,' Ed replies moderately, casting his arm over an array of flattened cardboard boxes and paint pots. He's clean-shaven and looks like an NPC. This was before he discovered the antiestablishment style of a seasoned activist, when he was still sporting the short back and sides of boyhood and wore blue jeans all the time. But despite his nondescript appearance, Ed's brown eyes were deep-set with determination.

'Join us at Whitehall at twelve tomorrow,' he says to the camera, then looks to me for reassurance. I nod my encouragement. 'It's time to tell the government that enough is enough – we need climate action *now.*'

There is a sheepish murmur of approval from the group. I smile and put my arm around him, thrilled with myself. My following was barely breaking a couple of thousand back then, and Travis was just a shadow in my comment section, yet I'm holding myself with the self-assuredness of a star on the rise. The shot focuses in on the placard I'm making. It says *THE OCEANS ARE RISING AND SO ARE WE* – a phrase I'd stolen from someone else – yet I'm grinning like I've just designed the next BLM fist.

I don't relate to this woman at all, to this *girl*. She's too readily perceived. She doesn't cover her mouth when she laughs, allowing a wad of pink gum to devour her upper lip and ruin her otherwise-acceptable face. But most pathetic of all, she thinks we actually stand a chance to change things.

'That's great, baby,' Ed says, leaning in to look at my placard. Our heads knit together, and he asks me what colour he should use on his. We opt for green, though I ended up painting it for him. He was never any good at that sort of thing. I was, as it turned out. I designed the RIOT 1.5 T-shirt he's wearing in the video. It's one of the ways I made my mark: not just by creating a logo but by convincing Ed that we needed one in the first place. He founded the Climate Change Prevention and Democracy Preservation Society at university and was committed to its deeply uninspiring name, calling it *credible* and *pragmatic*. I had a hunch that pragmatism was not the way to grow a movement, and when we moved to London to do just that, I made it my mission to get him to change his mind.

'But what are we rioting about?' he'd asked the day I suggested changing the name to RIOT. It was the first time we'd used Irie's conservatory, and he was stooped over the farmhouse table like an army general planning an invasion. 'It can't just be anything, Fi. We need to be more specific.'

That's when we landed on RIOT 1.5, a name that both suited Ed's wonkish leanings – referencing the need to limit global warming to 1.5 degrees – and my eye for catchy branding. It's what made us the perfect team. He had the facts and figures; I knew how to make things look good. He studied environmental sciences at the University of Edinburgh; I studied Photoshop hacks at the University of YouTube. He led the actions; I did the artwork.

I'm still proud of that logo. The *I* in *RIOT* is an exclamation mark, the point of which forms the dot in *1.5*. Ed called me a *creative genius* when I came up with that – two words that I retreat to whenever I need a reminder that I have, at one point in my life, *done something* worthwhile.

The video plays on a loop, and I watch again as Ed gestures over the table and announces the climate march. His white arms are bare, devoid of the botanical tattoos he later collected, and his awkwardness in front of the camera is endearing. He was a policy guy, not a campaigner. But as our numbers grew, so, too, did his confidence, and before we knew it, Ed was leading a national strike that got international news coverage.

A bubble of shame pops in my throat like the first throws of vomit. I flush it down with wine. I don't have it in me to dwell on the impact we once had – or, more to the point, the way Travis made me squander that impact long before Ed died.

I switch accounts and scroll through my posts in search of a photo of Bruce. I skim past videos of me flogging humidifiers and grow lights and plant scissors and pest control and moss poles and misters and 'niche-adjacent products' like plant-based skin care and natural deodorants and bamboo toothbrushes. Then, as if someone has built a virtual Hadrian's Wall across my account, the sales pitches stop. Now I'm scrolling past videos of me marching in front of Big Ben and handing out flyers in a polar bear costume, posted alongside repotting tutorials and houseplant tours and faux-candid photos of me looking wistfully at trees.

Before Travis, my bio was:

heart full of flowers, hand a raised fist

Since Travis, my bio is:

Houseplant guru
Eco beauty & fashion queen
Daily discount codes!!
For brand collabs, promos, reviews: travis@hypetribe.com

Finally, I find the photo I'm looking for. In it, I'm showing off my new kitten with the sincere glow of a mother holding a child. We were, after all, the sort of people who called our cat our *fur baby*. Bruce was the panther in our palm house. No, he was the sloth, because all he did was curl up in the plant pots and sleep. And now he's gone.

Now they're both gone.

The white whir of the fan touches my face and chills tears that haven't stopped since Tracy took him. *Neglect.* That's the word she used. *Neglect.* How long has it been since I filled his water bowl? How long since I fed him? I don't remember. I've lost entire days. Why couldn't Ed have died in the winter? In the winter, I could have opened the curtains and navigated loss by daylight. I could have ripped out grief by the root before it invaded the building. I know I could have.

I upturn my glass and wince at the vinegary afterburn. I lie down on the towel next to the standing fan. The knife I've been twisting all morning gets sharpened against my spine. It discovers a live nerve. It's been there since the day he died, the knife. First it cut the legs out from underneath me, then it robbed me of every last scrap of hope left in my possession. But it feels different this time. I don't feel disarmed by the pain. Rather, rage swells around the blade and subsides before crashing down with the blow of a clenched fist. The nerve is defending itself. It forces me to my feet.

I *tried*. I really fucking tried to *do something*, something that would make things better. We both tried so hard. I know Travis screwed me over towards the end, I know I let Ed down, but does that really justify the suffering that's been thrust upon me now? Isn't it punishment enough that I've lost my life partner, our sanctuary, my peace of mind, without losing the one creature that still bonds me to that time?

I need to channel this new sensation. I need to find somewhere to put it or else the horses will return and rage will become a fear so palpable that it will render me immobile. I pace around the suffocated dark, dodging boxes and mouldy mugs in search of some release. Leaves crunch underfoot and stick their sharp teeth between my toes. Vines brush against my face.

'Fuck off!' I scream, groping into the void for the offending plant. I pull it down. We trained devil's ivy to grow around the picture rail, so when I pull, it keeps coming like a magician's handkerchief trick. It rains dust in my eyes. The retaliation ignites a spark of resolve.

I have to get rid of these dead things.

Frantic, I grasp at the debris and drag it from its final resting place. A ceramic pot smashes on the floor. The knife loosens its grip slightly. I grab another pot and throw it. It shatters in a firework of terra-cotta shards and multipurpose compost. I do it again, sweat beading at my temples, then again and again and again. There are so many plants that I could rampage against them all day long and still have leftovers. Then a fist hammers on the ceiling, and my anonymous upstairs neighbour shouts, 'Shut the fuck up!'

The interruption makes me hesitate, pot in raised hand. I lower my arms.

We got this one at a fancy garden centre in De Beauvoir. It was before I signed with Travis's agency, back when we couldn't afford it.

'I don't know, Ed. Thirty pounds is a lot for a plant pot,' I'd said, my teeth anxiously pinching the insides of my cheek. We could barely make the rent, let alone splurge on overpriced ceramics.

'But it goes so well with this ficus, look.' He lifted a leafy tree into the pot and set it down on the shelf in front of us. 'They were made for each other.'

My impulse was to say *just like us*, but it felt too cheesy. I was still worried about coming on too strong. I didn't want to scare him away. But I couldn't help locking eyes with him and smiling, the sentiment captured in the little grin that brightened my face.

'Just like us,' he'd said, reading my mind. I nodded and smiled some more. Finding my coyness adorable, he grabbed me by the waist, tipped me back and kissed me with the inhibition of a US Navy sailor. My arms flung up to stop myself from falling, my right hand colliding with the shelf and knocking a ceramic bird ornament onto the floor. Despite our inflated overdrafts, we had to get the pot after that, and the bird ornament. It's still here somewhere, its wing reattached with superglue, its imperfection a testament to Ed's affection for romantic indiscretions.

I put the pot down and back away from it. My skin is crawling with foliage and bits of terra-cotta and sweat and soil. I search the room for something to wipe my face with. The curtain is the closest thing. Lifting it casts a splinter of light from a crack in the tinfoil. If Tracy thought things were bad before, they're a whole lot worse now. It looks like a fight broke out in the De Beauvoir garden centre. Plaster is crumbling from the wall, and the sideboard is buried underneath a mountain of rooty mud. The knife eases up again, my anger morphing into regret.

First I kill all of our precious plants. Then I smash them to smithereens.

What's wrong with me?

My tongue yearns for wine, but the bottle is empty. I look again at the bombed plant shop, then go into the kitchen for a dustpan and brush. I stoop down to open the cupboard under the sink, heedless of what I will find there.

I hid him after the funeral.

I couldn't bear it. Tracy put him in a *Pringles* tube, for God's sake. What was I supposed to do? I didn't think I was entitled to even a pinch of him, let alone half, but Ed's mum Florence insisted.

She'd fast-tracked the cremation and wanted to make sure I 'got my share' before she went back to Kent. But ashes aren't the easiest thing to divide, particularly not at a wake. Florence dithered over the urn with the uncertainty of an amateur baker until Tracy got impatient and rolled up an order of service.

'It's got a lid and everything,' she'd said jovially, funnelling the ashes inside.

When I returned home with nothing but a tube of Pringles to show for the love of my life, I had to get as far away from it as possible. So I hid it somewhere I knew I'd never look – the cupboard under the sink where we kept the cleaning products. And it worked. I forgot about it. But now I remember the crunch of crisps as my stepdad finished off the Pringles. I remember the smell of paprika on his breath. I remember the grey puff of smoke as Ed's remains hit the bottom.

I sit back on my heels, the wind knocked out of me.

The worst part is, Ed didn't even like Pringles. If he has to live inside a snack packet for the rest of eternity, he deserves something classy, like organic rice cakes from Whole Foods or a tin of M&S Parmigiano Reggiano bites. Not processed party food that Tracy got from the big Tesco when I asked her to sort out catering. But I know that's not what he would have wanted, either, M&S or otherwise.

He would have wanted to go back to his tree.

'It's that yew tree over there,' he'd told me, pointing to an evergreen that was spilling its copious branches over the boardwalk. It was the first time we had gone to Kew Gardens together. We'd just moved from Edinburgh, and Ed was taking me on a tour of his favourite green spaces. His aunt Beatrice lived in a Georgian town house in Richmond where he spent childhood summers roaming the park with his back-from-boarding-school cousin, Caspian. I didn't tell him that having an aunt Beatrice, a cousin named Caspian, and a summer town house right next to Richmond Park made him enormously posh until much later, once we'd dropped the pleasantries.

'Will dear *Beatrice* be present?' I used to tease him. 'What about darling *Caspian*? Oh, I do hope you boys won't be *beastly* to the staff!'

He just grinned and took it on the chin. Ed's family was *comfortable*, as they liked to put it, and lived on a private road in Broadstairs. It was one of the ways we were different. While Ed grew up wearing Billabong and eating artichokes, I grew up wearing stuff that Tracy got from car boot sales and hadn't even heard of artichokes until I was in my mid-twenties. But Ed soon learned to distance himself from his upbringing. When the world grew suspicious of posh white men, he started speaking with a clipped southeast Kent accent, telling people he was from Thanet (dropping the last *T*) and dressing in secondhand workwear.

'These aren't actually berries,' he'd said that day at Kew, plucking a red fruit off a nearby branch. 'They're called arils. They protect the seed.' He rolled the fruit between his fingers and crushed the flesh, exposing the pit within. 'The seeds are extremely poisonous, though, so watch out.' Then, with a mischievous grin, he flicked it at me. I ducked, snatching half a dozen arils to throw right back, only for him to run up the boardwalk and grab a handful of rotting leaves. What followed was a vigorous leaf fight that only ended when a woman pushing a pram rounded the corner.

That's when I added the word aril to the secret list of baby names I kept – *keep* – in my head. Aril joined Calathea (the first plant we bought together) and Bell (our favourite type of Scottish heather). Aril, Calathea and Bell.

What am I supposed to do with that list now? What am I supposed to do with these memories? Memories I've assigned to every other object in the flat. Memories which dig in like a crown of thorns and cut my head wide open.

I take the Pringles tube out from under the sink and carry it into the living room. That's progress, I suppose. I put it on the coffee table, directly opposite the crack in the wall where I flung the plant pots. It doesn't feel right, having Ed among all this filth. In life, he was house-proud – his Pinterest-worthy level of curation is one of the reasons our home became our income. I was, in my own way, buying ornaments from charity shops and any plant I happened upon, but Ed was neat.

'I'll tidy up,' I tell no one. Well, no one except for Ed. The Pringles logo has a moustachioed face on it that seems to be observing me. Judging me, almost. But the thought of actually tidying up is overwhelming. I have no idea where to start. I sit on the sofa with the Pringles tube turned to face me. Ed didn't have a moustache, his stubble giving way to a soft beard that joined the nape-length curly brown hair he lost his life with. But he did have eyes and a face, and that's enough of a parallel for me to delude myself into thinking I'm sitting across from my boyfriend.

'I miss you so much,' I whisper, my face a mess of muscle spasms. 'I can't do this without you, Ed. Why did you have to leave me?'

I wait in earnest for a response. When Ed first died, I heard his voice all the time. I'd have whole conversations with him and feel the weight of his body in bed like a phantom limb. But as time wore on, his voice faded, and the memory foam forgot. I'd give anything to hear it again.

'I'll get better, I promise,' I tell the Pringles tube, taking Ed's silence to mean that he's just as appalled by my lifestyle as Tracy is. 'And I'll take you to the yew tree. That's what you want, isn't it?'

But still, no reply.

I pick up the tube, gripping it in both hands. With Bruce gone, tonight will be my first night truly alone – not just since Ed died but since before I can even remember. I'd say that's reason enough to put off tidying until tomorrow and bring the Pringles to bed with me.

3

I've been feeling brighter since I started talking to the moustache. I know it's a bit weird but it's not just a tube of Pringles, is it? People talk to gravestones all the time. They sit on the ground in cemeteries and pour their heart out to a slab of stone, the perished remains of their loved ones encased in velvet six feet under. This is no different.

The jolly arch of the cartoon eyebrows on the Pringles logo surely means that Ed approves of life outside the cupboard. But, despite talking through every banal detail of my day like a diligent parent trying to get their baby to speak, Ed hasn't said a word. I can hardly blame him. He's emerged from three months of isolation to find all of our houseplants dead, Bruce MIA and his girlfriend indifferent to the state of the world. In this kind of oppressive heat, Ed would have led a mutual-aid initiative to check on the elderly and distribute water to the vulnerable, all while lobbying the government to take decisive action on climate change. Yet here I am, throwing plant pots against the wall, living in squalor and drinking too much.

When the doorbell rings, I collide with the corner of the coffee table and almost knock Ed over. That's two visitors in as many days. What is going on? I check my phone. Travis has gone quiet on me. Maybe Tracy's back. Maybe she's realised that stealing my cat was a cruel lapse in judgement and has come to return him. I take Ed downstairs, digging my fingers around the tube for courage, and steel myself to take her on. I'll be a lot firmer this time. I won't let her leave without returning Bruce. Then Ed will *have* to start talking.

I take a brief glance at myself in the hallway mirror, immediately regretting it. I look like I've been dragged through a hedge backwards. My face is smudged with soil, and my hair is a tangled nest of twigs. There are purple crescents under my eyes and trenches between my eyebrows – testament to not just my hangover but my premature ageing. I lean closer and spot a wiry silver wisp sprouting from my left temple.

The door opens to nothing but the sun's stiff heat. I squint up and down the street. It's just as hot and quiet as yesterday. More so, since there's no man pushing a wheelbarrow uphill. I bet that guy purchased the last bottle of water in London, and now he's sitting tight, waiting for the council to switch off the supply. Then he'll sell them for fifty quid a pop. I step back into the hall, the thought making me thirsty, then pause. There's something on the doorstep. It's a potted plant – flush with leaves and very much alive. It's in a fancy ceramic pot, just like the one Ed and I got from De Beauvoir. I put the Pringles down to pick it up. A small envelope is nestled amid the foliage. It's addressed to me. I tuck the plant into the crook of my arm and tear it open. Two words are embossed on the card in gold foil:

I'm sorry.

I turn it over. The other side is blank. I look around again, expecting to see at least a delivery van driving away. But it's just me, the plant and the Pringles. The dark green foliage looks so incongruous against the sepia tones of the city, like a relic from a bygone era. It doesn't resemble any of the plants we used to grow, with their glossy, tropical leaves belonging to distant climes. This one has a twisted trunk and carefully pruned branches. I carry it inside and put it on the coffee table beside Ed. I look at the card again.

I'm sorry.

Who could be apologising to me? The only person who's done me wrong is Tracy, and she's not the type to leave anonymous gifts, let alone apologise. Could it be someone expressing their condolences, three months after the fact? Could it be from Beth? The last we spoke, she sent me a link to an article titled 'The Paradox of the Sustainable Influencer' and accused me of greenwashing. This was during Earth Month, when I'd partnered with a clothing brand to promote their new eco line. Travis called it *one hundred and ten percent sustainable*, but as it turned out, the brand was *one hundred and ten percent problematic*. It caused a bit of a backlash, not just from Beth but from a handful of my followers who accused me of exploiting garment workers. It was my first and only foray into controversy. I made a donation to the Fair Wear Foundation and publicly apologised. But Beth said it wasn't enough – I couldn't claim to be an environmentalist if I was promoting consumerism. We bickered over WhatsApp for a few days until I stopped replying.

Her last message read, Please pick up, Fi. I just saw the news. I'm devastated. Please, talk to me. I love you. But I didn't want to talk. I didn't need her disapproval on top of everything else, not when disapproval was the poison that tainted so many of my final moments with Ed. So I ignored her calls, and I didn't invite her to the funeral. Eventually, she took the hint and left me alone. It was no major loss. Sure, we were inseparable as kids, but there's only so long a shared childhood in Strathyre can keep a friendship intact.

The glazed container is squat and cobalt blue, with a carpet of moss covering the soil. On closer inspection, the little tree appears to be a bonsai, its mottled trunk spiralling out of the moss in an elegant curve that extends to its outstretched branches. Each branch is decorated with a cluster of forest green needles. It's like a pine tree cross-pollinated with an English oak and stunted to the size of a beginner's houseplant. I look at the Pringles tube and shrug. If Ed were here, he'd know exactly what kind of plant it is, but I don't have a clue. I take a photo and scan it with Google Lens. When the search result loads, the gasp that escapes my throat is shrill enough to choke me.

Taxus baccata (English Yew)

I sit down, my brain thrumming against my skull. All I can hear is the sound of my pounding heart. My lips go numb. Heat rises and falls against my skin, leaving my arms prickled with goose bumps.

Beth didn't know about Ed's favourite tree. Tracy didn't know. Nobody knew except us. And wasn't it just yesterday that I was thinking about yew trees? That I was planning to spread his ashes at Kew? I look back at the Pringles, slack-jawed.

'H-h-how?' I hear myself stuttering, my voice raspy as my tongue sticks to the roof of my mouth. His inert moustachioed face gives nothing away. I check the results again. This technology isn't infallible. There were plenty of times in the past when I'd try to identify a wildflower on a walk, tapping the screen to focus on the petals and taking the result as gospel. But Ed would just scoff and pull out his trusty *Field Guide to Native British Plants* to prove Google wrong. So Google must be wrong this time. Because if it isn't, if a miniature version of Ed's favourite tree has materialised on my doorstep without a clue as to how it got here, I don't know what I'll do.

I am gripped then by an unfamiliar sensation – the urge to leave the house. I have to go to Kew Gardens. I have to see for myself whether this bonsai does indeed belong to the yew family. Because if I can see it, if I can confirm it, I can begin to make sense of it. And if I can make sense of it, I can figure out who is saying sorry to me and why.

There's going to Kew Gardens, and then there's *getting* to Kew Gardens. I have to take a bus to Seven Sisters, get the Victoria line to its namesake station and then ride the District line all the way across the city to Richmond. It's the farthest I've travelled since Ed died. It's the *only* time I've travelled since then. I'd order an Uber if not for the cobwebs in my bank account. It turns out there's no sick pay or compassionate leave when you're an influencer.

The empty District line carriage is suffocatingly hot and fumy, my winter-pale arms coated in a film of grimy sweat as I breathe through my mouth and count down the stations. It's usually impossible to get a seat, so I'm grateful to be alone, at least. Given that there's no one around to recognise me, I take off my oversize sunglasses. I'm not *famous* famous, but it's not unusual for someone to approach me for a selfie, and that was before Ed's death, which turned both of us into a household name.

Influencer Boyfriend Turned Eco-Terrorist Dead at 31

Boyfriend first, *eco-terrorist* second. I can't tell if that's a blessing or a curse. Almost every article was accompanied by the same selfie I took of us in Edinburgh. We were at the top of Arthur's Seat, squinting into the then-pleasantly warm sun with the twinkling eyes of the recently in love. The shadow of my arm covers the top half of Ed's head. His hair is neat and tidy. I'm dressed like a frazzled Englishwoman, but the pencilled arches of my eyebrows are a dead giveaway of the year: 2016. When Ed died, I couldn't understand why the press ran such an old photo. Now I think it's because they wanted him to appear like a normal, well-adjusted good guy, much in the way the media always treats dead white men. Not to say he wasn't well-adjusted, but by the end, he wasn't exactly law-abiding.

I interlace my fingers around the pot and take a deep breath. The plant is in my lap, and the Pringles tube is in a linen bag on my shoulder. I'm gearing up to do something that was unthinkable a few days ago. I'm gearing up to let go of his remains. I have to. I'm travelling all this way, and I highly doubt that I'll find it in me to do this again. But my gut is a mess of knots, and my heart is working double time. I want to go home, back to where it's safe and dark, where I don't have to confront the cruelties of the past.

I look at a tube ad to distract myself. In it, a woman with an undercut and a pierced nose is shouting angrily into a megaphone. The man next to her is holding a tin of paint, primed to dump it over the viewer. The slogan reads, 'Seen something that doesn't look right? See it. Say it. Sorted. Together, we'll put a stop to organised crime,' followed by the HM Government logo. I sigh bitterly.

Nothing's changed. Nothing will ever change.

That's when the rhythmic clattering of the tube intensifies, and the fumes tinge with red smoke. I shut my eyes and clench my jaw. All I can hear now are hooves hitting hot concrete and surging cries of disorder. I hold my breath, my mouth creasing into a grimace as the train hurtles through the tunnel. As soon as I hear, 'The next station is Kew Gardens,' I stagger to the doors. My surroundings have transformed into a thick fog, through which horses are charging down the carriage towards me.

After what feels like a lifetime, the doors finally slide open. I run.

I don't stop running until I'm surrounded by the heady affluence of Lichfield Road. I catch my breath and check that the plant – and the Pringles – have survived my desperate escape unscathed. It's too hot to walk at a pace, let alone run, so I balance the plant on a wall and reach into my bag for water. Ed is sitting at the bottom beside his *Field Guide to Native British Plants*, his lid firmly attached. His cartoon face provides some reassurance.

I'm not alone. I can do this. *We* can do this.

Detached houses with stained-glass windows tower behind wrought-iron fences, the naked branches of the adjacent London plane trees no longer the pleasant sight they once were. The road is lacking not only people but cars, the ubiquitous BMWs and Porsches vanishing along with their owners. Considering the quiet of Stamford Hill and the lack of commuters, this shouldn't come as a surprise, but the calm is disconcerting. It's like the entire population of London has evaporated during my three-month convalescence.

Once I've composed myself, making a silent vow to get an Uber home – overdraft be damned – I cross the street and approach the gates of Kew Gardens. The *closed* gates. Peering through them, I see that the ticket booths are empty. I didn't think to check whether they'd be open. I eye the wall beside me. It's too high to climb, especially with a houseplant in tow, but I've come too far to give up now. I walk the length of the wall. Ed always knew how to beat the crowds, entering via a side gate that was reserved for locals. I head in that direction and sure enough, the gate is ajar, locked by a loose chain that's just wide enough to squeeze under.

Kew Gardens is unrecognisable. The lush green foliage and vibrant flower beds have been drained of colour, leaving behind a parched expanse of land with skeletal trees that belong in a horror movie. I walk past the Great Pagoda and Queen Charlotte's Cottage, where the Woodland Walk begins. Although I've covered myself in SPF, my skin feels pinched already, the might of the sun radiating off every pore. By the time I'm halfway across the garden, I feel faint. The plant becomes a dumbbell, and my vision blurs with sweat. I take little sips of water, conserving it just like Wheelbarrow Man, before ducking into the shadeless woods. Up ahead, I spot a welcome sight. The evergreen trees have proven themselves worthy of the name. Somewhere here, among these hardy pines, is Ed's yew tree.

'There are better specimens, sure,' he'd said once we'd recovered from our leaf fight that day at Kew. 'Older ones – ancient, even. But this is the first yew tree that caught my imagination. Before they built the boardwalk, me and Caspian used to pretend it was our house. The trunk is hollow.' He struck his knuckles against the bark. 'You can climb right inside. That's why I love yew trees. When the trunk decays, the tree starts rooting inside itself. Regenerating.' He turned to face me, his eyes sparkling with boyish wonder. 'They never stop growing, even after they die. Pretty cool, right?'

They never stop growing, even after they die.

I look down at the houseplant, a thought suddenly emerging through my heat-induced malaise. A ridiculous thought. I shake my head, willing it away. I can't jump to conclusions. Not until I know if this really is a yew tree.

My feet hasten down the boardwalk, the clap of my sandals the only sound breaking the eerie silence. There's no birdsong, no squirrels rustling in the leaves, no squawking parakeets or chittering insects. The cacophony of Kew's wildlife has disappeared along with the restless din of its residents. I swallow against a surge of dread.

Then I spot the tree. It droops over the corner of the boardwalk like a weeping willow, creating a tunnel of evergreen branches that are just as alive and well as I hoped they'd be. I step off the boardwalk to reach it. When I push the branches aside, a canopy of feathery pine needles falls behind me like the closing of a tent door. The shade is an enormous comfort. Not just because of the reprieve from the sun but because it's dark.

And darkness means safety.

Just like Ed said, the trunk is hollow with a new tree growing right at the centre of it, its aerial roots sinking into the earth and shooting up branches towards the sky. This is a tree-lover's tree, rugged and wild like the highlands it hails from. I squeeze myself inside a split in the outer trunk, finding room enough to imagine that the dead heartwood could be a house after all. With the plant on my hip, my free hand traces the rough texture of the bark. Dry moss crumbles underneath my fingertips. My hand follows the curve of the trunk as I walk around its circumference, the internal growth close beside me like the axis of a revolving door. When I return to the entrance, I notice a carving near the ground:

E + C WOZ ERE

E and C. Ed and Caspian.

My body concertinas to the forest floor. With my knees at my chin, I hug the houseplant tight to my chest and trace the infant lettering with tears streaming down my face.

Ed carved these words. Ed loved this tree. He loved it long before I knew him. He loved it enough to claim it as his own. And that's when a deep sense of knowing calms me from the inside out. Ed wanted me to come here. Not just to spread his ashes but to see this inscription. To be reminded that, regardless of what happened between us, regardless of what happened to him, he left his mark in more ways than one.

I pick up a fallen sprig of needles. The shape and spread of the leaves really do resemble the potted plant. I pick up a twig. The fissured, reddish grain of the wood is indistinguishable with that of the carefully cultivated bonsai. I fumble in my bag for the field guide, search the index for *yew* and flip to the right page. I check the double-page spread against the houseplant. I look back at the sprig, comparing all three. There's no doubt about it. This is a yew tree.

I wipe my forehead with the back of my hand and look up at the boughs above me, racking my brain for answers. Why has this little link to Ed's childhood appeared in my life? Why did the card say *I'm sorry*?

That's when the ridiculous thought starts to crystallise.

That day, when Ed first showed me this tree, he wasn't the only one with insight. 'That's why I love yew trees,' he'd said, 'They never stop growing, even after they die. Pretty cool, right?' And I agreed that it was pretty cool, more so because I knew that yew trees weren't just botanical curiosities, they were once considered sacred.

When I was a kid, Dad worked in the local timber yard. He tried to quell his guilt about chopping down trees by campaigning to protect ancient ones, ones that were integral to the beating heart of Scotland's history. According to him and dendrophiles everywhere, yew trees were of special significance because, in the time of the Celts, druids planted them in circular groves to hold ceremonies and rituals. Without the blinkers of science, they took the regenerative power of yew trees to mean that in these groves, the spirits of the dead crossed over from the Otherworld and were born anew.

At the time, I didn't tell Ed. I didn't want to ruin the moment by talking about my dad, whose guilt endured to such a degree that he left his family to find something that would absolve him. I kept the Scottish folklore to myself. But now, even my old wounds aren't enough to stop me from drawing connections. Because whoever sent this houseplant couldn't have possibly known how much it would mean to me. So what if *someone* didn't send it?

Or at least, not someone who's alive?

As unhinged as it sounds, Ed has every reason to be sorry. Sorry for leaving me. Sorry for the cruel things he said one week before he died. Sorry that I have since turned into a cynic and recluse. And if, like the druids said, yew trees really are more than they seem, doesn't it make sense that Ed would reach out to me in this way? That he'd send me a plant long venerated for its lore of resurrection?

I take the Pringles tube out of my bag and clutch it with shaking hands.

'Did you send me the yew tree, Ed?'

He doesn't respond.

Instead, after ninety days of flat, relentless heat, a cool breeze blows through the canopy, stirring the branches to life and sending leaves swirling around the hollow trunk of the yew tree. My tear-streaked face breaks into a smile. I place a hand over the carving, my hair whipping up all around me, and just then I feel closer to Ed than I have since the day I watched him die.

After going all that way to spread his ashes, I couldn't do it. As much as Ed loved that tree, if I'd left him there, I'd have to take three modes of transport just to visit him again. It didn't feel right, especially not now that, for reasons as-yet unknown, a baby version of that same tree has become my responsibility.

Back among our fallen paradise, with its crumbling plaster and heaps of trash, my newfound belief in the druids has waned slightly. I think I got carried away. If by some major miracle Ed has found a way to send me a tree from beyond the grave, I need more proof. No doubt my heartbroken grip on reality has made me prone to wishful thinking. But there's one thing I am certain of now: I know what I'm supposed to do with his remains. I'm supposed to add them to this little yew tree, to this symbol of Ed's childhood, so that we can stay together.

I curl a fingernail under the Pringles lid and pop it off. I've never looked inside. I wait for the contents to settle, fearing that the suction from the lid will cause Ed to puff out and go up my nose. I tilt the tube and peer in. It smells faintly of incense and a lot like paprika. I gag and put the lid back on. I can't do it like this. I can't just dump him over the moss and be done with it. It needs to have a sense of ceremony, a sense of occasion. I need to light candles and get dressed in something nice. I need to play our song. I need to find the courage to tidy up, or else it'll be like spreading ashes in a landfill site. But first, if I'm going to keep this plant alive, I have to take the tinfoil down.

I have to let the light back in.

Once I start putting things in bin bags, I don't stop except to catch my breath when the heat threatens to dissolve my willpower. Everything has to go. Everything except the plant and the Pringles tube and a few other select items, like Ed's favourite mug, his earbuds, the bird ornament, the De Beauvoir plant pot, any receipt that sparks a memory of him, and any scrap of paper I find with his handwriting on it. I pull down the remaining vines and bundle them into bin bags, then scoop up bits of broken pottery and bone-dry root balls, throwing them out alongside every dead plant in the house. I strip the windows of tinfoil and squint, the sun's rays like laser eye surgery. I find plates so laden with mould that I have to ditch them, along with – shamefully – numerous cat turds. Dirty protests from Bruce which fell on unseeing eyes until Tracy took him away. Each time I find a turd, guilt spurs me on.

During my excavations, I unearth some RIOT 1.5 merch – tote bags, the stickers we used for guerilla marketing and a box of campaign T-shirts. All things that I designed. I take a T-shirt out and sniff it, hoping for Ed's green cedar musk. It smells box-fresh and is black with a white logo. I put it on and look at myself in the bedroom mirror. The last time I wore one of these, Ed was throwing black paint down the steps of BP HQ shouting, 'Climate reparations now!' while I filmed him. In my reflection I see Wednesday Addams after a coke binge – no longer the cute vintage girly who revived nineties fashion and made oversize cardigans look cool. I brush my hair and clip it up. It's the most I've tended to my appearance since the funeral.

I clear out Ed's bedside drawer and find an invitation from the last RIOT 1.5 event I organised. It was a party at East Peace one week before The Final Strike. Although I'd invited the whole collective, I organised the party for Ed. By that point, my job with Travis had drawn me away from activism long enough that I needed to prove myself – to show Ed that, although my involvement was limited, my heart was still in the right place. But it didn't turn out like that.

I crumple up the invitation and throw it in a bin bag, then find myself sobbing and retching on the bedroom floor. Ed's after-party insults reverberate between my ears. But I can't allow myself to go back there. I have to get better, just like I said I would. I rise to my feet and puff out my cheeks, clamping a hand over my heart to steady it. The threat of another breakdown recedes into the shadows. The striking of hooves on hot concrete fades.

Once the flat has been purged of decay, I prepare for the ceremony. It's been so long since I got dressed up that I find myself actually enjoying the process. I take a cold shower. I wash my hair. I moisturise my face. I pick out a white linen dress that feels best suited to the occasion, spinning around in front of the Pringles tube to show off my new look. There'll be no black this time. This isn't about mourning or loss or tragedy. This is about life and growth and fresh starts.

Unable to bear the heat of a flame, I substitute candles for battery-powered tea lights, dotting them around the coffee table and across the mantelpiece. Then I cue 'Our House' by Crosby, Stills, Nash & Young – a song I thought I'd never be able to listen to again. I press Play.

This was the song I'd have walked down the aisle to. It became ours by accident. We'd just moved in and were bickering about money. London felt like a change of continent in comparison to the relative comfort of Edinburgh, where we didn't have to compete in a battle royale just to get a roof over our heads. After losing half a dozen places to finance bros with infinitely more capital, I used my savings to double the deposit on this place. By the time we'd moved in, we couldn't afford it. We were worried we'd made a mistake. Then this song came on shuffle, and we both paused to listen. Ed put down the box he was opening and walked over to me. He took my hands and, quite spontaneously, we began waltzing around the living room.

When the song descended into a chorus of carefree la-la-las, we started skipping around the table, our arms in the air, our grins childlike. Then the dancing broke into a chase, and I ran through the flat scream-laughing until Ed caught me and threw me onto the bed.

'Everything *is* easy because of you,' he'd told me, his breath short from dancing and running and laughing with me. Then we made love in *our house*, and I knew that everything was going to be easy from now on. Because so long as I had Ed, and so long as he had me, we were safe.

'Nothing makes sense without you,' I croak now. I pop the lid and scoop out the ashes with a cocktail spoon. Without pausing to reconsider, I scatter them over the moss. The ashes amount to ten spoonfuls. Is that half of a man, or is that more? I decide it's just the right amount. I water his ashes in. Once the song has finished, something shifts.

God, I've missed you, Ed whispers from some far-off place.

It worked. His voice is back.

4

Travis has sent me a care package. Well, he referred to it as a *care package*, but really it's a thinly veiled warning: *Get back to work or else.* Among reams of pink tissue paper, there's a selection of cosmetics from my corporate sponsors, a brass watering can with bees on it, and a livestreaming body cam. I have to restrain myself from throwing the whole lot against the wall – the camera especially.

'You can get double – *triple* – the amount of followers from one livestream compared to regular in-feed content,' Travis used to rant, 'and it connects you more authentically to your audience. That's what people want these days, babe. De-influencers! It's a no-brainer.'

What he meant, I later realised, was that if I put my whole self online, I could more readily disarm people into buying things they didn't need. But by the time I'd figured that out, it was too late. I'd already signed the contract. A contract which, to this day, dictates not only what I can and can't sell online but what I can and can't say.

'You've signed a golden gag order,' Ed had said when Travis first vetoed one of my videos. 'Didn't you read the fine print? This contract is *predatory*, Fi.'

I didn't. I'd just been signed to a digital talent agency. I thought I was going to join Greta Thunberg in the Climate Activist Hall of Fame. After all, Travis said he *loved* my content, he said he loved *everything* on my platform. How was I supposed to know he meant the houseplant stuff, not my *unmarketable* posts about RIOT 1.5 or the protests we were organising?

The video in question wasn't even that divisive. It was from a rally outside the Houses of Parliament. In it, I'm holding a placard that says *1.5 TO STAY ALIVE*, and Ed is shouting, 'Climate change means system change!' into a megaphone. That's it. It's not like any of my older posts, when I was occupying fracking sites and making a real nuisance of myself. Still, Travis said it wasn't *on-brand*. He wanted me to be authentic, but within the confines of my sponsors' guidelines.

'It's not that *I* don't approve, babe,' Travis had said in a voice note afterwards, 'but you've got corporate clients to think about now. And as much as I bloody love the planet – because I do, don't get me wrong – protests are a bit naughty these days, don't you think? You see what they write in the papers. Criminals this, terrorists that. Not to mention the prime minister calling you lot a *plague* the other day. I was so flippin' *pissed off* about that, trust me, but our brands don't want to be associated with the plague, if you know what I mean? It's shit, babe, but it is what it is.'

Back then, the tide of public opinion had just turned against protesters. What once was a fringe cause that no one paid much attention to had become an outright provocation. We were, according to the right-wing press, progress-hating zealots who wanted to plunge Britain into darkness (rather than concerned citizens who wanted to solve an existential threat to humankind). When that didn't rile up enough hatred, they called us *terrorists*, and the prime minister likened us to a deadly disease. Just like that, the culture war was won.

I should have realised that by signing with Travis, I'd have to distance myself from those slurs. But, however naive it sounds, I sincerely thought that he understood what I was trying to do.

When I played the voice note to Ed, his brow furrowed so deeply that I thought his face was going to split in half.

'We still have a separate channel for RIOT,' I said, trying to pacify him yet quietly horrified that I'd been duped into becoming a glorified telesaleswoman. 'We can post whatever we want on that.'

'It's got less than ten thousand followers,' he'd said exasperatedly, looking down at his phone to check. 'How many have you got now?'

'I don't know,' I lied, my follower count exploding once Travis had paid to promote my account. 'About four, maybe five hundred thousand, probably less. Why does it matter?'

'We've just lost an audience of half a million, Fi. If you can't share the next action, no one will show up, I guarantee it. You have to quit.'

I've spent so many sleepless nights wondering whether, had I quit, Ed would still be alive. Because then neither of us would have had a point to prove. He wouldn't have turned to the sort of activism that stoked the flames of political intolerance, and I wouldn't have sat on the sidelines and watched. But after rinsing my savings to move to London, we needed the money. However radical our intentions, the rent didn't magically appear, and Ed was too focused on RIOT to get a postgrad job. Yet the one thing Travis *could* guarantee was a decent income – so long as I did what I was told.

More than anything, that's what I miss about social media – the money. And I suppose the daily validation from strangers didn't hurt, either. Maybe that's why I clung on for as long as I did.

Suddenly irate with myself, I dropkick the body cam under the sofa. 'See?' I tell the plant. 'I'm not doing it. Travis can get fucked.'

That's when I see something that makes me grab the headboard to stop my bones from turning to mush. The plant is on my bedside table. It's the first thing I looked at when I woke up this morning. In dreaming, I'd forgotten about Kew Gardens and the ceremony that had revived Ed's voice. When I rubbed the sleep from my eyes and remembered the gifts of the day before, I smiled, finding the plant's green countenance infinitely more in keeping with Ed's spirit than the Pringles logo ever was. Then the so-called care package arrived, and I jumped out of bed without noticing what I notice now.

The plant has *flowered*.

I pick up the pot and look closer. The flower perches on the tip of a woody branch and looks entirely out of place. It must be fake. It must have fallen out of an old festival head garland when I was tidying up. I touch it. It's real.

Cold sweat trickles down my spine. My eyes lose focus. I sit down on the bed and shake my head. Then, unexpectedly, I start laughing.

The flower has ruffled white petals, a checkered yellow centre and slender, pollen-tipped stamens that curl towards the light. It reminds me of the rhododendrons at East Peace, the ones that bloomed at the end of spring and daubed an entire corner of the garden in clusters of lily white. But what really amuses me is the way it sparkles. It's like flecks of glitter have been woven into the silky white surface of each petal, making the flower gleam.

But yew trees don't flower, do they? I reach for my phone.

The Royal Horticultural Society's website says, 'The yew tree is a gymnosperm and, as such, does not produce flowers.'

My eyes dart between my phone and the flower. I know for a fact that this is a yew tree. I went to great lengths to prove it. So how is it flowering when, according to the Royal Horticultural Society, this is something that yew trees simply do not do? I try Google Lens again. The result is inconclusive. Even artificial intelligence can't explain it.

People need to see this. I need to share this on social media, at least to find someone who can make sense of what's happening. The compulsion surprises me. Although every facet of my life used to be captured online, it's a long-dormant urge, and I push it down before it ruins the first laugh I've had in three months. My second impulse is to call Beth – another surprise. She's the only person open-minded enough to believe that this flower could be more than it seems. As teenagers, she took my affinity for witchy fashion one step further by dabbling in wicca. I gladly participated in the woodland rituals she copied off Tumblr, although I was more interested in the aesthetic photos than the promise of magic. And while her powers never came to fruition, she was still drying herbs and burning black-flame candles when we lived in Edinburgh. I know she'd understand. But that friendship is as lost to me as Ed is.

Or *was*.

The flight of fancy that gripped me at Kew Gardens returns.

I sprinkled his ashes into the soil. I heard his voice for the first time since those early days, when his presence never left my side. And now there is this enigmatic flower, this botanical anomaly.

'Ed?' I whisper, looking up at the ceiling with searching eyes.

I'm here.

'Oh my god, Ed. How? I don't understand.'

It doesn't matter, Fi. I'm here. You did the right thing.

My eyes find an untapped well of tears. I fill the room with wailing, squeezing the pot as tight as if I were holding Ed in the flesh. I suck air through clenched teeth and try to stop myself from having a panic attack. The shock is a body blow. I feel simultaneously worse and better than I have since he died. Because this changes everything. It puts everything into question. Magic belongs in fairy tales. It belongs to the stories Dad told me growing up, the ones about fairy queens and selkies and horselike water spirits. The things he told me about the druids were never meant to be true, were they?

I fall back on the sofa, the houseplant tucked against my stomach, and I sob out all the unanswerable questions until my spasming body forces me to sleep.

I awake at midday, the heat from the uncovered windows making sleep impossible. My eyes are inflamed, and my mind is blurry from emotional exhaustion. The flower twinkles in the sun, its delicate white petals like a postnap kiss on the forehead. I sit up, rub my eyes and stretch my back. I look around the empty flat. It's like waking in an unused exhibition space, the absence of plants robbing the place of character.

I hold the plant out in front of me and try to get my thoughts in order. A psychiatrist would tell me that my enormous guilt about neglecting Bruce has created an internal dialogue to comfort me. A psychiatrist would tell me that, if I'm hearing voices, perhaps I should consider medication. They would write the words *psychotic break caused by emotional trauma* in their notes and hand me a prescription. They'd make me medicate him into silence. *But what about the flower?* I'd say, the prescription scrunched up in my hand. *How do you explain that?* And they would look at me with pity and say that *It's just a flower, Fiona. Plants do that all the time.* But they would be wrong. Yew trees don't flower. No amount of psychiatric evaluation can make that fact untrue.

So what am I meant to do about it? How am I meant to proceed, now that a flowering yew tree has become a vessel for Ed's voice?

'Why did you send this to me?' I ask him, looking around the room for answers.

Am I supposed to fill this place with plants again? Am I supposed to rescue Bruce and reunite our little family? Am I supposed to go back to work? Ed's disapproval of my job surely extends to whatever mystical realm he now inhabits, but if I don't get back online soon, I run the very real risk of running out of money. His response comes as a distant echo.

You know why.

My mouth swings open. It's going to take a lifetime to get used to that. Light catches the petals. Specks of glitter glisten in my eyes.

'Do I?' I look up again, expecting to see his face looming out of parted clouds like a caricature of God, or a ghostly Mufasa.

Go back to where it all started, Fi. Then you'll see.

'Go back…?' I trail off and lean towards the flower, hoping to find a map etched into the folds of its petals. Go back to where *what* started? We started so much together. We started a life. We started a community. We started RIOT 1.5. But all of that is over. There's nothing left to go back to. I've lost everything…

I wrestle with a spike of shame and look away. All of a sudden, this strange flower feels sent to expose me. The petals radiate sun from the unveiled windows and shine light on all the shadows I have spent so many months hiding from. Because everything I've lost wasn't taken *from* me, it was taken *by* me.

With each sponsored post, the golden gag drew me away until I couldn't be part of RIOT 1.5 even if I wanted to. And by the end, I didn't want to. While Ed was lying down in front of traffic to no avail, my gains on social media were instant. I'd post a video, and in seconds hearts would flutter up my screen and the affiliate sales would roll in. On social media, there was no risk of being run over by a frustrated motorist. But that risk never stopped Ed. Even when they called him a terrorist, even when they took away his rights and ignored his every demand, Ed never gave in.

'I don't understand,' I say powerlessly. Ed's silence is loaded. I stare at the flower. Its white petals glow like an all-knowing yet evasive firefly. I am reminded again of the rhododendrons at East Peace, the ones that Irie rigorously pruned to stop them from taking over. I catch my breath.

East Peace was where *everything* started.

We went there not expecting to find a community. Dalston had an edge, like the past, present and future were fighting it out on the pavement in front of us. The luxury flats were punching down on the Afro-Caribbean hairdressers. Pret A Manger was butting heads with a family-owned Turkish restaurant. Whole Foods was striking a blow at Ridley Road Market. But like a poppy that grows from a crack in the concrete, East Peace flourished, providing a space where the past, present and future called a truce and found common ground. That common ground was plants.

'Irie?' I ask. 'You want me to go and see Irie?'

In the airless fever of our flat, I hear him say *Yes*.

The walk from ours to East Peace is down one long stretch of road that runs up the seam between North and East London. In that time, I can usually smell spray paint, popcorn, patchouli, cigarettes, exhaust fumes, BO, chargrilled chicken, vape juice, urine, shawarma, laundry detergent, weed, alcohol sweats, a multitude of spices and the occasional waft of sewage. I can usually hear saxophones, trains, heavy-duty machinery, sirens, helicopters, planes, car horns, reggae, bike chains, tattoo guns, swearing, laughing, tutting, revving, preaching, begging, bartering and catcalling – a lot of catcalling. But today, I could walk right down the middle of the street unimpeded except by the heat. I stick to the shadows of overarching buildings as dread creeps up on me again. I know this drought is hostile, but that doesn't explain where everyone has gone. I clench my swollen hands into fists and regret leaving the plant at home, longing for some comfort. The walk is decidedly less intense than the arid landscape of Kew Gardens, but I didn't want to risk damaging the flower. Then there's the delicate issue of how I'd explain it to Irie.

As I approach Kingsland High Street, I spot posters plastered over a wall on the opposite side of the street. They all feature the same linocut symbol: a shattered planet earth held together with a giant safety pin. I recognise it from somewhere, but I can't place it. I see a dozen more before I reach the gates to East Peace.

Ever since we found this place, this oasis blooming in the middle of urban sprawl, it's felt like home. Its surrounding fortress of office towers trap the heat and radiate it, creating a subtropical microclimate where palm trees and agave plants flourish. I open the gate and prepare my senses, hoping, however wishfully, for a riot of colour. But the micro has become macro. All that's survived are the tropical plants, and even those are clinging on for dear life. The ground is cracked like a shifting tectonic plate, the runner-bean frames and raised beds are bare and the remains of spring flowers are scattered about like crepe paper. I walk around with a stitch in my stomach. Four paths converge to a middle patio with a pergola at its centre. It's usually decorated with a blousy tangle of clematis and jasmine, without which it looks like an abandoned structure at a construction site. I glance down the end of the garden, towards the rhododendrons that brought me here. Given the time of year, the lack of flowers doesn't surprise me, but the fried leaves do. It's like someone has taken a blowtorch to the whole lot.

I wouldn't admit it to anyone, but I'm slightly relieved. This place no longer belongs to the evening of the RIOT 1.5 party, when I risked everything by organising an activist event that could have left me jobless. I set up the buffet table underneath the pergola and overcompensated for the stilted atmosphere by giving a speech. I wanted to boost morale before The Final Strike, to recognise the amount of work everyone had put in, to prove that I still cared. The party was supposed to do so many things. Instead, it did the one thing I didn't want it to do: it let Ed down.

I let Ed down.

The words echo in surround sound.

I let Ed down. I let Ed down. I let Ed down.

I stop underneath the pergola and touch a hand to my chest, yearning now for the weight of the plant to soothe me. The heat is a pestle, and I am the mortar. My windpipe shrinks. I stagger, uneasy on my feet. Not here. I can't fall to pieces here.

'Can I help you?' a voice says from behind me. I turn around slowly and dig despair back down into the ditch of my gut with a fake smile.

'Hey, Irie.'

'Fifi!' Her face lights up. 'Oh, love, it's been such a long time.'

Although I keep smiling, I'm alarmed by Irie's appearance. It's like ten years have passed since the funeral. Her usually rich black skin is ashen, and her lips are chapped, making her plum lipstick look like it was applied yesterday. Her locs are styled in a swirl on top of an open straw visor, now greyer than before, and her blue worker's smock is covered in dark patches of sweat. But most alarming of all is the skin that hangs in fleshy swags underneath each of her eyes. It looks like she hasn't slept in months. 'I'd hug you but I stink,' she says. 'I wasn't expecting to see anyone today.'

'Where is everyone?' I blurt out. Irie is the only soul I've seen in this city besides Tracy and Wheelbarrow Man. I have to know why.

'What do you mean?' Irie wipes her forehead with the back of her hand and readjusts her stance, uncomfortable in the mid-morning heat.

'The city is so quiet.'

'Have you been living under a rock?' She laughs. It is a sharp, mirthless shout that bounces off the surrounding buildings, trapping us in a mocking echo.

'I've been a bit out of it, since–'

Irie nods to save me from having to finish the sentence. 'Everyone left,' she answers plainly. 'The people who had someplace to go, at least. That or they've been arrested.'

'They left?' I ask, ignoring her point about people being arrested. I'm too on edge to risk engaging with *that* subject today.

'After the queues.'

'The what?'

'You really don't know?' There's that sharp yelp of laughter again. 'You have to queue for water in Brixton now. Take turns filling at a pump. Won't be long before it's the same here.'

I had no idea. I've been unable to attend to my own needs, let alone the anxiety coma that is the twenty-four-hour news cycle. But I knew something like this was on the horizon, not just because of Wheelbarrow Man but because, after almost one hundred days without rain, water restrictions are inevitable. But queuing for *water*? That's unprecedented.

I bite my lip and try to contain the swell of anger that heaves against my rib cage. RIOT told them. We said, if you continue business as usual, nothing will be safe, not even water. *We fucking told them.* No wonder, then – after everything we did, everything *Ed* did – I no longer believe in the power of collective action. Because look at where it's got us.

'That's absolutely horrifying,' I manage to say. 'Ed tried—'

'I know. You can lead a horse to water…' Irie baulks at the irony. 'No one tried as hard as you two.' She looks at me with a woeful expression, the heavy bags under her eyes suddenly evidence of her grief. I forgot that other people might be feeling it, too. Then her face becomes a picture of reassurance. 'But hey! All is not lost. Dissident Uprising is giving them a run for their money.'

'What's that?'

'The new activist group,' she tells me. 'Their posters are everywhere.'

That's when I remember where I first spotted the shattered planet symbol – on the matching T-shirts of the baby activists, the ones who were pepper-sprayed outside Number 10. The memory of their conviction and Irie's misplaced compliment makes my cheeks redden. *This* is why I don't want to talk about activism. Because sure, no one tried as hard as Ed did. But by the end, I had nothing to do with it.

'They're brave, I'll give them that,' Irie goes on obliviously. 'You can't so much as *look* at a placard these days without getting arrested, yet they're fighting for change *by any means necessary*.' She starts deadheading the rhododendrons, Dissident Uprising's slogan hanging in the air between us. 'I just don't know how they're doing it. The conditions in those prisons must be hellish.'

'What do you mean?' I ask before I can decide whether or not I want to know the answer.

'The prisons are full, Fi.' Irie stops what she's doing and turns to look at me. 'The media keeps harping on about it. Saying that so many *eco-terrorists*,' she makes exaggerated quotation marks with her fingers, 'are getting locked up that actual criminals are being let off scot-free. There's rumblings from Westminster that something big is coming. I predict a blanket ban on protests, for one thing.'

'Fuck.' I anchor my feet to the ground as shock is poised to knock me sideways. *This* is why Ed wanted me to come here. He wanted me to *go back to where it all started* so that I could see what's happening to our movement. But doesn't Ed realise that seeing these things, knowing about them, only makes me retreat into myself even further?

'Sorry, Fi.' Irie touches my forearm, seeming to sense my distress. 'This is probably the last thing you want to talk about. After Ed died, the way he went, I thought things would–'

'Please stop,' I cut over her, pushing my sunglasses onto my head and scrunching my eyes to rid them of the sight of Ed's bloodied face. His toothless smile.

'Let's change the subject. What brings you here?'

'I, um…' I don't know how to explain why I'm here without causing Irie to call the psychiatrist herself. *A yew tree appeared on my doorstep, and I felt the urge to put Ed's ashes in the soil, and then I heard his voice, and the tree flowered like the rhododendrons you used to grow, and he told me to come here.* 'I guess I just wanted to see how you're getting on,' I say instead. 'And to see the garden.' I glance at the drought-stricken scratch of mud behind her.

'It didn't stand a chance after the hose pipe ban,' she explains, turning to follow my eyeline. 'And can you believe, I haven't had a volunteer in over *five weeks*? I tried to keep the place going on my own, but after a while I had to accept defeat.'

'I'm so sorry, Irie,' I say, and to my surprise, the words actually sound sincere. I guess I'm still capable of empathy. 'This place was such a lifeline for me and Ed.'

'Speaking of which…' Irie turns her attention towards the house and perks up. 'Come with me. There's something I could use your help with.'

Irie leads me through the sweltering conservatory, where the shrivelled shells of geraniums tumble from dusty plant pots, and through a door that leads downstairs to a room I haven't been in before. It's a shady basement kitchen that reminds me of the servants' quarters in *Downton Abbey*.

'This used to be the staff kitchen,' Irie says, confirming my suspicions.

Everything in the kitchen looks like an original feature, from the wrought-iron bread oven to the inglenook fireplace. I touch it, enjoying its cool hard surface. The room is crammed with shelves displaying the kinds of tools I'd expect to find in a shed. It's big enough for a studio apartment, though considering I've been to Irie's ample townhouse in Clapton, she's got no need to squat in a make-shift shed.

'How do you afford East Peace?' I ask, probably rudely. The thought of Irie's townhouse and not-for-profit business, combined with my own border-line broke bank balance, has made me impolite.

Irie laughs. 'Oh, I don't pay for it, love! I knew the woman who owned this place. We met at a protest camp in the eighties – you'd have loved her, Fi. A proper socialist, a philanthropist.' She leans over a large flat cardboard box that's lying on the kitchen floor. 'She wanted the garden to become a social enterprise when she passed. I pitched her East Peace, and she left it to me. Not the whole house, mind you. Her kids carved that up into flats years ago, but I got the garden, the basement and a fair bit of cash to get the business going. God bless that woman.' Irie lifts the box onto its side with a laboured grunt. 'Anyway, you can help me build this. It's been sitting here for two months.'

'What is it?'

'A bench,' she replies, opening the top of the box with a flick-knife that she produces from her back pocket. 'For Ed.'

'A bench for Ed?' My tongue feels like sandpaper.

'Something to remember him by. He was such an integral part

of East Peace. Did you know it was his idea to build those raised beds out the back? He just appeared with a load of railway sleepers he'd found on the side of the road. Turned a bit of old mud into a pumpkin patch just in time for Halloween. Not to mention everything he did with RIOT. I meant what I said at the funeral, Fi. I was proud to know him.'

I don't remember her saying that. All I remember is standing in the corner of the crematorium with my hands in the pockets of my black pinafore, reeling from the imperfection of my reading while a long line of people I barely knew told me the exact same thing: *I'm sorry for your loss. Ed was a great man. Let me know if there's anything I can do to help.* I was too bewildered to think of anything anyone could do to help. I was too bewildered to process that Ed was gone and that the funeral was for him and that I would forever be known as his surviving girlfriend. All I wanted was to call him and tell him about the second-worst day of my life. Instead, I looked at my feet and tried to block out the sound of his wicker coffin receding behind a curtain.

Irie unpacks various slats of wood and lines them up according to the instructions. It's a classic park bench and smells like a pine furniture shop. She hands me a drill. I hold it in both hands, clueless. Irie picks up on my hesitation and drills the first hole. I follow suit, feeling a little jolt of excitement every time the screw spirals into the wood. We start building. During the process, we don't talk much. Irie slots the planks together, telling me where to drill, and I do so like I've been handling power tools all my life.

'You do the honours,' she says when the bench stands upright. I sit down slowly, and when my bum makes contact with the seat, I lift my legs and swing them.

'Feels like a bench.' I grin.

'Looks like a bench.'

'We built a bench.' I swing my legs again, a flicker of satisfaction making me uninhibited.

'We did.'

Irie sits down beside me. Her wide hips push against mine, and I move closer to the armrest. She smells like sweat and compost.

Her fingernails are deeply set with mud, and her palms are bumpy with calluses. I look at my own hands. In days gone by, I used to get manicures, pedicures and facials every other week. At the height of my online fame, I didn't even have to pay for it, so long as I posted the results and tagged the company. Now I am haggard and pale with peeling cuticles and nails that have been chewed to the quick.

'Time for the most important part,' Irie says, placing an encouraging hand on my knee. 'What message shall we put on it?'

'Message?'

'There needs to be some kind of remembrance message. I've been holding off building it so that you can decide.'

'I'm not sure,' I say quickly, the task feeling like a trap.

'Did he have a favourite quote? A poem?'

I clear my throat. I think again about my reading at the funeral. The way I couldn't get through the first two lines of poetry without breaking into ugly sobs. Ed's mum sprang out of her chair and handed me a near-empty packet of tissues. Everyone was crying. But for some reason, my spluttering rendition of Tennyson's 'In Memoriam' didn't feel right. It was too morbid. I shouldn't have picked it. Not when the crematorium was so packed that the service had to be amplified on speakers to reach the bloated crowd of mourners outside. I should have tried to uplift them. That's what Ed would have done. He'd have tried to make them see that his legacy would live on. But when I'd found 'In Memoriam' online, it was the only poem that made sense to me.

Old Yew, which graspest at the stones
That name the under-lying dead,
Thy fibres net the dreamless head,
Thy roots are wrapt about the bones.

The seasons bring the flower again,
And bring the firstling to the flock;
And in the dusk of thee, the clock
Beats out the little lives of men.

O, not for thee the glow, the bloom,
Who changest not in any gale,
Nor branding summer suns avail
To touch thy thousand years of gloom:

And gazing on thee, sullen tree,
Sick for thy stubborn hardihood,
I seem to fail from out my blood
And grow incorporate into thee.

I made myself forget that poem along with the Pringles tube under the sink. My mind rejected the memory to protect itself. Yet remembering those words now ignites every inch of my skin with pinpricks.

And grow incorporate into thee…

Does that mean what I think it means? *I become a part of the tree?* I picked that poem because it was about yew trees and death. That's the only reason it made any sense: Ed loved yew trees, and he was dead. Sorted. I just wanted to get the funeral over with so that I could crawl into a pit and shut the world out forever. Be done with the commiserations, the line of well-meaning strangers, and let sorrow swallow me whole.

O, not for thee the glow, the bloom…

I have to stop myself from audibly gasping. Even a poet writing in the nineteenth century knew that yew trees don't flower. Even *he* understood their incorporeal potential, just like generations of people who built entire faiths around the idea that these exceptional trees revive the dead. Who's to say that they were wrong, just because our cocksure, modern sensibilities have robbed life of mystery? The fact of the matter is: human history vastly favours the myth.

So if it's true, if the druids were right, wouldn't that explain why the plant showed up without explanation? Wouldn't that explain why I can hear Ed's voice again – why it flowered when I put his ashes in the soil, why it defied the laws of nature to do so?

I thought the yew tree was a *vessel* for Ed's voice. But what if it *is* Ed?

My heart rate hits the roof.

I have to go home. I have to ask him.

I mumble something to Irie about needing time to think and feeling unwell. She looks a little disappointed as I make my excuses, offering me a cup of tea, a snack, anything to keep me there a little longer. I don't have the headspace to wonder why.

I march into the flat, breathless and sweaty. The yew tree is standing in a tray of water on the mantelpiece. As I cross the living room, I swear I can see the flower turn towards me.

'Ed?' I say, picking up the plant and holding it close to my face. 'Are you…?' My voice wavers. I don't know how to articulate something so utterly implausible.

I am, Fi.

'You are? You're actually *here* here?' My eyes fill once more with tears.

As 'here' as I'll ever be.

I nod and smile and weep happy tears. My knees give way. I sit on the sofa and gaze at the flower as if I'm looking right into his eyes.

'You came back,' I croak, my bottom lip quivering. 'You came back.'

5

In the video, Ed is pretending to be a TV gardener, a Monty-Don-meets-David-Attenborough type that always made me laugh. For once, this video was just for us. Ed made me promise. Despite his playful nature, he took his public persona seriously and thought that, if he showed even a hint of weakness, his opponents would use it against him. It made him dry in interviews, sometimes surly. But secretly, Ed was a big kid. That's one thing he said he loved about me. I drew out parts of him that the world made him hide away.

The camera sweeps across East Peace and lands on Ed crouching beside a bed of daffodils. His muddied knees are at his chest, his face contorted into that of a wizened old gentleman and his voice croaky with the Queen's English of a national treasure.

'After the dreary bleakness of winter,' he begins, overemphasising his *B*s, 'the cheery faces of daffodils burst forth and glow like beacons of light through the dark. These bonny wee blooms herald longer, lighter days and the promise of green things to come. Listen!' He puts a cupped hand to his ear and expands his eyes. 'Can you hear nature revving her engine? Watch out, she's about to take her foot off the clutch. Steady now, mother eeaaarrrrth!' He mimes getting hit by a car and is left for dead among the daffodils. I can be heard snorting in the background.

I sound like such a twat, Ed says with a laugh, a laugh that resonates in my ears like a childhood lullaby. His leaves are momentarily animated, the fan buffering hot air towards us.

'No, you don't,' I tell him, turning the phone away in mock defence. I'm sitting in bed with Ed between crossed legs, my thumb sore from spending all morning scrolling through old photos and videos together. 'You sounded like a legend, thank you very much. Not a twat.'

You always loved that side of me, huh?

'I did,' I say with a fond smile. 'I *do*.'

I sit back against the headboard and take a deep breath. A warm tide of tranquillity washes over me like an oxytocin high. I feel content. More than that, I feel released. Because against all odds, we've found our way home to each other. This is how things were always supposed to be.

Then a clod of fear muddies calm waters. 'You're staying for good this time, right?' I brush my fingertips over Ed's sparkling white petals.

Hopefully, he says.

I uncross my legs and hold him out in front of me.

'*Hopefully?*' My contentment vanishes. 'What does that mean? Why not *definitely?*'

I don't have all the answers, Fi.

'Why not? *You're* the magical houseplant.'

The silence that follows gives me the impression that, if Ed were still a man, he'd be shrugging his shoulders.

'How can I keep you with me, then?' I ask, sitting forward, restless. 'What do I need to do? If you leave me again, I don't know what I'll–'

You'll figure it out, my love. You're smart like that.

It's so inexplicably lovely to hear him say that to me. I relax back against the headboard with a grin, then focus on his flower.

He bloomed for a reason, that much is clear. Because thanks to that first flower, I went to East Peace and realised something profound. Not just the truth about Ed, but a forgotten truth about myself: despite Travis and all he took from me, I am still capable. Capable of seeing Irie. Capable of building a bench. Capable of hearing about the state of the world. I didn't shut down when Irie told me about the water shortages or Dissident Uprising or the prisons. I didn't let the horses overpower me. And I think, in doing all that, I allowed a part of myself – a mere glimmer in the gloom – to reemerge.

So what if Ed blooms again? What if, with each new flower, the glimmer outshines the gloom until I let go of what happened to us and reemerge as the woman who Ed fell in love with? Is that how I'll get him to stay? But that logic relies on flowers – flowers that, in and of themselves, defy logic entirely. And Ed isn't some bog-standard begonia. It's going to take more than tap water and indirect sunlight to get an otherworldly yew tree blooming, to get someone like *Ed* blooming. In life, he had such high standards. Standards that I so often failed to meet.

But not this time. This time, I'll get it right.

That evening, I take off all my clothes and try to find some relief from the sun. I won't risk closing the curtains, not after what it did to all of the other plants, but the heat is almost enough to make me submerge myself in an ice bath until nightfall. I put Ed on the mantelpiece and set about making dinner. Before he came back, I ordered takeaways whenever I had the presence of mind to feel hungry, but I know he wants me to take better care of myself. With a frying pan in one hand and a wooden spoon in the other, I stand in the kitchen stark naked and try to remember how to cook.

Figured it out yet? Ed says from across the room.

'No. Maybe. I don't know,' I reply, softening my tone so that I don't sound as exasperated by that question as I feel. I put the kitchen utensils down and look out of the window, hoping to find an answer in the silent streets below. When I look back, I see something almost as astonishing as that first flower. The evening sun is bathing Ed's branches in golden light, casting a shadow on the chimneypiece behind him.

In that shadow, I see a shape.

I search the flat for a pen, my fingers frantic as I upturn drawers and rummage through keepsakes. My body is more sweat than skin and my bare boobs swing about like overripe fruit. My hands are shaking. I grip the black marker pen and take a deep breath. Then, with my tongue stuck firmly in the corner of my mouth, I trace the shape. The ink bleeds into the wallpaper. My heart pounds.

When I'm done, I move Ed aside and step back.

It is unmistakable. In the wobbly outline of my crude recreation, a cat is scrawled onto the chimneypiece like a minimalist work of art.

'Bruce,' I gasp.

Bruce, Ed confirms.

'You want me to go and get him?'

Of course he does. Of course *I* do. It's just that, with everything that's happened since Tracy took him, I've not had the time to entertain the possibility. Or, indeed, the courage. Because getting Bruce means going to Scotland. That's a whole lot harder than walking up the road to East Peace. It means taking a train, travelling across the country and confronting Tracy, a woman who knows exactly how to shatter my resolve. But there's no pushing it away when Ed's message is etched onto the wall in permanent marker. If I want him to bloom again, if I want him to stay, I have to go to Scotland.

I look up train tickets. It's one hundred and forty pounds for a single to Edinburgh. I open my banking app. Before Ed died, the rent and bills barely scratched the surface of my earnings. After three months with no income, the sole upkeep of this place is taking its toll.

Why didn't I save any money? Social media is such a volatile creature. There was no guarantee that I'd keep raking it in. I should have put some of it away. I should have invested it or done whatever it is that proper adults do when they're suddenly very wealthy. But once people knew my name, there was no going back to the frugal Fifi who got trinkets from charity shops and wore secondhand clothes. I had to live up to my freshly forged niche, to prove that my ever-increasing follower count was in tandem with my lifestyle. So I selected designer pieces that suited my brand, gravitating towards labels that used keywords like *artisanal*, *slow fashion* and *ethically sourced*. That's why I spent so much money. Because so long as I could keep up with trends, I could maintain my relevance. And relevance was an influencer's currency.

I eye my wardrobe with a guilty glance. I didn't touch my clothes when I gutted the flat. I couldn't bring myself to. Those expensive, beautiful things are all that I have left from that short time, when I felt important. But with Ed here, I can't wear that stuff again. Not when fashion was part of the arsenal of problems that drove us apart. Ed agreed with Beth: fashion was exploitative, whatever way you tried to spin it. He said I was fuelling consumerism. He said I was part of the problem, and he wore out his jeans until they were busted at the knees and left muddy trails of torn fabric at the heels.

I open the wardrobe. There are hundreds, if not thousands, of pounds' worth of clothes in here. That's more than enough for a ticket home. With Vinted downloading, I start taking out hangers and throwing them on the bed – brushed cotton dresses, naturally dyed linen trouser suits, pure silk slips, each piece handcrafted by an independent business who cared enough about their impact to say so. There was, of course, the brand I partnered with during Earth Month, but I gave all of that crap to a charity shop when the shit hit the fan. I really *did* care.

Then I land on the dress I wore to the East Peace party. It is a puffy, off-the-shoulder piece that was gifted to me by an up-and-coming designer. I thought I looked like a young Sophia Loren that night. Everyone else was wearing sun-bleached shorts and flip-flops.

I want to douse it in lighter fluid and start a small fire. Instead, I hang it on the bedroom door and take a picture. This will be the first thing to go. But before I can upload the listing, I get another unsolicited and entirely unwelcome visitor.

'You could have called ahead,' I say, hiding my phone in my back pocket where a stream of missed calls aggregate. Travis is standing on my front doorstep with his hand on his hip, a denim tote bag on his shoulder and his foot tapping on the step like an impatient cartoon. Propped beside him is an electric scooter.

'You never answer.' He sucks on what appears to be a pink kazoo but turns out to be a vape. An artificial cherry cloud escapes his mouth. His white skin is flushed red, and his Turkish hair transplant sticks to his wet forehead.

'I told you, Trav,' I retort, my voice tight with contempt, 'I need a break.'

'You've had a break, haven't you?' He leans in, his demeanour deliberately gentle. He's wearing slouchy jean shorts and a cropped T-shirt that shows off his belly button. 'Look, can I come in? We need to talk. And I *neeeed* to get out of this sun. The weather has zero chill – literally, ha!'

I can't think of a decent enough reason to turn him away. I *have* been avoiding him, and now that he's here in all of his extra pearlescence, closing the door would signal the end of my career. I cast my mind upstairs to the clothes scattered over the bed. Perhaps, if I can get him to give me an advance, I won't have to sell the only lovely things left in my possession. And Ed wants me to go on this trip. I can't find a new job or cash in my clothes while I'm in Scotland, can I?

'I've had a bit of a clear out,' I say to Travis as I lead him into the flat, attempting for my lack of emotion to diminish his own. But he makes a noise akin to someone squeezing air out of a taut balloon.

'Eeeeeeek! Wow. OK.' He takes a long drag of his vape, filling the room with the smell of a teenage girl's body spray. 'Where the *fuck* are all the plants, pardon my French?'

'I felt like a change,' I say with a casual bob of the head.

Travis gapes. It's like he's stumbled on a crime scene, his frenzied eyes taking in the extent of the moral degradation that surrounds him. 'But, babe, you're *Foliage Fifi*. Plants are your niche.'

I wince at the mention of my social media handle. 'Ugh, god. Can we not?'

'Can we not *what*? Can we not talk about your brand? Why do you think I'm here, hun?' He walks over to Ed. 'At least you've got *one* left. What even is this? This flower looks…' He extends a finger, his glazed expression like a hypnotised Sleeping Beauty reaching for the spindle.

'No touching!' I rush across the room and snatch Ed away with a nervous laugh.

'I don't get it. Why get rid of everything except this? And what's with the crazy doodle?' He eyes the shadow portrait of Bruce on the chimneypiece, then the cracked plaster.

I wrap my arms around Ed and rock him from side to side, ignoring the comment. I know what it looks like. Who else scrawls pictures of cats on the wall and wrecks it with projectiles aside from the mentally unstable? But Travis is the last person on earth who would understand.

'This is all very *odd*, babe,' he says, spinning around and setting his eyebrows in a Botox-inhibited scowl. 'I can't say I'm best pleased. You're known for plants. It's how I got all your sponsors.' He twiddles his wilting moustache, something he's grown since the funeral, and parts his glossy lips indignantly. He showed up to the crematorium wearing a crushed red velvet paisley suit accessorised with a gold curtain tieback. It was almost over-the-top enough to draw attention away from my insipid reading. I frown at the memory. No wonder I've been ignoring him.

'I couldn't take care of them all without Ed,' I admit, hoping that the genuine pain in my voice might soften him to my struggle.

'But what is Foliage Fifi without the foliage, you know what I mean? And what will your sponsors say? The Plant Pantry, for example. They won't be happy about this, babe. They won't be happy at all.'

'I don't know Trav. The truth is…' I hesitate, wondering whether I should be honest. Despite what Travis might think, this conversation isn't just between the two of us. Ed is here, observing the whole exchange, and I know for a fact that if I'm going to get him to bloom again, I can't let Travis bully me into submission. I have to bend him to my will.

Threaten to quit, Ed tells me.

'The truth is,' I say more firmly, drawing courage from the bulk of Ed's pot against my torso, 'I don't think I want to do this anymore. I don't think I *can* do this anymore. Too much has happened.'

'I totally get that, babe.' Travis takes a few strides towards me, his face warped with practiced sincerity. 'But there's the contract, isn't there? You have to give three months' notice.'

'*Three* months'?'

'It's all there in black and white, hun!' He laughs, a bursting guffaw that ruffles Ed's leaves and floods my face with the smell of his breath. Beneath the cherry vape juice, there is the mothbally scent of a man who doesn't floss.

'What happens if I don't?' I retreat into the kitchen. Being in such close proximity to Travis is jarring. He takes me back to the world I used to inhabit; the one of content quotas, ring lights and engagement metrics; where influencers called themselves *creators* and pretended to be impervious to like-counts but refreshed their feed every five minutes and deleted anything that didn't perform well. When I say *people*, I mean *me*. That used to be me.

'Let's cross that bridge when we come to it, shall we?' His smile is sickly sweet.

I can't believe I used to work for this man, that I allowed him to dictate my life and rob me of so much precious time. But once I'd signed the golden gag, I didn't have a choice. I had to upload three posts a day, seven days a week. There's only so much I could do in our flat, however impressive the plants, so I traipsed the city in search of inspiration. Ed tagged along at first, holding my bag as I posed outside the pastel-coloured terrace houses of Portobello Road and the cherry-blossom-clad restaurants of Covent Garden, but after asking him to stop one too many times, he lost interest. He'd sigh and sulk, his frustration peaking if I asked him to wait to start eating in a restaurant.

'The food doesn't disappear if you don't take a picture,' he'd snip at me, his eyes darting around in case anyone saw me acting like an influencer in the wild.

'They'll give us the meal for free if I post it,' I'd reason.

'I'd rather pay and eat hot food.'

After that, we'd eat in silence while I wrestled with whether or not to remind him that he benefited from free food just as much as I did, since I was the one paying the rent. Instead, I'd push salad around my plate and remember the meals we shared before Travis, when the food went cold because we were too enamoured with each other to notice that it had arrived.

'Now, listen,' Travis announces, forcing me back into the present.

'We can get all the plants back, no problem. The Plant Pantry can send a truckload tomorrow. Then we can restrategise, right? Resynergise. The plants are the jumping-off point. You know what I mean?' He walks around the sofa and peers out the window, as if expecting the truck to have arrived already. 'At the end of the day, hun, I just want what's best for you. All of us at Hype Tribe do. We didn't win Wellness Agency of the Year for nothing! That's why we've been so lenient. You've had the whole of Q2 off, you know?'

'But—'

'Listen, babe. I've got news. And I think you'll like it because funnily enough, it's not about plants. Where's Bruce?'

'I'm not sure.' I survey the empty living room, my stomach dropping into the flat below.

'Right, well, you're in for a treat, babe. Imagine this. You and Bruce in *You*.'

'You what?'

'*You magazine. Mail on Sunday* supplement. Old media, I know, but it's a great way to get credibility. Not that you're not credible, but it gets to the boomers – that's where the money is. And get this. They're doing a feature on creators and their pets. Guess who else is involved?'

'Who?'

'Go on, guess.'

'I don't know, Trav.'

'Mrs. Hinch. Mrs.-bloody-Hinch and Henry Hinch, her dog! They wanna feature all different types of influencers in different niches. The cleaner, the botanist, the candlestick maker. You know what I mean? It's the perfect PR for a comeback.' He takes a glass out of the kitchen cupboard and looks in the fridge. 'Where's your water?'

'What?'

'Your bottled water?'

'I don't have any.'

He laughs. 'So what've you been drinking?'

'Tap water.'

'Vintage,' he says dryly, leaving the empty glass on the kitchen counter. 'And no air-con, either. Anyway, this could go viral, I'm telling you, especially if we style you in something iconic. I'm thinking Vivienne Westwood – tartan, safety pins, maybe even one of her climate change pieces. I'm not saying we go full *eco-terrorist chic*, but something a bit punk for Ed. You deserve it, hun, after everything you've been through.'

I lick my lips, at a loss for words. Trust Travis to bend his own rules about overt displays of activism when it benefits him.

'Thank you, Travis,' he says, miming a talking hand. 'You're welcome, babe,' the other hand mimes back. 'You're a genius, Travis,' says the left. 'No, really, stop it, I'm just doing my job,' says the right.

'Bruce isn't here,' I admit, keeping my tone as matter-of-fact as possible. 'My mum took him to Scotland.'

'Why?' he practically shouts.

'To give me a break.'

'To give you a *break*?'

I nod.

'From your *cat*?'

'Yes.'

'Right…no plants, no Bruce. Are you trying to kill me?' He laughs again, all veneers, no humour. 'I get it. Times are tough. When my nan died, I was in bits. But we can't let that stop us from going on our own journey. You know what I mean? The universe has a plan, babe, and right now, the universe is throwing you a bone. A very big juicy fucking bone!'

'All right, Travis. I get the point.'

'So you'll go get Bruce?'

'Yes,' I say, my cheeks flushing pink when I realise that Ed is asking me to do exactly the same thing. The coincidence makes me giddy. Except it's *not* a coincidence, is it, Ed? Nothing is anymore. 'But only if the agency covers my expenses,' I add.

'No problem,' he replies without pause.

I squeeze the plant pot, pleased with myself.

Look who's the legend now, Ed whispers.

I smile so widely that Travis grins back with a hint of confusion, thinking I'm directing it at him. I make a move for the front door with Ed in my arms, desperate to get rid of Travis now that we've got what we need.

'How come you're still in London?' I ask as I shepherd him down the stairs. 'I thought you'd have a holiday home in Margate by now.'

'My new beau lives in Embassy Gardens.' He perks up, glad for an opportunity to talk about himself. 'Let me tell you, hun, it is *bouuuugie*. Air-con, temperature-controlled spa, sky pool. I'd be mad to give that up.'

'Sky pool?' I picture a levitating pool table.

'It's a floating pool between two skyscrapers. I can't believe my luck, to be honest. Everyone's got so much fucking money that they imported water *from the Alps* to fill it. And David, my beau David, he's shipped in crates of *jewellery water*, so we're hydrated to the hilt!'

'What's jewellery water?'

'It's from Japan. It's like, luxury water or whatever. I'll send you a bottle – if you behave.' He taps his nose and winks at me. 'Now, put that fucking plant down and go get the cat, OK? Or else we'll have to get lawyers involved, and that would be extremely cringe for the both of us.'

When I shut the front door behind him, I go upstairs and look out of the living room window to watch him leave. The view is unchanged, the metallic patchwork quilt blasting heat at my building and hiding any sign of the people who might cower within. Travis stands on his scooter, readjusts his tote bag and zooms off towards Central London, the cloud from his cherry vape puffing behind him like a steam engine.

6

All of the people who were missing from Kingsland High Street appear to be at King's Cross train station. Digital screens loom overhead, neon yellow text flashing *Delayed* across every destination. The murmur of the crowd rises and falls like the ineffable heat and fizzes with a tension that threatens to boil over. An amplified voice pleads wearily for restraint.

With my suitcase in one hand and Ed in the other, I raise my face parallel to the geometric ceiling and try to catch a breath that doesn't smell of other people. My ribs feel like they're going to erupt out of my chest and stick me in the neck, a feeling made worse by people's hostility. When the leaves of the plant brush against their skin, they snarl at me as if I've cut them with a razor.

'Stupid bitch,' someone says.

'Get that fucking thing out of my fucking face,' says another.

I apologise and hold Ed above my head, his flowers shining like Christmas decorations.

Yes, *flowers*, plural. He bloomed again this morning. When I spotted it, I screamed like a lottery winner, blasted 'Our House' and skipped around the coffee table like I did the day we moved in. I figured it out, just like he said I would. Because why else bloom on the morning I leave for Scotland if not to tell me that his flowers mean something? If I can just keep figuring it out, he'll keep on blooming, and that's how I'll get him to stay. I feel like the luckiest recently bereaved person in the world. Whenever my churning gut tells me to turn back, I focus on those two flowers and find the strength I need to push on.

Just then, there's a loud groan as all of the ticket gates swing open.

'The gates have been opened to ease congestion,' the weary voice says over the PA system. 'Please proceed to your platform in an orderly manner. The police are on standby.'

My heart lurches. I look over peoples' heads and try to spot rubberised vests and riot shields. If I know where they are, I can plan my escape. But all I can see are train guards in hi-viz jackets. The buzz of angry people fades as a familiar panic sets in. I close my eyes and huff the stagnant air. My mouth breaks into a frightened sneer. The horses—

'You OK, love?' A stranger puts her hand on my shoulder. I open my eyes to see a woman holding a child.

'Claus-tro-pho-bic.' I utter the lie as four separate words.

'Stick with me.' She loops an arm around my waist and nods decisively.

The crowd pushes forward. We are pressed on all sides against hot bodies that are moist with sweat and hard with tension. If I have to endure this for much longer, I'm going to break. I close my eyes and trust the woman to guide me and try not to think about the police. I wish I could put my arms down. I wish I could hold Ed close. I wish it wasn't so hot. The crowd carries us through the gates. The woman's child starts crying. She lets go of my waist, and I lose her in an instant. That's when I realise that I'm being dragged towards the wrong platform. I have to fight my way back, apologising to every other person as I squeeze myself between grown men and get stung by their insults.

'Delays have been caused by train tracks buckling between Peterborough and Stevenage,' the PA continues. 'We apologise for any inconvenience caused.'

By the time I'm on the train, there's nowhere to sit, not even the floor. At least I can put my arms down. I cradle Ed and check his flowers. As the train lurches away from the station, I stumble and almost drop him. My knuckles whiten around the pot. I look at the fortunate people with seats. Their eyes are fixed on their phones, ignoring the struggling masses around them. I watch the cityscape fading through the window, my nose almost pressed up against it. The train ploughs through a tunnel and past a protest camp. People have spray-painted messages onto bedsheets and tied them to the railings.

> *WE WILL NOT BE SILENCED*
> *RESIST POLICE POWERS*
> *DISSIDENT UPRISING*

There's that symbol again, the shattered planet with the safety pin stuck through it. I trace my eyes across the display for a glimpse of the RIOT 1.5 logo. We shoot past before I can spot one. I can't help but feel territorial. We were organising protests before Dissident Uprising was a twinkle in an activist's eye, yet that symbol is popping up around the city like a rash. Does that mean Ed's legacy is already fading? Is that where this is leading?

All in good time, Fi.

I nod and breathe deeply, his pot like a weighted blanket. All in good time.

The train pulls in after four. I messaged Tracy earlier and asked her to meet me in Edinburgh. I need a lift home – public transport is not a reliable way to reach the remote villages of West Scotland – but she was dumbfounded. *Why not come to Glasgow*, she fumed, *when it's only an hour away from Strathyre?* But Glasgow means nothing to me. Not compared to Edinburgh, with its gift bag of memories and cherished thoroughfare. Now that he's back, Ed deserves to see it. Tracy's irritation boiled over, saying that it was her birthday and she had plans and Edinburgh was too far and blah, blah, blah, so I resorted to a bit of emotional manipulation.

You were right. I'm not well. I need to get out of London, get my head sorted. Plus I can treat you to a birthday dinner. It's been so long since we did something nice together. Love you, Mum xxxxxxx

There was no arguing with that. I booked a table at an Italian bistro, a favourite date spot of Ed's, and sent her the location.

Now, with three hours to kill, I stand outside the station and take in my surroundings. The air has the slightest edge, a suggestion of coolness, and I feel calm. This is the city where we fell in love, where we sank our teeth into each other and spent whole days savouring the taste. I close my eyes and see an indie film montage of us kissing in the rain. We're hiking up Arthur's Seat and drinking in basement bars filled with cigarette smoke and stylish people. I hear 'Toothpaste Kisses' by The Maccabees. I feel the burgeoning potential of lifelong love, the way it enveloped us in its plenty and made so many promises. Back then, we were on the same page about everything. We got stuck into the kind of low-risk activism that we could both enjoy, before Ed started gluing himself to buildings and I started retreating into social media.

Remember how we met? Ed says wistfully.

'Of course I do.' I smile down at him.

The train station is a few minutes away from The World's End, the pub where it all started. I decide to stop inside for a drink, walking past medieval buildings that are dwarfed by the jagged cliff face of Arthur's Seat. We had a picnic up there once and got a bit carried away; our gin-in-a-tin lunch leading to passionate kissing that stopped short of indecent exposure when a gaggle of students crested the hill.

Fuck 'em. We should have gone all the way.

My stomach flips over and floods my body with heat. That's the most *himself* Ed has sounded since he came back. That's exactly what he would have said, were he walking beside me. When I get inside the pub, I find that I am very much in need of a large glass of wine to steady my girlish jitters. It's just as I remember it: dark oak panelling, raw stone walls, a pentagonal bar with a stained-glass frontage and the antique musk of age. This pub hasn't changed since the sixteenth century. I take my pinot grigio to a leather-bound booth in the window, placing Ed on the table and turning his flowers to face me.

When we met, Ed was in his third year at university, and I was working here. It was the only job I could get when I moved to

Edinburgh, the landlord taking a punt on me despite my complete lack of experience. Beth and I moved to the city when we were eighteen, both in search of some higher purpose. Dad had left Strathyre the year prior, packing up his meagre belongings to move to an island off the coast of the Inner Hebrides where, he claimed, he could live in harmony with nature. He was going to Banmora to plant trees and restore balance. 'Lucky you,' I told him. 'Go and isolate yourself instead of doing something actually meaningful.' Because it's all very well and good to leave your only child to seek out redemption, but I knew why he was really going there – to save himself. Wildfires had swept through West Scotland a few months earlier, licking the outskirts of Strathyre and tearing through the pine forest he felled for timber. He was frightened. But instead of joining a cause that would do something about it, he picked up sticks and ran away.

I went to Edinburgh to spite him. If he was going to manufacture a personal utopia that would protect him from climate change, I was going to face the threat head-on. I was going to join a cause – to make change happen. But that was easier said than done.

Beth and I moved into a one-bedroom flat above a fast-food restaurant where the smell of fryer fat forever lingered and looked for said cause. At first, we joined a fringe group that claimed to want *a just and thriving world*, but after a couple of fruitless meetings where people spent more time bickering about privilege than achieving anything tangible, we decided to branch out on our own. I spent quiet day shifts hunched over the bar, drawing posters with messages like *Let's Get Active to Stop Climate Change!* But I had no real sense of how to do that.

Until I met Ed.

He was the chair of the Climate Change Prevention and Democracy Preservation Society. They drank at The World's End once a week, but from where I was standing behind the bar, all they did was *prevent* the pub from making money by *preserving* their pints of ale. Still, their sense of purpose was intoxicating. The government had just introduced new police powers, and activists were up in arms. The right-wing media was praising the prime minister for his *decisive leadership*, and the fringe group was too worried about law enforcement to rise above their progressive showboating. But from what I overheard, Ed refused to be deterred.

I barely noticed him at first. He was wearing a navy blue University of Edinburgh hoodie and looked like every other library ghost with something to prove. But beneath his unremarkable appearance, Ed was surprisingly charismatic.

'You're really good,' he'd said, bending over the sketch of a peaceful protest I'd been drawing. I was mindful to include a range of ethnicities and body types – the fringe group had rubbed off on me – creating a diverse community of activists holding banners and megaphones. 'We could do with someone like you. I'm useless at this sort of stuff.'

'Thanks,' I'd replied coolly, hiding the scrap of paper behind my back. 'But it's just a doodle.'

I felt his eyes on me as I tilted a glass to pour his pint.

'That's a lovely accent. Are you local?'

'Oh, um, I grew up near Stirling. Well – Strathyre – but you won't have heard of it. It's near Stirling,' I repeated, stumbling over my reply. I was used to punters chatting me up, but students rarely showed an interest. They were too full of their own self-importance to notice a barmaid. The word *lovely* flustered me. I filled his glass with foam.

'Near the Trossachs?' he went on, ignoring my blunder. I nodded. 'That's so cool. I'd love to go there. I'm from Kent, land of roundabouts and industrial parks, so Scotland continues to blow my tiny mind.'

His tiny mind. I liked that. It put me at ease, as did his suggestion that my home was nicer than his. I poured out the foam and corrected the pint. Then he said, 'Maybe you could take me there one day?' Just like that. And it worked, because as I put the pint down on the bar, he turned from just another library ghost into a cute guy who made me feel like I mattered.

'If you play your cards right,' I'd replied, dazed by a bolt of electricity that flashed from his deep brown eyes into mine. The spark – that elusive thing that people on dating shows chased like an unattainable high – we had it.

I pull Ed close and find myself overcome with gratitude. Instead of being shattered by these memories, I know now that we never lost that spark, we just lost our way. A way that I am rediscovering, flower by gleaming flower.

The cool respite I felt on arrival vanishes, and I'm sweating and tipsy by the time I reach the restaurant (one glass of pinot at The World's End had turned into three). I check my reflection in the front window to see Tracy and my stepdad sitting at a round table directly behind it. They watch me trying to tame my frizzy curls and feign a smile. I adjust the hem of my turmeric-dyed shirt dress and go in.

They both stand to greet me. Ian looks like he's stumbled out of a department store clearance sale, and Tracy looks like she's just discovered Shein, her mass-produced synthetic clothing recognisable from a mile off.

'Fiona! How lovely,' she says, reaching for the plant. 'You never buy me birthday presents.'

'What? No.' I panic and yank Ed out of her reach. I haven't prepared an explanation. 'It's mine.'

'Oh. How silly of me to assume.' Tracy looks at Ian and scowls. She sits down without hugging me and reaches for the bottle of wine in front of her.

'Well, why the devil have you brought it all the way here?' Ian asks, his Scottish drawl present in every syllable. He has a monk's crown of white hair and the elongated features of a greyhound.

'To water it,' I say as plainly as possible, directing the statement to the centre of the table rather than his face. I look up at Tracy. 'You wanted me to take better care of plants, didn't you?'

'How long are you planning on staying?' Ian eyes my suitcase in disbelief.

'A little while, if that's all right with you?' The suitcase is empty. That's where I plan to stow Bruce if I can't find his carrier. Knowing Tracy, she'll have hidden it.

'Of course,' Tracy declares, her hand darting across the table to touch my fingers. She's had her nails done since I saw her last. They're metallic gold and glittery: birthday nails. 'Now, put the plant down, and we can order.' She purses her red lips – likely checking the filler hasn't dissolved – and opens the menu. I place Ed on the table beside me.

'Does it really need to be on the table?' Tracy reaches to put him on the floor.

'Yes,' I say, blocking her with my forearm. 'Otherwise someone will knock *it* over.'

Tracy tuts and buries her face in the menu. When the waiter arrives, I order spaghetti and another bottle of wine, just to be safe.

Tracy dominates the conversation. She tells me about some woman in the village who cheated on her husband; an old acquaintance who went bankrupt; a car accident on the A84 – forever delighting in other people's misery – while Ian and I take turns saying *How terrible*. When the food arrives and she pauses to eat, Ian jumps on the chance to air his own grievances.

'It's not right – reservoirs drying up, people queuing for water,' he moans between mouthfuls of calzone. 'I've never known anything like it. You're lucky to have left London, Fiona. It could've been you next–'

'Too depressing,' Tracy butts in, waving her hand in his face. 'It's my birthday. Lighten up. The weather's the weather. It comes and goes.'

'What does that m–' Ian attempts to ask.

'The best birthday pressie of all,' she cuts over him again, 'is my dear Fiona, home at last. We've been so worried about you.' She puts a manicured hand on top of mine and looks at me with dreamy, watery eyes. I think the second bottle of wine was a mistake.

'I'm all right.' I straighten my back. 'Fantastic, actually,' I add, remembering why I came here. 'I've sorted the flat. Look.' I show her photos of the living room and describe my incredible, newfound sense of wellness.

'But your message said you weren't well,' Tracy remembers. 'You said you needed to get your head straight.'

'Only because I'm missing Bruce,' I explain, my stomach lurching at the inconsistency. 'He's like a son to me and Ed. Imagine how you'd feel if someone took me away when I was a baby.'

'Chance would be a fine thing!' She laughs, then turns to see if Ian's laughing, too. He gives a tight-lipped smile and exhales through his nose.

'I'm fine, really. I just need Bruce.'

Tracy shakes her head and opens her mouth, primed to contradict me.

'The thing is, Mum…' I lean forward and clasp my hands on the table. I was expecting this. It's not in her nature to back down. But I have a card up my sleeve. Tracy is just about the only person who had a nice word to say about Travis, calling him *salt of the earth* when they met at the funeral. If the moral dilemma of stealing her daughter's cat isn't enough to sway her, his ultimatum might. 'I've been offered something really exciting. An interview with a big magazine – but I need Bruce.'

'Why?' She sits back and crosses her arms.

'The interview is about creators and their pets. *Mrs. Hinch* is involved.' I say the last bit with deliberate grandiosity, as if I've just announced that I'm working with Malala.

'Oh I see. So you want to *use* Bruce, is that it? You only care about him when it suits you?'

'I've been *grieving*, Mum, in case you forgot. Things got away from me a bit. But I'm feeling loads better now.' I give Ed a slight shake, hoping his flowers will persuade her. 'Look at how well I'm taking care of this little fella. This is a huge opportunity for me.'

'So do it without Bruce.'

'It's *about* Bruce. I can't go back to London without him.'

'We'll see.' Tracy pats my hand and nods, as if that settles it.

'I can't believe you.' I suck wine noisily through my teeth, the alcohol loosening my tongue. 'You've actually *stolen my cat*, you realise? I could report you.'

'Careful, now,' Ian says, putting a hand on Tracy's shoulder. 'Your mum just wants what's best for you, Fiona. We both do.'

I glower at him, sick of hearing that statement twice in as many days. How can Ian want what's best for me when he doesn't have a clue who I am? I can count the interactions I've had with him on one hand, but that's enough to know that he's as appealing as a bin bag and a total pushover. He'd have to be to marry someone like my mum. I thrust my chair back with a screech and pick up Ed.

'Where are you going?' Tracy asks.

'To the toilet, if that's allowed?' I hate the stroppy, teenage tone in my voice, but I can't help it. She brings out the worst in me.

'You're taking a *plant* to the toilet with you?' Her expression is caught between dismay and amusement.

Of course I am. I can't leave Ed alone with *them*. What if she picks a flower? I can just imagine it. I'll come back from the bathroom and she'll have one tucked behind her ear. She'll say, *Look, Fiona. It matches my blouse!* And then I don't know what I'll do.

'Yes,' I insist.

'Surely not,' Ian says, looking behind him to see if anyone at the adjacent table has noticed. 'Don't be silly, now, pet.'

'I'm not your *pet*.'

'Oh, come on.' Tracy stands and reaches for the plant. 'Give it to me.' She pulls the pot towards her. It almost slips out of my hands.

'No.' I pull back. 'Get your hands off him.'

'*Him?*' Tracy hisses under her breath, refusing to let go. '*Him?* Have you completely lost your mind?'

My stomach twists. I try to pry her fingers away but Tracy clings on, much like she did that day with Bruce. Why is she intent on confiscating the only things that bring me joy? We tussle with the pot, making more of a scene than if she'd just let me take him to the toilet, then one of Tracy's acrylics catches my skin. That's when I lose my grip.

Ed falls.

The pot hits the floor.

And just like all those long-dead plants that I threw against the wall, the soil, the ashes, explode.

Cutlery clatters onto plates. I drop to my knees. I try to hold the pot together, the blue shards of ceramic like splintered glass. It's in too many pieces. Ed's roots are exposed. There are pine needles everywhere.

'It was an accident,' Tracy spits out defensively. She kneels beside me to pick up the pieces. 'I'll buy you a new one.'

A throaty sob escapes my mouth. I bat her hands away. Ed's remains – falling into the cracks between the floorboards, drifting into the kitchen, dusting the chef's hat, seasoning the soup. 'It's Ed. Ed was in here.'

'Oh.' Tracy drops the shattered ceramic. She puts her hand over her mouth and then thinks better of it, wiping her soily fingers on a napkin.

'Well, do something, then,' Ian snaps, grabbing Tracy's mock-Mulberry handbag and rummaging inside. He finds a foldaway, cat-print shopping bag and shakes it out.

'Here,' he says, joining me on the floor. 'We'll put him in here until we get home.'

Ian cups his hands around the ball of roots and places the plant inside the bag with utmost care. Then we both scoop up the soil, picking out crumbs and other people's hair until a confused waiter brings over a dustpan and brush.

When it's done, I remain kneeling on the floor for longer than I should have. I stare at the flowers in my hand. The petals are bruised, their glittery iridescence gone.

7

Strathyre is strung along the east of the valley between Callander and Balquhidder. It has a dozen sandstone holiday homes, a village shop called The Village Shop and a primary school that, when I attended, had thirty-five students. Of those thirty-five students, I warmed solely to Beth, whose precocious nature and cackling laugh made compulsory education bearable.

Tracy has lived at Cleadale Cottage for over three decades, despite outgrowing it when she had me. It is a tiny two-up two-down gatehouse that's dwarfed by the houses on either side of it, and damp with a dodgy kitchen extension. Tracy hasn't let that limit her interior design ambitions, though. She's into shabby chic: the kind of junk you buy from a family-owned knickknack shop that survives one year and sells faux vintage signs. She's into those too, especially in the kitchen. There, one of many painfully kitsch signs reads, 'This house runs on love, laughter and prosecco.' It would be borderline acceptable if it weren't for the copious amounts of cat decor – her collection of brass cat ornaments, cat-shaped teapots and embroidered cat cushions cluttering up the place. This dedication to a theme makes Tracy easy to buy presents for, but it doesn't work both ways. There were many Christmas mornings when I'd awake to an envelope telling me I was the proud sponsor of Socks, the cheeky moggy, or Marmalade, the bossy tomcat. I did get a free cuddly toy and an educational activity pack, but I wanted a Barbie. I hid my disappointment. Tracy told me she was proud to have a family who cared so much about animals. She said it made us better than other people.

Ian's only mark on the place, as far as I can tell, is a giant smart TV and an impressive collection of scotch. He offers me a nightcap when we get in, but I head straight upstairs for Bruce. I find him nestled on my childhood bed. The room looks nothing like the one I left. It used to be Parma Violet purple with Groovy Chick bedding. Now it's Farrow & Ball grey like the rest of the house, with matching paw-print pillowcases.

'There you are,' I whisper, putting a bagged Ed down on the desk and sitting beside Bruce. He wakes with a start. I take a second to marvel at his feline features, the ones Ed captured in the shadow of his sun-struck foliage. 'We've come to take you home, baby.' I stroke him. He looks up at me sleepily, his brilliant green eyes coming into focus. Then he jumps off the bed. I pick him up and push my face into his long grey fur. He's been brushed and smells faintly of Tracy's perfume. He wriggles out of my arms. I put him down. He leaves the room, his tail swinging behind him.

It's OK, Fi. He'll come round.

I catch my breath and turn towards the desk, relief lightening the load of Bruce's rejection. Ed's voice hasn't left me despite the fall. That means I didn't lose as much of his ashes as I first feared. Still, he looks so naked without his flowers. He's just a yew tree again, potent with magic, but no longer decked out with the proof.

'I'll do whatever it takes to get you flowering again,' I tell him, running my hand lightly over his foliage. The bare floorboards are cold underfoot. This room used to be carpeted until I spilled a bottle of nail polish and destroyed Tracy's world for a day. She binned all my makeup after that. It was just cheap stuff from Claire's, but I was gutted. Then Dad gave me twenty pounds and took me shopping. He bought me brand new everything.

Ugh – *Dad*. It's hard to ignore the child he wounded when I'm in the bedroom I grew up in. If Edinburgh is a romantic montage stolen from an indie movie, this house is a black-and-white silent film. I'm the damsel in distress who's been tied to the tracks and the train is pummelling towards me, only instead of untying the rope, Dad adds more coal to the engine.

Ed never met him, though he was always interested in the place he ran off to. He, too, aspired to live in a passive house with a grey-water system and solar panels on the roof. The sustainability of Banmora, with its hydropower and community of like-minded doomsdayers, appealed. But I never took him there. I didn't want to give him any ideas.

Ian knocks on the door just then. I know it's him because Tracy doesn't knock.

'Yes?'

'Can you get the door?'

I reluctantly open it. He is holding a cup of tea in one hand and a plastic plant pot in the other. He hands me the tea. 'Milk, no sugar?'

I normally don't drink cow's milk, but today I can't bring myself to care.

'Thanks,' I manage, putting myself between Ian and Ed. 'Will he be OK?'

'It'll be fine. Just needs a wee bit of TLC.' Ian pulls a trowel out of his back pocket.

'Can I do it?'

'Sure.'

I take the trowel and scoop the soil from the bag and into the plastic pot that Ian has provided. It is substantially less tasteful than the blue ceramic number Ed showed up in. As soon as possible, I'll buy a more suitable replacement.

The pot isn't the problem.

I'm stumped by this. If the pot isn't the problem, what is? I'm not in the mood to decode more cryptic clues. I lift him out of the bag, his exposed roots akin to full-frontal nudity, and press him firmly into his temporary accommodation.

'There,' Ian says when I'm finished. 'Run it under the tap and it'll be right as rain. The pot's lighter, too. Easier for you to cart about the place.' He smiles without a hint of judgement. I can't help but warm to him a bit. 'What kind of plant is it, anyway?'

'It's a yew tree!' I gush, ecstatic for the chance to say so. Nobody has bothered to ask me that yet.

'Huh. Didn't know they came that small.' He bends down and squints at Ed. 'But aye, now that you mention it, it is. I used to canoe across the loch to Inchlonaig when I was a wee 'un. The Isle of the Yew Trees, we used to call it. Local legend had it that Robert the Bruce planted the trees himself.'

'Really?' My voice is high pitched with interest. 'In Loch Lomond?'

He nods. 'Aye.' I wait for him to say something more, but he just stands there with his hands in his pockets, barely able to make eye contact. I want to ask him what else he knows about yew trees, whether local legend didn't just credit Robert the Bruce but told of mystical, otherworldly forces that resurrected lost loved ones. I want to ask if he can explain why the tree had two flowers earlier this evening. But he seems to have forgotten all about them or didn't notice in the first place.

He clears his throat. 'I just wanted to say,' he pauses to listen for Tracy downstairs then says, 'when my Jan passed... well, I thought I'd never get over it. And I haven't–'

'That's encouraging,' I retort, my smidgen of warmth icing over.

'What I mean is... Yes, it still hurts. But over time, you learn to live with grief. It never goes away, I'm sorry to tell you, but it has less control over you. You adapt and you grow around it. You get bigger than the way it makes you feel, if that makes sense?' He gives this speech to the wall like a socially inept uncle trying to speak at a funeral. 'I guess what I'm trying to say is... I understand. I understand why this plant is important to you. I spread my Jan's remains at the top of Ben A'an. She loved the view up there. Now, every time I can manage the walk, it's like I feel her in the wind.'

I glance at his face. He snatches a wayward tear with his fingertip and turns away.

'Thank you, Ian. It's good to know that someone understands,' I say, touched by his sincerity, 'and thanks for the plant pot, too.' I smile and force the eye contact he's been avoiding.

He nods and leaves the room. That's the most Ian has said to me in private and the only time I've heard him talk about his late wife. I didn't even know her name was Jan. Ian has always been so painfully boomerish that I can barely bring myself to address him, let alone his past. When Dad left, Tracy's idea of comforting me was to swap husbands as quickly as possible in the hope that I wouldn't notice. They had this lavish barn wedding with bows on the backs of chairs, and before the leftover wedding cake had gone stale, I got on a bus to Edinburgh and never came back. But it's comforting to know that Ian has been through what I've been through. Not the houseplant-boyfriend bit, of course, but he knows what it's like to feel the presence of the dead long after they've passed. And he agrees with me: the plant is a yew tree, and that's coming from someone who grew up surrounded by them.

Although my reunion with Bruce has been less than amicable and Tracy very nearly returned Ed to the grave, I'm glad I came home – at least for the vindication.

I put Ed on the bedside table and pull back the duvet. The sheets are scratchy, the mattress is lumpy, and the pillow is rock-hard. I doubt anyone has slept in this room for years. After half an hour of restless tossing and turning, I press my face into the pillow and wait for my eyes to adjust. The room has the matte black quality of a pollution-free sky. I shine my phone torch to check on Ed. He's still alive.

The pot isn't the problem, he said. Does that mean I have to stop worrying about Ed's needs and more about Bruce's? In which case, he couldn't have cared less that I travelled the length of the UK to rescue him. Or is there some greater problem that I haven't figured out yet? Before the fall, Ed had two flowers. Does that mean something? Two flowers, one for each of us? But what about Bruce? I lie back with a frustrated huff.

Dad used to read me stories in this bed. He had an old, hardback book of Scottish fairy tales with a Celtic knot on the cover. He said that as Scots, it was our duty to reclaim the pagan oral histories that were lost to the church. The stories were always entwined with the natural world, evoking the ruddy countryside that surrounded us. I loved the way he brought them to life. Gruff-voiced goblins, whisper-quiet fairies and rasping hags with magical healing powers. He used to call me Fianna, nicknaming me after a legendary band of warrior-hunters who protected the shores of Scotland and Ireland from invasion.

Fianna, he'd say, *my little fighter*.

What a little fighter I turned out to be.

With nothing else to do but press on my childhood bruises, I reread his most recent text message to me. It was sent five weeks ago.

GREETINGS FROM BANMORA. NO RAIN AGAIN. MENDED CHICKEN COOP. HOW ARE YOU? TRIED CALLING. WOULD BE GREAT TO TALK SOON. LOTS TO CATCH UP ON. LOVE FROM DAD (JOHN).

I'm not sure what I find more irritating: the all-caps, the weird parentheses or the lack of effort. What hurts most, though, is that up until he left, he was a good dad. He was funny and kind, he was patient, he had a gentle tone of voice. He was the first person who stuck my hands into the soil and taught me how to love it. In fact, my earliest memory is in the garden with him. I'm about three years old, and Dad is showing me how to plant pansies into a hanging basket. He guides my dimpled toddler fingers as I pull a plug plant from a seed tray and try my best not to tear it. I remember being mesmerised by the technicoloured, smiling faces of those pansies. I remember telling him that when I grew up, I wanted to paint the flowers, since they could only be this pretty if someone was colouring them in. I remember him being delighted with me for saying that. But nothing I did ever delighted him enough to stay.

At first, he did ask me to come. When I was a teenager, Dad preached the virtues of Banmora like it was some kind of cure-all. If he and my mum argued, he'd tell her that they'd be so much happier on the island. If Beth and I fell out, he'd tell me that I'd make new friends on the island. If unseasonal weather decimated our hanging baskets or ransacked the village, he'd promise us that in Banmora, we'd be safe. But I never thought he was being serious. My adolescent brain couldn't comprehend that anyone would *choose* to move to a remote island thirty miles offshore – even if that island was carbon-negative and climate-proof.

'Imagine it, Fianna,' he used to say. 'We can live somewhere that runs on the wind and the sun. We can have four football fields of land, all to ourselves. And we won't have to worry anymore. If you could just *see* what they're doing out there to sustain themselves — it's remarkable.'

It sounded like another one of his fairy tales. But Tracy wasn't interested in fairy tales, especially if they didn't have cat sanctuaries, so Banmora remained a pipe dream. That is until a few months after my seventeenth birthday, when I watched from my bedroom window as wildfires blazed above the valley. The embers were still smouldering when Dad quit his job at the timber yard and left. I was almost an adult. It shouldn't have hurt as much as it did.

A needle of yearning sticks between my ribs. Ian's one attempt at paternal kindness has left me feeling raw. I start tapping out a response to Dad. I entertain the possibility of visiting him, of finally showing Ed around an island that I am yet to see myself. But I hold my finger on the backspace. Dad tried to reach out when Ed died, called me half a dozen times, sent a condolence card, but it wasn't enough. If my only child's partner had been killed, I'd have moved mountains to be by her side.

I swipe his message off-screen. I'm too agitated to sleep, so I do something that I've not done in months. I check social media. My accounts are jammed with people demanding an update, my DMs are fit to bursting and my mentions are higher than they were at the height of my success. One comment in particular grabs my attention:

What if she's topped herself?

I delete it, although there's really no point. There are thousands more suggesting the same thing. I flick through puerile stories from people I've never met, then switch apps. That's when I see that #StateOfEmergency is trending. I tap on the hashtag to reveal photos of the Thames. I sit up and switch the bedside light on. In three taps, I load a video and prepare myself for more bad news.

'If you thought things were bad before, guys,' a TikTok creator says, her head floating in front of a screenshot of a meteorological map, 'the shit just hit the fan. Because after a hundred days without rain, the Met Office says that London is gonna get railed by the worst flooding since records began.' I rub my eyes and shake my head, wondering if I did slip into a dream after all.

'I'm talking storm surge. I'm talking torrential rain. I'm talking Armageddon, baby. And before you come at me for catastrophising, apparently the Thames Barrier – the thing that literally stops London from flooding on the daily – might break. Folks have been saying it needs work for years, but surprise, surprise, the government has been too busy lining their own pockets to give a shit. And if the barrier breaks, let me tell you, we're doomed.'

I lock my phone and look at Ed. I don't know what to do with that information. I wait for him to say something.

Is *this* the problem? Is this why he made me leave London? To protect me from a flood? My heart climbs into my throat.

'Did you know about this?' I ask him.

The drought couldn't last forever, Fi.

'So you *did* know?'

This can't be happening.

I get out of bed and take Ed downstairs with me. I have to tell Tracy and Ian. If London is in a state of emergency, I'll have no choice but to stay longer. I find them in the living room watching a news anchor deliver the same announcement with infinitely more stoicism than the TikToker.

'The mayor of London is urging the government to initiate an evacuation plan for Central London. Meanwhile, the leader of the opposition has criticised the prime minister's inaction in preparing for extreme weather, despite continued warnings that the Thames Barrier requires urgent repairs. We go now to Gabby Pasticca who is with Thames Barrier engineers in Woolwich. Gabby–'

Tracy changes the channel with a 'Pfft.'

'Trace, I was watching that,' Ian says.

'Too depressing!' She bats him away with a flick of her hand. '*Gogglebox* is on.'

'What am I going to do?' I say from behind them.

'Bloody hell, Fiona!' Tracy yelps, clutching one hand to her heart while cradling a wine glass with the other. 'I forgot you were here!'

'Sorry, I just... I saw on my phone, about the flood.'

'It's just a load of old rubbish, darling,' Tracy says, reaching over the sofa to reassure me. She has a green face mask on and is wearing a fluffy grey dressing gown with cat ears on the hood. 'You know how the media is these days, overblowing everything. We survived the cyclone of '87, didn't we?' she says to Ian. 'And the drought of '76. It's just a storm.'

'But the mayor—'

'Mayor schmayor, Ian. It's all politics.'

'He's just listening to the meteorologists and the engineers, Trace,' Ian tries, 'the experts—'

'Oh come on, you can't believe everything you hear. Those so-called experts are paid off by the greenies to make things sound worse than they are. I watched a documentary on YouTube. It's deep-state stuff...' she says, trailing off vaguely.

Ian scoffs. A short pig-snort that is, to Tracy, a slap in the face. 'Sorry, Trace, but why the *hell* would anyone want to make things sound worse than they are? Ain't the truth bad enough? It's not rained for almost half a year!'

She rolls her eyes. 'Don't exaggerate, Ian. It's barely been a *third* of the year. And it's obvious, isn't it? To scare people. It's mind control.'

'You're just making stuff up now. Time to put the wine glass down, dear.'

'How dare you—'

That's my cue to leave. I take Ed into the kitchen and close the door behind me. I didn't know Mum was into conspiracy theories. She's become a bit right-wing in recent years – the sort of person who's happy to save cats but draws the line at refugees – but I didn't have her down as a climate change denier. It's one of the things she and Dad used to argue about. He said she was too easily led, that she couldn't see past harmful rhetoric, while she said he was a self-righteous, pseudointellectual who needed to get off his high horse. I always sided with him, leading to heated dinner table debates that ended with a tearful Tracy accusing us of ganging up on her. After Dad left, her right-wing leanings turned into outright cynicism. When we launched RIOT 1.5 online, she commented on all of our posts like they were personally addressed to her.

uh-oh! take it from someone who knows – there's no point!! world = corrupt
so protests = waste of time!!

    She never did explain how she came to be 'someone who knows.'
Back then, I tried reasoning with her. *Without protests, you wouldn't be
able to vote, Mum*, I'd say. And that's where the conversation ended.
She'd disengage, ignoring the myriad of proof that I'd link from
reputable sources. She didn't want facts. She wanted an opinion,
however contrarian. Eventually, I gave up trying and just muted her.
Maybe that's why the alt-right stuff is so jarring now. Maybe, if I
scroll through her Facebook profile, I'll see memes about 5G towers
and microchips in vaccines. But I don't need to expose myself to that
today. Not when I have to stay under the same roof as her.

    I put Ed on the kitchen counter and stare at him. He got me out of
London just in time. I wish I could hug him. I wish I could squeeze
his body and nuzzle my face into his chest and whisper about how
batshit Mum is acting. But in the fluorescent light of the kitchen,
it's clear that he's suffered more from the fall than I realised. One of
his branches is entirely bare. I touch the place where his flowers used
to be. I have to be more careful.

    But what am I supposed to do, now that London is in a state of
emergency? I thought the whole point in coming here was to bring
Bruce home.

    'What now?' I ask him. 'I can't stay here with *them*, Ed. I'll go
mad.'

    You don't have to.

    'What do you mean?'

    There's another way.

    'How? Who else is there?'

    He doesn't elaborate.

    Why can't Ed's clues be more straightforward, rather than this
trail of breadcrumbs that barely constitutes a dialogue? Because
despite returning, he's never once told me why he's here or what he
actually wants. I'm just making wild assumptions.

    'I get that you don't have all the answers,' I say with a frustrated
sigh, 'but I need more to go on, Ed.'

I gave you something to go on.

'You did?'

Think about it.

I check whether he's casting another shadow. No luck. I pull myself up onto the kitchen counter and massage my temples. Ed had two flowers before the fall. Two white flowers. Does that mean something? Who am I forgetting?

Then it dawns on me.

When Beth and I first moved to Edinburgh, we went to get matching tattoos. It was Beth's idea. She wanted something to symbolise our friendship – our shared childhood in the middle of nowhere and our burgeoning adulthood in the big city. And although neither of us admitted it, we wanted to fit in with the fringe climate group, whose members were adorned with the piercings and tattoos of the vehemently countercultural. So we chose white roses from a flash sheet. I watched as Beth winced through the pain, the tattooist wiping away the excess ink to reveal two flowers that looked like they belonged on a sailor. This was before tattooing became an art form, when the only choice was two-dimensional full-colour designs that adorned the skin of the sorts of people with tribal armbands. That's when I backed out. Beth called me a wimp, and I went along with it, pretending I was afraid of the pain and not the thought of having something so incredibly tacky inked on me for life. As far as I know, Beth still has those two white roses on her forearm – two reminders that her tattoo outlasted the friendship she wanted to immortalise.

'Beth?' I ask Ed.

See? You're good at this, he whispers.

My frustration dissolves, and I grin at him, wanting more than ever to feel the heat of his body in my arms.

Last we spoke, Beth was living in Kilmahog with her parents and working in their café, a tourist trap next to the woollen mill that's known for its paddock of highland cows. We spent so many summers loitering around that café, counting down the days until we could leave the Trossachs and make our way in the world. Now Beth is right back to where she started. Now I am, too. But we aren't speaking. I can't just turn up at her parents' house and ask to wait out the storm together.

'Who are you talking to?' Tracy says, coming into the kitchen. She clicks her fingers at me. 'Off the counter.'

'Oh, um…' I reply, jumping down. 'I was recording a voice note.'

She opens the fridge and takes out a cake tin, all the while singing 'Happy Birthday' under her breath.

I take the hint. 'Happy birthday, Mum.'

'Hmm.' Tracy opens the tin and cuts herself a piece of cake. The face mask makes it look like I'm standing in the kitchen with Shrek.

'It's gluten-free and fat-free, before you judge me,' she says with her mouth full. 'The frosting is quark.'

I wince at the joylessness of the statement and change the subject. 'Mum, do you still see the Mackenzies?' I shoot an acquiescent look at Ed. He's taken me this far, guiding me away from a city that could be underwater next week. I have to trust that he knows what he's doing.

'Nope,' she says, swaying a little, 'they were friends of your dad's. Dropped me like a stone, just like he did.' She's clearly drunker than she's letting on. Tracy never talks about my dad.

'Can we go to their café tomorrow? I could take you out for a post-birthday brunch? Get some mimosas?' Mackenzie's isn't the sort of place that serves mimosas, but I know that the mention of a bougie drink that she can post on Instagram will convince her.

She nods and wipes quark off the side of her lip, taking a bit of mask off with it. She puts her finger in her mouth and sucks. 'That would be nice, Fiona. Mummy deserves a bit of love, eh? I'm not a *gowk*, you know,' she slurs, overemphasising the Scots word for *idiot*.

'I didn't say you were.'

'Tell *him* in there, then,' she says, pointing a finger at the door. 'Acting like I'm a gowk.'

'You're not a gowk, Mum. Let's go to bed, shall we? Then I'll treat you to a lovely brunch.' I guide her out of the kitchen and lead her upstairs. She flops onto the bed. I take the face mask off with a wet flannel. It's like wiping face paint off an overtired kid after a birthday party. Then I tuck her into bed. She closes her eyes and smiles dopily.

8

It's the rearing of horses that wakes me. I can't tell if it's a part of my nightmare or if they're outside. That's the thing with horses. They could be anywhere. The sound of hooves on hot concrete is like someone loading a gun. Because when the horses come, so do the shields. And then I am trapped inside a recurring nightmare that comes at least once a week.

This time, though, it was different.

The horses were white and stampeding towards me as a wall of water, the sound of their fury echoing in the boom of a breaking wave. Ed stood there on the shore, motionless. He made no effort to escape them. He did not run. Not even when a maul of muscular horse limbs dragged him underwater. I dived in. I thrashed about. I cried out his name. But what I found wasn't Ed as a man. It was Ed as a plant, floating on the surface. I pulled him close and I held my breath as a swell of horses crashed overhead. I didn't have the strength to escape them, not with the weight of Ed in my arms, but I wouldn't let go. Then, from atop those beasts of burden came shield-wielding shadows who reached in and held me under. It wasn't until my lungs threatened to burst that I woke up.

My eyes are dazzled by a ray of sun cutting through the curtains. My temples are throbbing. It feels like the flu, the half-life of the nightmare trapping me in feverish limbo. The flood has already found its way into my subconscious, then. At least in waking, I know I'm safe. But I can't pretend that I'm not frightened. London is my home. It's where Ed and I built our lives together, where we found our purpose. And now the government is going to sit back and watch as the place we loved, the memories we made there, get washed away. I whiten my knuckles against a rush of outrage. If I'm not careful, anger will transport me right back to the nightmare, where the thumping of hooves exists to remind me that there's nothing I can do to stop this. I am powerless. Worse than that, I am complicit, because instead of joining Ed in the fight back, I was busy counting coins.

I move to get out of bed, then notice a warm weight at my feet. A grey ball of fluff is rising from the duvet like a discarded feather boa.

'Bruce?' I croak. He lifts his head and looks at me neutrally. I pat my chest to see if he'll come. He uncoils himself and stretches his legs. His fur lies flat against his body. I hold my breath and pat my chest again. He chirps, then pads up the bed. I suppress a sob, not wanting to scare him off. He bumps his head against mine with a purr.

'Oh, Bruce.' I run my hand down his back. He lifts his tail and starts kneading the duvet. 'Look,' I tell Ed without breaking my gaze, 'our baby's back.'

See? I told you he'd come round.

I raise my head to smile at him from his place on the windowsill. He is in silhouette, but even in shadow I can see that something has changed. I jump out of bed and open the curtains. Daylight rushes in, illuminating not one but *two* new flowers – just like Beth's tattoo.

I pick him up and spin around the room shouting, 'Yes, yes, yes, yes!' as euphoria cancels out the nightmare and Ed becomes a blur of white and green.

I'm proud of you, Fi.

The spinning stops. My breath catches in my throat. I sit down on the bed. My brain takes a few seconds to realign my vision.

He's proud of me.

I don't remember the last time I heard him say that.

'Thank you,' I whisper with a trembling voice. Bruce brushes his face against Ed's new flowers, saying hello, then squeezes himself behind the pot to curl up on my lap. I sit like that for a while, stroking a purring Bruce, holding a flowering Ed, the morning sun pouring over the three of us like a supernatural spotlight. And I feel that maybe, if I put all the pain to one side, if I zoom out and take stock of everything I've done since Ed came back, I might be proud of myself, too. There's strength in that feeling. There's resolve. I look down at Ed's flowers, his most definitive breadcrumbs yet. I have to make things right with Beth.

I take Ed downstairs with a spring in my step, Bruce following close behind. Tracy is at the kitchen table spooning sugar into a cup of tea with the expression of a dehydrated blobfish.

'Hanging?' I ask, searching the cupboards for cat food. Ian is standing by the counter frowning at a muted television that's mounted above the table.

'A bit,' she mutters, dropping her head into her hands.

'You still want to go for brunch? Hair of the dog?'

'Bloody hell,' Ian says before she can answer. I look up at the television. It's the news again. Captions flash across the screen. I reach for the remote to unmute it.

'There were scenes of pandemonium inside the House of Lords this morning as rioters disrupted a debate about new protest laws. The upper chamber was adjourned for half an hour while police removed fifty environmental activists, many of whom could be heard threatening peers and shouting insults at law enforcement.'

There is blurry phone footage of people wearing Dissident Uprising T-shirts. The shattered-earth symbol. They are being dragged across the floor. I take a step towards the television.

'The Unlawful Assemblies Bill is designed to crack down on guerrilla tactics used by climate activists,' the anchor goes on, 'with peers drawing parallels between extremist eco groups and organised terrorism. Critics, most notably the first minister of Scotland, say that the bill is an attempt to criminalise all forms of public assembly, but at a briefing outside Downing Street yesterday, the prime minister assured the public that the bill is designed to protect the nation's workforce.'

The screen cuts to footage of the prime minister standing behind a podium. His red tie looks tight enough to choke him. 'It is my solemn promise to hardworking people everywhere,' he says directly into the camera, 'that I will cure the activist plague that is blighting our nation.'

It cuts back to the news anchor. 'Meanwhile, there is growing pressure on the prime minister to solve the prison crisis, with officers reporting unprecedented crowding caused by the crackdown on public disorder.'

The prime minister reappears. 'I have dedicated a decisive new task force to tackle the issue,' he says, 'and in the coming weeks, I will announce a bold plan to address prison overcrowding. Rest assured, extremist zealots will feel the full force of Britain's world-leading criminal justice system.'

Ian and I exchange a fraught glance. Just like Irie said back at East Peace, the government is planning something big. She thought it was a blanket ban on protests. But this sounds like something bigger. Because what could a *bold plan* against imprisoned *zealots* be, aside from something drastic?

'Every time I think the English have reached the bottom of the barrel,' Ian says bitterly, 'the bastards find a new way down.'

'Do the crime, do the time,' Tracy mutters, less forceful with her opinions this morning but still unable to contain herself.

'Is that what you thought about RIOT?' I snap. My entire body is red-hot with rage. Rage at what the police did to those peaceful protesters. Rage at the way the media reported it. Rage at the prime minister's rhetoric. Rage at the fact that while the government puts all of its time and energy into suppressing fundamental human rights, a life-threatening storm surge is hurtling towards the city and no one seems to be doing anything about it.

'If you stick your head above the parapet, you're gonna get burned,' Tracy says. 'There are laws in this country for a reason.'

'Last night you were going on about deep-state mind control,' I hurl back at her, Ed's pride giving me the strength to speak my mind. 'And this morning you're pro law and order?'

Ian hides a look of approval in his coffee cup.

'I'm not in the mood for this, Fiona.' She pulls her cat ears over her head. 'I had enough crap last night from *him*. Are you taking me to brunch or not?'

From the outside, Mackenzie's looks just like I remember it. The highland cows are opposite the car park, and there's a garish sign outside that reads *Homemade Haggis & Tattie Scones*. It's one of the last cafés on the road to the Small Isles that can cater to a lot of people and, considering the number of tourists posing for photos with the cows, it seems as popular as ever.

But inside, things have changed. This used to be a baked-beans-and-builders'-brew joint, but now there's smashed avocado on the menu and an espresso machine hissing in the corner. Who knows, they might even serve mimosas.

Tracy chooses a table by the window and goes to drool-at-but-refuse-to-eat the pastries. I sit down with Ed and look across the car park at the cows. I try to maintain a quietly self-assured expression. I'm aware that at every turn, there could be someone I went to school with or an old family friend nearby. They'll want to make an assessment of how successful I am, since I think I'm 'too good' for Strathyre, so I've made an effort with my appearance today, wearing mascara, silver hoops and a summery wrap dress.

'Hey,' Beth says, appearing at the table with a pad and pencil. I almost don't recognise her. She's got a turquoise blue mullet and an eyebrow piercing that makes her look unapproachable. I scan her arms for the tattoo. She's covered herself in ink now, every inch of skin home to misshapen doodles that look like they were drawn by a toddler, but the roses are still there. I look at Ed's flowers on the table, then back at her tattoo. 'What can I get you?' she asks without looking up.

'Um…' I swallow hard. 'Do you do mimosas?'

'Bethany!' Tracy shouts from across the café. 'How lovely to see you looking so… blue!' Beth turns and clocks Tracy, then turns back and clocks me.

'Hey,' I twinkle my fingers, then hide my hands under the table.

'Oh, hi.' She steps back and barely glances at me or Ed before repeating, 'What can I get you?'

Tracy dashes to the chair opposite and flits her head between us like she's watching a game of Ping-Pong. 'Fiona is staying with us for a while,' she explains, her enthusiasm an attempt to smooth over Beth's indifference. 'And Bruce. The cat, Bruce!'

'Right,' Beth says. She strains her mouth into a nonsmile and taps her pen on the pad, looking distractedly back at the counter. 'So do you want anything or...?'

When Beth leaves with our order, Tracy leans across the table.

'What the *hell* was that about?' she snarls, Ed's foliage concealing the full extent of her dismay. A pine needle touches her nose, and she blows a raspberry at him.

'I don't know,' I say, moving him out of her way. 'We grew apart.'

'Nonsense. You're practically sisters.'

I shake my head, as if stumped by Beth's behaviour, and try to appear unfazed. But really, I'm hurt. I knew things with Beth would be awkward, but her complete lack of interest has thrown me. How am I supposed to make things right if she won't even acknowledge my existence? And how can I prove to Ed that I am, in fact, good at this, if I can't follow basic instruction? I have no idea why he wants me to see Beth or how it will keep him blooming, but I don't need to know. This morning, I found a wisp of peace. I found it because of *him*, because of the journey he's leading me on. After the profound misery that overpowered me in London, I'd follow him to the ends of the earth if it meant holding onto that wisp.

'Damn shame,' Tracy sighs, sipping the flute of prosecco and orange juice that's been placed in front of her by another member of staff.

'People change,' I say.

'She certainly *looks* different. That *hair*. And those *tattoos*. She looks like one of those rioters on TV this morning. A member of the wokerati.' Tracy glares at the ceiling.

'What's with the prejudice, Mum?' I ask, the wisp of peace evaporating. 'You realise that Ed and I–'

'I don't mean *you*, Fiona. At least you have a proper job, make decent money. And Ed wasn't always an extremist, was he?'

'He was *never* an extremist.' I put my fists on the table and lean towards her, my voice low but furious. 'Jesus-fucking-Christ, I didn't know you were so easily led.' This is precisely what Dad used to say. I know it will bruise her.

'Whatever,' she scoffs petulantly. 'Your generation might think you're *all that*, but I'm a damn sight older than you are, Fiona. I've been around the block.'

'So what? Does that automatically make you right?'

'You lot are so hysterical about everything,' she says, ignoring my question. 'Everything's *offensive*, everything's *oppressive*. Everyone needs to *change everything right now* or the world will end. But you didn't live through the war, did you? That's when there was real suffering in this country.'

'You didn't live through the war, either.'

'Which is why I'm grateful for my lot in life.'

'You're talking out of your arse,' I tell her, my volume fading as I reach the end of the sentence.

'What?'

'Nothing,' I back down, losing the will to fight when a waiter returns with our order. I look over her head at the counter. Beth is nowhere to be seen. Tracy drinks three more mimosas and takes a selfie with each one, her smile becoming less and less convincing whenever she raises a glass.

I know that coming to Scotland was the right thing to do. I know I have to rescue Bruce, fix things with Beth. But I wish I didn't have to stay with Tracy. I wish my dad hadn't left and moved to the middle of nowhere or that, at the very least, we were still talking. Because he would never have called Ed an *extremist*. He would have called him a hero.

That's when all the rage that's been bubbling in my gut comes to the fore. While I sit here and watch this charade from a woman drunk on misinformation, the storm amasses power and the city inches towards disaster. Meanwhile people – people who used to be just like me – are being detained in crowded cells for *doing something* about it. Anger burns in my chest like a box of lit matches. The last time I felt this way, I smashed a bunch of plant pots and found some much-needed relief. But aside from throwing my breakfast plate against the wall, there's no way out of this feeling.

I used to think that if I could paint the perfect placard or design the perfect poster, I could capture the injustices that are gripping this country and get people to understand. And if I could get them to understand, they would act. And if I could get them to act, we could change things.

Only, we won't, will we? Because I've seen what happens. I've seen that even when things do change, it's never in the way you intended. I've seen the way that change leaves you with nothing but the clambering of horses at night and a fear so immense it destroys you. I've seen that Tracy is right about one thing: there's no point in trying.

Because trying cost me his life.

9

I lean my rusty bike against the gate and take Ed out of the front basket, unsteady on my feet. As a kid, I cycled the nine miles between mine and Beth's house without breaking a sweat. Today, I feel as though I've lost the Tour de France. I blame the heat. That and the fact that I was so focused on Ed not falling out of the basket, I kept veering off the path. I look at my reflection in my front-facing camera. My face is beetroot-red and dripping wet. I lift my top to wipe my forehead. On the way here, I saw families on the shore of Loch Lubnaig. There were even swimmers, some of them standing right in the middle of the loch with their hands on their hips. The water used to be Baltic and six hundred feet deep, even in the height of summer. Now it's like Lake Garda.

I take my hair down, only to put it back up again, and wait for my heartbeat to slow. I'm nervous. What if Beth refuses to see me? What if her parents tell me off? I look at Ed's flowers and search for courage in his glittering petals. They are physical manifestations of Beth's tattoo, a tattoo she could have had covered up by now. After the way I treated her, she could have erased all trace of me and moved on with her life. But she didn't. That tells me something, doesn't it? In the not too distant past, Beth called me a corporate shill, yet she's still sporting the floral tribute to our friendship.

With my pulse thumping, I prepare a grovelling monologue. I know how deep Beth's grudges go. When we were twelve, she didn't speak to me for an entire term because I supposedly betrayed her trust. It was after a sleepover at her house. We'd watched a VHS of *Practical Magic* and decided that, to prove our friendship was for life, we needed to copy Sally and Gillian's bonding spell by cutting our palms with a butter knife and clasping our hands together. But neither of us had the guts to do it. Instead, we became spit sisters. We touched the tips of our tongues together, recited a made-up spell and burned tea leaves in a cereal bowl. I told a few people at school, thinking it made us sound like real witches, but they thought it was weird. We became known as the Spit Sisters and victims of the occasional gob on the head. Beth blanked me until the summer holidays. It was one in a long line of childish arguments that made our friendship the volatile yet enduring creature it was – until recent history.

How to explain why I didn't invite her to the funeral? How to make amends for blanking her for all of these months? I think if things with Ed weren't as bad as they were by the end, I wouldn't have been so sensitive about her messages during Earth Month. It was just too close to home. Ed and I were bickering relentlessly by that point, first about the ever-increasing risks he was taking, then about my 'sellout' job. I couldn't bear to hear it from her, too. Then he died, and the guilt was so all-consuming that I had to push her away to stop myself from joining him. If I put it like that, surely she'll understand? But I don't know how to *put it like that* without giving in to the worst of my intrusive thoughts.

I open the front gate. Beth's parents' house looks strangely unfamiliar. It's smaller and more run-down than I remember, with a mass of ivy choking the brickwork and threatening to break into the bedroom windows. My shoes crunch up the garden path. A dog barks. I hesitate. Then the door swings open.

'That can't be Fiona Reid. As I live and breathe. Carol!' Beth's dad Pete calls behind him. 'Come quick. You'll never guess who it is.' Pete is standing on the porch in his slippers. He has grown an unfashionably long, grey-streaked beard and looks like a modern-day druid. The resemblance makes me smile.

'Come in!' He touches my shoulder as I cross the threshold. A young golden retriever wearing a red bandanna jumps up and snaps their jaws at Ed. 'Get down, Vashti, that's a girl.'

I lift Ed over my head and turn my body away from the dog. Carol, Beth's mum, is standing at the foot of the stairs with a paintbrush in her hand.

'Fifi,' she says breathily, opening her arms wide, 'what a lovely surprise!'

I give her a side hug, the plant impeding any proper physical contact, and apologise for the unannounced visit. After a short squeeze, she holds me at arm's length to get a good look at me.

'Is Beth here?' I ask, hoping to skirt the inevitable commiserations.

'She's in the annex.' Carol studies me with large, glossy eyes, then says with eager solemnity, 'I was so sorry to hear about Ed.'

'Thanks.' I resist the urge to say, *He's right here, actually.*

'We'd have come to the funeral but we weren't told–'

'Sorry,' I lie. 'I did ask Mum to tell you.'

'It's not a problem, darling. I'm just so glad you've come home. When we saw the news yesterday about London, you were the first person we thought about, wasn't she, Pete? Thank god you left, darling.' She leans against the banister and gesticulates with the paintbrush. 'Miserable business, this storm surge, isn't it? And what they're doing to those poor protesters–'

'She's not come to chat about the weather, Caz,' Pete cuts her off with a chuckle. I almost want her to carry on, to cancel out Tracy's ignorance. At least Beth's mum has still got her head screwed on. 'Come on, Fi. I'll show you to the annex.'

I follow Pete and a bouncy Vashti through the house. I'm pleased to see that, unlike Tracy, they haven't drained the place of colour. The hallway is home to the same patterned wallpaper from my youth and cluttered with framed photos. I glance over them for pictures of myself. I don't see any. Pete leads me through the kitchen and over the checkerboard floor. It smells the same. A sweet, lived-in scent with the faintest undertone of spice. A smell that lingers, but not in an unpleasant way. We go out the back and into the garden towards a large shed. Pete knocks on the door. I wring my hands, anticipating her animosity. The door opens tentatively, then Vashti barges in.

'Someone here to see you,' Pete says, beaming at her. Beth stares at me, first confused and then, as expected, pissed off. Her blue mullet is sticking up at all angles and she has a shiny T-zone. I stare back, mouth wide as I search for something to say. Pete tugs at his beard, his smile fading when he realises that our reunion is not a happy one.

'I'll leave you to it, then. Let's go, Vashti.' The dog comes out of the shed with a pair of socks in her mouth and, after a small tug of war, drops them and trots off.

'Hey,' I say with a self-conscious wave.

'What do you want, Fi?' Beth replies venomously, though the question is softened by the abbreviation of my name.

'I want to be friends again. I want to make things right.'

'OK. All is forgiven.' She stretches her hands towards me with the virtue of a benevolent priest.

'Really?'

'No, not really, for fuck's sake,' she jeers, digging her hands into her pockets. 'You've been ghosting me for months, and now you just show up and expect everything to go back to normal? It's going to take more than a houseplant for me to forgive–'

'The plant isn't for you,' I speak over her, tightening my hands around Ed's pot in case she tries to take him.

'Oh, great. So what's it for, then? Is it the latest accessory? This season's *must-have*?' She lifts her eyebrows and crosses her arms, her lightning-quick disapproval reinforcing the very reason I've been keeping my distance.

'It's hard to explain. Can I come in?'

She sighs and flings her arm into the shed like a servant welcoming a member of the royal family. I cower as I cross the threshold, worried she'll change her mind.

Beth has clearly tried to make the shed look like a proper home, but the smell of WD-40 is a dead giveaway. She's stapled patterned fabric to the ceiling and traced the edges of the room with fairy lights. There's a pentagram made of sticks above a single bed, a nod to her wiccan past, and a Himalayan salt lamp on her bedside table. Underneath the window, there's a foldout table with an electric kettle and an ancient fan. She's decorated a side of the shed with photos and posters, surrounding herself with slogans like, *MOTHER NATURE IS A LESBIAN* and *FUCK THE CIS-TEM*. I look for pictures of myself but come up short again.

Instead, there are dozens of photos of Beth with a woman who I don't recognise. Her short afro is a different shade of pink in every photo.

'That's Celeste,' Beth says, noticing my interest. 'My girlfriend.'

'I didn't know you had a girlfriend.' Beth has never been in the closet, though there was zero queer scene to speak of in Strathyre, so exploring her sexuality had to wait until she followed me to Edinburgh. It's another way we drifted apart. She threw herself at the Pink Triangle and, when I met Ed, I threw myself at him.

'That's a pretty name,' I say, paying closer attention to the photos. Everything about Celeste's appearance is rebellious, from her tattoos and hairy armpits to an ever-evolving style that oscillates between masc and femme. She appears to be an avid climber, with shots of her scaling climbing walls and rappelling down rock faces. My eyes land on a photo of them wearing matching shattered-earth T-shirts and holding a sign that says SOCIAL JUSTICE IS CLIMATE JUSTICE. It looks like the rash of Dissident Uprising has stretched four hundred miles north to Kilmahog. I should be impressed. For some reason, it stings.

'She's French,' Beth adds. 'Moved here to study psychology at UoE.' She says this in a neutral way, acting like it's not enormously impressive to have a psychologist girlfriend when neither of us went to university.

'How long have you been together?'

'Almost a year.' She takes two tea-stained mugs out of a cupboard.

Almost a *year*? But we've only fallen out of touch since Ed died. Does that mean she's had a girlfriend this whole time and not told me? Or did I forget to ask? I decide to change the subject. 'Why did you leave Edinburgh?'

'We're saving for our own place.' Beth hands me a mug and sits on the bed. I put Ed on the table and take the sofa opposite. We are two strides away from each other, a tatty woven rug between us like a black hole of bad feeling. 'So what happened, then?' she says bluntly, done with small talk.

I'm not ready to explain why I've been ignoring her, so I

deliberately misinterpret the question. 'My mum showed up in London and took Bruce. She said I can have him back when I'm 'better,' but I'm perfectly fine. And now Travis – my agent – is threatening to sue me if I don't do this magazine interview with Bruce. That's why I came home – to get him – but she's acting like a complete twat. She's got into conspiracy theories, thinks the storm surge is some leftie mind-control thing. And she's drinking like a fish.' I pause for breath.

'What I mean is,' Beth crosses one leg over the other, ignoring everything I've just said, 'what happened between *us*? Why didn't you invite me to the funeral?'

I rearrange myself on the sofa, my body suddenly an assortment of sharp angles. I try to find the right words. 'I don't know.'

'Yes, you do,' Beth says.

Yes, you do, Ed echoes.

'OK, well… we fell out, obviously, about the Earth Month stuff, and after that, you know, Ed died and, um, seeing you would've just made me feel worse about myself, I guess. I was in a really dark place.' My throat tightens. I suck in a staggered breath.

'We've been best friends for twenty years, Fi. We've fallen out loads of times. That doesn't mean you can cut me out of your life. Like, I honestly can't believe you didn't invite me to the funeral. I loved Ed. Ask Celeste – I sobbed my eyes out when I saw the news. I was heartbroken.'

'*You* were heartbroken?' I snort.

'Yes, I was. Your heartbreak doesn't negate mine. I know you've been through hell, and I am so, so sorry, but ghosting me was wrong. For *you* and for me. I could have helped. I could have stayed with you, made dinner, watered the plants, fed Bruce. I could've taken care of everything and just let you grieve.' She starts crying then, her chin wobbling as tears flood her face. Her reaction shocks me. I was expecting a shouting match, not tears.

'I wanted to be there for you,' she sobs. 'I *needed* to be there, to feel like I had some way of being your friend, of holding that space for you. It's not fair to lock me out. It's really fucking cruel, actually.'

'I didn't mean to be cruel,' I mumble, trying to bury the shame the moment it flares up inside of me. I thought making things right with Beth might alleviate me of some guilt, not pile more on.

'Well, you were. I didn't deserve it. I might not agree with everything you do, Fi, but I love you. And that Earth Month stuff… I was just worried. Some of the things you were posting–' she looks to the ceiling and shakes her head '–it seemed so out of character.'

'I love you, too.' I make eye contact and try to forget that Ed once accused me of becoming a totally different person after signing with Travis. 'I'm sorry, OK? I am, Beth. I'm really sorry. All I can say is…' That's when my own tears break like a dam, and I give in. 'When Ed died, the world stopped. Everything just stopped. Losing him like that – watching him die – I think my brain shut down. And then everyone wanted in on it. Like, it was all over the news, journalists were outside my house, people online were harassing me – they *still* are. I just… I couldn't bear to be around *anyone*, if that makes sense?'

I could tell her that Ed and I were in a bad place. I could tell her that I made so many mistakes that hound me to this day and make me feel like I was to blame for what happened to him. But I don't. My guilt weighs so heavily that I can't say it out loud for fear that someone will tell me I'm right.

'It does make sense,' Beth's voice softens as she moves to sit next to me. She puts her arm around my shoulder. 'I can't imagine what that feels like.' She smells like the spicy sweetness of the house. I tentatively rest my head on her shoulder, waiting for her to tell me to back off. When she doesn't, I collapse into the hug and push my face against her chest. 'That's why I wanted to be there for you, Fi. To protect you from that bullshit.'

'I'm sorry,' I groan, my tears forming a wet patch on her T-shirt. I realise then that I *am* sorry. That I do need this. That it is good to be held and heard and taken care of. Maybe, if I'd let her in sooner, I wouldn't have lost so much in the fallout.

'It's OK,' she says. 'I'm sorry, too. I shouldn't have been so rude at the café. I was just thrown. You're the last person I expected to see yesterday.'

'You mean it?' I croak against her shoulder blade, worried that she's only accepting my apology because there's nothing else to say to someone expressing such abject sorrow. 'We're OK?'

Then, with a resigned sigh, she whispers, 'We're OK. Spit Sisters for life.'

I laugh and cry at the same time. Then I'm seized by a coughing fit, the duelling emotions clashing in my throat as I hack up a lung like a lifelong smoker. Beth hands me a glass of water and pats my back. Through snatched breaths and chest spasms, a rush of relief steadies my senses.

I don't know how Ed understands what I need more than I do, but I don't need to know. I'm just so grateful that he's back, and that I have a best friend again.

'I'd love to meet Celeste,' I say once I've composed myself. 'She seems really cool.'

'She's the best.' Beth stands to get her phone and taps out a text. 'We're about to go away, though. There's this activist retreat on the Isle of Banmora. We're staying with the person who founded Dissident Uprising.'

'Pardon?' My body tenses against a rush of disquiet.

Beth looks up from her phone. 'Yeah, it's funny you're here, actually. When we planned it, I was thinking about you. Your dad lives there, right?'

Nodding, I take Ed off the table. I lift his flowers to my eyeline, my mind sparking with an arsenal of questions.

'The heat wave's been really hard on Celeste,' Beth goes on, her tone drenched in loving concern. 'Her grandparents left Senegal during a drought, so it reminds her of what her family went through, you know? That's why I booked the retreat.'

I keep nodding, but I can barely focus on what she's saying.

There's something I've been missing.

When Ed first bloomed, he told me to *go back to where it all started*. I thought he meant East Peace, but now he's led me all the way home.

Go back, he said, *then you'll see.*

So now that I'm as far back as I can go, what *do* I see?

First Ed takes me to East Peace, where Irie tells me what's happening to our movement. Then to Strathyre, where the injustice of the storm surge and Tracy's denialism reignites the rage that used to drive me. Then to Kilmahog, where I see a picture of my best friend wearing a symbol that's followed me from day one; where I learn that Banmora – the island that ended my childhood – has become an activist retreat run by the person who likely created that symbol.

All this time, Ed has been leading me towards something greater. Because with a killer storm on the way, is it enough to say that I rescued Bruce and reunited our little family? Is it enough to let the light back in and mend my broken heart when people are being crammed into prisons for taking a stand? When I spent the last few months of Ed's life wearing a muzzle that continues to choke me? It can't possibly be. Not when Ed was so devoted to the cause that he went to The Final Strike wearing the same clothes he'd worn to the East Peace party, one week earlier. If I want Ed to keep blooming, if I want him to stay, I have to do more.

Deep down, I think I've always known that. It's been there from day one, when his first flower felt sent to expose me. I've just been unable to address it. Because building that bench with Irie might have reminded me that I'm still capable, but joining Dissident Uprising is another thing entirely. I don't belong with them. We had no part to play in mobilising those bright young things. That came after Ed, after RIOT 1.5 and all the ways we failed to make a difference. And that's the crux of the issue, isn't it? How am I supposed to *do something* when I know it's pointless? Should I just go along with it, keep my cynicism to myself and join something that I don't believe in? Will I finally redeem myself in Ed's eyes, even though my heart's not in it? People do that all the time. They participate in social conceits, they mask their contempt. But all of that overlooks the one thing I simply cannot mask.

The paralysing fear.

The fear that, if I step out of line again, the tattered fabric that separates my nightmares from reality will tear open. And in that torn-up place, the horses will descend, and I will be powerless to stop them.

10

The sun is still a way off rising when I tiptoe downstairs with Ed. I take Tracy's keys from the hook by the front door. She has a fluffy pom-pom keychain with a golden T charm and a paw-print door key. I carefully remove the car fob, my head darting behind me to check if either of them has woken up. I stuff it in my back pocket before I can change my mind, then I stick a Post-it note to the front door.

Gone to see Dad. Had to borrow car. Thanks for understanding x

Bruce is sitting on Tracy's gaudy Home Sweet Home doormat, watching me commit this act of theft with an impartial head tilt. I think about taking him with me. He can sit in the front seat with Ed and admire the views. I'm sure Beth and Celeste won't mind. Then again, having him loose in the car – not to mention taking him to a remote island where he could run off for good – feels like too great a risk to take. I shake my head and exhale. It feels miserable leaving him behind. He's only just started trusting me again. What if he thinks I've abandoned him? What if he decides that he's much happier at Mum's and I never get the chance to take him home?

But at least here, I know he's safe. And once I've done whatever it is I'm supposed to do in Banmora, I'll come back with the perfect bargaining chip. *The car for the cat*, I'll say. Then Tracy will have to hand him over.

I bend down and scratch him behind the ear.

'I'll come back for you,' I promise, a well of regret sparking in my eyes as he leans into the scratch with a purr.

I drive towards Kilmahog to collect Beth and Celeste.

After cycling home yesterday, I spent the rest of the afternoon deciding what to do. I paced up and down my childhood bedroom like a captive animal. Should I stay with Tracy and shoulder her abuse? Should I go back to London despite the impending flood? When I'd put it like that, Banmora seemed far less intimidating. Plus, neither of those things would keep Ed flowering. Neither of those things would be *enough*.

You're overthinking it my love, Ed had said from his spot on the windowsill. *Just listen to your gut.*

He was right. I'd been feeling slightly unhinged since leaving Beth's. Her casual revelation that the person who founded Dissident Uprising lives on the same island as my father sent my mind into a tailspin. But Ed is still speaking to me. He's still got two flowers. That has to mean something. And he'd never put me in harm's way like that. In fact, all Ed's done since he came back is guide me *away* from harm, away from gloom and towards fleeting moments of peace. I have to trust that he knows where he's taking me. And perhaps, when I get there, I'll find a way of making my peace last. So I put my faith in Ed once again and messaged Beth.

Thank you for today, I can't tell you how much it means to me. It's made me realise that I need to make things right with my dad. I could drive us to the ferry terminal, if you need a lift?

She replied in less than a minute.

OMG that would legit be amazing. We were going to thumb it the whole way!

In all honesty, seeing my dad is just an excuse to get to Banmora. I could tell her about Ed, about the yew tree that's guiding me towards some greater good, but I'm not ready. Our friendship is still too fragile to confide in her. And besides, I can't go all that way *without* seeing him. The island is tiny. I might bump into him at any second and be forced to explain myself. The worry from that alone would drive me crazy. But if I get it over with – see my dad, give him a piece of my mind and move on – I can focus on the much bigger challenge ahead.

My clammy hands slip on the steering wheel and my teeth churn the inside of my mouth to a pulp. The anxiety isn't helped by Travis, who's hounding me for an update, or my followers, who post constant speculation about my mental state and clog my DMs with pleas for a response. I have no idea what to say to any of them, or what this journey will mean for my job, or what I will do if I lose it, so I just focus on the road ahead and remind myself to trust the process.

I pull up outside Beth's house to find her standing in the front garden with Celeste. Vashti jumps at the gate. They both pick up their backpacks. I make a quick assessment of Celeste before getting out of the car. She has the complexion of a twenty-year-old but the heavy black eyeliner of an elder emo. Her septum piercing glints in the sun, and she has a golden snitch tattoo on her upper arm with the words *TRANS RIGHTS* scrawled over the top of it. But the most surprising thing about Celeste is the way she dresses. Most women want to flatter their body shape by making themselves appear as small as possible, but not Celeste. She has silvery stretch marks that contrast against her black skin and a soft, round belly that protrudes from her high-waisted shorts. I can tell that not covering up is as much a political statement as her *Babe with the Power* T-shirt, and Beth's nonconformist style starts to make sense. The sight of both of them makes me want to overhaul my wardrobe. The artisanal dresses are out. The Helena Bonham Carter hairdo is obsolete. I need to get an undercut. I need to pierce my nose. I need to ink my opinions all over me. Only then can I reclaim what it means to be an activist. I look at Ed's flowers, his gentle blooms of encouragement, and gulp down the intimidation. I get out of the car.

'Fi-fi!' Celeste says in an elegant French accent, making my name sound melodic. 'I am so pleased to meet you!'

Her warm smile loosens the knot in my stomach, and I return

her energetic hug. After brief introductions, they walk towards the car with the dog in tow.

'Vashti's coming, too?' I ask.

'Is that all right?' Beth replies, looking in the back seat. 'She's technically mine, and my parents are working all week. I can't leave her home alone.'

Tracy will already be incensed about me taking the car. Dog hair will make her catatonic. And the thought of being around a beloved pet again makes me uneasy. Vashti's shiny blond fur shows how well she's looked after, her red bandanna reminding me of the things I used to buy for Bruce. I struggle once more with shame. I shouldn't have left him behind. But Ed's motionless leaves and petals tell me that *Yes, Fi, it'll have to be all right*, so I nod and fix my face with a breezy smile.

'You can leave the plant here,' Beth offers when she sees him in the passenger's seat. 'I'll ask Mum to water it.'

'I can't,' I blurt in a panicked tone. 'It's special.'

'Oh,' she replies, sticking her head in the car to access Ed's apparent specialness. 'How come?'

Celeste casts me a curious but not unkind glance. I search for the right way to explain him. Maybe this is my chance to tell the truth. Part of me wants to. Ed's return is too miraculous a thing to keep to myself for much longer. Maybe they'll understand. But there's only so far out of my comfort zone I'm willing to go in one day, so I settle on a half truth.

'It's an urn.'

'Oh,' Beth repeats, standing straight.

'What a lovely thing.' Celeste's approval is surprisingly quick. 'That way he's always with you.' It strikes me as odd that she knows about Ed's death before we've had the chance to get to know each other. Then I remember that everyone in the country knows about Ed's death. My grief is a cautionary tale. Celeste walks around the car to look at him. 'What kind of plant is it?'

'It's a yew tree,' I say with a grin, my heart lifting. I pick up the pot and, buoyed with pride, reveal another little truth. 'It flowered when I put his ashes in the soil.'

'A flowering yew tree?' Celeste leans in to smell his flowers. We both know he doesn't have a scent, but she smiles as if she's just got a whiff of jasmine. 'Very lovely.'

'Thank you.' I beam at her. If I ever find the courage to share Ed's return with the world, I hope everyone will be this understanding.

'So that's why you've been carting it all over the place?' Beth quips, cancelling out Celeste's gentle acceptance. 'Like what's-her-face, in *Léon*?' There's a glint in her eye, telling me that she's only pulling my leg. Beth has always been a piss-taker.

'Natalie Portman,' Celeste answers. 'Classic French thriller.'

'Isn't she a child in that movie?' I ask, wondering what Beth is getting at. 'A *traumatised* child?'

'She's like, twelve,' Beth says, then quickly adds, 'Not that I'm calling you a child.'

'Just traumatised?'

'Exactly.' She smirks and elbows me in the ribs. Her normality towards me is a peculiar comfort. People tend to give grief a wide berth, but Beth isn't afraid to look it right in the eye. 'Ed can sit on my lap, then.'

I'm hesitant about letting her near him. The last time someone was, I almost lost him to a restaurant floor. But she just called the plant Ed. That means she understands how important he is. Maybe she even senses that the plant *is* Ed. I get into the driver's seat. As I drive away, I feel a single artery pump a little more easily, as if my heart has restored something of the person I was before.

The road to the Small Isles is famed for its views, and as we wind around a chain of lochs that end at the sea, Celeste's face is fixed in open-mouthed awe. With the Trossachs behind us, the low hills rise to become steep pleats that transform into craggy peaks. Waterfalls that used to roar now trickle down the mountainside, and free-roaming sheep give Vashti something to bark at. It's too hot to drive without air-conditioning so we keep the windows up and savour the fridgelike quality of the car against the scorching morning sun. Yet even the sting of the heat doesn't deter us from stopping every now and then to take pictures.

'Please, may we?' Celeste asks as we pass a scenic view. I get a kick out of pulling over and being the spontaneity-loving grown-up that Tracy never was. Dad, on the other hand, always followed brown tourist signs, especially ones with a blue thistle on them. He called them *a mark of Scottish quality* and made it his mission to visit every local attraction in the country. Tracy never understood the appeal.

It's just a sign, she'd huff when we pointed out the blue thistles, usually followed by *Peas in a pod, you two*, which is what she always called us. Because we were. And now I'm driving the same roads to reach him. At least I won't be in his company for long.

The crumbling stone bridges of West Scotland look like they were crafted by watercolour painters, and as we continue our journey, Beth puts on an Instrumental Ambient Folk playlist to heighten the mood. After long stints of stunned silence, Beth tells Celeste stories from our adolescence – like that time I intentionally capsized our canoe in a freezing loch to chat up a kayaker, or that summer we spent smoking crap weed and hitchhiking to and from Glasgow. The way Celeste laughs at all of Beth's jokes and touches her shoulder feels borrowed from the love life I used to have. My eagerness to please Ed. His eagerness to impress me. Now I'm bearing witness to it again. Except it's Beth's turn to fall in love. I feel a flash of jealousy. I hadn't anticipated that, by coming on this trip, I'd be playing third wheel.

When we reach Ben Nevis, Celeste asks to stop for a selfie. I lift Ed into the shot, my smile widening when Beth slings her arm around my shoulder. Her rose tattoo looks so at home against Ed's flowers that I wonder if she notices. Celeste starts tapping through her phone, choosing a filter for her stories. 'This one is never using social media,' she says, signalling to Beth, 'but I love to share these things. It's so exquisite here. Why would you not?'

'Is your profile private?' I ask, trying to sound casual but hearing the strain in my voice. The photo could be screenshot and shared by anyone.

'No, why?'

'Do you mind not posting it, then? If you do, there'll be headlines like Influencer Girlfriend of Dead Eco-Terrorist Spotted at Ben Nevis – Is She at the Summit of Her Grief? or something equally horrifying. I'm not ready for the influx of bullshit.'

'Of course,' Beth nods, 'I'm here to protect you from bullshit, remember? We'll remain incognito. Is that all right, Cel?'

'Fine by me! I forgot I'm travelling with an *influencer.*' She overemphasises the word, enjoying the novelty of it.

'I'm not looking very influential right now,' I join in, gesturing to my appearance, 'but you should see me on a good day. I influence the *fuck* out of people.'

'She's not wrong,' Beth adds. 'I'm so easily influenced by her that I'm considering getting a potted plant as a pet. *That's* the influence Fi has over me.'

As we get back into the car, laughter burns the underused muscles in my cheeks, and by the time the ambient folk playlist has started repeating tracks, we're only half an hour from Mallaig. We stop at a service station to grab some provisions. I ignore another phone call from Tracy, who's been buzzing on my dashboard all morning, and pluck up the courage to message Dad.

Dad, I'm home. Can I come visit?

Contacting him feels like a much bigger step than I anticipated. My heart pounds the whole way around Loch Eil. I'm almost too on edge to drive, and the apprehension only grows as we get closer to the ferry terminal. A few minutes later, my phone vibrates. Beth reads out his reply.

DEAR FIONA, MARVELLOUS NEWS. CHECK FERRY CROSSINGS AT MALLAIG. LET ME KNOW ETA. MEET QUAYSIDE! LOVE FROM DAD (JOHN).

We spend the final part of the journey dissecting the characteristics of boomer digital comms, and Beth invents the name Parentheses John. Celeste says he sounds like a very niche superhero, and their levity turns the cloud above my head into a soft mist. Before long, we're driving alongside the North Atlantic. I roll down the windows to enjoy the sea-cooled evening sun, the smell of hot salt like a summer holiday. A cluster of islands dot the horizon. I wonder if any of them are Banmora. I wonder what it'll be like, whether this self-sufficient community is enough to justify a man leaving his only child. I sigh a little too dramatically. Beth asks if I'm OK.

'Yeah, I've just been putting this off forever so it feels a bit…'

'Daunting?' Celeste suggests from the back seat.

'Yeah, very.'

'We could always come with you,' Beth says, giving my thigh a supportive squeeze. 'Or if things get too weird, you can come with us to the retreat. Don't worry, babe. We've got your back.'

It's an offhand comment, but tears prick my eyes. They've got my back. They support me, these two women who've shown up for me despite the fact I pushed Beth away. I stem tears and thank them, feeling swaddled by a sense of emotional intimacy that's been escaping me for too long. And without knowing it, Beth has foreseen the real reason I offered to drive – to go on the retreat.

To meet Dissident Uprising.

I try to picture it. The word *retreat* conjures up spa breaks and cucumber slices. I can't imagine Beth and Celeste wanting to go to a place like that. But if it's for activists, it'll probably involve kumbaya drum circles and gong baths. We'll take part in lentil-fuelled workshops about the theory of change, use ribbon dancing to cleanse our chakras, and lament the ills of late-stage capitalism while an old hippie teaches us to make kombucha. It'll be like a rehabilitation centre: if I attend enough workshops and ferment enough tea, I'll be a card-carrying activist again. I'll redeem myself in Ed's eyes without having to turn to the kinds of risks that terrify me.

We chase the sunset all the way to Mallaig. The sky is red and decorated with the whipped-cream clouds of the Inner Hebrides. The town sign announces itself as the *Gateway to the Small Isles*, and when I pull up the hand brake in the harbour arm car park, I feel almost at ease.

11

In our haste to get here, we failed to realise two things: one, the last ferry from Mallaig to Banmora leaves at 5:00 p.m. on Saturdays, and two, it doesn't run on Sundays. We're stuck here until Monday morning.

That night, we tread the pavement in search of accommodation and find only one option: the Mallaig Travellers Inn. It's a bare-bones, £15-a-night hostel right next to the boatyard. We are greeted by Dugald, a ruddy-faced middle-aged man with the rough hands and burly frame of someone more suited to life at sea. He welcomes Vashti like an old friend. The smell of diesel and fish saturates the shaggy red carpet, and the artex ceiling is matched in tastelessness by the textured wallpaper. He takes us up to the accommodation which consists of six rickety bunk beds and a shared bathroom. As the only guests, Dugald boasts, we have free run of the Common Room, with its faux leather sofas and DVD player. Not wanting to shirk his hospitality, we watch an old rom-com and share a rancid bottle of white zinfandel that Beth finds in the self-catering kitchen. That, combined with a dinner of service station sandwiches, leaves a bad taste in my mouth. A taste made worse by Beth and Celeste's near-constant PDAs. They pull their mattresses onto the floor to sleep beside each other. They share in-jokes and toothpaste and an obsession with Vashti, who they treat like their only child. When we say good night and switch off the light, they whisper and giggle for at least an hour before falling asleep.

I stare at the bunk bed above me and scowl. Although I'm not proud of it, being around them is starting to get to me. I'm happy for Beth. I like Celeste. They're clearly very much in love. But their chemistry only reminds me of what I lack. A plant can't kiss me or cuddle me at night. A plant can't replace romantic love. And even before, in the months leading up to Ed's death, we weren't bouncing off each other like this. We were barely making it through the day.

I roll over to look at him on the windowsill.

'Send flowers,' I mouth like a prayer. If I have to tolerate their love, I want to feel as close to him as possible. His flowers are the next best thing to real intimacy. So why hasn't he bloomed since the morning I went to the café? And why not, when I've done everything he's asked of me? The closer I get to my dad and Dissident Uprising, the more doubt creeps in. Because if Ed's not blooming, how can I be sure that I'm on the right path? How can I have faith that any of this is worth it?

When I wake up, the hammering of hooves merges with the sound of glass smashing. The bedsheets are damp, my body a white-hot heat source. I blink rapidly and try to scrub the nightmare from my memory. But it won't budge.

Ed was withdrawing from me behind the conservatory door at East Peace, his disdainful expression mirroring the look he gave me the night of the party. I watched through the glass as he built a barricade to keep me out, using boxes of RIOT 1.5 merch and the portable speakers we used to take to marches. I don't need a dream expert to figure out the heavy-handed symbolism, especially not after my envy-induced mood last night.

I put a pillow over my face and groan. The heavy-handed symbolism didn't end with the barricade. As I hammered on the conservatory windows and promised I'd do more, the sound of my fists were joined by hooves that shattered the glass house and descended on him in a chaos of steel horseshoes.

I sit up, almost hitting my head on the bunk above me, and remember where I am. Beth and Celeste are curled up on the floor with Vashti on her back between them, her tail wagging as she dreams. I exhale shakily, the jumble of their limbs and their soft breaths temporarily restoring my peace of mind. The horses recede. The final shard of glass falls to the ground. I unclench my jaw. There are horizontal shadows across the wall from the blinds. I look to the windowsill for more reassurance. What I see next makes my heart triple in size.

'Oh!' I wail, my morning throat like a bullfrog. Beth and Celeste sit bolt upright. Vashti jumps to her feet.

'What's happened?' Beth shouts, her hands in a fighting position.

'He's flowered!' I fall out of the bed to get to him. I yank open the blinds. Beth complains at the sudden burst of light. 'He's flowered! He's actually flowered!'

The flower glows with the same lustre as the adjoining blooms, but it's bigger. Blousy, even, the ruffled white petals curling towards the light like a lacy handkerchief. I count them. One flower, two flowers, *three flowers*.

Then I hear his voice.

You're on the right path. And you know I'd kiss you if I could.

He speaks with such startling clarity that I spin around to check whether Beth and Celeste can hear him, too, but they just look bemused.

I giggle through my nose. He'd kiss me if he could. A rush of delight courses through me, feeling very much like the intimacy I've been craving. *He'd kiss me if he could!* My giggle turns into a yelp, and Vashti springs up and down, the only one matching my elation. I grab her front paws and dance in front of the window like a kid on Christmas morning. Celeste laughs.

'He's *magnifique*,' she says, heedless of how much that means to me.

He. She said *he.*

With a whole day ahead of us, we decide to go to the beach. I hesitate about bringing Ed. The heat could dry out his soil and the salt air could damage his flowers. But leaving him feels like an even greater risk. Anyone could come into the dorm room and take him. I could stay behind and feign illness, but Ed's new flower is explicit: I can't lock myself away again.

After breakfast, I ask Dugald if he has an umbrella I can borrow. He calls me a *strange wee lass* but hands me a collapsible one with a Scotland flag on it. I put my bag on back to front and lower Ed inside, then open the umbrella and tuck it into one of the straps. I catch sight of myself in a hallway mirror. The umbrella makes me look like a tourist who's just hit up a souvenir stand, and the bulge of the bag against my torso gives me the profile of a heavily pregnant woman, but I don't care. The bag will protect his soil, the umbrella will protect his leaves, and I'll have my hands free to protect his flowers.

Vashti leads us along a well-worn path to Camusdarach Beach, tracing the frilly edge of the west coast with its sublime views across the archipelago of the Inner Hebrides. In the far distance, there are two islands side by side. One is entirely flat, and the other looks like a cluster of Egyptian pyramids. Parentheses John once told me that Banmora was built on a single slab of volcanic rock. The flat one must be Banmora. That means that somewhere out there, on that vast stony expanse, my father is waiting for me. Dissident Uprising is waiting for me. I look to Ed for comfort. He told me that I was on the right path. I breathe deeply into that knowledge, his comment about kissing me still sending little bolts of joy dancing around my body. The morning sun is almost pleasantly warm, the ocean is as blue as Beth's mullet, and all around us, butterflies and bees bumble in and out of wildflowers. I close my eyes and bathe in it. Just a few days ago, I was trapped inside a dungeon of my own making. Today, I am walking to the beach with my friends.

'Did you hear about the storm surge?' Beth asks, unknowingly spoiling the moment.

'No,' I reply, my eyes snapping wide.

'They think it could happen next week.'

'Really?' I say shrilly. Beth and Celeste nod. Clearly, they took the time to catch up on the news this morning while I was celebrating a flower.

'And then there's your maniacal twat of a prime minister with his big, bold plan to *cure the activist plague*,' Celeste adds, her face alight with righteous indignation.

'Has he said what the plan is yet?' I ask.

'No,' Beth replies, kicking a clod of dry mud, 'but whatever it is, it can't be good.'

'Maybe he's waiting for the weather to turn,' Celeste says, her voice sarcastically upbeat, 'and then he's gonna throw us all off Tower Bridge.'

'Yeah,' Beth laughs, 'he'll make us walk the plank, one by fucking one.'

'I wouldn't put it past him,' I chime in with a fake laugh, trying to match their flippant tone. Then the laugh peters out and I ask, 'But wait – isn't the plan about prison overcrowding?'

'We're taking the piss, mate,' Beth cackles, punching me softly on the arm.

Her mirth does nothing to reassure me.

We walk in silence for a while, each stewing on what the big, bold plan could be. I feel an old frustration reemerging. I can't even enjoy a day at the beach without existential dread lurking close behind me. It's the curse of caring, and precisely why I disconnected as readily as I did. First, I abandoned the news, unable to stomach its myopic agenda, then I abandoned social media – not just because it had become an emblem of my failure but because of its horrifying, daily dose of dissonance. An unprecedented wildfire, *swipe*, a fancy birthday dinner, *swipe*, an infographic about genocide, *swipe*, a photo of a dog better-loved than those experiencing aforementioned genocide, *swipe*. My nervous system couldn't handle it. Compassion was simply incompatible with a broken heart. But now that I'm with Ed again, and now that I'm following the direction of Beth and Celeste's moral compass, I think my capacity for compassion has grown. Because despite the dread, I think I want to know. I think I'm ready to reach outside of my own suffering and engage with the world, even if it taints the present moment. It is a profound shift. I look down at Ed and give a resolute nod.

Up ahead, there is a stile bordering a meadow. Beth and Celeste climb over it, but I falter, restricted by Ed's protection devices. When they look back, their expressions are pitiful. I must look absolutely mad. But if anyone has licence to act like a kook, it's the recently bereaved, and they seem to agree. Because instead of drawing attention to my burgeoning eccentricity, Beth helps me over the stile while Celeste holds the umbrella.

'Thanks,' I say.

There is a moment of quiet, a held breath. I know what they're both thinking: *What's really going on with the plant?* But thankfully, the walking recommences.

'So tell me,' I say with the breezy cadence of someone trying to move past an awkward encounter, 'how did you guys meet?'

'In the back of a van,' Celeste replies with a quick grin and sparkling eyes. 'What do you call it? A meat van?'

'Meat *wagon*,' Beth laughs.

'A police car?' My pulse increases.

'We got arrested at the same protest,' Beth explains, moving to put her arm around Celeste. 'When I met this dream boat, she had cable ties around her wrists and blood on her face.'

'Truncheon,' Celeste says, lifting her upper lip. Her front tooth is discoloured, as if a bruise is trapped beneath the enamel. It's such a shame. She has otherwise beautiful teeth.

'Oh my god, Celeste,' I gasp. 'I'm so sorry. Where was this?'

'At a RIOT protest, actually,' Beth answers. 'I went to a few of the Edinburgh meetings.' Then she shoots me a fretful look. 'We don't have to talk about it.'

'It's OK,' I say despite my quickening pulse. If I'm going to embrace compassion again, I can't keep avoiding these conversations. 'Why did you get arrested?'

'We blocked Canongate,' Celeste says. 'Right outside the parliament building – sat on the ground for hours. Then the police got bored.'

'Did you get charged with anything?'

'They tried to give me a caution,' Celeste replies, 'but I refused. No comment, no caution.'

'UNDER WHAT POWER?' Beth shouts, raising her fist. It's a phrase that's been chanted at many a London protest, too.

'So they're taking you to court?' I ask Celeste.

'I guess, although they arrested so many people that day. I doubt it'll happen any time soon.'

'It's so fucked,' Beth seethes. 'They just took my thumbprint and let me go.'

'As is the way on this racist little island of yours.' Celeste looks out to sea and frowns with the bitterness of a lifetime. 'But it was the same in France. My mother used to take me to protests in Paris. Thousands of white people would march in the streets, set fire to cars, throw bricks – typical French resistance. But guess who they always stopped for questioning?'

'That's awful,' I reply, though the response doesn't feel nearly enough. 'Didn't it put you off going?'

'It made us wary, sure. But we're always wary. And my mother was a child of climate refugees. She knew what it was to be displaced. That kind of upbringing makes you want to fight back, you know?'

'Beth mentioned your grandparents. What happened, if you don't mind–?'

'It's a long story,' Celeste says with a sigh.

As we continue along the trail, the might of the sun loses its pleasant warmth, and Celeste's long story slowly unfolds. I learn that, when Senegal was a French colony, local farmers were forced to expand their peanut farms at the expense of the ecosystem. Entire forests were razed to the ground, the soil was eroded, and the wildlife vanished. That would've been bad enough, but in their frenzy for a lucrative cash crop, the French failed to prepare for the fact that peanuts need a lot of rain.

'So when a drought hit in the late sixties,' Celeste explains, 'a lot of the farmers were left destitute, my grandparents included.'

When she speaks, it is with such self-assured intellect that I feel stupid by comparison. She tells me that her story is one in a tome of stories that have been shaped by climate change, a crisis that has already altered the lives of those whose autonomy was taken away. If the peanut farms were never forcibly expanded, Senegal wouldn't have experienced the kind of deforestation that left them vulnerable to extreme weather. Her grandparents wouldn't have been forced to leave their home.

'They got a visa to go to Paris,' Celeste goes on. 'Started a café in the *Goutte d'Or*. Tried to make the best of it. But they always struggled. And the French treated them like shit, of course.' She curls her top lip, revealing the bruised front tooth beneath.

'Even though they were the reason your family had to move there in the first place,' Beth adds with a mocking snort.

'Right,' Celeste says with a nod. 'The whole thing is insidious. That's why my mother raised me like she did.' She smiles fondly then. '*Si ce n'est pas nous, qui alors?* she always says. *If not us, then who?*'

'She sounds incredible,' I respond, masking my own embarrassment with praise. In the thick of organising RIOT 1.5, Ed and I never talked about these things. We didn't take the time to understand the issue we were both so passionate about. We just threw ourselves at the cause. Perhaps I should have participated in the progressive showboating of the fringe group after all. I might have learned something. Instead, I drew inclusive doodles that represented an ideal I had no part in creating. Then I think about Celeste's mum, about her rallying motto, and feel ashamed twice over. Because my own mother lacks both the courage and conviction to believe in change.

And so do I.

Across the meadow, we reach another field. This one is dominated by an enormous spire of stone that breaks through the earth like an ancient weapon. The path gets swallowed up by overgrowth, and Beth realises that we've wandered off-trail. While she checks Google Maps and Celeste takes a picture, I walk around the stone. Behind it, there's a waterfall and a gentle stream. The water is cold and clear. I taste it to check that it's fresh, then take Ed out of the backpack and dunk his pot in.

When I stand up, I realise that I'm not alone. There is a horse standing a couple of metres upstream of me. It is a white horse. A wild horse. It has a shaggy marbled torso and a long white mane that reaches down its broad back. It looks up at me, then turns its enormous head away. That's when I spot a whole herd of wild horses trotting close by.

In another life, I would have found the horses to be majestic. I would have thought that they each looked like a wingless Pegasus.

But in this life, the horses are lethal.

Beth and Celeste come running towards me. Their arms are extended, their faces distressed. Vashti jumps up and paws at my chest. The first horse whinnies and charges back to the herd, sending the rest of them running off into the distance. I can't hear my own voice, but my mouth is stretched into the shape of a scream. All I can hear are hooves and fear and pandemonium. I can see a red flare soaking the skies above me. The past clamps its jaws around my brain while Beth tries to hold me in the present, her hands on my waist, her eyes wild and round and pleading.

Help me. Dear god, somebody help me.

He's bleeding.

12

Later, I find myself in the bottom bunk at the hostel. I sit up and grumble as pain pulses behind my eyes. My brain is in a vice, and my body is aching all over.

'Hey,' Beth says softly, her head dangling down from the top bunk. 'How are you feeling?'

'Ed!' I shout, my hands frantically feeling around the bed.

'The plant's right here,' Beth assures me. She jumps off the top bunk and kneels in front of me, pointing to the windowsill. And there he is, his three flowers as bright white as ever. 'I managed to get it off you before you collapsed.'

'I collapsed?' I mutter, the wild horses returning to my memory. One minute, the herd was there, the next, I was here.

Beth nods, her expression full of gentle understanding. 'I'm sorry, babe. I didn't know there were going to be horses.'

'Yeah,' I say, running my hands over my face, 'neither did I. I've got a bit of a phobia now.' It's a coward's understatement, I know. But I already feel far too exposed to tell Beth about the visions that hound me during the day and invade my dreams at night. Because to tell her would mean to speak it into existence, to risk the horses smashing down the hostel doors and crushing the both of us.

'That's totally understandable.' Beth takes my hand and holds on tight. I steal a quick glance at her.

'And also…' I start, then turn away. I want to open up. I want to offload some of the weight that has made this journey so much harder. I'm just not sure how to anymore. Not after spending three months hiding from truths I can barely acknowledge in private. But if I'm going to go to Banmora and be a better version of myself, I have to try.

'It was just upsetting,' I admit, studying the folds in the thin hostel duvet. 'Hearing about how you and Celeste were arrested. I've never put myself on the line like that.'

Beth sits beside me on the bunk bed. Her voice is tender, trying to console me, but she says just about the worst thing possible. 'Oh, babe, you shouldn't feel bad about that. You used to do so much.'

Used to. Past tense. Just like Ed said the night of the party, when the tension between us finally erupted, and he uttered so many terrible things. I bury my face in my hands as Beth's concise summation of my failings barges down my defences.

'Hey, hey.' Beth moves closer. 'I'm sorry, I didn't mean–'

'You know when we had that fight about Earth Month?' I cut over her, speaking through a crack in my hands. 'You called me a *corporate shill*. Is that what you still think?'

'No, of course not,' she tries to convince me, although I know she's only saying what I want to hear. 'I shouldn't have said that. It was just jarring – seeing you behave like that online. One minute you were occupying fracking sites, the next you were doing sponsored ads for dodgy brands. I didn't understand, that's all.'

'Ed felt the same way,' I weep, wringing my hands and averting my eyes from the plant on the windowsill. 'He–' I stop myself from saying something I've never said to anyone. Something that I buried in my mental graveyard the day it happened. But then it forces its way out of me, the truth desperate to be heard. 'He wanted to leave me.'

'He did?' Beth puts her hand on my knee, urging me to carry on.

'He said–' my voice breaks between sobs '–he said he didn't love me as much as he used to.' I wail the words, the truth unearthing all of my shame. That's why I let the plants die. That's why I neglected Bruce. That's why I locked the world away and lived in squalor. Because it took every ounce of effort I had to stop those words from killing me.

'Oh, Fi.'

'He wanted to leave me,' I repeat over and over, the sentence morphing into a garbled string of pitiful sounds that echo down the halls of the hostel and exhume a memory I have spent so many months repressing.

In the video, I'm wearing the puffy off-the-shoulder dress that I came so close to selling. Ed is wearing grubby overalls. We're standing by the buffet table at East Peace. I'm smiling as I show him the cake I'd ordered for the occasion. It's a three-tier lemon and elderflower drizzle with the RIOT 1.5 logo bursting out of the top like the title of a superhero movie. Ed is smiling wanly. He looks exhausted. The Final Strike is seven days away. He keeps checking his watch.

The video was shot by a friend and uploaded to their stories. I had to ask them to take it down. I was happy to organise the party, happy to show my support, but I couldn't be seen there. By then, my sponsors had adopted the same stance as the media: The Final Strike was an illegal riot designed to stoke civil unrest. That meant that any contact with RIOT 1.5 was a breach of contract. I organised the party to prove to Ed that I was willing to take that risk, although I'd mitigated it by printing signs that read, 'No photos or videos for security reasons.' Still, it was a risk. You can't trust activists to stick to the rules.

The camera zooms into a bespoke balloon featuring the RIOT 1.5 logo, then a stack of branded gift bags containing protest badges and CLIMATE ACTION NOW mugs. In the background, waiters dish out vegan light bites and flutes of English sparkling wine that I'd sourced especially for its carbon neutrality.

The party was attended by everyone involved in the London group – a mix of ages, from kids fresh out of school to retired folks who'd been protesting since the Free Love movement. Most of them looked like they'd be more comfortable with a can of lager than a champagne flute, but I wanted it to feel special. The upcoming strike would be nationwide and, despite every effort to quash it, seventy-five towns and cities were taking part.

But morale was low. The government had just announced plans to impose tougher restrictions on public protest, giving police the power to shut down any gathering that they deemed disruptive or noisy – i.e., every political demonstration in the history of time. The heat wave was branding its irons around the city, and people were losing their right to demand action.

Looking back, I realise that the movement was being gagged just like I was. But instead of cowering before the whims of the establishment, the people at that party weren't afraid. They were burned-out, they were heartbroken, but they were still going to fight like they could win.

Once everyone had a glass of bubbly in hand, I gave a speech underneath the clematis-covered pergola. I don't know why I felt the need to draw attention to myself. I guess I just wanted everyone to know that I'd organised the party, that I was still part of RIOT 1.5 – despite my participation being in secret.

'I just want to take a minute to really reflect,' I began, nodding and smiling with the serenity of Gwyneth Paltrow at a Goop wellness resort. 'RIOT 1.5 started as a University of Edinburgh society called the Climate Change Prevention and Democracy Preservation Society. Catchy, eh?' There was a smattering of laughter. 'But thanks to the generosity of people like Irie, who lets us use this space for free, and the sheer determination of people like Ed, who has been relentless in his pursuit of change, we've been able to grow this into a national movement. Next week, thanks to all of you, this country will come to a standstill, and the government will have no choice but to meet our demands.' I paused for the assurance of whoops and cheers, but the murmur that emanated from the crowd was tepid at best.

'That's why I wanted to get everyone together,' I pressed on, brightening my tone against the frosty reception, 'to have a little celebration, a pat on the back, before the big day. Thanks so much for coming, everyone! Don't forget to take a gift bag at the end, and as a reminder, please don't share any content on your socials. Thank you!'

I searched the crowd for Ed and smiled at him, hoping for an approving grin in return. Instead, he upturned his glass and downed the £55-a-bottle wine with the zeal of a disgraced banker shooting whisky. Irie was standing next to him, gripping the stem of her flute with both hands. She and Ed exchanged an awkward glance. After that, he disappeared. I searched the garden for him, worried that I'd said the wrong thing, but instead found Irie by the rhododendrons.

'This party is quite something,' she said.

Quite something didn't necessarily mean *something good*. 'Have you seen Ed?' I asked, brushing over the insinuation.

'Not since your speech.'

I waited for her to suffix the statement with a compliment, but she just took an hors d'oeuvre from a passing waiter and stuffed her mouth. She hadn't bothered dressing up, either, wearing her usual straw visor, gold crucifix necklace and faded blue worker's smock that did nothing to flatter her pear shape.

Before I could respond, Ed appeared from the conservatory.

'Time to wrap this up,' he said matter-of-factly, an empty flute in hand.

'There you are!' I beamed, not clocking what he'd just said. 'Where have you been, babe?'

'I've been celebrating.' He tipped his glass upside down.

'What's the matter?'

'You tell me.'

'What's that supposed to mean?'

Irie began inspecting the rhododendrons. Then Ed made a beeline for the speaker.

'Excuse the charade, you lot,' he said, projecting his voice across the garden and switching off the music. 'I know we've all got better things to do than act like elitist pricks, so you're free to go. I'll be in the conservatory if anyone needs to go over logistics for next week.'

Everyone froze, their faces caught in various states of confusion. I strode over to Ed, my heels clipping against the pebble paving, and grabbed his forearm.

'What's going on? What's happened? We haven't even started the fireworks yet.'

Ed laughed – properly laughed from the pit of his stomach – and walked into the conservatory, closing the glass door with a bang.

Later that night, I arrived home drunk. After Ed's outburst, I went to an influencer event in Shoreditch and threw back cocktails like it was my last night on earth. But as I dropped my keys at the front door and tripped over the threshold, I wished I hadn't had so many. The flat was dark and smelled like warm terra-cotta pots. Light from the kitchen told me he was still awake. I went into the bathroom to delay the confrontation. My reflection in the cabinet mirror was blurry. My fake lashes were peeling at the corners. I took them off, enjoying the drag on my eyelid. Then there was a rap at the door.

'Yes?' I said, wishing I didn't sound so timid.

Ed appeared in the mirror wearing his bathrobe. I didn't turn around to face him. 'Good night, was it?'

'Don't,' I snapped, twirling my carefully straightened hair on top of my head.

'We can talk about it now or we can talk about it in the morning, when you'll be hungover. Your choice.' He leaned against the door frame and crossed his arms, performing the role of a disappointed parent. This was often our dynamic by then. Me, the school kid on the naughty step, and Ed, the worldly grown-up training me to be a better person. I pouted and opened the bathroom cabinet. His reflection vanished.

'I tried my best,' I said, rubbing cleanser over my face. 'I don't get why you're so upset.' I washed the cleanser off and finally faced him. The bathroom was cupboard-sized, made smaller by the number of plants we'd squeezed in. I felt cornered. A tightness appeared in my chest. 'Excuse me.' I ducked around him and went into the kitchen, skincare abandoned.

Before the kettle had the chance to boil, Ed was leaning against the kitchen counter. 'It was totally over the top, Fifi – the waiters, the gift bags, the fireworks. We're a grassroots activist organisation, not a marketing company.'

I concentrated on making tea. The longer it took to do that, the more time I had to plan my line of defence. I made a point of putting only one mug on the kitchen counter and concentrated on not spilling the oat milk – no small feat given my drunken double vision.

'I can't believe you made a scene like that,' I spoke into the steam. 'You showed me up.'

'I showed *you* up?' he spat, raising his voice. 'I've never been so embarrassed in my life! Those fucking signs, Fifi. What were you thinking? Did you really think people would fall for that?'

'Fall for what?'

'No photos or videos *for security reasons*? You tried to con people into thinking there was some kind of surveillance risk when you just didn't want to be seen there.'

'I'm not supposed to even *go* to activist events,' I said in a small voice. 'We've talked about this. It's part of my–'

'*Contract!*' he shouted, then snarled, 'The golden fucking gag. I keep forgetting you're Travis's little lapdog.'

It was just about the cruellest thing he'd ever said to me. 'Ed! How can–'

'You know what makes me *sick*, Fi?' he cut over me, his voice thick with resentment.

'I'm sure you're about to tell me.'

'How much did you spend on that party tonight? Go on, tell me. How much?'

'I don't know.'

I did know. The sparkling wine alone had cost one thousand pounds. I took my tea into the bedroom, desperate to get away from him, but he followed me, his eyes wild with adrenaline.

'That cake must have cost – what? Three hundred pounds? Four hundred? It was a *wedding cake*, for fuck's sake. Did you stop to think that maybe that money could have been spent elsewhere?'

'Like...?'

'Like, oh, I dunno... The Final Strike, perhaps? The biggest national strike in the history of the UK? Sound familiar? Instead, you spent an obscene amount of money on a party that no one asked for, just so you could feel better about yourself. Do you know how many people there tonight are scraping a living? Do you know how uncomfortable you made them feel?'

'I was trying to be supportive!' I started shouting then, the accusation making my heart race. 'You go on and on at me for signing that contract and for *abandoning the movement*, but when I put my career on the line to support you, I'm *still* a bad person? There's no winning!'

'That money could have been used elsewhere,' he scolded me. 'We don't need fancy parties or fireworks – which are terrible for the environment, by the way – we need boots on the ground.'

'You know I can't,' I said, sitting on the bed and drawing my legs underneath me.

'You can if you quit.' He sat down then too, ready to reach a resolution, but his suggestion made me livid. That's when I lost my temper.

'Who's going to pay the rent then, Ed? Or is it your turn to sell out while I fulfil my hero complex?'

'A *hero complex*, now, is it?' he said derisively, standing up again. 'When we met you didn't seem to think so. I remember you acting like I was God's gift to women for caring as much as I did, back when you used to give a shit.'

'I still do—'

'Oh come off it. All you care about is how many followers you've got and how much money you can make doing *product hauls*,' he seethed, mocking me in a grotesque baby voice.

'You're just being mean now.'

'No, Fifi, I'm being honest. For once in my life, I'm being brutally honest. Ever since you signed with Travis, you've become a totally different person. I feel like we're not even on the same planet anymore.' His volume lowered then, reaching the tone of someone who was coming to an overdue realisation. 'What are we doing?'

'What do you mean?'

'Why are we even together? We've got nothing in common.'

'Don't say that!' I jumped off the bed and reached for his hands, suddenly petrified. 'Please don't say that, Ed. We've drifted apart, but that's natural for long-term relationships, isn't it? We can't always like the same things. That would be boring, wouldn't it? And even before Travis, I wasn't brave like you. I did the artwork, you did the actions. That didn't come between us before, did it?'

'I don't know, Fi…' He shook his head and turned away from me. 'Tonight made me think that we're just not working. Like, the older I get, the more radical I become. I'd call myself an anarchist now. Would you?' His voice was softer, returning to the man I knew, which made what he was saying all the more hurtful.

'I don't know, I haven't thought about–'

'It's all I ever think about, Fi. Night and day. Whereas as you've gotten older, you've gone in the opposite direction. You're happy with *this*.' He gestured around the room, referring to our home, to the paradise we'd built together. 'But I feel trapped. I don't want *things*, I don't want *money*, I don't want *fame*. I want a liveable planet. I want a future. I want–' He took a step away from me and sunk his hands into the pockets of his dressing gown. 'Look, we're not in our twenties anymore. I think maybe, as adults, we're just not compatible.'

'That's not true!' I ran across the room to reach him, quick tears flooding my eyes. I knelt down, my hands clawing his chest as sobs snatched away every word. 'Please, Ed. I love you.'

'I just…' He looked down at me, his face grim with indecision, then covered his eyes with his hands. He took three laboured breaths, building up the courage to say something that he knew would break my heart. Finally, when he took his hands down, he said, 'I don't know if I love you as much as I used to.'

'No!' My mouth was sticky with saliva and tears, my face a wretched stretch of emotion as my heart tore a fault line right through my body. 'Please Ed. I'll be different. I'll come to The Final Strike, OK? I'll be there. I don't care who sees me. I don't care what Travis says. Just please, don't leave me. I love you. Please, please, please!'

I was drunk and distraught, my hands clinging onto his legs, my voice shrieking like a skidding tire, my body rocking back and forth as I begged him to stay. I can't imagine how tragic I must have looked, how utterly pitiful, but whatever Ed saw in that moment, it made him change his mind. He knelt down and put his arms around me. I fell into him. Then he said, 'It's OK. We'll figure it out.'

But even through the veil of my despair, I could feel him withdrawing. I could sense the space he was creating between us, the door he was retreating behind. It was clear in what he didn't say.

I love you, too.

13

The ferry feels more like a cruise ship than I expected. There's an indoor seating area with rows of cushioned seats and a café that serves filter coffee and plastic-wrapped cakes. There's even an outside deck with sun loungers and mounted binoculars for passengers to search for increasingly lesser-spotted whales and dolphins. I balance Ed on the railings and breathe in the gentle breeze. The boat glides through the glassy ocean. My mind conjures up visions of white-capped waves, and I sink into the shadows, my stomach threatening to send my breakfast overboard.

Beth is standing at the prow of the vessel like a blue-haired captain. I watch as Celeste comes up behind her. She lifts up Beth's arms and puts her hands around her waist.

'Close your eyes. Don't peek,' Celeste says.

Catching on, Beth says breathily, 'I'm flying, Jack!' They both burst into laughter and kiss like it's for the first time. I have to look away. They seem to realise because they separate and join me.

'You feeling OK?' Beth asks.

'Just a little seasick, I think.'

'We're almost halfway there,' Celeste says, looping her arm through mine. They're now insisting on taking me to Dad's house, still clueless to the fact that I'm only seeing him so that I can focus on the retreat. But I can't blame them for wanting to accompany me. My breakdown in Mallaig made it clear that I'm in no fit state to go alone.

I suppose one good thing came from it: I no longer have to fake my well-being. Beth now knows the full extent of my pain, how complex it is. She knows that I didn't just lose someone I loved that day, I lost someone I loved who didn't love me. That kind of rejection turns loss into a minefield, denying me the purity of platitudes like *At least we'd never been happier*. But now I want to tell her the whole story. I want to tell her that Ed's come back, that he's given me a second chance to become the sort of woman he'd never leave. I want to tell her that I'm coming with them to meet the founder of Dissident Uprising, to go on the retreat and drink as much kombucha as I can stomach in a bid to rehabilitate myself. But knowing Beth, she'll make a joke of it. She'll call me a *plant pervert* or something equally irreverent, and I don't think I can cope with that today.

The sky and sea stitch together around the cresting island, creating the illusion of a fallen gravestone hovering in the middle of a blue abyss. The sun hums off the water, doubling its intensity. It's hard to believe that next week, London will be ravaged by a storm. I've become so used to arid heat that rain feels like a nostalgic childhood memory.

Celeste's phone doesn't leave her hand as she takes photos of the view. It's interesting to be around someone who uses social media again. I was always made to feel like a pariah for how much I shared online, but Celeste is unashamedly a fan of selfies, grinning into her front-facing camera with the ocean sparkling behind her. It's reassuring, actually. Because although I've tried to crush the impulse, I've spotted multiple places I'd shoot content, from the sun loungers on the top deck to Beth's spot at the prow. In a past life, I'd have asked Ed to take my picture there. He'd have soured and made me regret asking, then I'd have reminded him that my cringey job paid for his free-loading activism. The rest of the journey would have been spent in aggravated silence, building up to an argument that would have ruined the holiday.

It wasn't always like that, Ed reassures me. *What about Islay?*

'Oh yeah,' I say softly, the memory smoothing out the creases of my gloomy hypothetical. 'You were so funny that day.'

Before Travis, there was never any friction when we went away. We'd sworn off flying, so aside from the occasional overland trip to France, we spent our summers exploring the Scottish isles – Skye,

Iona, Arran. With so much natural beauty on our doorstep, staying home never felt like a sacrifice. Islay, with its whisky distilleries, golden eagles and pristine beaches, was one of Ed's favourite islands. That made it one of mine, too. We stayed in an old stone cottage and took a boat from a drizzly Port Ellen to visit a seal colony. Ed was wearing a yellow waterproof jacket that made him look like a fisherman.

'When do the geese migrate back to Greenland?' another passenger had asked him. Ed looked from left to right, certain she was directing the question at someone else. But she was turned to face him. I noticed then that all of the tour guides were wearing yellow jackets.

'Oh, um...' Ed cleared his throat.

'Yes, when *do* the geese migrate back to Greenland?' I pressed him, stroking a hand to my chin and raising an eyebrow.

'In the spring,' he said eagerly, rounding out his shoulders and doing his best David Attenborough impression. 'It's a sight to behold, let me tell you. They take to the sky in their thousands, traversing vast distances to reach their breeding grounds. A true marvel of nature, indeed.' He pursed his lips and squinted his eyes, transforming into an old man. 'A reminder, one might say, of the *rich* yet *fragile* tapestry of all life on earth.'

'OK,' the woman said, her eyes darting about awkwardly. 'Thanks.'

I pulled the hood of my raincoat over my face to cackle. The woman turned her back to us, evidently not seeing the funny side, and Ed spent the rest of the boat trip presenting a nature documentary just for me.

'On the rugged shores of this remote coastline,' he said once we'd reached the seals, 'a bustling colony thrives. Here, amid the crashing waves and jagged rocks of the Southern Hebrides, these remarkable marine mammals gather in their droves. But don't be fooled by their seemingly charming nature – these seals absolutely fucking stink of their own shit.'

When things were good between us, no one made me laugh like Ed did.

After a three-hour journey, the ferry docks at the harbour. For the first time, I see the island that robbed me of my father. But it's not the picturesque, eco-oasis I had in mind. The flat slab I could see from the mainland is several hundred metres high, surging out of the ocean like a tsunami of stone. Swarms of seabirds fly in and out of its craggy rock face, reminding me of pterodactyls in silhouette, and the only sign that people actually live here is a cluster of granite cottages that are dwarfed by the monolith that surrounds them. On first impressions, Banmora appears to be a bleak, prehistoric outcrop that's better left to the birds.

People start to disembark. I cling onto Ed and hesitate at the top of the gangway. I texted Dad our arrival time, but he didn't reply. Now my heart is pinching my rib cage, and my every instinct is to tell the captain to turn this thing around. Because getting off this boat means committing. It means committing to seeing my dad, to meeting Dissident Uprising, to visiting this inhospitable lump in the middle of the sea. How can I find the courage to do any of that when the memory of that night is at the forefront of my mind? If Ed didn't love me as much as he used to, if he wanted to leave me, why do I think I'm suddenly capable of living up to his expectations?

I didn't mean what I said, Fi. I love you. Of course I do.

'Really?'

Really.

That revelation is enough to make me drop to the deck, curl up in the foetal position and weep for the rest of the day. But I know that isn't what Ed wants. He wants me to be brave. To commit. And now more than ever, I have to listen to him.

I walk off the ferry with renewed conviction and trot to catch up with Beth and Celeste, who are waiting for me on a long cement jetty that connects the harbour to the land. I scan the faces of the people gathered there. None of them are my dad – unless he's turned into the late-thirties white woman who is now striding towards us.

'I'm Jenny,' the woman says, holding out her hand. I shake it. She squeezes my fingers with the grip of a CEO. 'It's lovely to finally meet you.'

'Uh, you too,' I say politely, trying to hide my confusion. 'Where's my dad?'

'He's at home,' she explains, as if that's a perfectly valid reason for not meeting me here. 'I've come to collect you.'

'Oh. OK. These are my friends,' I tell her, splaying a hand in the general direction of Beth and Celeste, who wave back. 'They're here, um…'

'On holiday,' Beth chips in. 'Just want to say a quick hello to John – he's a family friend – then we'll be out of his hair.'

'Sure thing,' Jenny replies, patting Vashti on the head. I give them both a quick, grateful smile. Thank god I don't have to do this on my own.

We follow Jenny down the jetty and pass a Welcome to Banmora sign. Then I spot something that makes me backtrack. There's a sticker next to the word *Banmora*. It's positioned like a full stop and features a shattered-earth symbol. If this is where the founder of Dissident Uprising is hiding out, I shouldn't be surprised, yet the sight of that symbol makes me chew what's left of my fingernails. Those baby activists, the ones I saw get pepper-sprayed in the face, are within touching distance.

Beth and Celeste wait for me to catch up. Jenny marches ahead. She's wearing a khaki-green men's shirt tucked into beige linen shorts, brown walking boots and white socks pulled up to her calves. Her light brown hair is scraped into a low bun, and she has the frown lines of someone who has spent their entire life outside.

'She's giving Miss Trunchbull,' Beth whispers when we catch up with her. I clap my hand over my mouth to stop from laughing.

'Your dad's no good with houseplants, I'm afraid,' Jenny says, turning to look at Ed.

'It's not for him,' I reply with a now-foolproof explanation. 'It's an urn.'

Jenny simply bobs her head and looks away. She leads us to a pickup truck and motions for us to climb in. I have no idea who this woman is or why she knows about my dad's incompetence with potted plants, but I suspect it's going to sting when I find out. The wounded child, the one I left in my Palma Violet bedroom, reappears. He said he'd be here.

We ride in the back of the truck and hold on as Jenny swings around the numerous U-bends towards Dad's house. With the jetty behind us, we follow the base of the stone ridge until the land opens up and away from it. Swathes of heather bloom in every direction, smothering the island in an abundance of purple.

It is bell heather.

When we lived in Edinburgh, Ed and I climbed Arthur's Seat as often as we could. From the peak, we could see the castle, the ocean and the indigo blue of distant pine forests, but Ed was more interested in the tiny bell-shaped flowers that grew in clusters all around us. He'd crouch down among the purple bushes and tell me about the power of heather to withstand wildfires and its symbiotic relationship with fungus. That's when I first thought about having a baby with him, so that someone could inherit his reverence for the earth. A baby named Bell.

I raise the plant over the lip of the pickup truck to show him the view. His three flowers dance, and I feel him smiling at me, his pleasure radiating from every petal. Then the truck hits a pothole, and I have to snatch him down to avoid another incident.

Close shave, he says with a laugh. I start laughing too, relief and love making me giddy. Beth and Celeste look at us with their usual mix of amused bewilderment.

The truck climbs a hill where the north of the island comes into view. A crescent moon of sand curls around a bay. Beyond it, there is a short channel of ocean separating Banmora from the pyramid island I saw from the mainland. As we descend a steep, winding road, a scattering of houses appear, each with four football pitches of land, just like Dad said. I wonder which one is his. The crumbling cottage? The stately house? Or the wind-battered trailer by the beach? I've spent so many years imagining him here, but it's always in my childhood home.

Then Jenny pulls up in front of a building that doesn't look like anything I've seen before. The roof is alive, bursting skyward with grasses and ferns that remind me of the cress heads we used to grow at school. The house has an oval front door and arched windows, all irregularly shaped. On second glance, there isn't a single straight line to speak of. The terra-cotta walls are lopsided, as if someone had taken three hand-thrown bowls and smooshed them together. There is a veranda made from tree trunks and green bottles sunken into the walls like stained-glass windows. I don't for one second believe that my father lives here.

'Is this–?'

Jenny nods before I can finish my sentence.

'It's incredible,' Beth gasps.

We follow a brick path and dodge chickens who flap and squawk at Vashti. For once, my nerves aren't overwhelming me. Because none of this is real. This house belongs in a theme park. In fact, I'm pretty sure that when Jenny takes us inside, cartoon bluebirds will put flowers in my hair. But then the oval door swings open, and there he is, standing in the light of the sunken green bottles, looking at me with the expression of a man who has just been caught doing something out of character by the ghost of a dead relative. Because he *is* doing something out of character. Something stranger than living in a cress head house.

He is holding a baby.

There I am, cradling my boyfriend, my most cherished thing in the world, and there he is, cradling a baby, his best-kept secret. We stand there, the door between us like a referee, and stare at each other. Jenny, Celeste and Beth linger behind, watching this standoff unfold. No one moves. Dad is wearing a backwards cap and three-quarter length shorts. He looks like an elderly skater dude who's just kidnapped a newborn. I'm so stunned that I forget myself and tip Ed sideways, almost losing his soil to the doorstep.

'Meet your sister,' Jenny says, coming up behind me. 'Her name is June.'

'*Sister?*' I splutter.

'You didn't tell her?' Jenny asks, her voice tight.

We both glare at Dad.

'Fiona,' he starts, crossing no-man's land, 'I've been wanting to tell you for months, but you don't return my calls. I didn't want to tell you over text message. I know it's a lot to take in, but yes, this is June, your sister. And Jenny, my partner.'

'Jenny?' I repeat, my mouth open wide. 'John, Jenny and June?'

'Yes.' Dad nods and takes another step closer. 'It was quite by accident, really.'

The sense of rejection is a body blow. It tears a hole right through me. My legs turn to jelly and I stumble backwards, then feel Beth's hands as she steers me into the house and positions me on a jaunty chair with a love-heart design. She takes Ed and puts him on the table. I look up and try to regain control of myself. The roof is supported by beams of wood which twist into the shape of a mandala. The house is single-story but there's a mezzanine accessed via a spiral staircase that wraps around a gnarly tree trunk. The rest of the space is just as confusing. Someone has painted ornate floral patterns around the arched windows and made a garland over the kitchen table from dried herbs and flowers. There's an oven that looks like it was moulded from mud and a polished slab of wood that serves as a kitchen counter. A collection of copper pots and pans hang from hooks, above which a set of shelves display earthenware crockery and jars of pulses and rice. All around there are colourful glass jars filled with sprigs of heather.

What is going on? I grew up in a house with magnolia walls until grey became the must-have monochromatic of the season. How has my dad created a space with so much *whimsy*? And why would he build a house stolen directly from the pages of my childhood fairy tales without me?

Jenny retrieves a whistling orange kettle from the stove. I sit and watch as Beth and Celeste exchange pleasantries with Dad while gawping at the baby. I can tell they're trying to be polite despite the hostile atmosphere, saying all of the things you're supposed to say when you meet a newborn.

'She looks just like you!'

'She has your eyes!'

'She's big for five weeks!'

'Most importantly, how's Mum doing?'

Mum. Jenny is Mum, June's Mum.

Dad is Dad, June's Dad.

June is Sister. My Sister. I have a sister. Me – an only child who grew up lonely.

Why couldn't he have just texted me?

DEAR FIONA. I HAVE IMPREGNATED A YOUNG MISS TRUNCHBULL AND WE ARE HAVING A BABY IN A GIANT CLAY CRESS HEAD. NO ACTION NECESSARY. LOVE FROM DAD (JOHN).

I've been picturing this moment – our reunion. In my fantasy, Dad rolls out the welcome mat. There are banners saying *I'm sorry* and *I missed you* and a big dinner in my honour. Then he'll show me to the room he's been saving just for me, and there'll be a lovely bunch of flowers in a vase.

Instead, there is Jenny and June and the misshaped roof they all live under.

A wet nose touches my forearm. I look down to see Vashti with her head between my legs, her giant orblike eyes gazing at me with heartfelt sympathy. I ruffle the fur on her head and long once more for Bruce. A cup of tea appears in front of me, then everyone sits down and starts chatting about the house like everything is completely normal.

'We made it out of cob,' Jenny answers Celeste, 'a mixture of sand, clay, straw and water. Did you spot the trailer by the beach? That's where we lived while we built it. This place has only been habitable for the last few months. The view down at the beach is amazing, so we were in no rush. But then this one rushed us along…' Jenny touches my dad's arm and leans over, pulling down the baby's swaddle to look at June's face.

I hide my lips inside my mouth and sink my teeth in. They make for an unusual looking family. My dad, a pensioner. June, barely a dot of a human being. And Jenny, a surly headmistress with the attitude of someone much more senior than she appears.

'How old are you?' I cut across the table, my eyes trained on her.

'Thirty-eight,' Jenny replies with a slight lift of the eyebrow.

'Do you know how old I am?'

'In your thirties, right?'

'You're six years older than me. You don't have a problem with that?'

'Not really,' Jenny says with a shrug. 'Age is just a number.'

It feels like she's testing me, measuring how progressive I am against my evident discomfort with the age gap. Then the baby wakes up. She screeches like a crow, her face a tomato. Jenny unbuttons her military shirt and takes out her boob, then Dad hands her the baby.

In a matter of minutes, I have reunited with my father, discovered I have a sister and met my dad's new partner. And now I've seen said partner's engorged nipple.

'We met at the plantation,' Dad tells Beth and Celeste with an overabundance of smiles. 'Fiona knows all about it. That's why I moved here – to replant the pine forest. Jenny's a tree surgeon. She came to clear the land, and I guess we bonded over our mutual guilt from cutting down trees. Ha!'

I sneer.

'I don't cut down any old tree, John,' Jenny rebuts. 'But I'll get rid of conifers if it means planting native species.'

'How noble of you,' I snort. Beth and Celeste squirm.

Dad clears his throat. 'Jenny campaigns for the Landworkers' Alliance,' he explains, glossing over the barbed statement. 'Fronting up their forestry division.'

'Oh cool!' Celeste swoons. 'I've seen their banners at climate protests.'

Jenny nods while June slurps contentedly. 'Yeah, we go to a fair few of those – much good it does. I've spent years lobbying for better land use in Scotland, trying to improve working woodlands, make them actually function as carbon stores. But it's an uphill battle. I'm sure you're well aware, Fi.'

I ignore her attempt at connection. Of course I'm well aware.

'When I heard about what your dad was doing here,' she continues, 'I jumped at the chance to get involved. I never planned to stay but, you know, it's impossible not to fall in love with this place.'

'I had nothing to do with it, of course,' Dad jokes.

'None whatsoever,' Jenny grins back.

I won't lower myself to the petty theatrics of a teenager, but right then, I very much want to mime gagging.

'And she's downplaying it,' Dad adds, putting his arm around her. 'Jenny is basically an expert on sustainable forestry. It was love at first sight!' Another stupid laugh. I can't bear much more of this.

'Why didn't you meet me at the jetty like you said you would?' I ask him, redirecting the conversation away from Jenny's fabulous achievements.

'I was nap-trapped,' Dad replies.

'Excuse me?'

'The baby fell asleep in my arms.'

'So?'

'She's a very light sleeper,' he explains. 'I thought it would be better if Jenny came to collect you, rather than wake her.'

And so it begins – Dad is putting his new daughter's needs above my own. My antipathy towards the three of them radiates off me like a bad smell. Beth and Celeste stare into their laps and try their best to become invisible. I put my hands around Ed and draw him in closer. Is *this* why he wanted me to come here? To show me that I have a sister?

My jelly legs force me to stand. 'I need some air. Beth? Celeste?'

They dither in their seats. I worry for a second that their politeness will outweigh their promise to protect me. But then Beth nods, and they both move to join me. We head for the front door. It is as highly decorated as a wedding arch, with folksy flowers wrapping around the frame.

I resist the urge to kick it down.

14

With the colossal stone plinth behind us, the ocean wraps around on all three sides. We head for the curl of white sand that I spotted on the way down. Vashti charges ahead, dipping her snout low to take in the new environment, and the three of us walk in a solemn row behind her, sighing in quick succession.

'That was a lot,' Beth says, breaking the sigh-off. 'You really had no idea?'

'Zilch,' I reply, not knowing that word was even in my vocabulary. A sea breeze rustles Ed's leaves, and I cup my hand around his flowers, wishing I'd brought Dugald's umbrella for shade.

'It's so thoughtless,' Celeste says. 'He had no reason not to tell you.'

'I *have* been dodging his calls.'

'He could have written. He could have told your mum. He could have come to London. There's no excuse for ambushing you like that.' She seems genuinely upset for me, and I realise then that I like her a lot.

When we arrive at the beach, Vashti runs straight for the ocean. Beth chases after her, stripping her clothes midrun and dropping them on the wet sand. She crashes into the water with her arms above her head. I look down at my feet. I don't know if I'll ever stop associating waves with charging horses. The beach is expansive and has the fine white sand and turquoise waters of a tropical island. The shore is flanked by a ribbon of sand dunes where wild grasses grow. I climb one with Celeste and sit down to watch Beth and Vashti swim. I dig a small trench in the sand and lower Ed into it, then build a mound around his pot, securing him against the breeze.

'You're very tender to your plant,' Celeste remarks.

'You probably think I'm mad,' I say with a weak smile, finding that, for once, I don't care if that's true.

'Not at all,' she says. 'I had a little cactus when I was in halls. I loved it very much. Too much. I overwatered it, and it died! How I wish I had your green thumb, your *main verte*. I just don't have the knack for it.'

'I'm not that green-thumbed,' I admit, my eyes downcast as her praise reminds me of the botanical catacomb of my past. 'We used to have a lot of plants. This is all I have left.'

'Well, no wonder you take such good care of it, then.' She smiles warmly and turns to look at Beth and Vashti playing in the surf. I am struck again by the urge to tell the truth. Celeste seems to understand just how important the plant is to me. Perhaps if I tell her everything, she'll understand why. I open and close my mouth. When the words fail to materialise, I reach for low-hanging fruit.

'I didn't just come here to see my dad,' I say on an exhale.

'No?' She turns to look at me again.

'I want to come to the retreat, if that's all right? I don't want to crash your holiday. It's just, after seeing my dad and the baby and everything...' I trail off. Even if Ed brought me here to meet June, I can't stay with them. All I want is to get as far away from my dad as possible. And in a horribly childish way, I want to prove to Jenny that I give a shit about the world, too. I want to prove that once upon a time, I was doing much more than her.

'It's not a holiday,' Celeste says, dropping her voice and shifting towards me in the sand. 'Or a retreat. It was just called that online to avoid tipping off the police.' She lowers her voice even further, and I have to strain to hear her. 'It's an activist boot camp. A place for people who want to join Dissident Uprising and train for their next action. We need to figure out where it is first – they didn't reveal the exact location and the organiser is anonymous – but you're welcome to join us, if that's what you want? If you want to join Dissident Uprising?'

My mouth opens and closes again, my inability to speak fast turning me into a hooked fish. I pinch the bridge of my nose and grapple with what she's just told me. So much for my assumption that the retreat would be a ribbon-dancing, gong-bathing, chakra-cleansing rehabilitation centre. No kombucha, either. I feel a bit disappointed. I was starting to look forward to it – the well-meaning nonsense, the vegan stews, the characteristic kindness. I thought it was going to be a gentle return to activism, Ed's way of easing me back in. But this is right in at the deep end. A lump appears in my throat. Then I remember what Celeste said when we walked to Camusdarach Beach – that she'd refused a caution, that they'd assaulted her.

'Aren't you going to get into more trouble if you join Dissident Uprising?' I ask.

'If the police find us, yeah. But they won't. Not out here.'

Fear returns to the hard-set clench of my jaw. She can't be sure that the police won't find her. Dissident Uprising hasn't exactly been discreet about it. They might not have called it a *boot camp*, but they still told people to come to Banmora. And what about the government's big, bold plan? What if they're going to infiltrate Dissident Uprising and are on their way here right now, wearing the Doc Martens and temporary tattoos of committed activists but carrying the firearms of a special assault team?

Ed's toothless smile flashes before my eyes. I grind my teeth and scrunch up my face, willing the white light behind my eyelids to scrub out the memory. But it sits heavy on my chest and pounds its hooves against my ear drums.

Coming here felt like such a fail-safe way to please Ed. The retreat felt attainable, moderate enough for me to actually succeed at without putting myself in harm's way. But this? I watched Ed die for the crime of *doing something*, something that was, I'm sure, a lot less illegal than whatever Dissident Uprising is planning now. How can he expect that three months after the fact, I'd be willing and ready to join a group that is being pepper-sprayed outside Number 10 and violently evicted from the House of Lords?

I snap my eyes open and shudder. I need to tell Celeste the truth. This whole time, I've had no one else to talk to about what's happening to me. I've figured out everything on my own. It's gotten me this far, but now that the opportunity to join Dissident Uprising is being handed to me on a plate, I need to know if that's what Ed really wants. Because if it is, how am I supposed to say no?

'Can I tell you something?' I blurt, drawing my knees to my chin and squashing my panicking gut against my spine.

'Sure.'

'It's not just a plant,' I force myself to say, finding that I can't look at her when I do.

'Yes, you called it an urn, right?'

'It's more than that. Like, I don't know where it came from.'

'What do you mean?' She squints at me, her interest piqued.

'It appeared on my doorstep the day after my mum took my cat.' I speak as objectively as possible, hoping that if I sound reasonble, she won't think I've lost the plot. 'I was beside myself. Then this plant showed up. This yew tree. Ed's favourite, like I said.'

'Someone must have sent it, no?'

'But who? No one knew about that tree but me and Ed. And then I had this feeling... like I was supposed to put his ashes in the soil. And when I did, it flowered, just like yesterday. Yew trees don't flower.'

'That *is* strange.' Celeste studies Ed with keen interest.

'And last night at the hostel,' I continue, 'I asked the plant to flower, I asked Ed to, and he did.'

'Wow.' She smiles and looks up at me. 'So you think Ed's been reincarnated?'

Reincarnation. It's a word that has evaded me until now. But it's a word that makes the fear lift slightly. Because it's a word that explains everything.

'Yes,' I say, pulling Ed out of the hole I dug in the sand. 'I do.'

Celeste doesn't say anything. What can she say? What is the correct response to a near-stranger telling you that a houseplant is the reincarnation of her dead boyfriend, besides stunned silence?

'I don't know if Beth told you,' I add, sidestepping her hesitation, 'but things sort of ended badly between us. I've been trying to make it right. That's why I left London. That's why I'm *here*. I thought Ed wanted me to go on the retreat but now...' I sigh all the air from my lungs. 'I guess I didn't think he'd ask me to do something so dangerous.'

Celeste continues searching for something to say. Her face is lost in thought and impossible to read. That's when I remember that she's training to be a psychologist. Does that make her the ideal person to talk to, or the worst? She could pathologise my beliefs. She could call Ed a trauma response and shatter my trust in an instant. I curl my toes into the sand and wait, unease gripping every tensed muscle.

'Why do you think Ed wants you to go on the retreat?' Celeste asks, her voice cautious.

'It's hard to explain.' I return her caution, my guard suddenly up.

'I'm here if you want to try,' she says, resting a hand on my shoulder. 'It can't have been easy, going through this alone.'

I huff and shake my head. It's not been easy. I've been second-guessing myself for days, and I'm tired of it. That's when her empathy loosens my tongue.

'Well, there've been all these signs. And I've heard his voice. He told me that I was on the right path.' I wipe sand off Ed's plant pot and laugh wryly. 'Bet you think I'm crazy now.'

'No,' Celeste insists. 'I don't like that word – crazy. There's nothing wrong with you, Fifi. Take it from a psychologist.'

'Thanks.' I nudge my shoulder against hers in sheepish gratitude.

'I guess all I'd say is…' Celeste chooses her words carefully, like she's trying to get it right. 'You don't have to do anything you don't want to do. Ed would want you to go at your own pace, wouldn't he?'

I bite my lip and shrug, wanting that to be true.

'And you know,' she goes on, 'activism doesn't have to be dangerous. Like, I know it is these days by association, but if you choose to come, you can take a look around and make up your own mind. I think that's what's important.'

I let out a breath I didn't know I'd been holding. I really needed this. I really needed to let someone into the chaos that has been my mind of late. And given how quick Celeste was to believe me, perhaps a loved one being reincarnated as a houseplant isn't so ludicrous a proposition after all? Perhaps I can tell Beth without her laughing in my face? Perhaps not. But I don't need to tell anyone else right now. It's enough that Celeste knows.

All I hope is that she's right. I hope that out here, away from the mounted police and the pepper spray, I can find a way to keep Ed flowering that doesn't put me in the firing line.

When we arrive back at Cress Head House, Jenny acts like nothing is amiss and asks if we'd like a tour. Beth greedily accepts, her fascination with the place overriding our unspoken agreement to detest her. Celeste, Ed and I tag along, our newfound understanding giving me the strength I need to rise above it.

Jenny explains the grey-water system and shows us the external compost toilet, then we look at the chicken coop and admire a vegetable patch that is somehow still producing food. Bar the shiny row of solar panels, it feels like we've stumbled on a settlement of early man. Each dwelling has been made by hand; each off-grid contraption rejecting modernity in favour of a simpler life. There's no denying it. This place is infinitely superior to the one-bedroom, fourth-floor dump I wasted so much time affording. Then Jenny takes us to one building that doesn't look plucked out of the Stone Age. She says it's her *studio* – a converted shipping container that looks like the last resort of someone who couldn't get on the property ladder. It's split into two rooms with windows cut into the corrugated metal. She tells us she's an artist. Beth and Celeste coo over her collection of natural dyes and abstract designs, but to me, it seems no more skilled than if someone had covered their bum in beetroot juice and sat on a piece of paper.

Then Jenny leads us into the adjacent room. 'You'll like this, Fiona,' she tells me presumptively.

Hung on the wall of that room is a fabric banner. On that banner is a hand-painted symbol. It is a symbol of a shattered planet with a safety pin stuck through it.

'This is the centre of operations,' she says.

On one side of the room, there is a large table covered in papers. On the other side, there are two sets of bunk beds that remind me of the hostel in Mallaig.

'I never planned to start something like Dissident Uprising.' Jenny walks around the table and points at the banner on the wall. 'But after The Final Strike, I wanted to step up, especially with June on the way. I felt like I owed it to her, you know? And it made sense to organise it from here, away from London, where the police couldn't trace me.'

'You founded Dissident Uprising?' Beth asks, her face a jumble of confusion that mirrors my own. Because I can't make sense of a word that Jenny is saying. Why did she mention The Final Strike? And why is she talking about Dissident Uprising? She's a tree surgeon who makes natural dyes and lives in a cress head with her elderly lover. She couldn't be further removed from those baby activists who were abused in London.

'I did,' Jenny says. 'Glad I've maintained my anonymity!'

'Oh my god, Jenny, we came here to go on the retreat!' Celeste laughs and claps her hands to her cheeks. 'The *boot camp*, we were gonna find it after this.'

'This is the boot camp!' Jenny laughs, too, bending double to cackle across the room. 'So that's why you came to Banmora? You as well, Fi? I thought your visit was a bit sudden.'

I lean against the steel wall and press my free hand onto the heat of the metal. I don't say anything.

'How're you planning actions in London from way out here?' Beth asks with over-the-top enthusiasm.

'It's a self-organising system,' Jenny replies, her eyes glistening. 'Anyone can act under the Dissident Uprising name, so long as they share the same ambitions. Most of what I do *here* is facilitating others to do the real work out *there*. I know a fair bit of campaign strategy, thanks to the Landworkers' Alliance, so it's been good to flex those muscles. But the next action is different. It's a logistical nightmare. Hence the boot camp.'

'I can't believe you've done so much in three months,' Celeste gushes.

'I can't believe it, either.' Jenny puts a hand on her forehead and shakes her head. 'It's completely snowballed. But a lot of people felt the same way after The Final Strike. They wanted to *do something*.' There's that phrase again. 'And now, well, what we're planning is next-level. I'm out of my depth, to be honest.' She looks down at a number of blueprints strewn across the table with humility. 'It's great you're all here – you especially, Fi. You know more about this stuff than anyone.'

'What is it?' I find the gall to say, digging my fingers around Ed's pot as her misconception hits me like a fist in the stomach.

'What is what?' Jenny asks.

'What are you planning? What's the action?'

'I can't say right now. Our comms aren't secure. But I'd love to run the whole thing by you. You know, it was RIOT 1.5 who–'

I walk out of the shipping container with Ed. This is too much. This is fucking ridiculous. I've officially reached my limit. I search the grounds for somewhere to hide and find one room with a lock. I put the wooden lid of the compost toilet down and breathe through my mouth. I try to compose myself and cling to the clarity I found on the beach. Celeste said I could make up my own mind. She said I could take things at my own pace. But how can I say yes to joining Dissident Uprising when Jenny is planning something that requires a boot camp and blueprints to pull off? I've never been that kind of activist. Then again, how can I say no, how can I be the one who opts out, when Beth and Celeste are willing to put their lives on the line? Because that's what they'll be doing. They'll be risking everything. I know that better than anyone.

Why did it have to be *her*?

Why this place, this fairy tale that my father built without me?

That's when the wounded child, the one that Dad left behind, collides with the wounded adult, the one that Ed did, and I crumble. I watch clarity sift between my fingers like sand. Then I land on two words that sum it all up.

'I can't,' I tell the plant on my lap.

Yes, you can, Fi.

No, Ed. I can't. It's not even about the golden gag anymore. I don't care about that. But I can't suddenly find it in me to throw caution to the wind and do something this dangerous, not after last time.

You told me that I needed to do more, that I needed to give more, care more, be more, so I went to The Final Strike, and I tried in earnest to be that woman again. I went there *for you*. And look at where it left me. It left me traumatised and alone and hopeless. It left me lost.

I can't do it. I don't have what it takes. I'm not enough.

You are enough.

No, I'm not, Ed. I used to be, like Beth said. *Used to* be. But I'm not that person anymore. I'm the person you didn't love as much, remember? I'm the person your death turned me into.

Because they didn't just kill one activist that day.

They killed two.

15

The crowd was swollen like a body of water and flowed from the open-top campaign bus in Trafalgar Square all the way to the Houses of Parliament. Hundreds of thousands of people were gathered in Central London that day, joining millions around the country who were downing tools and demanding change. The atmosphere was electric. I'd been to enough protests to know that most of the time, people were tired of chanting and marching to no avail. But The Final Strike was different. It was thirty-five degrees in the middle of May. The media was calling it a *summer scorcher* and running pictures of kids eating ice cream while the government was approving new oil and gas licences. People were hot, people were worried, but above all, people were angry. Maybe that's why the atmosphere was heightened. And the name, too, the sense of finality, like this was our last chance to be heard – after this, the window of opportunity would close, and climate chaos would take hold. Maybe that's why, after Ed's speech atop The Final Strike bus, chants echoed across Trafalgar Square with the boom of a rocket launcher, and I finally understood the difference between a parade and a protest.

We marched down Whitehall towards Parliament Square. Ed smiled at me with wide, defiant eyes and squeezed my hand, any tension between us evaporating.

'We've done it!' he said.

'*You've* done it,' I corrected him, pulling my face mask down to smile back.

'Go on, take that thing off,' he urged me.

'You know I can't.'

He strode a few paces ahead, the tension reemerging as quickly as it had dissipated. He'd been nagging me all morning to show my face, calling me a coward when I stepped out of the flat wearing an N95 and sunglasses. I called him self-righteous for judging me when he knew I didn't have a choice. But still, I was aware that I'd reneged on the promise I made after the party. In grovelling desperation, I said I'd go to The Final Strike regardless of who saw me there. I begged him to love me by vowing to break the gag. But when it came down to it, I couldn't risk it, not when doing so could have stripped both of us of our security. Ed didn't see it that way, of course. He thought that marching in the streets only counted if people knew you were there. We took the tube into Central London without speaking another word to each other.

As we passed through the crowd, people slapped Ed on the back and shook hands with him. One woman asked for a selfie. When he obliged, I thought about telling her that he hated selfies and was only going along with it to spite me, but I held my tongue. We arrived at the square to find a group of drummers striking out a frantic beat. As the rhythm picked up pace, hands were splayed, feet thrashed the ground, and people yelled their rage into the sky. Ed raised his fist and joined in with the chants that moved through the crowd.

That was when I remembered that, despite our differences, Ed was exceptional. He came alive when people took a stand. He dedicated his life to speaking truth to power. He would always be the first to *do something*. I took a candid picture of him, capturing him in his element, and I had no way of knowing that it would be the last picture of him alive.

'Fifi, it's Celeste. Breathe with me, OK? Breathe in, one, two, three, four, five–'

I am cold. I am sweating. I am trapped somewhere far away. I can see my dad standing with the compost toilet door between both hands. It's been taken off its hinges. I can see Beth and Celeste squatting in the dirt outside the toilet, their hands reaching for the person within. Jenny is there. She is holding Ed in one arm and the baby in the other. I want to scream at her *Don't touch him!* But the only sound that escapes my mouth is the grating squeak of hyperventilation.

Then I am back in the crowd. Back in London. Where the chants swept across us like a current and with them came a warning we should have been expecting: *'Police!'*

Ed craned his neck to look over the sea of miscellaneous faces. The chant changed again. This time we heard the word *kettle*. Ed told me to get on his shoulders. I got up, assisted by half a dozen people around me, and saw a line of riot police pushing people back from Westminster Bridge. Mounted police trotted close behind.

'Why are they kettling?' I asked him. 'We're being peaceful!'

I wonder what was going through his head right then. He'd organised The Final Strike. He was responsible for anything that happened there. And if the police were using a tactic like kettling, things could go from peace to pandemonium in the blink of an eye. Then the chants stopped, and the sounds that rippled across the square were cries of disorder.

Ed bent forward to put me down. He held my hand. 'Come on,' he said, pulling me through the crowd. He was taking me away from the police, away from danger.

'Where are we going?'

'I have to speak to them.'

He was taking me *towards* the police. We didn't have to fight hard to get there. As Ed made his way, people let him through.

'Why are they doing this?' protesters hounded him. Ed just furrowed his brow and pushed on. I noticed a difference in the body heat then. And the smell. The thousands of people that were on Westminster Bridge were pushed against the thousands of people outside the Houses of Parliament, making the already overheated, dehydrated crowd reek from the struggle to stay upright.

That's when the wall of riot shields came into view. It advanced with the slow but mighty force of a hydraulic press, the police moving as one. The crowd bloated against the cordon, and when the momentum inevitably crashed back against the shields, the police lifted their truncheons. 'Back! Get back!' they shouted, their voices loud but robotic.

Then the crowd erupted, chanting, 'Shame on you! Shame on you! Shame on you!' Hundreds of phones were extended in the air alongside outstretched hands that were grasping towards the sky. We broke through the final row of people and found ourselves face-to-face with riot gear. The police were wearing hi-vis jackets and navy-blue helmets with plastic visors over their faces. The mounted police were perched above them like knights, the horses wearing just as much armour as their riders.

'I'm Edward Galbraith,' he said to the police officer in front of us, expecting his name alone to put a stop to it.

But the police officer just responded with a contemptuous, 'Back!'

'I organised this. There's no need–'

'Get back!'

Hundreds of people around us saw this happen. They saw Ed trying to reason with the police. They saw the police ignoring him.

Then the chants changed again.

'Scum! Scum! Scum!'

That's when Ed abandoned reason and started raising his voice. 'What the fuck do you want? We're being peaceful. We've done nothing wrong!'

A police officer pushed him with his shield, sending Ed flailing into the crowd. The chants disintegrated, and a growling uproar filled the skies. The crowd pushed forward and the police brought down their truncheons. People ducked and dived. The line of hi-vis jackets merged with the multicoloured masses. Everything seemed to be descending into chaos all around me. Then someone ignited a red flare. I looked behind to see a woman being crowd-surfed towards the police, then away from them. She was unconscious. It was too hot. People were passing out. I saw so many panicked faces. The police seemed to be picking people off, dragging them over the cordon and onto the ground where the horses were. The *Press* vests disappeared, followed by the *Legal Observers*. I saw a police officer jab her truncheon into someone's face like she was hammering on a door with a stick. One person threw a bottle, then projectiles were coming left and right as the kettle declined into full-blown fighting.

'There's no need for this!' Ed cried.

'We need to drop back!' I begged him, my face mask gone, my sunglasses crushed underfoot. But there were too many people. It was impossible to move.

Then something happened. I don't know what caused it.

I don't think I'll ever know.

'Breathe out – one, two, three, four, five,' Celeste is saying, her pursed lips encouraging me to do the same. 'Come on, Fi, we're right here.'

'This is worse than last time,' I hear Beth tell Jenny. 'She had an episode before we got here. She collapsed. We should have told someone, we should have taken her to a doctor, we should have–'

'It's not your fault,' Jenny says, 'it's mine. I wasn't thinking.'

I don't know what she means by that. I am shaking with the ferocity of a wild rabbit and unable to focus on anything but the broiling crowd. A wretched noise escapes my mouth. One single word.

Ed.

Hooves hit hot concrete. The police jumped aside to avoid the impact, sending the horses careering into the crowd.

'We need to drop back!' I insisted as a hoof flailed inches from my face. Ed didn't say anything. That's when I noticed that Ed wasn't there. I screamed his name. So many people were screaming. Then I saw him.

He was on the ground.

I watched it happen in slow motion. I watched it happen in double time. It happened before I could do anything. I could have done something.

A horse pounded its hooves into Ed's face.

Once,

twice,

three times.

A shriek so guttural it tore the corners of my mouth wasn't enough to silence the turmoil that surrounded me. I threw myself over him. His left eye had burst and sunken into the socket of his broken skull. The skin on his right cheek was split clean open. Some of his teeth were missing. His beautiful face was ruined. I didn't care. I didn't care about any of it, so long as he was alive. And he was. He was trying to say something. I couldn't hear him. His tongue explored his mouth and found the empty, bloody spaces where his teeth used to be. He smiled. I don't know if it was shock, but for some reason he smiled.

When people saw what had happened, hysteria set in. In the ensuing fight for justice, I was able to pull Ed clear of the horses, clear of the protest, and onto Westminster Bridge. A handful of people followed, the cordon completely abandoned, and they crowded around with their phones, but no one called an ambulance. I thought we'd escaped the onslaught, but I looked up to see another line of mounted police crossing the bridge. No. They were charging. I thought about jumping into the Thames. If I could just get Ed over the side, we could go down together. We might survive the fall.

Then a man started shaking me. 'There's a hospital on the other side of the river!' he yelled, his hands digging into my shoulder blades. 'We have to go. Now!'

Before I could make sense of what was happening, people were picking Ed up and carrying him away from me. I grabbed his hand. I looked at his face. I told him *Everything is going to be OK. There's a hospital on the other side of the river. Everything is going to be OK.*

The group crouched behind a safety barrier to avoid the charging horses, our once-peaceful protest now a medieval battleground, then we ran. Ed's tongue was still poking around the new holes in his mouth. He raised his hand and touched the place where his eye used to be. It was only when he felt the crack in his head that he started panicking. And when the panic started, the pain set in.

But he didn't die on that bridge.

We carried him to St. Thomas's Hospital. We pulled him through the doors of A&E. We got him onto a stretcher and into a ward. *Everything's going to be OK,* I told him, *I love you, please don't leave me. I'll be better. I'll do more. I'll be the person you fell in love with. Just stay.*

And that's when he had a brain haemorrhage.

And that's where he died.

In a hospital opposite the Houses of Parliament, overlooking the River Thames.

'Ed, Ed, Ed,' I hear myself whimpering. Beth takes the potted tree from Jenny, the little miracle, and pushes it into my hands.

'He's here, Fi,' she says with tears in her eyes. She clasps my hands around the pot and holds them there. 'He's right here.'

16

Falling into mental oblivion while locked inside a compost toilet is a new low, even for me, and not how I foresaw my first day on Banmora going. What must Jenny think? I came here to meet her, to put Ed's signs into action and follow the shattered-earth symbols all the way back to myself. I thought I was going on a retreat, that he had found a way to restore my convictions without tipping me over the edge. Instead, he wants me to do something even worse than The Final Strike. Because what we did back then had only just been criminalised, but what they did to him was unheard of. No one had died for their right to speak out about climate change. No one knew it was even a possibility. Until they did it to Ed. Then his death kicked their rampage into overdrive, creating the kind of hostility that will, no doubt, boil over with the government's big, bold plan. Why would Jenny be willing to take that risk? Why would Beth and Celeste? Why would anyone?

Despite what happened in the toilet, Beth and Celeste move into the shipping container that night. I feel their loss like an amputated limb. The concrete weight of loneliness has only just crumbled, yet their sense of purpose is rebuilding the wall that once surrounded me. I don't want to go back to isolation. I don't want to lose the confidante I found in Celeste, the vindication of her belief. There is still so much to tell her. But taking a bunk in that shipping container means joining Dissident Uprising. Celeste said I was free to make up my own mind but clearly, my mental instability has made it up for me. I simply don't have the strength to join them. No one asks me to, of course, but that doesn't stop Jenny from talking about it at dinner.

'We'll get you knowing that floor plan back to front,' she says to Beth and Celeste, alluding to the secret action that is only revealed to Dissident Uprising members. Dad doesn't seem to know what they're planning, either, but I can't bond with him over our mutual ignorance – not when he spends all of his time taking care of June. That leaves me with Ed. Yet I am more at odds with him than ever. After all this time, we're still butting heads about the very thing that came between us in life: my inability to act. Back then, it was about the golden gag. But it's different now. I want to help. I want to be the sort of person who can overcome my past, who can find a hidden well of courage, an untapped vault of hope, and *do something*. It's why I came to Banmora to begin with. But wanting doesn't change the fact that fear has extinguished the fire. Not even a flowering yew tree can change that.

With Beth and Celeste in the shipping container, I sleep on the sofa with Ed on the coffee table beside me. I dream of an empty prison cell that gradually fills with people. Among them are Beth and Celeste. I watch from a raised platform as they are trampled underneath the masses, human feet becoming hooves as red smoke floods the cell and chokes them. I wake throughout the night, my jerking muscles warning me of danger, but the nightmare returns whenever I close my eyes. I am relieved when the sound of a whistling kettle announces morning. I sit up with a crick in my neck and an aching back. Maybe I should have accepted a bunk bed after all.

I see Dad pottering around the kitchen. Then I hear the baby cry. I keep forgetting that she exists. The wounded child bubbles up again. He started a whole new family without me. I look to Ed for sympathy – and that's when I see his disappointment laid bare.

He has lost all three of his flowers.

The petals are brown, their lustre fading overnight, and when I check the soil, I see that he's lost a few pine needles, too.

'Ed?' I mumble, drawing the plant close. 'What's happened?'

He doesn't respond.

'Ed? I can't hear you. Speak to me.' Careless with panic, I shake his pot and shout his name again. Pine needles rain down onto the moss-covered soil.

That's when I give in to the darkness that stole my sanity in the toilet. I scream and I throw myself on the floor and I tear at my hair. Then I am surrounded by people who put their hands on me and tell me to calm down. *He's dying,* I tell them. *He's dying because I failed. Just like last time,* I say. *Last time he asked me to change, he told me to be better, to care more, to give more, then he was taken away.*

I failed, I tell them, *I failed.*

They lay me back down on the sofa. Vashti puts her head on my lap. I can see that I am scaring her, but I can't stop crying.

Celeste takes the flowers and puts them between the pages of a book. Then she puts the book between more books and says, *That way, they will last forever.* Jenny says she has fertiliser and *Maybe the plant would like that,* and Beth says, *It's the heat wave, all the trees are dying, it's not your fault Fi,* but that doesn't make me feel better because I am too weak to do anything about dying trees or impending floods or overcrowded prisons. I fall asleep with wet tears on my face, and when I hear the horses charging, I struggle awake to find Dad stroking my hair. *It was just a nightmare,* he says, *you're safe now.*

I lose the whole day like that.

When I come to, I hear the scraping of cutlery. Their voices are low so as not to wake me, but I can hear every word they say.

'It's looking like early to mid September now,' Jenny says.

'At least that gives us more time,' Beth says.

'Is the Thames Barrier still broken?' Dad asks.

'As far as we know,' Celeste says.

I roll onto my side and look at Ed on the coffee table. I study the bald patch where his flowers used to be. I watered him every day. I took him everywhere with me. I listened and I tried. Why isn't that enough? I look across the room to the low-lit kitchen table.

'They're building a new prison,' Jenny says.

'One just for protesters,' Beth says.

'Do you know where it is?' Dad asks.

'We do,' Celeste says.

The smell of their dinner makes my stomach complain. I've not eaten since yesterday. But I'm too humiliated to join them. If Jenny thought I was unstable after my charade in the toilet, she must think I'm a total lost cause now. But they don't understand. No one besides Celeste could possibly understand the significance of those three flowers.

Unless I can *make* them understand.

Unless I can claw back one ounce of their respect by telling them what I told Celeste on the beach. I have to make them see that, although I might be weak, I'm not crazy. And perhaps, if they all believe me, it will cast the spell that brought Ed back to me. I'll hear his voice again. Because wasn't it Ed who told me that yew trees keep growing even after they die? I just need to figure out how to make that happen. I haul myself up off the sofa and go over to the table with Ed in hand. I feel light-headed and foggy.

'Look who's awake,' Dad says, pushing back a chair for me. 'Feeling better?'

'Sort of,' I manage, the light from the kitchen feeling like an interrogation tactic. I sit down. Jenny puts food in front of me and touches the small of my back. Beth reaches across the table to squeeze my hand. Celeste smiles affectionately. They're all being very nice.

'Good, good,' Dad says, nodding energetically. They recommence eating, although I notice that their quick-fire conversation does not. I look at the food on my plate. My appetite vanishes. I can't eat, not until I've told them.

'I need to say something,' I announce, standing up and reaching for Ed. I wish he had at least one flower to encourage me. But Celeste will back me up. She's a psychologist. They'll take her word for it. 'I need to explain why I was so upset this morning. Celeste already knows,' I add, gesturing in her direction.

She blinks up at me and doesn't nod like I'd expected her to. Instead, she shares a fretful glance with the rest of the table – a glance which tells me that they, too, know something I don't.

I stumble through my announcement. 'This plant. It's more… It's not… I know how it sounds but… The plant…' I take a deep, frustrated breath. 'Dad,' I try again, 'remember what you used to tell me about yew trees? About the druids? How they thought yew trees were sacred because they helped the dead cross over?'

'Yes…?' he replies with a confused frown.

'Well, the druids were right. Because this is a yew tree.' I lift up Ed.

'Is it?' Dad scratches his forehead. 'Yew trees don't flower.'

'Exactly!' I cry out, my heart racing as a tangle of words erupt from my mouth. 'They're not *supposed* to flower. And it turned up out of the blue. There was this anonymous card. There were all these signs. I knew it had to be from Ed. So I put his ashes in the soil, and the plant flowered, and he started talking to me. He said he loved me. He said I was on the right path. He said–' I catch my breath, the explanation running away from me. 'The point is, this *is* a yew tree, OK? You can see that for yourself. But it's more than that. It's Ed. He's been reincarnated. Hasn't he, Celeste?' I give her a hopeful look.

Her mouth swings open, at a loss for words.

Then Beth speaks for her. 'We know.'

'You know?' I repeat, looking to Celeste again for answers.

'I told them,' she admits. 'I hope that's OK. You didn't say it was a secret.'

I'm surprised but not necessarily annoyed. If she's already told them, they already understand why I reacted the way I did. That explains why they're all being so kind to me.

'Well, I guess that's OK,' I say, sitting down. 'I'm just glad you all know the truth.'

I pick up my knife and fork. The anticlimax is confusing. I thought there'd be a little more fanfare about the reincarnation of my beloved boyfriend. I cut up the food on my plate, but I don't eat it. The atmosphere feels oddly loaded, like they're waiting for something else to happen.

'Look, Fifi,' Beth says eventually, her forehead bearing the frown lines of performative compassion. 'We know you've been through a lot. But this thing with the plant–'

'Just let her process this–' Celeste interjects.

'Stop encouraging her, Cel,' Beth fires back.

'If we can just validate her–' Celeste starts, but Dad cuts her off.

'Fiona. We're worried–'

'Let Celeste finish,' I say. I have to know what she means about validating me. She's the only person who's made me feel safe enough to let my guard down. Her acceptance at the beach – it meant more than anything. Dad gestures at Celeste to continue, but Beth speaks on her behalf again.

'She thinks we should all go along with it because she's doing her dissertation on psychosis. But this is too much, Fi. Your reaction this morning was really disturbing. And what happened in the toilet… We're all concerned that you–'

'Your *dissertation*?' I spit at Celeste. 'You said you believed me.'

'I do,' Celeste jumps up and moves around the table. 'I believe that *you* believe it's true. It's a perfectly valid response to trauma, Fi. You've suffered so much, and I think coming here, meeting June, finding out about Dissident Uprising, I think it's triggered some sort of episode. We don't blame you. There's no judgement here.' She talks with the intonation of a TV shrink. I leave the table and back away from her with Ed in my arms.

'You said you believed me!' I shout this time, moving towards the front door.

'I was trying to make you feel accepted.' Celeste follows me across the kitchen with entreating hands. 'So that you can move through your feelings and process this.'

'You *lied* to me?' I yell, my face flooding with heat. 'I'm not one of your fucking *case studies*, Celeste! You're the one who brought up reincarnation!'

'I was trying to help. I'm sorry if I overstepped. I'm still learning–'

Before she can finish trying to justify herself, I walk out of the front door shouting, 'You're fucking outrageous, Celeste!' Then I slam it shut.

I shouldn't have trusted her. I should have known it was too good to be true. She was far too understanding. I bet she was taking mental notes the whole time. I bet she wrote them up later on – used *my grief*, *my redemption*, to pad out the arguments in her lousy dissertation.

Psychosis? How dare she.

How dare *any of them* speak to me like that.

When I first went to Mum's, Ian said he could feel his late wife in the wind. That's the same, isn't it? That's not psychotic. But aside from calling him for consolation, I have to find someone else who gets it. Someone who isn't just trying to *validate* me. Because if no one believes me, what if they're right?

What if I am having a breakdown?

It's crossed my mind. Of course it has. But what about all the signs? And what about how far I've come since he came back? All of that can't have been for nothing.

I walk uphill in search of someone, anyone, who might understand. The sky is purple like the heather underneath it and streaked with delicate clouds. The road is steep, and my breath is short. When I get to the top, a broad heath rolls out before me. There are no houses up here. I could be walking for hours and find no one. I stop to catch my breath. Then my phone vibrates in my pocket. I look at it. My screen is flashing with notifications. I haven't had any signal since we got here. I look around for the source. There is a shed in the middle distance with an antenna on the roof. I walk towards it. The signal flickers like a sputtering candle. Foliage pokes my sandal-clad toes as I walk off-road. The shed looks like it's been abandoned; the padlock rusted shut. The signal vanishes. I turn back to face the road. Then the signal reappears. One bar at first, then two. I freeze, suddenly invested. My phone pings for a solid two minutes. I slide down the side of the shed and sit on the grass with my knees at my chin. I scroll through the notifications. I have over thirty missed calls from Tracy and a litany of furious texts. I ignore them and check social media. My followers are still circling the carcass of my profile, hungry for a sign of life.

There are five hundred thousand people here.

Surely one of them will believe me.

17

I could fill five Wembley Stadiums with my following and still have a queue of fifty thousand people waiting outside. Celeste's not got a clue. None of them do, because I'm gracious enough to not rub it in their faces. Don't they realise how many people value my opinion? Don't they know how many brands are lining up to partner with me? If I promote something, it sells out. Because people like me. They trust me. They've never once told me that I am having a *psychotic episode*.

My thumb hovers over the Share button. I make an internal list of pros and cons.

Cons: Posting this will end my sponsorship deals and any relationship I have with Travis. Posting this will mean that I have no job, no source of income, no security. Posting this could have legal consequences (Travis threatened to get lawyers involved). I could get sued. And if the absolute worst happens, if no one believes me, posting this could ruin my reputation. It could cost me my platform.

Pros: I'll finally drop Travis. I'll regain my freedom. I'll find someone who believes me. And most importantly of all, I'll prove to Ed that I've changed, that I'm willing to break the gag regardless of the consequences. He might bloom again.

My thumb trembles.

'What should I do?' I ask him. No response. But I already know the answer to that question. Ed never once cared about the cons.

I hit Share. The video uploads.

I hold my breath. It feels surreal to post something after all this time, especially since I know people are desperate for me to come out of hiding. If the media coverage about Ed's death was framed through my success, this will no doubt be another major news story. When it finishes uploading, the video auto-plays.

'Hey guys, it's been a while. I look like a mess, sorry.' I watch myself wipe my hand over my face and flatten my hair. In the fading dusk, the glow from the front-facing camera washes out my skin and accentuates my eye sockets. 'Sorry for the radio silence. I needed to get offline for a bit. Get my head straight. Sorry if I worried you. I'm OK, I just… I had a lot of healing to do. I had to do that on my own. But I'm not on my own anymore.' I look off-camera and lick my lips, my eyes darting back to the screen. 'That's why I'm posting this. I need to share something with you. It's gonna sound a bit mental, but I wouldn't say something like this unless it was true. So please, be kind.' I lift Ed into the frame and push my face against his sparse leaves, hoping that my confident grin will convince them. 'This is Ed. He's been reincarnated. And I can prove it.' I go on to talk about yew trees and druid mythology and magical flowers and unexplainable origins. I talk about his childhood carving at Kew Gardens and a poem by Tennyson and spreading his ashes and hearing his voice as if from an otherworldly dimension. I talk about the journey he's taking me on and the connection I've felt and how this is our chance to start over. Then I look down the lens with a soft smile.

'So yeah, I know it's a lot to take in, but I hope you guys understand. OK, that's all for now.' I throw up a quick wave and say, 'Bye!' in a weird singsong voice.

The video loops back to the beginning. I chew a layer of skin off my lips. My explanation sounds like the deranged rambling of a social outcast. My bare skin and bloodshot eyes make me look extremely unwell. I consider deleting it. Then a comment from Travis appears:

????????????????????????

I lock my phone. It vibrates. I reject his call. Lucidity flashes its light into my eyes.

Maybe they're right.

Maybe I do need help.

I unlock my phone. I have over one hundred notifications already. I delete the video.

That was a mistake. That was a stupid mistake. But it was only up for a few seconds. It'll be fine. Everything will be fine.

I stand up, desperate to get away from the shed and return to the disconnected void of the house. The sun has set, and the moon is a way off rising. I fumble forward in the dark, my phone torch barely punching one pace ahead. I feel turned upside down, the screen time making me cross-eyed. The ground is rough underfoot. I look for a trail to follow, but there is none. I turn around to go back to the shed and retrace my steps. It's gone. I walk into the inky dark. I stumble, something catching my foot, and narrowly miss falling over. I shine my light on the ground. It's covered in brambles, the trailing kind that are thorny and invasive. I'm walking right through a patch of them. A thorn snags my sandal. I stop to untangle myself. What if there are adders? The thought frightens me and I trip, the ground falling away.

This is it, then. The earth is devouring me whole. But no. I'm rolling down a hill. I wrap my arms around Ed and land flat on my back with a whomp, the wind knocked out of me. Everything stops spinning. I catch my breath. Pain sears from head to toe. My face feels like it's bleeding. But the biggest casualty of all, I'm sure of it, is Ed. There's no way he could have survived a fall like that. Before I can sit up and assess the damage, a wild animal pounces from the dark. I scream and thrash around, waiting for the rabid teeth of a wolf to rip out my windpipe. Instead, it starts licking my wounds.

'Vashti?'

The beam of a torch traces the landscape. I hear Beth calling out my name, followed by a dog whistle. Vashti springboards off me and runs back into the night, then returns with Beth. 'Hey Fi,' she says, her voice drenched in kindness.

But instead of sounding like a friend, she sounds like a nurse.

I follow her back to the house, where they all apologise for being tactless and upsetting me, although no one backtracks on what they said. Who can blame them? I just rolled down a hill. I'm not exactly acting normal. Jenny dabs tea tree oil onto my bramble scratches and says I'm lucky I didn't break anything.

But I did. One of Ed's branches has snapped clean off the trunk.

I've lost control. I don't know how it happened. A few days ago, he had three flowers. He told me I was on the right path. Now his flowers are dead and his leaves are dropping and he's lost a branch and he won't speak to me. A pitchfork of anxiety wheedles its way through my chest. How long did I leave that video up for? Long enough to watch it from start to finish. Long enough, then, for an internet sleuth to download it. I could pretend I've been hacked. I could say that someone created a deepfake and that none of it is true. But why would I, when there's still a chance that someone will believe me? Because right now, it feels like my brittle state of mind is hinging on just one person telling me that I'm OK.

When I approach the shed the next morning, I am bombarded with notifications. I take a deep breath and return to my spot on the floor. I unlock my phone. My accounts are jammed with DMs. Some people are expressing concern, begging me to get help. Some people are sending me links to articles that I don't read. Some people are telling me to kill myself. Then I see that my worst fear has come to fruition.

Someone has reuploaded it.

ECO-INFLUENCER THINKS DEAD ACTIVIST BOYFRIEND HAS BEEN REINCARNATED AS A HOUSEPLANT!!!

There I am. My face sallow and pale. The light grainy. My eyes twitching. I check the view-count. Five million. Against every instinct, I tap on the Comments:

tough watch - get help

Me when I need to go to the psych ward

That's mania bestie

I know you like plants but this is taking it a bit far babes

WTF are you on about???

Don't do drugs kids

GIRL CHECK INTO A HOSPITAL

Are you gonna shag a plant then???

it's giving mentally ill

just sad

looking like a hot mess

I don't want to laugh but damn

fucked up fifi more like

My mum came back as a block of cheese and I ate her on toast

I shake my head, and somehow, I laugh. But it is not a happy sound. It is a bitter, broken one that descends into drawn-out, rhythmic sobs that remind me of the noises I used to make. The ones in the days immediately after The Final Strike, when I thought grief was going to finish me.

I don't understand. I don't understand how I can be so sure about something and yet, at every turn, have people tell me that I am not only wrong but insane. I fly through thousands of comments searching for a name that I recognise. I don't know any of these people. They don't know me. They don't know what I've been through. Then I spot one comment that makes me incandescent with rage:

Ed is cringing in his grave mate

With furious tears and flared nostrils, I punch out a response.

How fucking DARE you. I KNOW what I KNOW and I don't need low life SCUM like you trying to ruin it for us. In fact, I feel fucking sorry for you, 'mate.' You'll never have the kind of love that me and Ed have because you're a worthless piece of shit!!!!!

I hit Send, lock my phone and slam it into the ground.

'FUUUUUUUUUUUUCK!' I roar, the sound reverberating off the hills and sending a flock of birds fleeing into the sky. I toss around like a toddler having a tantrum in the dirt, kicking my legs and punching my thighs and pounding my back against the side of the shed. I abandon myself to despair. I lose control in a way that I never have. Not even after The Final Strike. When my throat is red raw and my limbs are bruised, I stop.

Why isn't Travis calling me? Why isn't he trying to fix this? Why isn't he coming to my defence at the one time I actually need his help? I catch my breath and think again. *Why* isn't Travis calling me? I unlock my phone, swipe my comment off-screen and check my emails.

Dear Fiona (@FoliageFifi),

Following negative attention in the media, combined with your lack of communication, off-contract activity and drop in followers, we have made the decision to terminate your contract.

As per the terms of your contract, your sponsorship deals with The Plant Pantry, SOS Swimwear, Orgaknix Skincare and Kind/Botanic are also terminated. We wish you the best in your future endeavours.

Regards,
Hype Tribe

In the email signature, there is a gold crest logo marking their achievement as the Wellness Agency of the Year. I look ahead. The sun hovers in a flat blue sky and makes the view look two-dimensional. Up here, there is no sea breeze to take the bite off the morning heat. Sweat coats my skin. The fight drains out of me.

It's official.

I've cut ties with Travis.

I've done what Ed always wanted.

I wait for relief to lighten my mood, but I wait in vain. Because instead of freedom releasing me, I just feel completely and utterly lost.

18

From the shed on the hill, I can see right across the north side of the island to the curl of white sand where I told Celeste the truth. I've not budged since this morning. It's like I'm trapped in a state of digital sleep paralysis, my fingers buzzing with RSI as I trawl through thousands of comments eviscerating my character and calling me every mentally ill slur under the sun. Ed droops in the dirt beside me, his deterioration reflecting my own, his silence growing louder by the second.

You sound like an absolute nutter, I read.

I thought we were an enlightened generation. I thought we were proactively dismantling stigma and liberating ourselves from shame. Isn't that what being a millennial is all about? Breaking generational trauma? Gentle parenting? Body positivity? Or was that all a lie? Because right now, I am being made to feel like a forties housewife who's been accused of hysteria and is on the waiting list for a lobotomy.

I suppress the urge to post a follow-up video – something articulate and levelheaded that will expose my naysayers as backward, misogynistic trolls who make the internet such a loathsome place to be a woman. But even if I effectively feign articulation and levelheadedness, I don't trust myself to get it right. Replying to that egregious comment about Ed only added more fuel to the fire.

What hurts most is that a few days ago, my followers claimed to care about me. They were calling Ed a climate hero and sending me long, thoughtful DMs about how much we both meant to them. At one point, they were even rallying for a wellness check. If they were that concerned, why are they now abandoning me in droves? I've lost mountains of followers overnight.

I mute the apps and resist doomscrolling. But every five minutes, the phone is in my hand, and my heart is in my mouth. My impulse is to throw it over the hill, to destroy the evidence of my downfall and pretend like I was never an influencer in the first place. But before I can do anything hasty, a shadow appears in front of me.

'There you are,' Dad says, his body silhouetted by the sun. He's holding a small plastic box and has Jesus sandals on. 'Beth said I might find you up here.'

'What do you want?' I cuddle Ed and don't make eye contact.

'I just came to check on you.'

'Check on me? I'm not a mental patient.'

'No, of course. I mean, see how you are. See how you're getting on.'

'I'm fine. Where are the others?'

'Planning the action. There was an announcement yesterday that kicked things into overdrive.'

'I overheard you talking. They're building a new prison, right?'

'The prime minister didn't call it that. He called it a Dissident Detention Centre.'

A bolt of panic robs my lungs of air. So that's the big, bold plan. All-out criminalisation of dissent. Surely that means that anyone associated with Dissident Uprising is at risk? That means Jenny. That means Beth and Celeste. It makes my online humiliation seem pathetic. I've been mourning each lost follower like a vital organ, meanwhile the others have thrown themselves at organising something that could land them in a detention centre. And what even is a detention centre? A prison? Worse than a prison? What will happen to June if Jenny gets locked away? What will happen to Celeste? She couldn't even attend a protest without being physically assaulted.

I look at Ed's pitiful branches and take a staggered breath. I've been so wrapped up in my own problems that I've forgotten all about the storm surge and Dissident Uprising. No wonder he's dying. My priorities haven't changed one bit.

'What's the action?' I ask then, reaching for a quick fix to my shortsightedness. 'What are they going to do about it?'

'You'll have to ask them,' Dad says. 'It's all very hush-hush.' He bends down and takes the lid off the small plastic box. 'Anyway, I brought you some lunch.' He takes out a sandwich wrapped in waxy fabric, a bunch of grapes and two cans of off-brand coke. 'Jenny doesn't like me having fizzy drinks, but I've got a secret stash. No telling.' He puts a finger to his lips. It reminds me of the pacts we used to make when I was younger, back when we were two peas in a pod. Tracy didn't like me having sugar, either, but Dad had a sweet tooth. Whenever it was just the two of us, we'd stuff our faces with Tangfastics and destroy the evidence.

He hands me a coke. It is ice cold. My mouth waters at the prospect of its sugary fizz. Then he sits down beside me and opens his can. 'Well, cheers then,' he says, lifting his drink. I open mine, and we sit in the dirt and drink cokes and look at the view. His bare legs are marked with lightning bolt varicose veins. The skin around his kneecap is creased and baggy. He's getting old.

'Fiona,' he says once we've sat in silence for a few minutes, 'if you've not got too much on today' – I have no idea what he thinks I'm doing up here – 'I'd like to take you somewhere. Just you and me. There's something I'd like to show you.'

With the memory of those sour sweets pinching my cheeks and the sugar from the coke rushing through my veins, the wounded child reemerges, and she says, 'Yes please, Dad. I think I'd like that very much.'

Parentheses John walks along a row of tree stumps with his shoulders stooped and his hands clasped behind his back. He's driven me to the west side of the island, down a dirt road and through a farm gate. We're in a field where all of the trees have been cut down. For a second, I wonder if he's taking part in illegal logging. But there's a polytunnel at the back and rows of plant pots, reminding me that it's going to be replanted.

'This spruce plantation was a tax dodge,' he explains, gesturing at the stumps like a tour guide. 'Back in the day, millionaires could invest in woodland and just write it off. Terrible practice. Created monocultures all over Scotland. This one was especially bad, though. It sucked up all the groundwater and dried out the bog. It's an SSSI, our bog. A Site of Special Scientific Interest.' He pulls his cap over his eyes and squints at me. 'We've got sphagnum moss. That's why we're working hard to restore it.'

'Cool,' I say cautiously, my hand shielding Ed from the harsh midday sun. 'But wait. Didn't you used to work in a timber yard that harvested pine? A monoculture?'

'Well, yes. Commercial forests can be sustainably managed, though.' His posture stoops lower, and he clears his throat. 'But you can't beat the biodiversity of wild forests, that's for sure. We're growing native species here.' He points to the wall of plant pots at the far end. 'Alder, birch, hazel and yew.'

'Yew?' I perk up.

'Yes, that's why I wanted to show you,' Dad says with a smile. He picks up pace and walks towards the nursery. 'This is where we propagate everything.'

Trees of varying sizes grow in rows. Some of them are in the kind of seed trays you sow sunflowers in, but there are more advanced saplings in pots even bigger than Ed's. I scan them in search of the features that I have memorised from his *Field Guide to Native British Plants*. I stop in front of a small cluster of sprouting pine needles that look as healthy as Ed did the day he appeared on my doorstep.

'Have these flowered?' I ask.

'Like I said, Fi, yew trees don't flower. They grow little red berries called–'

'Arils,' I cut over him curtly, 'I know. They're not actually berries.'

I want to demand an explanation. I want to say *Why is Ed flowering, then? Where did he come from? Why, until just yesterday, could I hear his voice? Go on, admit that my yew tree is special. Admit that everything you told me about the druids was true.* But I think I might wither into dust if just one more person calls me crazy.

'Yours does look remarkably *like* a yew tree,' he says, trying to placate me. 'But I think you're overwatering it. May I?' He reaches for Ed.

'If you must.' I reluctantly hand him over. Then I watch in horror as Dad sinks his fingers into the soil. 'Don't do that!' I yelp, yanking him back.

'Sorry, sorry.' He puts both hands up in surrender. 'I was just checking for moisture. It's saturated. Most plants need to dry out between waterings. That's all I was going to say.'

I touch a fingertip to the soil. It seems, in my mission to keep Ed flowering and learn from the mistakes of my plant-killing past, I have been a little overgenerous.

'If it *is* a yew tree,' Dad adds, touching the pine needles in his nursery, 'it'll be incredibly hardy. I've always admired that about them.'

I don't respond. I can't. Because I hate how much he sounds like Ed. It's like seeing into a future that was supposed to be mine. An old hippie with a reverence for trees and a commitment to something meaningful – that would have been Ed, were he granted the privilege of a long life. The thought makes me heartsick and confused.

'Shall we?' Dad points at two plastic chairs underneath an old parasol. 'This is where Jenny and I have our tea breaks.'

Without the shade of trees, the plantation is unbearably hot, and I'm glad for the chance to escape it, even if the plastic chair sticks to my bare legs. After a brief pause, Dad leans against his knees and says, 'You know, Jenny was so excited to meet you. I think she was a bit intimidated, to be honest. She wanted to impress you.'

'Intimidated?' I straighten my back and scrunch my nose. 'By me?'

'Of course. You were the reason she started Dissident Uprising.'

'*What?*'

'She didn't tell you?' He turns to me, his hands in touching distance. 'When I first met Jenny,' he begins, motioning towards the trees she cut down, 'it was *me* bragging about *you* that broke the ice. I read every article, Fiona. I watched every interview.' He leans closer. '*My* daughter, the founder of RIOT 1.5. I told anybody who cared to listen. And Jenny cared. Then, when Ed died…' He bites down on his bottom lip. Dad has never once acknowledged Ed's death to my face. 'I'm so very sorry for your loss, Fiona,' he says eventually, resting a hot hand on top of mine. 'I tried reaching out to you so many times.'

'What's that got to do with Dissident Uprising?' I snatch my hand away. I don't need his long-overdue commiserations. Not when he lacks the spiritual intellect to accept that Ed is sitting right here on my lap.

'Well,' Dad sits back, taking his cap off and fanning his face with it, 'after The Final Strike, after what happened, Jenny wanted to do something. She didn't want Ed's death to be in vain, I suppose. What I'm saying is, without RIOT 1.5, without you, there'd be no Dissident Uprising.'

'Without Ed,' I correct him.

'Without both of you.'

I sit and stew on that information. Dissident Uprising bloomed in the wake of RIOT 1.5. In death, Ed unknowingly handed the baton to Jenny – a baton that would have remained unclaimed had my dad never met her. Because I wasn't exactly scrambling to pick it up, was I? I was, and still am, doing everything in my power to avoid touching that baton ever again.

'I really thought you and Jenny would get along,' Dad adds on a disappointed exhale. 'You've got so much in common.'

I audibly scoff. He hasn't got a clue how much that statement overestimates me.

'But then everything went to pot,' he goes on. 'Finding out about June the way you did… Well, that was a failing on my part.'

'How perceptive,' I murmur, turning my face away from him.

'I regret the way things turned out,' he says, seizing the arm of my chair. 'All of it, Fiona. I feel terrible about the whole thing. I always intended for you to live here, you know that? That was the plan. But your mother insisted you stay in the village.'

'That's not true.' I turn back to glare at him. 'I didn't want to go.'

'Well, the intention was there, I promise. I hated leaving you–'

'Clearly not enough to stay though, right?' I snap, my chin

jutting out in furious objection. 'Clearly not enough to stop you from abandoning your only kid. But I guess that doesn't matter anymore. You replaced me. I'm surplus to requirements.'

'Not at all,' Dad says with a measured calmness, as if he's been preparing to shoulder my accusations. 'June was never part of the plan. Neither was Jenny. I came here to help, you know that. You saw how unhappy I was in Strathyre, how much I hated my job. There's no way to feel worse about climate change than chopping down trees.'

'You came here to save yourself, Dad. Admit it. You were scared. Why else leave right after the wildfires?'

'That was part of it,' he concedes, his eyebrows heavy with shame. 'I *was* scared. Who wouldn't be? But it was more than that. I wanted to find like-minded people. Everyone in Strathyre was so…' he searches for the least condescending word '…oblivious.'

'What about me?' I drop my voice and pick at my cuticles, the furious adult deftly replaced by the wounded child. 'I wasn't oblivious.'

'You were just a kid, Fiona. I didn't want to burden you with my existential dread any more than I did your mother. You remember the rows we used to have. That wasn't good for anyone, was it? You especially.'

There was a time when they didn't row. There was a time of harmony, when Dad enjoyed Mum's eccentricities and vice versa. Then there was a time when the only way they knew how to communicate was with raised voices.

'What happened, then?' I probe, knowing the answer to that question but wanting to hear it from him. 'Why did you leave her?'

'Oh, you know.' He rolls a pebble under his sandal and starts pushing it backwards and forwards. I watch, momentarily distracted by the motion of his foot, then nudge him to continue. 'Your mum wasn't always so cynical. She cared about things – went to protests against animal testing, worked for that cat charity in Stirling. But as we got older, I noticed a limit to what she was willing to care about. That's when things got difficult for the both of us.'

'She's worse now,' I tell him, irritated that I feel even a glimmer of guilt at talking about her like this. 'She's sort of a climate sceptic.'

'That's very sad to hear,' Dad says, shaking his head and sighing, 'but I'm not surprised. She was going that way years ago. After the first recession, that's when things started going downhill.'

'Why would the recession make any difference?'

'She got made redundant from Cats Protection, remember? We lost a lot of money. Almost lost the house.'

'I don't remember,' I reply, casting my mind back to 2008. I would have been a teenager then, too absorbed by the ups and downs of adolescence to pay attention to a global financial collapse.

'I'm glad you don't remember.' Dad pats me on the knee. I let him. 'It was a tense time. After that, she struggled to get another job, and that's when she got sceptical. The world was moving on without her, and according to Tracy, that meant there was something wrong with the world.' He kicks the pebble and runs a hand over his damp face. 'But I don't blame her. I think it's safer to become a cynic. That way, you don't have to put your heart on the line and have your hope dashed to pieces.'

I look at my feet. My ears burn. If Ed and my dad share similarities that are uncomfortably close to the bone, Tracy and I do, too. I might not have descended into the sort of ideologies that led her to the underbelly of the internet, but I am cynical. My hope has been dashed to pieces.

'That's how I feel,' I admit with a whisper, my shoulders hunching over as my body concaves. All this time, I've been too disturbed by that belief, or lack thereof, to come clean. But I've lost so much these last few days, weeks, months. I simply don't have it in me to go on pretending. 'I don't see the point. Not after what happened.'

'That's perfectly understandable, Fiona.' Dad speaks with a gentleness that reminds me so much of the man I grew up with. 'I think it's OK to withdraw for a while. It's necessary, actually, to heal. But just make sure the light doesn't go out. That's when you're playing right into their hands.'

'What do you mean?' I tuck my hair behind my ears, the burn emanating down the sides of my face, and allow myself to look at him.

'Well, the system loves a cynic, doesn't it? They don't challenge the status quo. They're angry and they're lost, but ultimately they're powerless. They believe nothing and everything all at once. But beneath every cynic is a disappointed idealist who used to hope for more. Be disappointed, Fiona. What happened to you was barbaric. But don't give up hope. That's the only thing we've got over them.'

His insight astounds me. It reaches down into the ditch of my gut and upturns every fear I've left festering there. Dad sits with his hands in his lap and watches me cry. Then, when I start sobbing – big, painful, heartbroken sobs that boom across the plantation and fill the space with sound – he shuffles closer. Then, carefully, slowly, he puts his arm around me.

I've let the light go out. I know I have. I've let Ed's death replace hope with fear and fool me into believing that I have no power, that failure is a foregone conclusion and that Dissident Uprising will die trying. I've poured everything I have left into a plant to find some way of moving through this world without him. But despite everything I've achieved since he came back, despite taking the tinfoil down and living in the light, I've never once internalised it. The darkness persists. And like all of those plants trapped inside the gloom of our blighted paradise, the darkness is killing Ed all over again.

'How?' I splutter then, wiping my eyes on my forearm.

'How what, Fi?' Dad asks, his hand on my back, his face close enough to see a burst blood vessel on his cheek.

'How can I have hope again?'

'It won't be easy, I'm afraid. But grief never is. I know it feels like there's nothing left to look forward to. But so many people love you, Fianna. We'll help you find the way.'

When I smile, it is with wobbling lips that can barely rise at the corners, but it is a smile nonetheless. He hasn't called me that since I was a child. *Fianna. Little fighter.*

'Just look at what we're doing here,' Dad continues, casting an arm over the plantation. '*Planting trees under whose shade we will never get to sit*, as someone much smarter than myself once put it. That's how I harvest hope when the stores run dry. I think about these trees and the people who will enjoy them, long after I'm gone, and I know that at least here, on this little island, life will go on. That's something worth fighting for, don't you think?'

I look across the empty plantation. I look at the nursery where Dad harvests hope. I look down at Ed. My little, overloved yew tree. If I can save him, he will outlive us all. That's why the druids revered them as much as they did. That's why they believed that these ancient trees could supersede the limits of human frailty and let their spirits live on. Yew trees sprout roots from within their own decay and live for thousands of years. They've borne witness to generations of human life on earth. They've survived famine and disease and war, the rise and fall of entire civilisations – civilisations who no doubt believed that the world was ending, yet sought shade under the same evergreen trees as I do now. That is something worth fighting for. There is hope in that.

It is dull, dimming the moment it emerges, but it's there in the shadows.

As we wind around country lanes towards the north side of the island, Dad looks at me every so often and makes a pleased little *hmm* sound. There is a stillness between us that hasn't been there for years. I rest my head against the open window and close my eyes. A warm breeze soothes my tear-stung skin. I breathe relief in and regret out. When my phone vibrates, I switch it off without looking at the screen.

We return to find the house a hubbub of activity, with half a dozen strangers crowded around a free-standing whiteboard. It seems they've outgrown the shipping container. The table is covered in blueprints and paperwork, on top of which a woman is talking into a MacBook with a Dissident Uprising sticker covering the Apple logo. I look over her shoulder to see twenty-odd faces displayed in rectangles on her screen. It's all a bit *Ocean's 8*, and I wonder if they're planning to steal some priceless jewels. But their severe expressions and restless legs ground the moment in reality.

I take my packed lunch to the sofa. Jenny eats standing up, glancing at a diagram that's been sketched onto the whiteboard and nodding as she goes over the logistics in her head. It's hard to believe that this woman was ever intimidated by me. Knowing that, I can't help but want to live up to her perception again, to return to the rosy-cheeked idealist who fought like she could win. I want to ask Jenny what the action involves. Now is as good a time as any. I clear my throat and open my mouth. Then Jenny is called back to the table, and the moment has passed.

'Help me put this on June, please,' Dad says once I've finished eating. He is holding up a baby grow. I don't know the first thing about newborns and have so far successfully ignored June's existence. But I've come back from the plantation with a different state of mind. Babies are well-documented fountains of hope. For Ed's sake, I have to find out if that's true. I watch Dad wrestle her pink limbs into the onesie and help with the snaps. Then he picks her up and hands her over.

'She won't hurt you,' he says, placing her in my arms. She is scrunched up and impossibly small, the baby grow covering her hands and feet. 'Make sure you support her head. That's it. Now, tuck her in close. Look, she's not been that quiet all day.'

I look at her face. She is nondescript in that way that all newborns are, but I do think she has my dad's eyes. Which means she has my eyes, too. She relaxes, her body like a sun-warmed pebble, and Dad shows me how she likes to be rocked. Then she falls asleep.

'Nap-trapped, see?' he says gleefully. 'You've got the magic touch.'

I smile, the corners of my mouth sticking firm this time, and walk around the house with her. The urgent tones of the activists wash over us, and I find myself soothed by the weight of the baby in my arms. Something changes then. Something minuscule, barely detectable, but it glimmers like it did at the plantation. I think it's the realisation that June is innocent in all this. She is blameless; a nascent sprout pushing through the sod of my childhood hurt. It is the feeling that perhaps, if I can open myself up to it, being her big sister is something worth investing in after all.

19

One morning later that week, I get up hours before everyone else. A soft, milky light radiates through the sunken green bottles, casting a duck-egg hue, and I stand at the kitchen sink, taking in the birdsong of Banmora at dawn. This house does have a certain magic to it, especially at this hour. There's harmony to be found in its hand-hewn walls and decorative flourishes. It's like it's always been here. Or that it's supposed to be. That's something I never felt about the buildings in London.

I set about tidying up, careful not to wake Jenny, Dad and the baby, who are all asleep on the mezzanine above me. Since coming back from the plantation, I've tried to make myself useful. I've helped Dad in the garden, harvesting salad leaves and collecting chicken eggs as he weeds the flowers. I've made a couple of meals, finding their homegrown produce incomparable to the drab stuff I buy from supermarkets. I've looked after June, bathing her in the sink and enjoying the way her wispy hair moves in the water. I've walked Vashti on the beach, and when that inevitably sparks yearnings for Bruce, I've consoled myself with the fact that Tracy is, above all else, very good with cats. And at night, with my phone now banished to the bottom of my bag, I've found that I sleep better. The change from that alone is striking. I wake up well rested. I wake up *well*. Or at least, my body feels well.

I move through the room collecting mugs from the day before. The number of people taking part in the action has grown, and there are upward of ten activists crowded around the table at any one point. Until now, my view has been shielded by a wall of hard-set backs so, with no one else around, I take a quick look.

At the centre of the table, there is an enormous blueprint of a building with rooms and corridors etched in white ink against the cobalt background. Red stickers plot what I assume to be entrances and exits, and a trail of cotton thread has been tacked from one red sticker to the other, marking the way in and out. I look at the whiteboard. It's covered in a wild diagram of arrows and counterarrows. In the top left-hand corner, it reads:

CODE NAME: JUNIPER

PRIMARY LEAD: JENNY

AUXILIARY LEAD: WELLSPRING FARM – TBC

HEAD COUNT: 582

ETA: 8 – 10 DAYS

It's sweet that she's named the action after June, but nothing else on the board makes sense to me. I guess the blueprint is of the Dissident Detention Centre, but Jenny had it in the shipping container long before the *big, bold plan* was made public. Did she know about it prior to us? How? And where did the blueprint come from? And what is the purpose of Wellspring Farm? And have they really recruited five hundred and eighty-two activists? Because last I counted, there were ten.

Dizzy with questions, I take the mugs to the sink and start washing up. Then I hear June grumbling and the soft steps of someone coming down the mezzanine steps.

'Morning,' Jenny says through a yawn.

'Morning.'

I leave the sink to light the stove. They could easily have an electric kettle in here, but I suppose it would spoil the back-to-basics aesthetic. Jenny pushes my blankets off the sofa and sits down, June already latched onto her breast. She stifles another yawn and gives me a grateful smile when I bring over a cup of coffee.

'Thanks for taking care of things,' she says, tilting her head towards the kitchen.

I'm quick to shrug off the compliment. 'No problem.'

'How's the plant?' she surprises me by asking. Since I told everyone about the reincarnation, no one has paid Ed any attention besides me. I haven't been able to take my eyes off him. Every day, I touch a finger to his soil to see if he's dried out. I inspect his branches for a sign of life. I move him around the house to find the perfect light. I plead with him to talk to me. But Ed's condition remains unchanged, his voice inaudible.

I know what he's waiting for me to do. I'm just waiting for myself to be able to do it.

'He's – *it's*,' I correct myself, unable to stomach her judgement this early in the morning, 'it's no different.'

'Sorry to hear that,' Jenny says, looking down at June and manoeuvring her nipple. She doesn't sound especially convincing. I go back to the sink. Through the jaunty window, I can see the chicken coop and, beyond that, the colossal stone plateau towering over the garden. When I've finished the washing up, I make my way to the back door to let the chickens out.

'Fi,' Jenny whisper-shouts across the room. I turn around. 'Look, while we're alone, I just wanted to say,' she waves me closer, 'I think we got off on the wrong foot.'

I stare at her blankly.

'I know how shit it must've been to find out about us the way you did.' She lifts June up slightly. 'I was livid at your dad for not telling you sooner.'

The only word that escapes my mouth is 'Oh.'

'I wanted to for ages. I almost called you myself. But you know what John's like – he can be so nonconfrontational. I should have listened to my gut and reached out to you. I'm really sorry I didn't.'

'That's OK,' I struggle to say after too long a pause. 'It wasn't your job to tell me.'

'Yeah?'

I nod and go over to the kettle to make myself a coffee, needing something to occupy my hands. But it's not OK. Not really. Not when my dad kept her and June a secret for as long as he did. Not when Jenny is young enough to be my sister and June my own daughter. Not when he had another baby, whereas I'll never get the chance at one with Ed. 'Well, no,' I find myself admitting, the stolen hours of dawn making honesty less of a challenge. 'It's a bit of a mindfuck.'

'Yeah, no, I get that. It is for me, too.'

I take my coffee over to the sofa and sit down beside her. She starts patting June on the back and then asks if I'd like to hold her. I take her in my arms and rest her on my chest. She dozes happily.

'Why was it a mindfuck for you?' I ask in a measured tone. There's no way her feelings can possibly compare to mine.

'Well, I never planned to get pregnant,' she says while reattaching her nursing bra. 'Fuck, I never planned to stay on this island, never mind meet someone like your dad. I know the age-gap thing is hard. My last boyfriend was thirty-five.' She laughs self-effacingly. 'But it just happened. At first, I wasn't gonna have the baby. I was just gonna go back to the mainland and forget about the tree-obsessed guy I met in Banmora. Because even before I met your dad, I wasn't sure about having kids. Not with the way things are. Do you know what I mean?'

It seems like a sincere question, one that takes no measure of soul-searching for me to answer. I've always been sure about having kids. Aril, Calathea and Bell. That was always on the cards for me. Before things went sour, it was on the cards for Ed, too.

'I want them,' I say with a resigned sigh. 'We both did.'

Jenny shakes her head. 'Shit, sorry, I wasn't–'

'It's OK.' I brush over the sting. This is too fine a morning to dwell on the imaginary children who I still pine for. 'Why did you have June, then, if you weren't sure?'

Jenny stretches her legs across the coffee table and balances her cup on her postpartum belly. 'Well, I was of two minds about it. Like, the second I got pregnant, my body wanted it, my heart, but my head thought it wasn't the right thing to do. Not because of the population or anything stupid like that, but because it didn't seem fair to the baby. But then I thought, well, the rest of the world is carrying on regardless of climate change – babies are being born, people are dying, just like they always have, and I'd be denying myself something I wanted because I was scared about making the wrong choice. But what is the *right* choice, you know? Have kids and teach them to be better? Or not have them and leave the people who don't question these things to raise the next generation?' She lets that question hang in the air for a moment. Then, with the force of someone trying to swing a jury, she says, 'I think if people like us stop having kids, we're accepting defeat.'

'You don't need to convince me,' I say with a nod. 'I've met a few activists who think having a baby is like blasting a hundred hairdryers at an iceberg. But that never sat right with me. Like, our wombs are not your battlegrounds.'

Jenny nods back. 'Right? And they're taking the heat off the actual problem. It's not about individual responsibility. It's about–'

'Changing the system,' we say in unison.

'Exactly.' Jenny follows up with a smile. 'You get it.'

Just then, in the duck-egg light of daybreak, she looks incredibly vulnerable. She is shattered, her face papery with the first throws of age and her hair a confusion of grease and knots. When we first met, she seemed to possess superhuman stoicism. Maybe I was just too angry to see her struggle.

'How are you holding up?' I ask, genuinely curious to know. 'It can't be easy, organising Juniper *and* being a new mum.' The code name feels foreign on my tongue.

'Uh,' she exhales and rubs her eyes, 'yeah, it's fucking hard. I don't know why I'm doing it to myself. I'm barely sleeping.'

'If there's anything I can do...' I abandon the platitude midsentence. I don't mean that. I can't mean that, because there are all sorts of things she might ask me to do that are outside of my mental capacity. 'When it comes to the baby,' I clarify.

'Well, yeah, actually. Your dad and I were talking about it last night.'

I fidget uncomfortably. 'About what?'

'It's a bit morbid, but we need to update our wills. If anything happens to me during Juniper – and I'm not saying anything will, but there's a chance I'll get arrested, at best – your dad will be June's sole carer. That's fine, but you know, John's no spring chicken. So if anything happens to him, we'll need someone to look after June.'

'You want me to be June's legal guardian?'

'I know it's asking a lot, but it's just a precaution. You're her only sibling so–'

'I'd be happy to,' I accept quickly. Then I dwell on what she's just told me. Jenny could be arrested *at best*. What's *at worst*? It doesn't bear thinking about. Then there's my dad. He's sixty-five. Will he be able to take care of a ten-year-old on his own at seventy-five? I doubt it. I look at the baby asleep on my chest. Of course I'd take care of her if I had to. But the prospect of anything happening to Jenny or my dad is deeply unsettling. And, more to the point, why have they chosen *me* as June's potential guardian, when I've been nothing but a complete mess since I got here?

'If you trust me,' I add, fishing for reassurance.

Jenny grasps my hand. Her fingers are rough and callused like Irie's. 'Of course we trust you. You've had a hard time, Fi. No one can judge you for that. But, correct me if I'm wrong, it seems like you've turned a corner these last few days?'

'Yeah, I have.' It feels good that someone else has noticed.

'Well, there you go. And it was your dad's idea. He thinks the world of you.'

I look up at the mezzanine where Dad is still sleeping. It hasn't felt like that for years. Then again, I never gave him the chance to tell me otherwise. I opted out the day he left. Just like I did with Beth. I opted out of our friendship. I punished myself with loneliness because I thought that I deserved to suffer. And now Jenny, a woman who has only ever seen the side of me that suffers, is inviting me to opt back in.

'Why don't you try to get some sleep?' I offer, wanting to repay her kindness. 'I'll take care of June. The others won't be up for a few hours.'

'Are you sure?' Jenny asks as a polite formality, since she's already getting up off the sofa.

'I'm sure. It's my legal obligation now.' I grin. Jenny grins back.

'Thanks, Fi.'

Halfway up the mezzanine steps, she stops and hangs her head over the gnarly wooden banister. She'd look like Rapunzel if not for the ravages of parenthood.

'Help yourself to anything,' she whispers. 'There's a fresh batch of kombucha in the fridge.'

She looks perplexed by my explosive laugh – a laugh which I catch in my hands to avoid waking up the whole island. At least I got one thing right.

20

Temperate water soothes my skin as I float on my back and focus on the clouds above me. Even before my nightmare, I've never been one for sea swimming. The ocean frightens me – the impossible expanse of it, the unseen depths – but I couldn't resist cooling off after another disgustingly hot day. Beth and Celeste are bobbing in the gentle waves beside me while a soaking-wet Vashti barks on from the shore.

I take a moment to observe my weightlessness. I am small. Yet in the sea, I am part of something bigger. I am grateful to have the clarity of mind to appreciate it. As the days go by without incident, stillness prevails. Granted, Ed isn't flowering, and I have no idea what I'm going to do for money, but I have the sense that if I just focus on getting better, everything will fall into place. After making up with my dad and building a bridge with Jenny, I no longer feel out of place here. My guardianship of June has made all the difference on that front. I wonder if that was their intention – to coax me away from the darkness by giving me someone to get better for. Whatever their reason, it appears to be working.

Beth, Celeste and I have buried the hatchet, or at least tacitly agreed to ignore it. Despite the secrecy surrounding Juniper and their preoccupation with it, the three of us have rediscovered the friendly rapport we built on the way here. I never want to go back to the state they found me in in the toilet. Or, indeed, the toddler tantrum I had up at the shed. At least no one was around to see that, and I have no intention of ever telling them. That would mean explaining my digital downfall, and I've found that the only way to maintain my well-being is to pretend like the internet was never invented, and that no one has ever heard of Foliage Fifi.

After swimming, Dad, Jenny and the baby join us, and we play rounders on the shore. June sleeps on a picnic blanket beside Ed while Vashti chases the ball, and when I make it around four bases before Celeste can catch me out, our cheers rival the waves. We make a barbecue with a bag of coal and a shovel, then chargrill vegetable kebabs and whole ears of corn in the husk. Dad, Jenny and June go back to the house after dinner, leaving the three of us drinking beer and talking.

It's hard not to give myself over to this place, to the undeniable charm of the island and the allure of Dad and Jenny's simple way of life. Because with sun-soaked, sea-salted skin, honest food and easy company, I'd dare say that right now, I feel happy.

It's an odd sensation, one that seems poorly timed given the enormous challenges to come. The storm surge is imminent, activists are being detained and Ed has, once again, abandoned me. Yet the light that my dad spoke of has turned from a glimmer into a glow.

How can that be, when there's still so much to worry about? I look at Beth and Celeste. They're about to risk everything, yet they seem as relaxed as I am. They're not closed off to joy. Maybe that's the answer. Maybe the only way to maintain the will to fight for this life is to love it.

With that sentiment in mind, we sit back to watch the sunset. A gradient of colour makes a canvas of the sky, the dusky pink of day fading into the indigo blue of night. The adjacent island, with its many peaks and rock faces, stretches across the horizon. As the sun dips behind it, rosy fractals of light cut through the low mauve clouds and dazzle off the ocean. It is profoundly beautiful. After so many years in London, it's easy to feel like the whole country has succumbed to concrete and chaos, that the skyscrapers have won and that every last inch of the natural world has been sold to the highest bidder. Yet still there are places that speak to the potential of coexistence, places where people live in harmony with nature instead of trying to conquer it. Since the beginning, that's all nature has ever asked of us – harmony. Surely that's something we're still capable of?

It seems a lifetime ago since nature reached out to me in this way. Since I had the wherewithal to reach back. When did I stop taking stock of what it was we were trying to defend in the first place? It was views like these. It was sunsets on the top of Arthur's Seat and the trees in Kew Gardens. It was the hand-painted perfection of pansies. And now, sitting here on this extraordinary beach, I see that, while I succumbed to grief, nature carried on. Despite all the ways we have tried to contain it, extract it and obliterate it, nature has not let loss stifle its will to survive. It endures. And with that being so – with nature enduring despite our every effort to overthrow it – how can I possibly give up hope?

I can't.

I grab on to the feeling with both hands. I internalise it. I store it in the place where the light is glowing, where I know it will stick. Then, before the shadows have a chance to register the change, I follow through with it.

'Are you going to tell me about Juniper?'

Beth and Celeste turn to look at me, surprise written all over their faces. The blues and pinks of their hair look so at home against the luminous sky, making them appear one and the same with the setting sun.

'Do you really want to know?' Beth asks sceptically.

'Yes,' I reply with more conviction than I thought myself capable.

'She deserves to know,' Celeste tells Beth, shuffling closer. I move closer, too, eager to be let in on the secret.

'But what about your, uh… episodes?' Beth says, her eyes darting about with discomfort. 'I don't want to upset you.'

'I can take it,' I tell her, putting my beer bottle down and folding my arms. 'These last few days have been good, Beth. I've been feeling better. I'm ready.'

'OK,' Beth concedes, her tone still uncertain, 'but if at any point you want me to stop…'

I nod, urging her to continue.

'So you know about the detention centre, right?' Beth hunches her shoulders, her voice low and vigilant, as if she suspects that someone on this vast expanse of sand might be listening.

'Right.'

'A whistleblower shared some information with Dissident Uprising,' she says before taking a long swill of beer. A whistleblower. That explains the blueprints and Jenny's prior knowledge of the detention centre. Someone on the inside has been leaking information.

'We've been told,' Celeste takes over, 'that the detention centre has been built on the Isle of Dogs. All of the so-called ecozealots in the south are being moved there.'

'South London?' I ask.

'South of the *UK*. Like, hundreds of people.'

'Why?'

'Think about it,' Beth says. 'Where's the Isle of Dogs?'

'Um, near Greenwich?'

'Where's Greenwich?' she presses.

'In London? I don't know! Come on, Beth, drop the cryptic crossword. Just tell me.'

'The Isle of Dogs is upriver from the Thames Barrier, Fi,' Celeste says. 'They're moving prisoners there, right before the storm surge. So if and *when* the barrier fails, all of those people could drown.'

'You can't be serious.'

Beth and Celeste nod gravely.

I picture a map of the Thames and try to place the Isle of Dogs. The first thing that comes to mind is the title sequence in *EastEnders* – a soap opera that Tracy used to watch with a near-biblical obsession when I was a kid. I'm pretty sure that the island is on the bend in the river, near Canary Wharf. But that area is so built-up. Where could they possibly have put a detention centre? And why there, when Canary Wharf is right on the floodplain?

'You know what the worst thing is?' Beth adds. 'People won't care. You've seen how the media is. The public will probably be relieved. They'll say good riddance to bad rubbish.'

'So what are you going to do?' I ask, my tongue swelling in my mouth. I turn once again to the sunset, imploring its ever-changing beauty to maintain my peace of mind.

'We're going to free the activists,' Beth says with a slight lift of her shoulders.

'From prison?'

'From the detention centre, yeah.'

I anxiously rub at my temples. 'Let me get this straight. You are going to break hundreds of people out of a detention centre on the Isle of Dogs?'

HEAD COUNT: 582. That's the number of prisoners they're planning to rescue. Five hundred and eighty-two people. I shudder.

'Yup,' Beth confirms with the sobriety of someone sharing their summer holiday plans. 'Well, us and a few others. We've recruited about thirty people now.'

'And you're going to do this before the storm surge?'

'Yup.'

'Which is forecast to happen imminently?' *ETA: 8 – 10 DAYS.* So that's what the whiteboard meant. That's the estimated time of arrival for the storm surge. Less than two weeks. I feel suddenly untethered from reality.

'Yup.'

I can't take another *yup*, so I try not to ask any more questions, but my entire body is now throbbing with enough stress to cause a heart attack. I stand up. My limbs feel light and detached from my torso. I pace up and down the beach in front of them. My footprints in the sand are the only proof that I am actually moving.

'You could get hurt,' I say, the questions leaving me thick and fast as I try to mentally lasso my brain back down into my skull. 'What if they have guards? What if the barrier breaks while you're in there? What if you don't make it out in time? What if…?'

Now I see why Jenny wants to update her will. My promise to take care of June, should anything happen to the two of them, feels like an all-too-real eventuality.

Beth pounces to her feet and stops me from pacing. 'Jenny's

thought of everything, OK? We've got intelligence, we've got blueprints, we've got backup plans. We've thought of everything.'

'You could get hurt,' I say again.

'What are we supposed to do, Fi?' Celeste gets up too, the three of us standing there like a coven of witches performing an evening ritual. 'Leave all of those people to drown? Those are our people, Fi – those are *your* people. A lot of them were arrested at The Final Strike.'

'Really?'

Beth nods. 'We have to *do something*.'

Again, that phrase. But this is far bigger than anything I imagined. I thought they were planning a protest, not a prison break. I feel horror grip my throat. Horses. Hooves. Pandemonium. Ed's toothless smile. His battered face. His empty eye socket. The smell of hot bodies pressed too tightly together. The sound of people panicking as the force that had sworn to protect them put their lives in danger. The way I thought about jumping off Westminster Bridge. The way that man dug his hands into my shoulder blades. The way I walked into the ward with the beaten body of my boyfriend. The way I left that ward without him. I couldn't wash his blood off my clothes. I couldn't get it out from under my fingernails. I didn't want to. I wanted to. It happened before I could save him. I could have saved him.

I ball my hands into fists. I hold my breath. I look up.

A freckle of stars decorates the skies, night waiting in the wings. I feel the earth reaching out to me again. Holding me. Grounding me. And I hear my father. He is saying *Be disappointed, Fiona. What happened to you was barbaric. But don't give up hope. That's the only thing we've got over them.*

'What can I do to help?' I hear myself say.

'Fifi, it's OK,' Beth replies, shaking her head. 'You've been through enough–'

'No,' I insist, courage bubbling up from a place I thought had frozen over. 'I want to help. I *have* to.'

'There is one thing,' Celeste admits, looking at Beth. She sighs and takes a step back, yielding her reservations. Then Celeste looks at me. 'We need a place to stay. The guy who was going to put us up was arrested yesterday.'

'You can stay at mine, no problem,' I promise, the offer seeming entirely inconsequential in comparison to what they're planning.

'It's not just the two of us,' Beth adds. 'It's all of us. All thirty of us.'

'Oh,' I say feebly, realising that my flat isn't nearly up to the task. But now that I've found the courage to offer my assistance, I can't let the moment slip through my fingers. My sprout of hope is as nascent as June. The only way to maintain it is to follow through with it. I hug my arms around myself and draw in a long, ragged breath. Then, on a slow exhale, I say, 'I can go back to London. I can find you somewhere to stay.'

It's Celeste's turn to shake her head. 'We can't ask you to do that. The storm is going to be absolutely brutal.'

'I can't stay here forever, Celeste.' I drop my arms and square my shoulders in a show of resolve. 'You're both going to London, aren't you? I can't just play rounders on the beach while you both go into the literal eye of a storm. And I've lived there for years. I know the city. I can do this.'

'You wouldn't need to go right away,' Beth assures me, a quiver of doubt still perceptible in her voice. 'We can wait a few days to see if something else comes up. We have time.'

'OK.' My eyes are blinking excessively. I hold them firm, I set my lips hard and I nod. 'Just say when.'

What I don't say is that I have no idea how to do this. I don't know anyone in London with room enough to accommodate thirty people. There's Travis and his precious penthouse, but he's the last person to share his home with activists. The thought of Embassy Gardens and the rich people within makes my skin crawl. Because they won't be sending lifeboats when the storm takes down London, will they? They'll be perched in their sky pools at the top of their towers, watching their wealth swell like the water all around them, while people in the detention centre drown for the crime of *doing something*.

At least I finally have a role to play. At least I've finally found the courage to accept the truth: Ed came back to get me to join

Dissident Uprising. If our own people are being locked in the detention centre, waiting for their turn to drown, the only way to save *him* is to save *them*.

I look at Ed's naked branches. They poke out of his pot like a petrified hand. I just hope that it's enough.

21

Dad asks me to help him put the chickens away. I take it as my chance to tell him that I'm leaving the island. I'm not sure how he'll receive the news. We've only just reconnected – our moment at the plantation giving me the strength I needed to get to this point – so I know he won't want me to go. Not just because we've got more mending to do, but because of the very real risk of drowning. I squash that irrational thought before it has the chance to germinate. I've said I'll do it. I can't back out now. They're relying on me. Ed is relying on me. And I'll be leaving here with something I never expected: a chance to release the child trapped inside the Palma Violet bedroom. A chance at a future that features my dad.

Most of the animals trot into the coop as we approach, but there are a couple of *tricky buggers*, as Dad calls them, that we have to chase. It ends up feeling like a comedy bit, with Dad cornering a chicken against a fence post as I run to catch another, only for both of them to flap off in the opposite direction. By the time we've closed the coop, we're out of breath and walking towards the house with clownish grins on our faces.

'Fiona,' Dad says, his smile vanishing as we approach the back door, 'before we go in, I need to tell you something.'

'I need to tell you something, too.' I wring my hands. 'You first.'

'I spoke to your mother on the landline while you were at the beach.'

'What?' I freeze, his news almost outdoing my own.

'She's not called me for years, so I was just as surprised as you are. She said she's coming to the island tomorrow. She's coming to take you back to Strathyre.'

'*What?*' I repeat, louder this time.

'I told her that there's no need, that you're doing fine, better than fine, but you know what she's like, she wouldn't take no for an answer.'

'But why?' I hear the panic in my voice, and the irritation, too. Tracy has never shown the slightest interest in coming to Banmora. Why now?

'That's where it gets a bit sensitive, I'm afraid. She said that you stole her car. And she thinks that you're… Well, she used the word *unstable*. She suggested we get doctors involved. I said no, absolutely not, but she was quite adamant.'

'I didn't *steal* her car, Dad. I borrowed it. And why the hell would she think I'm unstable? I haven't spoken to her since I got here.'

'Well, she told me that you put a video up on the internet about the, um… about the plant, and that it's caused a bit of a stir. I don't know the first thing about it, but she seemed very concerned. She read that you'd been fired because of this video. That's not true, is it?'

My eyes widen as the real world and the internet intersect. I hadn't stopped to think that Tracy would know about the video. But of course she would: she stalks my profile more than my most prolific followers. I blocked her once, embarrassed by the way she rambled on in my mentions, but she kicked up such a fuss that I had to let her back in. I wish I hadn't. Because now she's using my fall from grace as collateral to get her car back.

'I can't go with her, Dad,' I say, ignoring his question. 'She makes me feel so much worse about myself.'

'I understand that, Fiona. But she gave me the impression that if you refuse, things might get a bit nasty. She mentioned admitting you to hospital.'

'She wouldn't.'

'It seems like she would. But if you just give her the car back, maybe she'll forget about the whole thing? If she can just come here and see for herself how well you're doing—'

'But what if she doesn't, Dad?' I talk over him. 'What if she goes through with it?'

I rake my hands through my hair and try to compose myself. He's skirting around the issue, but it sounds like Tracy is threatening to have me sectioned. Because what else could she mean by admitting me to hospital, if not to force me into a ward against my will? How can my own mother be so callous? And what will happen to Beth and Celeste if I can't make good on my promise to find them a place to stay? What will happen to all of the other activists who are now relying on me?

What will happen to Ed?

'What time?' I ask impatiently. 'What time does she get here?'

'She's booked the first ferry in. It arrives at nine o'clock tomorrow morning.'

'When does the first ferry leave here?'

'Nine thirty, love. There's only one vessel.'

I walk through the back door with a plan already formulating. If I can just hide by the jetty until the ferry arrives, I can sneak on as she gets off, then I'll beat her back to the car and be home in time for dinner. But Ian will have a set of car keys. What if she suspects that I'll try to escape and moves the car before she gets on the ferry? As I rack my brain for a plan B, Vashti puts her head between my legs. I stroke her absent-mindedly, willing the answer to present itself. Then I remember.

Bruce.

He's still at Mum's. I can't go back without him.

'Shit,' I say under my breath.

'Everything OK?' Jenny asks, looking up from the blueprints on the table.

'Not really. Did Dad tell you about my mum?'

'She sounds like a handful,' Jenny replies with a commiserate nod.

'That's putting it lightly.' I put my hands on the back of the sofa and lean over it, my body at a right angle, my breath short. 'I don't know what to do. I need to leave before she gets here, but she's taking the first ferry out. I don't know how I'm going to get home.'

'You can't go back to London,' Dad says, coming through the door behind me. 'Not with the forecast.'

'What other choice do I have, Dad?' I turn to him with my arms flung wide, stress giving way to melodramatics. 'And I spoke to Beth and Celeste. I'm going to help you find a place to stay,' I tell Jenny, 'but I can't do that if I don't have the car.'

'You are?' Jenny says. 'I was going to ask, but I wasn't sure if–'

'I'm OK. Like you said, I've turned a corner. I want to help. But not if Tracy has any say in it.'

Jenny looks at me with an expression that I've not seen her direct at me before. It's a mixture of gratitude, relief and, most notably, respect. I reflect the esteem back at her, our eyes locking in a moment of mutual recognition. Then Beth and Celeste, both fresh from the outside shower, come into the house with towels around their heads.

'What's happening?' Beth asks, sensing the tension in the room. When I tell them, they look just as horrified as I feel. They sit around the kitchen table and try to think up ways around it. Everyone seems invested in helping me, especially now I'm helping them, and I try to take solace in the fact that at least I have their support, if not that of my own mother. Eventually, once we've gone around the houses and come up with nothing, I sit on the sofa with my head in my hands and groan.

That's when Dad sighs defeatedly and says, 'I know someone with a boat. He might take you out tonight.'

'You do?' I snap my head up and let out a shrill squeak. 'Why didn't you say that right away?'

'Because I don't want you sailing at night, Fiona. This is madness. You'll be a lot safer if you just stay here. And your mother's not a monster. She'll see reason.'

'You've not been around her for years, Dad. She's the opposite of reasonable. She stole my cat, for fuck's sake!'

'All right, less of the language, please. I just don't like the thought of you going all that way on your own–'

'We'll go with her,' Beth says, looking to Celeste for approval. She nods.

After a brief silence, Dad throws his hands up in defeat and heads into the kitchen. 'You'll need sandwiches for the journey, I suppose.'

Wes's caravan is pastel green with 1940s stylings. Not in a cute, vintage-revival way, but in a battered, unhabitable way. That's the least of it, though. His garden looks like a cross between a salvage yard and a nautical sculpture park, with an array of upcycled art installations displayed among discarded buoys and ropes and stacks of lobster pots. The most notable sculpture is a plastic monstrosity at the centre of the garden. It has fishing-net hair, lighters for eyes, fish tackle earrings, a toothbrush smile and a Scottish flag scarf that reminds me of Dugald's umbrella. I give it a wide berth and scan the assortment of objects for a boat. The only one I spot has been cut in half, turned on its side and made into a bench. I shake my head and try to knock some sense into myself. *The boat will be moored at the jetty, idiot.*

Dad knocks gingerly on the door, worried about waking Wes. Beth and Celeste linger in the yard with Vashti, looking similarly bemused by the collection of objects. I stand next to Dad with Ed on my hip.

'Thanks for this,' I tell him. Then the door swings open, and a topless man with skin the colour of printer paper appears.

'What's all this, then?' Wes says, rubbing his chin and looking at the motley crew assembled in his garden. 'All right, John? And who are all these lovely ladies?'

I cringe and eye Beth and Celeste. They cringe, too. If my dad can vouch for this man, who looks like a half-naked barnacle on the bottom of his proverbial boat, I have to trust him, too.

We follow Wes into the caravan. It's barely big enough to accommodate one person, let alone all of us, yet every surface of Wes's home is brimming with stuff. Mostly it's things he's found around the island: rocks, shells, driftwood, fossils, pine cones. But there's a whole shelf dedicated to bits of plastic. Wes spots me looking and jumps on the opportunity to explain.

'The ocean is the dustbin of the world, and we're the poor buggers who have to sort through it. That's why I turn it into art.' He hands me a toy car he's made out of a plastic bottle, four lids and some straws. '*From disposable to collectible*, I like to say. But *this* is one of the best things I've found. I keep meaning to add it to Big Bess outside.'

I assume he means the plastic monstrosity. He takes down a battered Darth Vader mask. 'I am your father,' he says in a croaky voice. 'It's original. Might be worth a few bob, if it weren't for the water damage. That's the thing with plastic. Never goes away – just washes up someplace else. When I first came here in '98, most of the flotsam was biodegradable, no trouble at all. Now it's like a deluge. You go down there one day, clean it up, next day it's back. At least if I make it into art, the problem ain't all bad, you know?'

It's like he's giving an informal TED Talk on plastic pollution to an audience he's trapped inside his caravan. I wobble my leg impatiently and eye the rising moon.

'Look, Wes,' Dad says, cutting to the chase, 'I need to ask you a favour.'

'I was wondering when that was coming,' he replies with a chuckle. 'What do you need, mate? I can do you ten quid on the lobster pots. Three for twenty, seeing as it's you.'

'It's not that. I was wondering if you could take the girls out on your boat?'

'Ah, I should have known. Want to see the sights do you, ladies? I know where the last pod of dolphins are, the porpoises, too. Not the minke whales, mind. They've been few and far between since–'

'Not whale-watching, mate. They need to get back to the mainland. Tonight.'

'Tonight?' He rubs his stubbly chin again. I can't tell how old he is. He's either a sixty-something man who's led a very hard life or approaching his deathbed. His wispy hair sticks up at all angles and is the lightest shade of strawberry blond I've ever seen. 'Tonight's pushing it, John. It's already past my bedtime.'

Dad puts his hand into his back pocket and takes out his wallet. He presents Wes with two crisp fifty-pound notes that look like they've never entered circulation.

'Now, this,' Wes laughs, his eyes lighting up, 'this is my kind of plastic.' He swipes the money out of Dad's hands and smells it with the grandiosity of a sommelier. 'Looks like we're going night fishing, ladies. Hope you've brought your sea legs.'

Wes's boat is called *Fishful Thinkin'* and bobs in the water like a kid's bath toy. It's small, with a deck at the back and a cupboard-sized wheelhouse with room enough for the captain. He beckons to it from the jetty as if unveiling a solid-gold statue, then hops aboard with surprising agility before busying himself with preparations to make the place 'fit for three princesses.' This comment causes Beth's eyes to roll clean out of her head, but she doesn't say anything, instead hauling Vashti onboard and making a point of not being a princess by sitting on a seaweed-encrusted lobster pot. Celeste boards with just as much ease, leaving me standing on land with Dad and Ed, eyeing the gap between the jetty and the boat.

'I'm still not comfortable with this,' Dad says, looking in the direction of the mainland. 'You'll call me the second you arrive?'

'I promise. And I'll send you the money—'

'My treat,' he insists. 'Call it a going-away present. And this, too.' He hands me a Tupperware box and a thermos of tea. 'There's only two cups so you'll have to share.'

'Thanks, Dad.' I make an effort to look him in the eye. 'Thanks for everything. I think I'm actually going to miss you, you know?'

'Well, blow me down with a feather, Fianna. Things certainly have improved. Just don't be a stranger, please. Answer the phone when I call you, OK?'

'OK.' I put Ed on the ground to say goodbye properly, feeling my eyes water when the hug turns into a meaningful squeeze. 'Love you,' I manage to say.

'I love you more.'

'Hop on, then,' Wes shouts from the wheelhouse, the engine already spewing diesel. Beth reaches out her hand. I brace Ed against my body and step over the gap. Then Wes blows the horn and sails away into the black shroud of the night.

22

*F*ishful Thinkin' is a lot slower than I expected, trundling along at the pace of a narrow boat as Wes shouts in excruciating detail about the varieties of marine life he's caught. The ferry from Mallaig to Banmora took three hours. In *Fishful Thinkin'*, it could take double that time. It'll be morning before we arrive. What if Tracy's already there? I gnaw at the tender flesh around my fingernails as a bitter taste fills my mouth. Why, on the one day I feel genuine contentment, does she have to rear her ugly head again? Why has she never once asked me what I actually need, instead staging histrionic interventions that do nothing but push me away? Then I think about my dad, about the sandwiches on my lap and the things he said to me at the plantation, and some sweetness returns. Somehow he knew exactly what I needed.

Wane light from the wheelhouse lamp illuminates the deck. It is the only unnatural light for miles, the boat chugging through an expanse of obsidian that is slashed from one end to the other by the Milky Way. Beth and Celeste are sitting opposite me with their faces turned skyward, their mouths agog as they take in the celestial display above them. There's sweetness here, too. They're choosing to sail through the night with me. I know it's partly because they need me back in the city, but still, we're in this together again.

'Are you coming to London?' I ask when Wes pauses his fish chronicles long enough to get a word in. The noise of the engine snatches my voice, and I take two perilous steps across the deck to reach them, flask in one hand, Ed in the other. They secure a lobster pot for me to sit on. I steady my legs and sit with Ed gripped firmly between my feet.

'Not yet,' Beth says, taking the thermos and unscrewing the cap. 'There's still some final prep to do, but we won't be far behind you.' She pours a cup of tea and hands it to Celeste. The liquid jumps in time to the motion of the boat.

'This is the last thing you need, then,' I say with a tut. 'I'm sorry.'

'Don't be,' Celeste replies. 'You're doing us a massive favour. And anyway, we need to get some supplies from the mainland, so it's all good. Happy to go night fishing with you, babe.' She grins and raises the plastic cup of tea like a champagne flute. 'What are you going to do in London? Besides finding us a five-star hotel?'

'I don't know,' I admit with a half-hearted smile, the joke making me nervous. I don't know if I can find them a shoebox to stay in, let alone a hotel. Back when I was an influencer with cash to burn, I could find half a dozen boutique B and Bs willing to do me a deal, but those heady days are history. Maybe I've been hasty. The hope I felt on the beach was delicate, barely punching through the fog of my fear, and now I've embroiled myself in something that I have no idea how to follow through with.

'What about your job?' she asks, blowing on the cup and settling in for a night of ambling conversation. 'Your *influencing*?'

'I just lost my job, actually.'

'What?' Beth looks up from the flask midpour and it overflows. She narrowly misses scolding her fingers. 'Why?'

'I posted a video about the reincarnation,' I confess, looking out to sea. 'I was desperate, I guess, to find someone who believed me. But it totally backfired. People called me a nutter. Like, thousands of people. Then my agent dropped me.'

'Oh my god, Fi.' Beth reaches for my hand. 'Why didn't you tell us?'

'Why do you think?' I say, aiming for vulnerability but sounding jaded. There is an awkward pause as Beth and Celeste squirm on their lobster pots, their mistreatment of me finally coming to the fore. 'Anyway,' I push on, 'that's why Tracy is threatening to have me *admitted* – she thinks I've lost it. Or that's her excuse.'

'I handled that whole thing really badly,' Celeste says, reaching for my other hand. 'I was just worried. I wanted to help.'

Beth nods. 'Me too. I've never seen you that low. I've never seen *anyone* that low. But it was fucked up to corner you at the dinner table. I should have listened to Celeste.'

'What, you should have gone along with it to *validate* me?' I take both of my hands away and lift Ed onto my lap.

'Yeah, no, I don't know.' Beth struggles to find the right way to put it. 'I didn't know what to do. But like, what did you expect us to say?'

'I expected you to believe me,' I snap. 'Of all people, I thought my friends would.'

'But I do believe you.' Celeste puts her hand on my leg, unwilling to forgo physical affection. 'Whether or not it's for the reasons you want me to, I completely understand, OK?'

I don't say anything. I don't want to get into another argument. Because with Tracy on her way to have me sectioned, I can't stomach Celeste's clinical approach to my situation. Can't she see the enormous gulf between actually accepting Ed's reincarnation and treating me like one of her test patients?

'So is Ed–' she falters, glancing down at him and then back up at me with a deliberately neutral face '–is he still talking to you?'

'Yes,' I lie. If they know he's gone quiet on me, it will only reinforce their disbelief. And if I say it out loud, it will only stoke my fears that he's really, truly gone for good this time. It makes no sense. I'm sailing through the night to reach Tracy's car. I'm driving back to London to help Dissident Uprising. I'm entering the eye of a lethal storm to *do something* worthwhile. Why won't he bloom again? Why won't he talk to me? Or have I simply left it too late?

'At least there's a silver lining,' Beth changes the subject when I fail to elaborate. 'You've got rid of that dickhead. What was his name? Your agent?'

'Travis.'

'God, he was the *worst*,' Beth jeers. She might think it's a silver lining, but her hostility towards Travis and what he represented does nothing to reassure me. Instead, it makes all the same old insecurities come rushing back.

'You sound just like Ed,' I mumble.

'He didn't approve of your influencing, then?' Celeste asks, her voice bright with interest. 'He *doesn't*, sorry.' She corrects herself like someone getting a pronoun wrong. I appreciate the effort, but it doesn't help. Shame is reemerging as a monstrous, multiheaded beast, made more powerful by the fact that I've never talked about this to anyone.

'Not at the end, no.' I lick my lips and take the cup that Beth passes as a peace offering. 'My approach to activism changed, and we were at odds about that sometimes. Like, he thought you couldn't change things from the inside. You had to totally reject the system.'

'Don't you agree?' Celeste replies, maintaining her guise of neutrality.

'To an extent, yes. But one of us had to pay the rent, you know? You can't change the world if you've got nowhere to live.'

'You were paying *all* the rent?' Beth raises her voice.

'I paid for everything, Beth. I didn't mind. I was making more than enough, and it meant that Ed could focus on RIOT full-time. But still, he grew resentful.' Revealing this buried conflict feels like betrayal. The public display of our demons will not get him growing again. But at the same time, it feels cathartic. I've spent so long keeping these things to myself, letting the friction blister and burst until it became a long list of ways I let him down. Sharing it is an unexpected tonic.

'I didn't know that,' Beth softens. 'There's something gross about a man relying on a woman to support his ambitions and then making her feel bad about it.'

'Right?' I agree, although I've not thought about it like that before. Ed was entirely reliant on me financially, yet he not only ridiculed my success, he never once acknowledged it. 'And you know,' I add, 'I do think change can come from the inside. Like, how are corporations or politicians going to take us seriously if we don't meet them on their level? Protesting isn't exactly doing us any favours right now.'

'But it's their level,' Celeste counters, 'that's fucking up the planet. If we play by their rules, aren't we also to blame?'

I want to defend myself. I want to tell them that I was manip- ulated by Travis. He told me that all of my corporate sponsors were sustainable. He told me that I was part of the green revolution and that by influencing people to make ecoconscious choices, I was on the right side of history. But I saw enough *Made in China* labels to know better. Combine that with my political disillusionment and there's no defending it.

I was part of the problem.

I think back to what I said to Tracy at the café, when I acted like I was above her because I wasn't so easily led. But that's not true. I'm no better than Tracy. In fact, I'm worse. Because unlike my mum, I'm fully aware of the true corruption at play. I've seen how capitalists maintain the status quo by turning people against environmentalists. I've seen how they manipulate the media and puppeteer politicians. I've seen the very worst of that agenda. Yet despite seeing it, I gave up. I retreated into myself, into social media, and I *liked* it. That's the bit I can't forgive myself for. Because yes, I had the burden of our finances to bear, but I wanted the protection of the golden gag. It gave me the perfect excuse to opt out – just like Ed's death did with Beth, and Banmora did with my dad. I don't know why I'm so intent on isolation.

'I don't think social media is all bad,' Beth says with a contemplative sigh. 'I just think you have to use it on your own terms, not theirs.'

'And how do I do that?' I ask, mimicking Celeste's even-handed affectation.

'Well, like you were before, I guess.' Beth braces herself against the side of the boat as we navigate a rocky patch. 'Before the sponsored content, I loved following you. I loved seeing all the ways you were *stickin' it to the man*,' she laughs. 'Like, when you occupied that fracking field, I shared that video with everyone.' Her voice is warm and full of admiration, then she exhales heavily and says, 'I was a bit jealous, actually.'

'You were?'

'I was. You were making change happen, Fi.'

'Can I see?' Celeste says, pushing her shoulder up against mine in an excited jostle. 'Can I see this video?'

I take out my phone and scroll through my camera roll. Celeste and Beth shuffle closer, dropping their heads to look at the screen. The three of us huddle around the phone, the blue light illuminating our faces so that from a distance, we must look like a cluster of stars. I press Play.

In the video, I'm lying in a field with my arm through a tube. The tube has a metal bar inside that my wrist is hand-cuffed to, around which three inches of concrete anchor me to the ground. I am joined by dozens of RIOT 1.5 activists who are similarly indisposed, each talking to the police in a pleasant way. That was our tactic back then – kill them with kindness – and the police acquiesced, seeming to enjoy a break from actual crime to babysit a bunch of harmless hippies.

The protest was part of a nationwide movement to ban fracking, this one taking place at a contested fracking site in Lancashire. In the background, the famous yellow-tabard-wearing 'Nanas,' women who'd dedicated their retirement to the cause, sip tea from cracked mugs and hand out Lancashire roses, their long-standing camp visible behind them. Ed is locked onto the same tube as me, our fingers touching as we politely decline to give the police any personal information. The field was owned by a farmer who had leased it to Cuadrilla, a ruthlessly extractive company with a Disney villain name to match, and the farmer was angry. For months, people had been breaking injunctions and sullying his good name. And that day, he snapped.

In stark contrast to our serenity, the video pans to show the farmer hurtling towards us in a tractor. A tractor is arguably an effective way to disperse a protest, given its power to crush people, but the farmer chose to up the ante, bringing a slurry tank for good measure. He circles around our gentle demonstration, at first relying on intimidation, but when we don't budge he starts spraying putrid cow shit. There is a chorus of *No*s as campers emerge from their tents and come rushing to our defence. That's when the farmer notices people recording him, and he hesitates, his potentially lethal behaviour now captured on film. Then he turns the tractor around, and the video ends.

'After that action,' I tell Celeste, 'fracking was banned.'

'That's amazing, Fi. You were so brave. And that farmer! He could have killed you!'

I try to take Celeste's praise to heart. It's not something I give myself enough credit for. The drills fell silent, the ground remained intact, and another extractivist giant was defeated. While most people were looking the other way, I was standing side by side with tireless locals and *doing something* about it.

'That would get you thrown in a Dissident Detention Centre now,' Beth says gloomily. 'It's crazy how quickly things have changed.'

It's a sobering thought. The fracking ban was a huge swing in the right direction. Then the pendulum of progress was pushed back with such force that it criminalised the means that made the ban possible. That's the thing with progress. It's never linear.

I restart the video and watch again as the farmer races across the field. If it weren't for the people who filmed that day, there'd be no record of what we did. Our peaceful demonstration would have failed. Because it was *this* video that was embedded into news articles and reposted by the masses. It was *this* video that showed how, in the face of such unwarranted aggression, we remained entirely non-violent.

By the same token, it was social media that told the truth of Ed's death. While the media defamed him as an instigator, the public told a different story. That's why the police got rid of the press and the legal observers that day. They wanted us to retaliate, to justify the crackdown. But they didn't account for the fact that people filmed every second of Ed's death and uploaded it in real time. Before the incident had been reported, it was viral. There was footage of Ed trying to reason with the police, footage of Ed on the ground, footage of Ed being carried over the bridge, footage of Ed's final, toothless smile. The police couldn't spin the story with that much evidence stacked against them. It didn't make a difference, of course. The government still took our rights away. But at least people knew that Ed was peaceful.

I turn my face to the charcoal-black sea and close my eyes. Ed always made me feel like social media was a necessary evil, only tolerable if it kept a roof over our heads. Even then, I think he'd have been happier living in a squat if it meant I didn't have to compromise my beliefs. But, looking back, I don't think I was compromising. Yes, I sold some crap on the internet and wasn't willing to glue myself to buildings. But my job allowed Ed to do those things. I was *doing* the *something* that allowed him to *do something* of his own. And if I give myself the grace of objectivity, so much of RIOT 1.5's success online was down to me. What Ed lacked in cultural literacy, I made up for in spades. I made viral videos that people wanted to share. I designed a logo that people wanted to be seen wearing. It was my idea to change the name of the group in the first place.

What a bittersweet awakening. If only, when Ed was alive, I'd had the self-esteem to realise that I enabled so much of what he achieved. Maybe then, grief wouldn't have been tainted by remorse and made so much harder to process. Because for too long, I have carried shame around like a bag of cinder blocks. It has made loss a soul-crushing struggle. Under the strain of those blocks, I have allowed myself to believe that I was somehow to blame for what happened to Ed, that the golden gag made those horses get up on their hind legs.

But that's not true, is it?

That's when, on an exhale, I tip the bag of cinder blocks overboard. I hear it crash into the water. I let it go, surrendering shame and all of the ways it has deceived me to the bottom of the ocean. I straighten the arch of my back. After so many months spent toiling underneath the weight of those blocks, my body feels featherlight. I look at the sky. A meteorite streaks across the Milky Way, its bright golden trail drawing a line above what now relinquishes below.

23

After drifting in and out of turbulent sleep, I open my eyes to see that we've pulled into the harbour. When I get my bearings, I realise that we aren't in Mallaig. We aren't even on the mainland. The island has a long cement jetty that looks like the one we left behind, but that's where the similarities end. On a hill overlooking the bay, I can see a sprawling, two-story castle with turrets on either side. It is nestled atop a rolling hill that is dotted with sheep and pine trees. Raucous birdsong heralds dawn, and when I look at my phone, I see that it's five in the morning. Tracy boards in one hour. For reasons as yet unknown, we are nowhere near the ferry terminal.

Stranger still, I'm cold. A blanket of cloud smothers the sky, and the boat bobs in choppy grey waters. Compared to the turquoise tropics of Banmora, it seems like Wes has left the North Atlantic. When I look across the ocean, I can make out land in the near distance, but it is barely visible through a thick veil of sea mist.

It's happening, then. The heat wave is easing its grip.

I lean forward to shout into the wheelhouse, impatient to give Wes a piece of my mind, but he isn't there.

'Wake up,' I tell the others.

Vashti stirs from her spot on the deck as Beth and Celeste, their heads piled on top of each other like a totem pole, take turns blinking and yawning.

'Have we arrived?' Beth asks croakily, wrapping her arms around herself as she registers the change in temperature.

'We've gone to the wrong place.'

'What?' Celeste says, rubbing her eyes. 'Where are we?'

'I've got no idea.'

I put on my bag and clutch Ed to my heart, foreboding like an unplugged sink in my stomach. My first thought is that Wes has brought us here with ill intentions. Why else sail to some random island when he was supposed to take us to Mallaig? I breathe through the discomfort and take in my surroundings. *Fishful Thinkin'* is dwarfed by a supply vessel that's moored behind us. I look for a sign of life within, but all I can see is a stack of crates and an industrial spool of rope. A flock of terns flies overhead, their frantic squawks providing a choice soundtrack.

We head for dry land, the jetty leading to a deserted car park that feels oddly soulless given the rugged scenery. There, a tourist sign reads 'Welcome to South Skye: The Sleat Peninsula,' and a modicum of tension leaves my shoulders. Skye is the closest island to the mainland. We're not far. But without Wes, that changes nothing.

I walk at a pace to reach the quayside, followed by Beth and Celeste who won't stop staring at the darkening sky. They're thinking what I'm thinking. We're running out of time. We reach a wooden cabin with a coffee menu nailed to a closed shutter. When I walk around the back, I find Wes sitting at a picnic table between two strangers. He has a paper cup in one hand, a bacon bap in the other and a half-smoked cigarette behind his ear.

'There's my sleeping beauties!' he says with his mouth full, HP sauce dripping down his wrist.

'What the hell, Wes?' I stride over to him, anger making my voice bounce off the adjoining beach. 'You were supposed to take us to Mallaig.'

'Ran out of fuel, didn't I? Not much I can do about that, lovey. Kim was nice enough to open the caf early.' He gestures his bap towards the homely old woman sitting beside him. 'Thought I'd grab a bite before Steve gets up.'

'Who's Steve?'

'The fella with the fuel, that's who. He'll be up and about in a couple of hours.'

'A *couple of hours*?' I parrot, going bug-eyed. I'd forgotten this about travelling in Scotland – the way everything and everyone moves at a snail's pace. They're in no rush to get anywhere, the lack of basic amenities making the locals go with the ebb and flow of the ocean. But if I don't get to Mallaig before Mum, I might not get the car. And if I don't get the car, I won't get back to London.

'We need to arrive before the first ferry leaves,' I tell Wes.

'Not possible, lovey. At least not in ol' *Fishful*. Ralph here might be willing to help a damsel in distress.' He nods to the person on his left, a wiry-haired man wearing a weather-beaten hi-vis jacket. 'You're going that way, eh?'

'Eh,' Ralph grunts, his nicotine-stained fingers gripping his coffee cup. I can't tell if *eh* means *yes* or *no*. Then he says, 'It ain't the Britannia, but yeah, I'm going that way. You can sit behind the crates.'

I guess that means we're going on the supply vessel moored next to Wes's boat. It's not ideal, but at this point I'd go on a pool float if it meant getting back in time.

'How long will it take, do you think?' I ask, lowering my voice so that I don't sound too demanding.

'Half an hour,' Ralph mutters, 'if the weather holds. Storm's comin' in.'

I know that already. I've known that for weeks. But hearing Ralph deliver the forecast with such dry indifference makes it chillingly real. That's when, after over one hundred days without rain, I find myself longing for the heat wave to continue. Because the longer the heat is in charge, the more time I have left.

The mist clears as we gain on Mallaig. I cling onto the railings and wish we'd thought to bring a couple of Wes's lobster pots to sit on. The supply vessel is a decidedly less hospitable mode of transport. Ralph insisted we wear life jackets so the three of us are decked out in garish orange gillets that pinch at the cheeks. Despite the circumstances, Celeste asks for a selfie, the novelty of the situation making her giddy. I smile at the camera with as much cheer as I can muster, leaving Ed on the deck so that his twiggy branches don't feature.

As the harbour grows on the horizon, I pick him up and look at him in daylight. He is barely alive. I wish I could ask him why or at least stop myself from obsessing over every naked branch. But his condition speaks volumes. If the police come down on Juniper with as much force as they did at The Final Strike, it's simply not enough to say that I found Dissident Uprising a place to stay. He expects me to go with them. To scale a prison wall with the sole intention of breaking people out. But the thought of *doing something* that extreme makes stomach acid race up my throat. Because I'm not brave like that. I never have been – not even when I was occupying that fracking field.

Because the truth is, while I couldn't bring myself to admit this to Beth and Celeste, when that farmer was speeding towards us in his tractor, I wanted to run. I would have, if not for the tube I was locked onto. Maybe, if I'd been prepared for such an adverse reaction, it wouldn't have rattled me as much as it did. But I was never supposed to take on that role. I'd bought pots of paint and planks of wood. I was going to help the Nanas make signs to decorate their camp and film interviews for our socials. Then someone dropped out and Ed begged me to take their place. He practically twisted my arm into that tube.

Everything's fine, he'd told me on the train home to London. *We're safe.*

But being safe didn't change the fact that for a split second, we'd faced the very real threat of being crushed underneath a tractor while gargling cow shit. As the train pulled into London, I couldn't get the farmer's face out of my head, the way rage distorted his features into a caricature and deprived him of reason. Ed was unfazed. He'd encountered enough men to know that, oftentimes, violence is the only way they know how to resolve conflict. But I'm nonviolent in the truest sense of the word: I can't even bear to witness it. That is, until I was forced to witness it in the most barbaric way imaginable. So how can I, whose tender heart was shaken by a farmer and shattered by a police horse, even consider breaking into that detention centre when violence is an inevitability?

'Aren't you scared?' I say abruptly, the bite of the wind prickling my summer skin.

'About what?' Beth asks, grabbing the railing as the boat crests a wave.

'About Juniper?' I hold Ed close as we ascend another. 'About what might happen? The last time you were arrested, Celeste, the police hit you in the face with a truncheon, and that was just at a protest.'

'Of course I'm scared,' Celeste replies, her eyes fixed on the burgeoning horizon. Then, with equal parts defiance and resentment, she says, 'But if Black people stopped trying because of the threat of violence, we'd never get anything done.'

The gravity of that statement hangs in the air between us, heavy and loaded with subtext. Because once again, I have centred myself, my fears, my apprehension, without stopping to realise that Celeste is facing a far greater risk than any of us.

'Do you know who first said *by any means necessary*?' Celeste asks while Beth and I remain in dumbstruck silence.

'No,' I admit.

'Malcolm X.' She turns to face me. 'He said that in *the sixties*. So, you know, there's only so long you can beat on the doors of liberation before you have to kick them down. And in this case, literally. Because I can bet you anything that the first people in those detention cells were people of colour.'

Celeste crosses the deck to the opposite side of the boat. She turns her back to us and looks out to sea. Beth and I trade troubled frowns, then wordlessly agree to leave her to her thoughts for a while.

I always considered Ed to be the most principled person I'd ever met. But Celeste has raised the bar. Her principles are profound in a way that Ed's could never have been. Because as far as I know, she was the only person who left that Edinburgh protest with an injury. She was singled out. She was profiled. At The Final Strike, the police might have used an inordinate amount of force, but they didn't target Ed. What happened to him was an accident. It's not something I've allowed myself to accept until now. Ed got away with as much as he did because he was white. In fact, I think he had the audacity to think himself capable of reasoning with the police because of that same privilege. That's why he dragged us *towards* danger – not away from it. He told them his name was Edward Galbraith, and he expected that alone to put a stop to it. He thought he held that kind of power because nothing had ever made him believe otherwise. Yes, the police were to blame for losing control of their horses, but no one was supposed to die that day.

So if Celeste, whose blemished tooth is a daily reminder of the injustice she faces, is still willing to go over the wall, who am I to say that I won't?

The harbour arm is in spitting distance. I can make out Dugald's hostel.

It's a quarter to six. Tracy's ferry leaves in fifteen minutes. She'll be there already. And I bet she'll have moved the car. There's a group of people waiting on the quayside. I trace the harbour for sight of her.

I swallow a surge of panic and turn to Beth and Celeste. 'I don't have a plan.'

'Just leg it to the car,' Beth says. 'We'll make sure she doesn't follow you.'

'But how–?'

'Just trust us,' Celeste says. And I find that I do.

The boat begins to dock. Beth grabs my hand and squeezes. That's when I see Tracy and Ian approaching the terminal. She's brought her husband for back-up. How disappointing. Ian said he understood. He said he knew why the plant was important to me. He said he could feel his late wife in the wind. Now he's standing by her side, ready to board a ferry with the sole intention of telling me I'm mad.

There's no way to get off the vessel without walking past them, so we do so in tandem, Celeste and Beth flanking either side of me and Vashti trotting close behind. Tracy looks shocked to see me. Then shock turns to a sickening expression of glee. If I'm in Mallaig, that means she doesn't have to trek all the way to Banmora after all. I grip onto Ed with one hand and hold Beth's in the other.

'Well, well, well,' Tracy says as we approach them. 'Trust your father to stab me in the back.'

'I'm not going anywhere with you so you can just piss off.' The words leave my mouth before I have a chance to consider whether swearing at her will only add to the acrimony.

'Unstable as ever, I see,' she hits back, taking a step closer. 'You know, you're lucky I didn't call the police, Fiona. You can't just *steal my car* to go on a jolly with your friends. After all I've done for you!' She is practically frothing at the mouth, proving my suspicion that this whole charade is just a ploy to get her car back.

'You're not well,' Ian adds meekly, reinforcing the conceit. 'We've come to take you home.'

'You've got no idea how I'm doing, Ian. If you'd just bother to ask—'

'We saw the video,' Tracy cuts in. 'You're clearly having a breakdown. Throwing your whole career away for a bloody houseplant. Which, I see now, you're no better at taking care of than you are yourself.'

That stings. That really fucking stings. Tracy sees how much it stings. The glint in her eyes makes me detest her. The next few seconds drag on for a lifetime as I wait for Beth and Celeste to intervene. I shift my weight from foot to foot and try to visualise my way back to the car. If I can just shove Ian out of the way, I might be able to make it. But before I can rugby-tackle him to the ground, Celeste starts screaming.

'She can't swim! She can't swim!'

I turn to see Beth thrashing about in the petrol-slick water of the harbour arm. Then, with a brave bark and a helicopter tail, Vashti leaps off the edge to join her. For a second, I think that it's Beth who's lost it. Tracy and Ian lean over the railings to see what the commotion is about. Celeste shouts at them to get a life ring. Then I realise what they're doing. Now's my chance.

I run.

Seagulls screech from above. I dash across the forecourt towards the car park. A man pushing a pallet truck steps out in front of me. I shove my way past him, shouting an apology. The car park is full.

Where did I leave the car? It feels like a lifetime ago. I search for the familiar shape of Tracy's pride and joy. She's moved it. I know she has.

But Tracy clearly doesn't have my forethought. It's exactly where I left it.

I pat my pockets furiously. The key. The key. Where the fuck is the key? The key is in my hand. The lights flash as the doors open. That's when I dare to look back. Tracy senses it. She turns. We lock eyes across the forecourt, just long enough for her to let the spite seep out. Her nostrils flare. Her eyes bulge. Her mouth warps as she shouts at Ian to go after me. I give her the middle finger, then I get in the car and drive.

24

The video is a black-and-white supercut cataloguing Ed's entire journey of activism, from the early days of RIOT 1.5 to his speech atop The Final Strike bus. I edited it like the end of a documentary, the text on-screen celebrating the life and times of a climate hero turned community gardener who just wanted to make a difference. With three million likes, ten thousand comments and fifteen million views, it's RIOT 1.5's best performing content of all time. People flocked to it – they still do. I can't blame them. It's like an emotional enema, the sombre greyscale filter accompanying shot after shot of an extraordinary young man whose integrity cost him his life. The end of the video borrows two words from Tennyson's poem:

In memoriam.

Even though I'd made the video, I wasn't allowed to share it. I wasn't even allowed to *like* it. That's how strict Travis was about the contract, especially after I was spotted at The Final Strike and got into trouble with my sponsors. Travis found it in his heart not to fire me, given my recent and highly public bereavement. He just restricted my freedom to talk about it.

I should feel remorseful watching it again. But I've unlocked the scold's bridle that was shackled to my mouth the day I signed the gag. I've sent it overboard along with everything else. And today, despite my fatigue, I'm finally ready to do what I should have done all those months ago.

I lock my phone to mentally compose a caption, putting my drive-through coffee in the cup holder. The service station is as quiet as the roads, people ducking for cover now that the clouds have come. It's taken hours off the journey back to London, but still I am completely exhausted. Bruce looks up from the passenger's seat with an irritated flick of the tail, loathing the drive just as much as I am.

'Not long now,' I say, scratching him behind the ear.

I saved him on the spur of the moment. With Mallaig firmly behind me, I realised that I'd be driving right past Cleadale Cottage. I couldn't leave Strathyre without at least checking if he was OK. After making sure that Ian wasn't tailgating me, I pulled up outside the cottage and peered through the letter box. Unsurprisingly, the front door was locked. I wish I'd thought to bring Tracy's entire set of keys. Around the back, I saw that my bedroom window was ajar. As a teenager, I'd snuck out often enough that I knew exactly how to sneak back in. I put a garden chair against the kitchen windowsill and hoisted myself onto the flat roof of the single-story extension, feeling every bit the adolescent rulebreaker I was all those years ago. When I climbed through the window, I found Bruce asleep on my bed. I wasn't sure how he'd act towards me, not since I'd abandoned him twice over, but he chirped and kneaded the duvet, as pleased to see me as if no time had passed at all.

Now, with petrol-station cat food in the boot and several hours of driving ahead of us, the sight of his sweet little face is the only thing keeping my eyes open.

'We're finally on our way home, baby.'

I look at Ed in the footwell for a sign of his approval. It was in his shadow that I first knew I had to come to Scotland. It was rescuing Bruce that kick-started this whole journey. Now that I have, I expect at least a leaf of gratitude. Still nothing. His stubbornness is starting to grate on me. It's planting a kernel of doubt. I smother it with a weary sigh and unlock my phone. I tap on my account and avert my eyes from the notifications. One thing I do check, however, is my follower count. I've lost almost one hundred thousand people since Reincarnationgate. Even so, there's still an audience here – a big one. I reupload the memorial video and fire out the caption.

Ed's death was more than a tragedy. It was a direct consequence of the government's assault on democracy. Yet this storm surge proves that Ed and @RIOT_1.5 were right all along. The people in power need to WAKE UP. They need to stand with protesters – not against us – before it's too late.

Join me and @DissidentUprising in demanding urgent climate action – by any means necessary.

It's not lost on me that I'm using Dissident Uprising's slogan at the end. I'm affiliating myself with them, despite the risk of doing so. My heart races as I hit Share. But it's not with fear. It's with exhilaration. I've forgotten just how empowering it can be to freely share my views with the world.

We press on to London, arriving at nightfall to find the streets as deserted as the motorway. It feels like returning to a house fire, the dip in temperature not yet making its way down south. That means we have more time. With the roads devoid of traffic, the air is fresh enough to put the windows down. I breathe in the familiar scent of melting tarmac. The orange streetlights suffocate the buildings in their dreary glow. There were no streetlights on Banmora. And no adverts, either. Funny that I didn't notice until I came back to the city. I miss the way the wilderness never tried to sell me anything.

I drive past Tottenham Marshes. The grass is crisp and yellow. The trees are mostly bare, their remaining leaves staggering towards the decay of winter. I glance again at Ed. He looks just like them now, succumbing to the false autumn that evergreens should be immune to. I drive past the remains of a protest outside Seven Sisters police station and glimpse a sun-bleached *FUCKING DO SOMETHING* placard wedged into the wrought-iron fence. The placard is surrounded by hundreds of other hastily scrawled cardboard messages about the flood. Were all of those people arrested? Will they be taken to the Dissident Detention Centre on the Isle of Dogs? Will I be able to live with myself if I don't do anything meaningful about it?

I spot road signs for Stamford Hill. Adverts shout their abuse in technicolour, capitalism the only force strong enough to withstand a natural disaster. There are sandbags piled outside front gates and shop windows. Something about it feels wartime, like the area is primed for an attack. I see a poster at a bus stop that says, 'Don't Leave It Too Late – Buy Your Sandbags Today!' That explains why not every house has a proper flood defence. Some people have made barriers out of household items – furniture, rolled-up rugs, old paintings – anything to keep the water out. It's a stark reminder that, when it comes to climate change, the odds are not evenly weighted.

I pull up right outside my flat – once unthinkable in this car-crammed city – and head inside with a restless Bruce in one arm and Ed in the other. The hallway is littered with leaflets – adverts from Flood Tech Ltd., flyers from community aid initiatives and a government-issued postcard that says:

We are taking every precaution and prioritising the well-being of the most vulnerable.

I put Ed and Bruce down to rip it in half. When will people learn that saying the right thing is not the same as *doing* the right thing?

Upstairs, the flat is as stifled of character as it is oxygen, my crude recreation of Bruce's shadow the only decoration to speak of. I watch him trot around the living room with an extended tail, taking in his now-unfamiliar surroundings. Last time Bruce was here, this place was little more than a landfill site. I'm glad that's no longer the case. I feed him and refresh his litter tray, then collapse onto the bed. But the heat is like a syrup that I can't wash off. I've forgotten that, too – the way the drought forced me to fester underneath frozen flannels on the floor. I go into the kitchen and check the freezer. I fill a bowl with ice cubes and switch on the fan. Then, with Ed close beside me and Bruce curled up on the sofa, I return to my frosted solitude.

But something has changed. This method used to provide such rapid relief that it would switch off my brain. The flannels would cool my skin and power down my thoughts, and until the ice melted, I was momentarily released. But I've come back from the island with an even busier mind than when I'd left. Because now I have to think about Juniper, about how I'm going to find Dissident Uprising a place to stay and whether I'll ever summon the strength to go with them. I have to think about Ed, about his refusal to flower, about whether joining Dissident Uprising on the frontlines is the only way to please him, about whether there's any pleasing him at all. I have to think about Beth and Celeste, about whether they'll break into the detention centre only to end up inside it, about whether my standing alongside them will help or hinder the cause. I have to think about Jenny and my dad, about my promise to look after June, about the circumstances that would make that promise come to fruition. I have to think about my mum, about whether she'll show up again and try to take Bruce, about her car parked outside and the relationship that might be beyond saving. I have to think about the storm surge, about the waters that will wash the most vulnerable away and leave the rich afloat. About the earth. About the gift it gave me on the beach. About the one thing it asked me for: harmony.

The tap sputters and chokes, threatening to run. After a few cursory drops, it dries up. I try the shower, turning the valve from hot to cold. Nothing happens. They've switched off the water supply. Suddenly thirsty, I search the cupboards for a drink. I should have been stockpiling like Wheelbarrow Man. I bet he's laughing now. I find a carton of oat milk and undiluted squash. At least that's enough to save me from dying of thirst for a few days. I check my phone to find it jammed with responses to my memorial video. I swipe them off-screen and see that I've been added to a group chat called 'Banmora Babes.'

Beth: did you get back OK Fi?
Celeste: any luck finding accommodation? sorry to pester but we're en route to London tomorrow given the forecast!! love you xxxxx

I open the weather app. Where the sun icon once reigned for months on end, the rain icon takes its place, with a bolt of lightning striking at the end of the week – days sooner than Jenny predicted.

I'm working on it, will let you know asap. Love you too xxx

I sit on the sofa with Bruce on my lap and look around the flat, wondering whether I could fit thirty people in here after all. If two people slept in the bath and a few on the kitchen counters, I might be able to make it work, but being crammed inside a hot box is not how the activists will want to prepare for Juniper, I'm sure. There are plenty of empty houses since most people have left London, but adding breaking and entering to their list of crimes isn't ideal, either.

At a loss, I look at Ed's brittle branches. He bears almost no resemblance to the flowering yew tree that appeared on my doorstep all those weeks ago. That first bloom felt like such a blessing, without which I wouldn't have gone to see Irie and understood the true meaning of the plant.

Then I realise – Irie.

She might still be in London.

I pull on my sandals and grab the car keys, for once electing to leave Ed behind.

25

Last year, Irie invited us over for an East Peace volunteer get-together, and upon seeing her house for the first time, I wondered whether she was secretly wealthy. The garden isn't exactly a profitable enterprise, and her Victorian, three-story terrace house, with its bay windows and wrought-iron fences, must be worth a couple of million. Then Ed told me she'd bought it in the seventies for twelve grand. If it were anyone else, I'd probably resent them for that. But Irie has spent her life giving back. She's earned every brick ten times over.

Her house is near the narrow-boat-lined River Lea. It would be an idyllic location, but with a storm surge on the way, the flood risk outweighs the bird-spotting benefits. The front gate is blocked by a mountain of sandbags and straddled by a step ladder. I descend it and knock on the door. The sandbags mean she hasn't left the city, surely? Because if she has, I haven't got a backup plan – aside from suggesting we pitch thirty tents in the East Peace garden and hope the torrential rain holds off. I glance up at the sky. There is cloud cover over the sun-battered city of London. The weather is turning.

'Fiona,' Irie says with a smile when she opens the door. I'm relieved to see her, then worried. She is wearing a baggy, unwashed T-shirt, a loosely tied silk bonnet and slippers with a hole in the left big toe. She looks uneasy, the bags under her eyes protruding in heavy curves and her cheekbones abnormally gaunt. My face must bear a similar degree of unease, because Irie's smile quickly vanishes. She urges me inside.

Back during the volunteer get-together, I enjoyed Irie's maximalist decor. She had an abundance of pattern-clashing soft furnishings, an impressive collection of amateur art hanging from every available wall space and a lifetime's worth of trinkets. But beneath the curated chaos was a fastidiously tidy house. Now I mask my shock as Irie leads me down the hallway and into the kitchen.

'I wasn't expecting company,' she explains.

The kitchen table is covered in stacks of newspapers, piles of crockery and unopened packages. It reminds me of the state my flat was in when Tracy took Bruce. I half expect a neglected cat to come out of hiding. I want to hug her and tell her that I understand. I want to ask her if she's let the place go ever since Ed died, and if so, to say that there's nothing to worry about because he's been reincarnated. Then I remind myself that he hasn't spoken to me in days, much less flowered, and is doing the one thing that yew trees aren't supposed to do: die. So I stand awkwardly among the detritus and watch as she tries to clear a space for me. She grabs a heap of laundry off the back of a chair and shoves it into an already-overloaded washing machine, then reaches for a bottle of multipurpose cleaner.

'Don't do that on my behalf. I don't mind.'

'I do,' she says, wiping down the surfaces. 'Can't get much done without water, that's all. Are you hungry?'

'Oh, no, I'm good. Don't go to any trouble–'

'I'll heat some soup.'

Irie takes a plastic container out of the fridge and pours the contents into a saucepan. She gets a loaf of bread out of the cupboard and cuts four generous slices. I sit at the table and look around the room, searching for a place to rest my eyes that won't embarrass her. Irie tuts and sighs while she's preparing lunch, like the etiquette of hosting is a chore she could do without.

'Are you OK?' I ask evenly, fidgeting in my seat.

'Not really,' she replies, stirring the soup with a ladle. 'How can I be?'

'Because of the storm surge?'

'Because of *everything*, Fi.' She turns to scowl at me, irritated by what I thought was a harmless assumption. 'The storm surge, the water shortages, the detention centre. It's like the whole city is falling to pieces and no one is doing a *damn thing* about it.'

'What about Dissident Uprising?' I reply, waiting for the right time to tell her that they're planning to do something inordinately brave about it.

'Much use they are in a prison cell.' Irie swings the ladle when she speaks, sending droplets of soup splattering across the work surface. 'And where's the pushback? Where's the people saying *No, this is not OK. You can't suppress our rights and get away with it*?'

I look down at my lap. I know she's generalising, but it feels like Irie's disappointment is directed solely at me, at my failure to do anything but bury my head in the sand.

No, that's not true. I came here to help. And not just because I want Ed to bloom again, but because it's the right thing to do. I ready myself to tell her everything. Knowing how disillusioned she is, I'm sure it will be welcome news.

But before I can get a word in, Irie continues, her voice quivering with candour. 'I've spent my life building a community. I've poured hours into creating a space where people look out for each other, where they grow something greater than the sum of its parts. But where's that community now?' She pauses to bring the soup to the table. When she sits down, it's like her entire body deflates into the chair. 'They've all left, Fi. And until today, I thought you'd left, too.'

'I did,' I admit, taking a bowl and smiling at her gratefully. 'For a while. But I came back to–'

'In my day,' Irie goes on, in the full swing of a rant now, 'we stayed and we fought until the bitter end. Me and the Greenham girls – we never called it quits. Not once in twenty years. But it's everyone for themselves now. Because the people who care enough to speak out are being locked away, and everyone else is either abandoning ship or praying to the heavens that they float.' She tears off a chunk of bread and shoves it in her mouth with a bitter sigh.

'Sorry,' I say, 'I don't follow. Who're the Greenham girls?'

'You don't know?' Irie asks between angry chews. When I shake my head, she kisses her teeth and says, 'See? Things really have gone to the dogs. There were thirty thousand women and girls there at one point.'

'Where?'

'Greenham Common. You've really never heard of it?'

I shake my head again, unsure whether I want to wade into unfamiliar territory when Irie is so clearly at her wits' end.

'It was during the Cold War,' Irie explains, sitting up straight and swallowing. 'Back when the whole world was about to blow up. The Americans were holding cruise missiles at Greenham. A group of women marched there in protest. They set up camp and they stayed until 2000.' She dips bread into her soup. I do the same, savouring the wads of hot butter. I find that I am hungry after all.

'I camped there for about seven months in all,' she tells me, her tone warming as she retreats into the memory. 'I'll never forget it – cooking around a fire with a group of women I'd never met. Women from all over the world. And the smell of woodsmoke. The way it would get into my hair until it felt like I was part of the common. I'd have stayed a lot longer, except my husband wanted me home. It was a good thing he did. He died a few years later.'

'Oh, I'm sorry.' I put down my spoon and look at her sombrely. The expression feels forced – I'm unversed at giving other people commiserations. 'I didn't know.'

'Paul died in 1988, love. I've been without him far longer than I had him.' She hesitates, retreating even further into the past, then pushes on with gusto. 'Anyway, the police treated us like we were the ones with missiles, of course. Hundreds were arrested, put in prison. It wasn't dissimilar to the political climate now. The media called us a bunch of filthy, rotten lesbians, and Thatcher was PM, so say no more.'

'People went to prison?' I lean forward, captivated.

She nods. 'There was a pamphlet that did the rounds at the camp: "Holloway for Beginners." That's how many of us were arrested. Not me, luckily, but I climbed on the roof to give them what for.'

'You climbed onto the *roof of a prison*?' I ask, my voice shrill as the parallels between Juniper and Greenham Common arise.

'I did, Fiona. Believe it or not, I was once a loudmouthed punk who scaled Holloway Prison to protest the mistreatment of my incarcerated sisters!' Irie laughs, and thankfully, some life returns to her eyes. She leaves the table and returns with a hardback book. It looks decades old with well-thumbed pages and a faded cover. She opens it to a crack in the spine, revealing a double-page spread of a black-and-white photograph.

'That's me,' she says, pointing to a woman with an Afro. I take the book and look closer. In the photo, a young, barefaced Black woman is stretching out her arms towards three helmet-clad policemen. She's wearing a baggy roll-neck jumper, black jeans and beaten-up Doc Martens. The three policemen are dragging a white woman through the dirt, while a fourth officer, his back to the camera, is poised to restrain Irie. In the background, there is an enormous barbed-wire fence, behind which a group of soldiers wearing camouflage and berets look at Irie with mild amusement.

'How have I not heard about this?' I gasp. 'I had no idea you were such a badass!'

'I still am, my dear.' Irie smiles ruefully. 'I'm just weary. World-weary and bone-tired. Because no one remembers what we achieved. And trust me, we achieved a lot. Reagan signed a nuclear treaty, and the Americans moved the missiles. Of course, they gave us no credit. But that's how it starts, isn't it? They don't acknowledge your power, then they scrub it from the story entirely.' Irie wraps her arms around herself and purses her lips together, clearly trying to keep her emotions in check. I've never known her to be this vulnerable. 'That's why I'm struggling, I think. Because here we are, over forty years later, with history repeating itself. They've smeared Ed, robbed him of his legacy and arrested anyone who gets in their way.'

We sit quietly for a moment, the atmosphere heavy with Irie's resentments. I flick through the book. There are photos of women sitting on top of a bus with the words *ADMIT DEFEAT, BOYS* spray-painted across the windows; women knitting inside makeshift plastic tents and feeding their babies around a fire; women grinning while they do the conga around the fence, then grimacing while they pull the fence down. I think about my realisation on Wes's boat to Skye: that progress is a pendulum – it always swings back before it can swing forward. With every laboured step we take towards justice, there is a fortress of muscle, ready to stop the pendulum's trajectory. After four decades of that push and pull, no wonder Irie's spirit is waning.

'Did you go back to the camp after Paul died?' I ask, my eyes feasting on an archive of resistance that I had no idea existed.

'I thought about it,' Irie says, running her spoon around the bowl. 'But I couldn't face any more upheaval. That's when I started East Peace. For him. And for Greenham.'

That puts her support of RIOT 1.5 into sharp focus. She, too, was part of a movement for change, then she built a space to keep that change alive. East Peace was the first place in London where we felt like we belonged, without which we wouldn't have been able to get RIOT 1.5 off the ground, yet I'd made no effort to get to know the woman who made us feel so welcome. A flash of guilt makes me close the book. Then guilt gives way to a moment of clarity. Irie must have been around the same age as me when her husband died. She didn't let loss turn her into a cynic. She grew roots from within decay and cultivated something meaningful.

I hand the book back and lean closer. 'Irie, do you believe in reincarnation?' The question is a bolt from the blue. It seems to give Irie conversational whiplash.

'Uh, um... that's quite a philosophical question for lunchtime.' She laughs through her nose and considers the question. 'Um... I suppose, when Paul passed, I used to feel his presence, if that's what you mean? He was there in the small things – cologne, mint chocolate, Motown. He's become quieter over the years, but I still can't hear Smokey Robinson without thinking about Paul, about the night's we spent in Ronnie Scott's, dancing like we had all the time left in the world.'

Her wistfulness reminds me of Ian, who spoke so candidly of Jan and his grief; who said he understood, at least in private, why I needed the plant to be Ed. Tracy might have corrupted his attempt at connection in Mallaig, but what was he supposed to do? Support me instead of her? It's clear to me then that bereaved people share an unspoken understanding. It's like we're all members of the worst club in the world, and everyone else, the hapless fools yet to get their membership, cannot fathom the desperate depths the heart can go to until their love is snatched away.

'Why do you ask, anyway?' Irie says with glassy eyes.

'Oh, no reason.' I shrug, stopping short of telling her the truth. All this time, I've been desperate to find someone who believes me. But with Ed's presence weaker than since before he died, I don't know how to lay claim to my beliefs without disproving them. And more to the point, it's not why I've come here. I've come here to do something useful, in the hope that it will inspire me to do something uncharacteristically brave. And I'm wasting precious time.

As if on cue, a rumbling noise makes both of us hesitate. I look out of the kitchen window. The light has changed. The garden is in shadow. The clouds are heavy and low. Without saying a word, I follow Irie out the back door. We turn our faces to the sky. My skin is nipped by windchill. I wrap my arms around myself and swallow.

That's when I feel a single drop of water on my cheek. I put my hand there, the sensation shocking me. Then, like a multi-car crash on a motorway, a blast of thunder rings in my ears. Irie grabs my forearm. We glance at each other, then up again at the sky. I hear the sound of tinfoil being peeled off a hundred windows. Then that long forgotten smell – the smell of hot wet concrete, the smell of hot wet earth, the smell of trees sighing, of dust being washed into drains, of city steam, of fear. Because just like they said, the rain has come. We know what happens next.

I turn to her and inhale. 'Irie, I need to ask you a favour. A big one.'

26

I pull down the attic ladder and climb it with a torch in hand, emerging into a dark, musty space with slanted eaves. It is filled floor-to-ceiling with boxes, suitcases, books, furniture, picture frames, bags of clothes and thick swags of cobwebs. Irie's house is pristine by comparison. The rain drills into the rafters, and the wind whistles through the roof tiles. I climb out of the hatch and trace the light from one end of the attic to the other.

According to Irie, there are a dozen or more sleeping bags up here from her Greenham days. I don't know where to begin looking. I find a string light switch and pull it. The attic is lit by a single bare bulb that throws shadows over Irie's forgotten possessions. It's eerie up here – the sort of place I'd expect to find the skeleton of a missing relative. But despite being spooked, I'm in a good mood. When I told the Banmora Babes that I'd found Dissident Uprising a place to stay, Beth replied with a champagne GIF from *The Office*, and Celeste sent me a voice note of singsong admiration that made me glow with pride. Beth called me an *icon*. Celeste called me a *queen*. They both said that they couldn't wait to see me.

But to be fair, Irie didn't take much convincing. Knowing what I do now about Greenham, it doesn't surprise me. Activism is what gets her out of bed in the morning. The suppression of it is what keeps her there. So the chance to get stuck into something as wildly ambitious as Juniper was like offering her an all-expenses paid holiday to the Maldives.

'I can't tell you how much that's lifted my spirits,' she'd said to me once I'd filled her in. 'It means people are still *trying*, Fi. It means there's still hope.' Then she put on an apron and started cleaning.

I rummage through the clutter in search of the promised sleeping bags. I unearth memorabilia from Irie's days as an anti-nuclear campaigner. I find the hand-sewn Greenham Common banners I saw in the book. I open archives that contain speeches Irie gave to politicians and testimonies she gave to the police. Clearly, she's a much bigger deal than she's letting on. That or history hasn't held her in the high esteem she deserves, as it hasn't so many Black women who took on the system and won. I wonder what significance the camp would have been given in the annals of civil resistance if men had been involved. Instead, they were playing chicken with big red buttons.

I leaf through a box of news cuttings. Most of them are on the verge of disintegration and feature articles about the camp, one claiming it was a 'hotbed of lesbian sex.' I press my lips together. If social media had been a thing back then, perhaps these women would have been able to push back. That's one thing we've got over traditional media these days: the power to tell our own stories. If they'd been able to spread their message beyond the confines of the camp, maybe their legacy would have lived on. Then I spot one news cutting that isn't addled with age or attic dust.

Eco-Terrorist Dies after Instigating Violent Riot

The article features the same photo as all of the others: the selfie I took of us on the top of Arthur's Seat in 2016. The caption says:

> *Pictured here with influencer girlfriend Foliage Fifi, Edward Galbraith was an environmental sciences graduate at the University of Edinburgh before getting embroiled in eco-zealot ideology. His professors describe him as a 'dedicated student,' who was 'simply concerned about climate change.'*

The headline makes it sound like he just dropped dead on the spot. It makes no mention of the police horses or the dangerous kettling that caused the so-called riot in the first place. If they'd just left us alone, Ed would still be here. And his professors got it exactly right. He was simply concerned about climate change. Yet still the media calls him a zealot, as if anyone who dares to care is an extremist. In the eighties, they were calling the same people lesbians, using the era's affinity for homophobia to discredit them. And today they are terrorists.

Maybe, in a more enlightened era, when we realise just how wrong we got it, we'll look back on this moment with regret. Maybe Ed will be pardoned for his fabricated crimes and seen as the hero he was. But I don't hold out much hope. The Greenham women were never given such good grace.

I fold the cutting in half and put it back in the box with steady hands. Yet the horses are relentless. They see my strength, and they despise it. Because the rain slamming into the rafters turns into the sound of hooves hitting hot concrete, and the attic fills with red smoke. I sit down in the dust and put my head between my legs. I breathe like Celeste showed me in Banmora.

Breathe in – *one, two, three, four, five.*

Breathe out – *one, two, three, four, five.*

When that doesn't work, I try something new.

'Leave me alone!' I scream, my head still clamped between my knees. 'LEAVE! ME! THE! FUCK! ALONE!'

The noise detonates from my throat. I picture Beth and Celeste on the beach. I picture Vashti playing in the ocean. I picture June, her scrunched up body, her oversized baby grow. I picture Irie at the peace camp. I picture my dad and Jenny. I picture myself standing in front of the setting sun, surrounded by the people who love me. And I see those rosy fractals of light, the sunset that changed my state of mind, and when I dare to look up, the red smoke has receded. The hooves fall silent, until all I can hear is the gasping of my breath and the clamour of the weather outside.

'Are you OK?' Irie asks when I return with the sleeping bags. 'I heard shouting.'

'I am now,' I tell her. And although I'm under no impression that I've defeated the horses for good, I know that I can finally outwit them. Because I've absolved myself of wretchedness. Not just the wretchedness from that day, but the wretchedness that made me feel powerless long before Ed died. The wretchedness that told me that nothing changes, so why bother?

After uncovering the extent of her activism, Irie's past has put my present conflict into much-needed context. Because just like us, she grew up being told that the world was doomed, so she joined a movement of women who said *no*. And despite the establishment doing their damnedest to repress their right to say *no*, they kept shouting because they knew that their voices mattered. So they shouted in handcuffs and they shouted in prisons and they shouted from rooftops. Because they knew that nothing was lost, not so long as there were people left trying.

The same is true of Juniper. Once again, we are facing insurmountable odds and government cruelty, yet still there are people left *doing something*. Still there are those who will dig their heels into the dirt and push back with every last drop of sweat they possess. People who have the courage to face insurmountable odds and cruelty and wretchedness with conviction, not cynicism – for they love life enough to imagine a future where we are free and the land is free and both are symbiotic.

Those people are *my* people.

Those people are me.

That's when I know that I have to do more, that finding Dissident Uprising a place to stay is just the start. Juniper can't become another buried relic of the past, a moment of immense bravery that the system hides away. The world needs to know. They need to see the lengths people will go to take wretchedness and turn it into action. They need to understand that wretchedness isn't the end of hope. It's the beginning of change.

I go home to make a plan, arms laden with Irie's stash of bottled water. After feeding and fussing over Bruce, I pace the flat and scan its empty walls for inspiration. It's time to seriously consider whether I have what it takes to go all the way, whether I can finally lay my fears to rest and join Dissident Uprising like Ed so clearly wants me to. But what if the horses snatch away my sanity before I can even get inside the prison walls? I might have defeated them in the attic, but coming face-to-face with riot shields is another thing entirely. If I do go, there's a strong chance I'll become just another person who needs saving.

I pick up Ed and search his branches for some guidance.

'Talk to me,' I beg. 'I don't care if you don't flower. Just say something. Help me.' I realise then that, to all intents and purposes, I am begging a stick to engage in conversation. A ripple of disbelief makes me put the plant down and shrink away from it, doubt now firmly planted. All this time, I've been waiting for flowers to show me the way. But everything I've done has been because *I* found the strength to do it. I found the strength to leave this flat. I found the strength to make things right with Beth and go to Banmora. I found the strength to post that video, to sever ties with Travis and get my freedom back. I found the strength to stop Tracy meddling in my life and return to London with Bruce. I did all of that. Someone who had my best interests at heart would be praising me for how far I've come, not punishing me by refusing to grow.

Right now, the last thing I need is doubt. I put Ed back on the mantelpiece and unlock my phone. I check my follower count. It's unchanged, although my notifications are in the thousands. I've put off checking the response to my memorial post. It's the first time I've talked about activism since the golden gag, and I have no idea how my followers are going to take it, especially not after Reincarnationgate. I start scrolling. There's the usual river of shit from people calling me crazy, but there's a glut of heart emojis, too. I spot the occasional supportive comment – people lamenting Ed's loss, people who are just as angry as I am. One comment catches my eye:

Welcome back.

Without stopping to think, I start archiving posts. I get rid of the sale pitches and the product hauls, I wipe my profile clean of sponsored content, and I don't stop until I get to Hadrian's Wall – the one that I built with Travis, brick by virtual brick. Soon, all that's left is content from before the contract, when social media was an extension of my activism. More than that, it was a tool for joy. Because without it, we'd never have grown RIOT 1.5 or found people who wanted to foster something good. And I'd never have been able to share not only the losses facing our world but the joyous moments when we won.

Is there joy to be found in Juniper? Irie seems to think so, but my anxiety has said otherwise. Yet there's always the chance that they will succeed, that the prisoners will survive and that Dissident Uprising will show the public that change is possible. We just need to make them see.

I need to make them see.

Despite being trolled into oblivion, I still have a bigger platform than anyone I know. I'm free to use it however I want again. And what better way to harness that freedom than to tell Dissident Uprising's story? The Greenham women didn't have the tools to do that. They couldn't pin the peace camp on the board of human history – not when their opponents were curating the truth, trashing the stories that didn't serve them and spinning the ones that did. But I have the tools. Whatever happens during Juniper, whether it's a joyous victory or a stain on the public consciousness, I can hold the authorities to account like so many phone cameras did at The Final Strike. I can show four hundred thousand people that *nothing* is inevitable – not the atrophy of our civil liberties, not the degradation of truth, not even climate change – so long as there are people left trying.

I search the flat for Travis's care package, my hands fraught with adrenaline. It might have gone in the bin along with the rest of our belongings. Then I remember kicking it under the sofa. I lie flat on the living room floor.

The box reads *Livestreaming Body Cam – Live Life Live*.

I open it. It's got everything I need inside, including a body harness to attach the camera to and integrated data. I thumb through the manual. Travis hounded me to start livestreaming. I wonder what he'll think when he sees my first foray into live content.

But I don't need to worry about him anymore. I get to decide how I use my platform again.

And I know exactly what I'm going to do with it.

27

The rain that started at Irie's house was a puddle in comparison to the torrential fury of Storm Enlil. Google tells me that they've named it after a Mesopotamian god who destroyed the world with a flood. Whoever came up with that at the Met Office must have been very pleased with themselves. But *rain* is no longer enough to describe what's happening outside. On the drive over this morning, I had to make two U-turns to avoid floodwater and one to avoid a fallen tree – a tree which I very nearly crashed into because visibility was so poor. I saw road signs bent like question marks and windshields smashed by wayward roof tiles. And this is just the beginning. The storm isn't even surging yet. It's just ramping up to the main event. I dread to think what's to come.

Irie watches the news with the same morbid fascination as Ian, her armchair pulled precariously close to the television so that she can absorb every detail. I've had the opposite strategy in recent months, feeling that the only way to survive the daily barrage of bad news is to look away, but there's no looking away now. Not when my plan to help Dissident Uprising is all about exposing the truth. So as we wait for the activists to arrive, I sit with Irie and watch back-to-back coverage that has the sycophantic zeal of a royal funeral.

'When the barrier was built in 1982,' an engineer says, the defences gleaming behind him like modernist river guardians, 'nobody had heard of climate change. Now, with sea-level rise, it's simply not fit for purpose. The barrier was closed *sixty times* last year – that's way above the maximum threshold. The Met Office is predicting a once-in-five-hundred-year weather event. We're simply not prepared.'

Footage cuts to members of Dissident Uprising occupying each of the ten sector gates on the Thames Barrier. They're holding up banners that say *FIX THE BARRIER, STOP THE FLOOD* and bracing their bodies against the gale-force wind. I don't know where Jenny's found the time to organise another protest. Then I remember what she said about the self-organising system. These people are doing this under their own steam. And they're doing it despite the obvious outcome – an outcome which unfolds when the police arrive in inflatable boats and arrest them all. *That's at least twenty more people left to drown on the Isle of Dogs*, I think grimly. Twenty more people who need saving.

A few hours later, Irie's doorbell rings, and I jog down the hall to answer it. I open the door to find Beth and Celeste cowering underneath a misshapen umbrella alongside a very wet Vashti and a backbreaking load of duffel bags. The roaring rain drowns out their hellos, then Vashti barges through and leaps up to lick my face. Beth hugs me with the might of a long-lost sister. Celeste squeezes my face.

'You're a superstar,' Beth says, dropping her bags in the hallway. 'I knew you'd find somewhere.'

'This place is massive,' Celeste adds, eyeing the stairs that lead to the second and third floors. 'Honestly, Fi, we can't thank you enough.'

'It was nothing,' I tell them. And I mean it. Because finding the accommodation was easy, but what I'm planning next could be the difference between Juniper being repressed and it becoming a moment for the history books. I just need to find the right time to tell them.

I lead Beth and Celeste into the living room to find Irie waiting with a stack of fresh towels. She introduces herself and hugs them with just as much familiarity as I did, already leaning into her role as Dissident Uprising's host.

'Thanks so much for letting us stay,' Celeste says, drying her hair. She's redyed it hot pink since Banmora. Beth is wearing heavy black eyeliner. I've also made an effort, wearing black-and-white striped tights and all my silver jewellery.

'It's the least I can do,' Irie says. She's reapplied her distinctive plum lipstick and changed back into her blue smock. It looks like we're all drawing strength from our appearance today. 'If there's anything I can do to help–'

'You've done more than enough,' Beth replies, wincing as Vashti jumps on the sofa and shakes her fur.

'Don't worry, that sofa has seen its fair share of wet dogs.' Irie gives Vashti a pat on the head. The atmosphere feels oddly festive, like we've all come together dressed in our best for a party. We sit down to catch up, but before we've had the chance, Jenny bursts into the living room. She's wearing a khaki poncho that makes her look like a leatherback turtle. Beth and Celeste rush to help her, lifting the soaking mass of tarpaulin to reveal June tied to her front and a giant bag on her back. I hadn't expected to see my baby sister.

'I'm still breastfeeding,' Jenny explains as I help untie the baby from the sling. 'Your dad sends his love.'

I take June in my arms. It looks like she's grown already. Her eyes are darker, and her little cashew-nut fingers are the size of baby carrots. I remember what I felt the first time I held her – that being her big sister might be enough. Then I remember that, should anything happen to Jenny, I'm one step closer to being June's sole carer. That sucks the festivity out of the room. This isn't a party. This is a rescue mission. And everyone arriving today is risking their lives.

'Who's this?' Irie gasps, her excitement counterbalancing my fatalism.

'This is my sister, June,' I say. Jenny gives me a little grin, then Irie takes June out of my arms with the face of a lottery winner.

'You didn't tell me you had a sister!' Irie gasps again, her pupils dilating as she touches June's nose and smells her head. 'Full of surprises, isn't she, little one?'

'A lot has happened in the last few weeks…' I look at the others. We share a knowing smile. 'This is Jenny, commander in chief.'

Jenny extends her hand, forcing Irie to wriggle her fingers from underneath the baby to shake it. Jenny calls Irie *a literal lifesaver* and starts talking through logistics, telling her who's arriving and when. Irie says she's not sure how she's going to feed everybody, but Jenny quickly reassures her, sending Beth and Celeste to get a bulk load of provisions from the car. Just like that, Irie's home is the centre of an illegal activist organisation. If things go badly, she'll be arrested for aiding and abetting. I will, too. But if Irie is fazed by the criminality of hosting, she doesn't show it.

With introductions out of the way, I open the door to an endless stream of people carrying bags and boxes. Each new face is dripping with rain and brimming with purpose, though none of them look capable of what they're about to do. The majority appear to be in their thirties or forties, bar a fifty-something woman with a shaved head and a much older man wearing walking boots and binoculars. A handful of them give me a brisk nod, but no one seems to recognise me. I had thought someone would. There's the online fame, for one thing. But more so the notoriety. Ed used to be a symbol of the movement, his death representing all the injustices that activists were facing. In fact, had he not died, Jenny would never have started Dissident Uprising. None of us would be here.

Feeling slightly overlooked, I go into the kitchen to get Ed. A man with stretched earlobes is setting up a piece of equipment at the table. It looks like a big walkie-talkie covered in antennas. He puts each antenna at a different angle and adjusts some cables.

'Scrambler,' he says, as if that's supposed to mean something.

I nod vaguely and collect Ed from the kitchen windowsill. When I turned up with him this morning, Irie said he was the sorriest yew tree she'd ever set her eyes on. Then, when my face drained of colour, she apologised and patted my back. I told her it was an urn; today is not the day to go into specifics. She reassured me that yew trees are impossible to kill and that mine will be just fine. I'm counting on that being true. Because bringing him here, showing him what I've done for Dissident Uprising, what I'm *going* to do, is my last-ditch effort to revive him. All that's left is to go through with it. I clasp the pot against my collarbone and watch the storm strike against the kitchen window. I take a deep, grounding breath.

I tell myself that if everyone in this house has what it takes to break into a prison, then so do I.

'Can I have everyone in the living room please?' Jenny calls into the hallway. I hook Ed under my arm and join them. The windows are fogged up with condensation as the chatter of thirty people fills the room.

'Thank you all for coming despite the last-minute change of venue,' Jenny says, projecting her voice. An abrupt hush sweeps across the room. 'Thank you, Irie, for offering your home.' She gestures to Irie who is sitting on the sofa with June. A round of thanks rises from the group. Irie smiles and bobs her head. 'And thank you, Fifi, for facilitating.' She gestures to me. I freeze as a room full of strangers turns to look. They thank me. Beth and Celeste throw in a couple of whoops.

Facilitating. It sounds so fancy.

'Now, listen up,' Jenny continues. 'According to the latest reports, the storm surge will hit in three days. That means we've got two days to get this done.'

People nod. Someone cracks their knuckles. Vashti wags her tail, oblivious to the severity of Jenny's speech.

'Let's not forget why we're here,' she says. 'As of this morning, there are six hundred and three people locked up at the Dissident Detention Centre on the Isle of Dogs – just over two miles west of the Thames Barrier. We've been given intelligence that the authorities intend to leave these people there, if – and when – the barrier fails.' She pauses for dramatic effect. I wring my hands. Everyone else, though grave, appears composed.

'Some of us have loved ones who have been detained,' Jenny goes on, 'some of us have been arrested ourselves, but whatever your motivation for being here, please don't underestimate the risk we are all taking. Please also bear in mind that, though we've been told that there will be no armed guards, we can't rule it out.'

Armed guards? My blood runs cold. I push my body into the corner of the room, the walls digging into my shoulder blades. I search for the nerve I found in the attic, when I defeated the hooves and regained control. But armed guards are so much worse than police horses. And my livestreaming idea seems so trivial now. Why would they make time for social media when they're facing this level of threat? And how can I even entertain the idea of wearing that body cam when, in Banmora, my mind was shattered at the mere mention of Juniper? I picture myself inside the prison, the body cam strapped to my chest as I tiptoe down a concrete corridor in search of the prisoners. Then a guard angles a sniper at me and pulls the trigger with the indifference of a boy playing Laser Quest.

Vashti trots over and puts her head between my legs.

'If you have any doubts,' Jenny says, 'you are free to go, but this will be your last opportunity.'

What the hell is that supposed to mean? What will happen if someone pulls out later on? Will she tie them to a chair? Force them to participate? Throw them in the Thames? There is total silence. Eyes scan the room, waiting for someone to crack. I hold my breath, willing myself not to back out before I've had the chance to tell anyone that I'm in.

Jenny continues. 'Good. Now, most of you know your roles already, but this is our first opportunity to go over the logistics as a group. Richard has set up the scrambler, so our comms are secure. You can speak freely. The auxiliary team is already at Wellspring Farm, so if, for any reason, you need to communicate with them, ask Richard.'

Richard, the man with the mutant walkie-talkie and baggy earlobes, salutes the room. I guess that means the scrambler is some kind of anti-surveillance device and not, as I suspected, a breakfast-making implement. I still have no idea what the purpose of Wellspring Farm is.

'Organise yourselves into your teams,' Jenny says in conclusion, 'walk through your roles, confirm your timings and check your gear, then we'll regroup and train as necessary. If you're new, come to me and I'll assign you a role.'

There is an upsurge of activity as everyone follows Jenny's orders. I am stuck in the corner, a spectator who has done her one useful act of facilitation and is no longer required. If I'm going to tell Jenny what I have planned, now is the time.

'Jenny,' I call out to her, 'Jenny, I–'

She leaves the living room. It's not deliberate, I'm sure, but it trips me up. I should follow her. I want to, but it feels like the armed guard still has his gun pointed right at me. People rush past and set about their tasks, each one exhibiting the bravery that I am so clearly lacking.

Just then, I feel invisible, the weight of Ed's pot no longer the comfort it once was.

28

I walk through the makings of a pre-raid military base with the camera box gripped tightly in my hands. Each room of Irie's house is occupied by different teams undertaking their final preparations. In the hallway, the shaven-headed woman is fitting dozens of people with climbing harnesses. In the dining room, the furniture has been moved aside to test retractable ladders and fit them with straps. In the study, someone is organising black clothes into piles while another person labels them. A man sits in the corner of the kitchen, silently untangling a maze of rope. No one looks up when I search the rooms for Jenny.

After the briefing this morning, I drove home to feed Bruce and pull myself together. As I got out of the car, the howling rain slapped me around the face like a frustrated accomplice. *There's no time for inferiority complexes, Fi!* Yet nothing could have prepared me for just how intimidating Juniper is. The gravity of Jenny's speech, the stoic expressions, the knuckle-cracking. How can they maintain such restraint in the face of a potentially deadly prison break? And when I go with them, how can I maintain the ability to function?

I find Jenny on the living room sofa next to Richard, the scrambler guy. He's projected a floor plan onto the chimneypiece and is using a laser pen to trace the two-dimensional corridors like an architect pitching for a job. I blink quickly, trying to erase my vision of the trigger-happy guard. Beside the coffee table, the binoculars man is inputting something into an ancient computer and talking into a head mic. After spending so much time with the women of Dissident Uprising, it's strange to see two men at the centre of operations. I'm grateful, at least, to see Irie, who is standing at the bay window with June in her arms. It adds a touch of normality to the otherwise pressurised scene. Still, I find myself hovering at the threshold, drumming my fingers on the box and waiting for the right moment to interject. Then an astronomical boom of thunder beats me to it. It shakes the windowpanes and startles June, who retaliates by screaming.

'Take five,' Jenny says to the men as Irie passes her the baby. Jenny unbuttons her khaki shirt and, when June latches, sits back on the sofa and sighs. 'Can I ask you a favour?' she says. I look around for Irie, but it's just the three of us now. 'Can you get my breast pump? It's on the sideboard over there.'

When I hand it over, she takes out her other breast, attaches the cup of the pump to her nipple and switches on the machine.

'Why are you expressing?' I ask, the pump sucking and whirring in an atonal rhythm.

'For Juniper. I'll be gone five hours max so you'll need to feed her.'

'Me?' I look down at the baby, then back up at Jenny.

'Yeah, sorry. Is that OK? I just assumed, seeing as you're not–'

'Oh… yeah. I guess that makes sense.' I sit down beside them.

'Unless you want–?'

'No, it's OK–'

'I don't want to impose–'

'You're not–'

'Irie can–'

We talk over each other. I pull at a tear in the cardboard box and twist it in my fingers. Why is this so fucking hard?

'Fifi,' Jenny says forcefully, putting a hand over mine, 'what is it?'

I look up at the ceiling and inhale. For some reason, I'm on the verge of tears. I swallow. My lungs feel like withered raisins.

'It's just, um…' I open the lid of the camera box. 'I've had an idea, and I wanted to run it by you. It's probably nothing.'

'For Juniper?'

'Yeah.'

'I'm all ears,' Jenny says, looking at the box curiously.

'When Ed died…' I begin. Here goes nothing. 'The only reason we were able to implicate the police is because everyone had their phones out. They captured the whole thing.'

'Right?'

'So what if the police come down hard on you, but there's no one around to record it?'

'The police won't be there.'

'But what if they are?' I press.

'Our intel isn't based on some flimsy rumour, Fi. The whistleblower *works* at the detention centre.' She adjusts the cord on the breast pump and checks the bottle of breastmilk, tipping it on its side. 'Obviously we can't guarantee anything, so if the worst happens, we have what's called a *kill cord* – a sort of press release that's automatically sent to the media if it all goes tits-up.' She looks down at June and smirks, momentarily lightening the mood. 'Does that answer your question?'

'Sort of,' I say, thinking on my feet, 'but the media has their own agenda, don't they? They'll just make out like we're all criminals, and the public will believe them. Like, if they're calling us terrorists now, I can't imagine what they'll call us after Juniper.'

'What does that matter? Same shit, different day.'

'Well, what if we could share what's happening in real time? That way, no one can spin the truth – the world will see exactly what the government is doing, and if things do go tits-up–' I can't help but smirk back '–there'll be thousands of people watching.'

'And how would we do that?' Jenny asks evenly.

'By livestreaming it.' I take the body cam out of the box and put it on the coffee table. 'If you broadcast Juniper live to the world, there'll be no hiding. Whatever happens, people will know the truth.'

'Hmm…' Jenny puts June on her shoulder and starts patting her on the back. 'Someone had that idea already.'

'Oh.' I drop my shoulders, the wind well and truly knocked out of my sails.

'But I said it was too risky,' Jenny adds. 'We don't want to be incriminating ourselves any more than we have to. And, you know, call me old-fashioned but I don't see how social media is useful in this instance. Not when there's so much at stake.'

I'm not sure how to answer that. To me, the benefits seem so obvious. Without social media, RIOT 1.5 wouldn't have become the group that inspired Dissident Uprising in the first place. And *with* social media, Irie might have been remembered for the activist she is. We might have been able to learn from what she and so many women achieved.

'Have you heard of Greenham Common?' I ask then.

'Of course,' Jenny says. 'I was born in the eighties.'

'A lot of people haven't. I hadn't until Irie told me about it. But imagine if they'd had social media back then. It would be in the public consciousness more, and who knows, we might not be in the position we are now. Because if people remembered the truth about Greenham Common – that it was a community of regular women who took on nuclear weapons and won – maybe they'd feel less cynical. Like, maybe they'd understand that all of us, every single one of us, has the power to fight back, if we just believed that was true.' It's an overstatement, I'm sure, but I can't give up now.

'OK…' Jenny says with a slow, conceding nod. 'I get what you're saying. But that relies on a lot of people watching it, right? Dissident Uprising has barely got a social media following. We've not had the time. Or the inclination, to be honest.'

'I've got a following,' I reply, trying to sound as humble as possible. 'I think that's what will make this work. Four hundred thousand people follow me. A livestream could get thousands – if not millions – of views.' What I don't say is that the story will have a far greater reach if it comes from my account. A bog-standard jailbreak might make a headline three scrolls down a webpage, but a jailbreak that's being livestreamed on a disgraced creator's channel will be a national news story.

'You'd be willing to do that?' Jenny asks, picking up the camera. 'You'd be willing to wear this thing?'

This is it. My mind races over my options. If I say yes, there'll be no backing out. If I say no, she'll think less of me and Ed will be lost forever. I visualise myself scaling the prison walls, dressed in black and wearing a mask of bravery borrowed from my Juniper comrades. But beneath that mask, the face I see isn't mine. It's Ed's. Ed would scale the wall. He wouldn't think twice about it. But I'm not Ed. I never have been.

And, after everything that's happened to me, I think that's OK.

It takes a village to change the world. In that village, there are leaders and fighters and scrambler-guys, but there are people like me, too. People who harness their softness to tell a story. People who stay behind and make sure that the bravery of their neighbours doesn't go unrecognised. Without people like me, the village is just shouting into the void, unable to contend with the might of their invaders, who know exactly how to flip the script.

When measured against the leaders and the fighters of the world, when measured against Ed, I've always seen my softness as a failing. I stayed behind so many times while he led from the front. I painted placards while he lay down in front of traffic. I kept myself gagged for as long as I did because I was too frightened to join him. But surely, maintaining a tender heart in a world of violence is its own sort of resistance? For isn't it the tenderhearted who can imagine change, long before anyone has thought to *do something*?

'No,' I say boldly, the word feeling more monumental than anything I've achieved so far. More than leaving the flat or going to Scotland or seeing my dad or defying Tracy. More than hauling myself up out of the pit of my despair and letting the light back in. It means that I have the presence of mind to know my limitations, and the self-worth to assert my strengths regardless. 'One of the climbers will need to wear it. But I'll set it up and launch it on my account, then I can manage the stream from here.'

Jenny wipes milky dribble from June's mouth and starts rocking her. I cross my arms and brace myself for the backlash.

'If a lot of people watch it,' she says instead, nodding in time to the rocking of the baby, 'we not only protect ourselves against the media, we spread our message. It's a good idea, Fi.'

'It is?'

'It is. That's one thing I've not had the time to think about – how we grow Dissident Uprising beyond Juniper. Because once the cat's out of the bag, there's a window of opportunity to reach new people. Having a livestream on your account could make that window much bigger.'

'That's what I thought,' I say with the smile of a school kid who's just got an A.

'I'm glad you're here,' Jenny says, lifting up the body cam and looking at it like it's an alien life-form. 'I don't know the first thing about this stuff. I've never even used Facebook.'

I suppress a laugh, Jenny talking about a dated social media platform like it's the latest in modern technology, then pick up the livestreaming manual.

'Who's going to wear it, then?' I ask, flicking through the first few pages.

'Celeste can. She's the lead climber.' Jenny pops her shoulders and puts the camera down. 'This is exciting, Fi. It adds a whole other dimension to the action. Let's see how those bastards try to defend themselves now.'

She scrunches her nose. It softens her face, revealing the light-hearted woman within, and tells me that I might be living up to her expectations after all.

29

If Irie's house felt like a military base yesterday, it feels like a trench today. There is no more training to do. There are no more preparations to make. All that's left is to wait until the break of dawn, when Jenny will give the order to go over the top.

I can't stop thinking about the people left behind, those whose paltry flood defences are straining against gale-force winds. The once-ubiquitous sirens have fallen silent, the shutters of social welfare have been locked, and the helicopters have whisked the billionaires away. I wonder if, before boarding, they stopped to think about what they've done? They kicked the nest while harvesting the honey because they thought they were above the sting. But when will they realise that sooner or later, the swarm is coming for them, too?

If that thought weren't dire enough, I'm finding the shift in climate hard to process. During the heat wave, there was little in the way of actual destruction. Heat can't tear down buildings or submerge cars; it can't pull up trees or overwhelm waterways. Its force was palpable, trapping the city inside a terrarium, but it felt moderate by comparison. Then I think back to my days behind those tinfoil-clad windows, when the only way to survive was by living in the dark, and I wonder if that's really true.

But there's no time to adjust. Before tomorrow morning, I have to fit Celeste with the body cam and set up the livestream, then broadcast for at least one minute to test the connection. I'm trying not to think about that bit too much. Despite the relative success of my memorial post, there are still thousands of trolls baying for my blood. I know that if I go live even for one second, they'll be salivating at the chance to lay into me. But I can't forget what I've learned these last few days: social media exists to serve me, not the other way around. And like Jenny said, it differentiates me from everyone else here. Although Beth, Celeste and the others are brave enough to break into the detention centre, I'm the only one who can amplify that bravery, who can make sure that Dissident Uprising gets the visibility that Greenham Common so deserved. It's a sense of purpose that is reflected back at me by Celeste.

'I think this is a great idea, Fi,' she says as I tighten the harness onto her shoulders. 'I think it's genius, actually.'

'Genius?' I clip the camera in. 'I'll take that.'

'It is! We wouldn't be able to pull something like this off without an *influencer* in our midst.' She grins affectionately. 'Way to give your platform to the cause, babe.'

'Took me long enough.'

'There's no time like the present,' she assures me, expanding her rib cage to see if the harness fits right. She moves her shoulders from left to right, getting used to the weight of it against her chest, and nods to tell me that it's comfortable. I plug a micro-USB into the camera and connect it to my laptop. A blue light appears on Celeste's chest. My screen goes black. I cluelessly press some buttons and look back at the manual, my tongue fixed in the corner of my mouth.

Once I've grasped the tech, Celeste checks the robustness of the body cam by running up and down the hall, chased by an overly excited Vashti. It's designed for outdoorsy travel influencers to film rock-climbing videos, so it's well-suited to a prison break.

Then it's time to test the livestream. Celeste ushers me into the office with a hand on the small of my back, sensing my hesitation.

'Just get it over with, then we can have dinner.'

I shut the door behind me. The desk is piled high with supplies. I move everything onto the floor. I stack some books in the middle of the desk and use a paper weight to prop the camera on top, fixing it with a wad of blue tack. I link the camera to my account. It has built-in data to run the livestream, so I'll be able to launch it from my laptop without stepping a foot outside.

With everything ready, I take a deep breath to centre myself. I've not scripted anything. I'm going to be *authentic*, just like

Travis always wanted. I press the button. The title on top of the screen changes to @FoliageFifi is LIVE. My stomach lurches. I mask my unease with an impassive face and sit up straight. My heart is beating so loudly that I'm sure the first couple of hundred viewers can hear it. Then it's one thousand. Six thousand. Ten thousand viewers. A flush of hearts floats up the screen, followed by an excess of thumbs-down emojis. I recognise the handle of one viewer.

@HypeTribeTravis has joined the stream

Then the comments start:

About time bitch!

what rock u been hiding under???

This'll be good lol

It's giving YouTube Apology

fucked up fifi's back in the building

Where's your leafy lover boy

I pull the laptop screen as close to the keyboard as possible without shutting it.

'I have an announcement to make,' I say straight down the camera lens. 'Lots of you have been DMing me, asking for an explanation, calling me a crazy bitch or whatever. But Ed really *has* been reincarnated. And I have proof.' I utter the lie without blinking. I know what it takes to get people watching – bait them with schadenfreude. That's the thing with following influencers. There's only so long you can stomach the artifice before you're clamouring for their downfall, before you want to pry back the polished veneer of their content and see them for who they really are – a fucked-up mess who's no better than you. Or ideally, who's worse than you, who allows you to revel in the superiority you were sure you had over them all along.

'So tune in tomorrow morning,' I conclude, 'for a special livestream where I'll set the record straight. Just tap the bell icon to get notified. See you tomorrow, then, bright and early. Bye!' I wave at the screen, close the laptop and exhale. That was barely fifteen seconds, but it'll do. The body cam works. The livestream works. This is going to work.

Five minutes later, I open the laptop to check the engagement. Seventy-three thousand people have watched it already. Not just that, I've gained nearly eight thousand followers. I try not to let that please me too much.

We can't all fit around the kitchen table so people have splintered off into groups, turning the living and dining rooms into impromptu picnic areas. There is a festive atmosphere again, like we've all agreed to replace fear with joy before the immense undertaking of tomorrow. In the kitchen, Jenny, Beth, Celeste and Irie sit around the table, leaving a seat open for me. I put Ed back on the windowsill and join them.

'Shhh,' says Irie, producing a bottle of red wine. 'There's not enough to go around, so keep it on the down-low.'

We drink out of mugs to remain incognito. June is sleeping beside Jenny in a car seat on the floor. Vashti rests her head in my lap. I sneak her a handful of pasta. Beth puts a bread roll on my plate. Irie fills my mug. Celeste grates cheese. Jenny hands out bottled water. There is a gentle murmur of chitchat. The only thing spoiling the intimate atmosphere is the storm, which rages against the kitchen window and finds its way into every crevice of this draughty old house.

'I wonder how bad the weather is in Banmora,' Celeste says.

'I haven't heard from John,' Jenny replies, buttering a bread roll. 'But that's not unusual. There's never any signal down at the house.'

'What was it like when you left?' I ask, instantly worried. I haven't had the headspace to realise that my dad is facing the storm alone.

'It was raining pretty heavily. But you know your dad – he was over the moon. Means he doesn't have to trek to the plantation to water the saplings.' Jenny smiles, alleviating some of my concern.

'I miss Banmora,' Beth adds with her mouth full. 'London is a hellhole in comparison.'

'Less bashing of my beloved city, please,' Irie scolds her with a good-natured wag of the finger. 'London has its merits.'

'Such as?' Beth asks playfully.

'Well, all the lefties live here, for one thing. There's a great sense of community. Or there was, before the heat wave.' Irie glances at me and smiles. Just then, she looks so different to the lonely, despondent woman I found when I first arrived. 'And you know, community is vital at a time like this. That's why I stayed in London.'

'Go on,' Jenny presses, urging Irie to say more.

'Well,' Irie says, clearing her throat and sitting back, 'take Chicago, for example. You lot won't remember, but in 1995, there was a killer heat wave. And I mean *killer*. Seven hundred odd people died. It was fifty degrees, much hotter than it ever got here. What they later realised was that in proper communities, fewer people died. In these parts of the city – which were majority white, might I add – people were looking out for each other, checking in, sharing air-con, that sort of thing. Their kids went to the same schools, their streets were safe, they had no reason not to open their doors. But in the poor side of town, people had nothing to share. They lived alone, they were old or sick or simply isolated, and they cooked.'

'God, how awful,' Celeste says, putting her knife and fork down. 'That's the thing with extreme weather. It just speeds everything up – the problems that've always been there, the things that don't get acknowledged, they become tragedies.'

'Indeed.' Irie nods. 'And some have the ignorance to call climate change *the great equaliser*. It's the great magnifying glass, let me tell you. My point is, being part of a community is how we survive this thing. I know the impulse is to give up on society, to live on an island and stick your fingers in your ears, but you're denying yourself social cohesion. That's what they called it after the

Chicago heat wave – *social cohesion*. Without it, we don't stand a chance.'

The scrape of cutlery against plates is all that can be heard as we process what Irie has just told us. For one thing, she's debunked Dad and Jenny's way of life; their off-grid solitude in the middle of nowhere. Jenny doesn't seem primed to defend herself. After all, she might lack a next-door neighbour, but she's made her own sort of social cohesion in Dissident Uprising.

Then I think about my own isolation. Before Tracy took Bruce, my solitude was so absolute that I didn't even have myself for company. That is until a houseplant appeared on my doorstep and I allowed myself to believe that love could surpass death and guide me out of the abyss. But I think I've always been lonely. I grew up an only child. I've never had meals like this, where multiple people break bread and share ideas. It was just me and two unhappy parents. Until it was just me and Tracy. And even at East Peace, when I had the chance to join a community, I opted out and surrendered myself to social media. Online, I could connect with people, but only on the surface. It felt safer that way.

The conversation moves on. Celeste and Beth tell the story of how they met. Jenny tells the story of the first time she got arrested. Irie tells the story of Greenham. I melt into the background and observe them. The wailing of the storm subsides. Their warmly lit faces glow. They share wine and laughter and ease – an ease that emanates from around the dinner table and directly into me.

How did I come to be among these remarkable women? Women who breastfeed while leading a civil resistance. Women who camp outside military bases to protest nuclear weapons. Women who love each other enough to link arms and scale a prison wall.

That's when the flame that I've been nursing catches. It spreads, and it burns from deep within me. It thaws out the parts I still have hidden away. The parts I associate with the woman I was before, when the rosy idealism of youth sparkled in my eyes and I felt love without knowing loss and I threw myself at changing the world because I didn't believe that anyone had the right to stop me.

I take the fire home with me. I curl up in bed with Bruce, and I soothe myself to sleep with it. In the morning, my community will be doing whatever it takes to defend our movement. Meanwhile, I will be broadcasting live to the world the idea that, despite what the system may tell you, despite how they may try to contain you, the power was ours all along.

30

My alarm goes off at four thirty in the morning. The dawn light is dampened by the storm, a storm which seems to have taken on a ferocious new edge this morning. Tracy's car is buffeted across the road as I drive to Irie's house, the windscreen wipers barely able to contend with the monsoon. I peel off my raincoat in the hallway, the few paces between the car and Irie's front door having soaked me to the skin. I sneak past rooms of snoring people in sleeping bags. Irie is in the kitchen, her hair wrapped in a silk bonnet and her holey slippers slapping on the stone tiles. We smile but don't speak. It's too early. I take out five loaves of bread and start slicing. Irie pours oats into a saucepan. At five o'clock, a chorus of alarms goes off. People start filing into the kitchen. Everyone is wearing black. We dish out toast and porridge and coffee. People sit around the table or stand by the windows to eat, grimacing, because who wants to eat at this hour? But they force it down nonetheless. It would be foolish to break into a prison on an empty stomach.

The hushed voices and sombre garb make it feel like we're eating breakfast at a wake. Beth and Celeste look as blurry-eyed as each other. I focus on pouring bottled water into the kettle, firing a guilty glance at Ed on the windowsill. I forgot to bring him home with me last night. With everything that's been going on, it's been hard to keep up with his care, especially since I'm no longer obligated to water him every day. But it's not just that. I'm officially a member of Dissident Uprising. I'm doing my bit – a bit that Celeste and Jenny tell me is vitally important. So why haven't I heard his voice since that day in Banmora, when he lost his flowers and made me feel like I was to blame? I can't help but be resentful towards him for that.

More so because, after his signs sent me all the way to Scotland, everything I've done since then has been of my own accord. I've not needed a single bloom to show me the way. If Ed was as proud of me as I am of myself about that, surely he'd send flowers.

Once everyone has had something to eat, I fit the body cam to Celeste and balance my laptop on my hip to adjust the settings. I must look like the tech person of the group – the vigilante computer whiz who's going to hack into the mainframe. It's not a persona I'm used to. I'm normally in front of the camera, not behind it. But with my moonstone necklace and crochet cardigan, maybe I'm giving Willow in *Buffy* rather than basement-dwelling doxxer. A blue light glows on the front of the camera. My chest and chin appear on the laptop screen. When Celeste turns, the on-screen video pans in real time.

'That blue light means the camera is connected,' I tell her. 'A flashing red light means you're live.'

Celeste nods and takes a staggered breath. 'Do you really think people will watch this?'

'I think *a lot* of people will watch this, Cel, so don't say anything you don't want them to hear.'

Celeste nods again and clenches her jaw.

'You look like Iron Man with that thing on,' Beth says, finishing her toast.

'Iron *Woman*,' the three of us say in unison.

Then Jenny enters the room. 'The situation has escalated,' she announces. 'The tidal surge started this morning. One of the sector gates on the Thames Barrier failed to close.' She is wearing a spotty grey pyjama top, giving her speech a faintly ridiculous air. 'I've spoken to our contact, and according to their estimates, it's releasing about fifteen thousand gallons of water into the floodplain every hour. There have been reports of minor flooding already.' She pauses and looks down at her top. Two dark blooms of moisture spread from her nipples. Irie hands her a dish cloth to pat herself dry. 'For that reason,' she says, dabbing at her chest, 'we have to launch Operation Grus. That means I will be pulling out of the main mission. Celeste, are you still willing to front the entry team?'

People gasp and shake their heads. Celeste freezes. I have no idea what *Operation Grus* means or why it would put Celeste in charge. From the looks of her wide-eyed alarm, she's just as shocked as I am.

'Yes,' she says with the pitch of a hummingbird. Jenny hands Celeste a credit card. Again, the reason for this is entirely unclear to me.

'It is now absolutely crucial that the prisoners are on the opposite side of the compound once they leave the building. Is that understood?' Jenny says to her. 'Me and Richard will do the rest.'

'Yes,' Celeste reiterates. She puts the credit card into her trouser pocket, then thinks better of it and puts it in the front pocket of the black utility vest she's wearing. Her fingers fumble with the zip.

'I'll repeat that,' Jenny says to the room. 'We are launching Operation Grus. This doesn't affect transport plans to Wellspring Farm. Now, gear up. We leave in five minutes.'

Celeste takes two steps back and puts a hand against the doorframe.

'You OK?' Beth asks, touching her waist. Celeste closes her eyes. I have so many questions. Is Operation Grus more dangerous? If the barrier is already failing, doesn't that make Juniper riskier already? If the Isle of Dogs is right on the floodplain, will it be underwater by the time they get there?

With Celeste's eyes still closed, I adjust the camera harness and triple check the settings. She's already taken on more responsibility by agreeing to wear this. Why would she take on even more? And why, when she knows the risks of retaliation better than any of us?

'You OK?' Beth repeats.

'Yep, just needed a sec,' Celeste replies, opening her eyes.

'Has Jenny put you in charge?' I ask.

'Yes.'

'Why you? You've only just joined—'

'I offered,' she says plainly. 'Jenny needed a stand-in, in case this happened.'

'But what if—'

'There's no point in what-ifs, Fi. Someone had to put their hand up. It might as well be me. Is the camera ready?'

'You're good to go,' I confirm, wishing I could find some way to keep them with me for a minute longer. But with one gate down, they should have left an hour ago.

'It's time,' Jenny says, coming back into the room with black clothes on. 'June's asleep in the living room,' she tells me. 'She'll need feeding at about seven.'

'No problem,' I say with a soldier's nod.

'My hero.' Jenny hugs me, then we all hug each other.

'Good luck,' Irie says as they leave the kitchen.

'Break a leg,' I say, regretting it the second it escapes my mouth. Then they're gone.

Irie and I sit in the living room. June is in a travel coat next to the sofa. Vashti is asleep on the floor. The TV is showing the news on mute. The coverage is around-the-clock, with footage of the broken sector gate played on a loop. My laptop shows a chest-height view of the seat in front of Celeste. It's upholstered in a jazzy pattern that belongs in the nineties. Whenever she turns to face Beth, we get an up-close shot of Beth's chest. It's hard to tell if the audio is any good given that no one in the van seems to be talking. My cursor is flashing over the Go Live button, ready to click the second they descend the wall.

'The detention centre is in the middle of Mudchute Park,' Irie explains, having attended all of the logistics briefings. 'It used to be a playground, but they've built a sort of aircraft hangar there. Two, actually, although the second one hasn't been finished yet.'

'So how are they going to break in?' I ask, embarrassed that I still don't know.

'Well, first things first, they have to get over the fence,' Irie says, erasing the image of the stony castle barricade I've been picturing. 'It's similar to the one at the nuclear base – twenty feet high, chain link, pitched posts, barbed wire – the whole gambit. But unlike

Greenham, it's got a ten-foot steel parapet all the way around, so they can't just take wire cutters to it. They have to climb.'

'Hence the ladders.'

'Hence the ladders.'

On-screen, Celeste opens her tool belt and checks the contents. Her hands are shaking. She takes out a bolt cutter, a window hammer, a metal hook, a knife, a pair of climbing gloves, a torch and a flare gun.

'What are those things for? The knife? The flare gun?'

'It pays to be prepared,' Irie replies vaguely, looking between the laptop screen and the television like someone trying to keep up with two tennis matches. Celeste fumbles with the flare gun and drops it underneath the seat in front. Beth picks it up. She takes Celeste's hands. The whole frame shakes.

'You've got this,' Beth says, and we hear the quality of the audio for the first time. It's tinny, but it'll do. 'You're the strongest person I know.'

'I'm scared,' Celeste whispers. 'What if the police come?' The question makes my heart lurch from one side of my rib cage to the other. Jenny said there'd be no police. She *guaranteed* it. Why is it suddenly a possibility?

'They won't,' Beth comforts Celeste and, unknowingly, me. 'Especially not now the barrier is failing. It's too dangerous for them to come this close to the river.'

That response seems to calm Celeste, because she puts the flare gun away and the frame steadies. I wish I could look out of the van window to see how close they are. Without traffic, it shouldn't take longer than twenty minutes to get to the Isle of Dogs. We sit in silence and listen to the sound of the engine as a van-load of people sit in silence, too.

'Look,' Celeste says eventually. 'We're at Canary Wharf.'

'Is there flooding?' Beth asks.

'Yes.'

'How bad?'

'The water's going straight over the South Dock.'

'That's not good.'

'No.'

Irie and I exchange a fretful look and lean closer to the screen. A few minutes later, the van stops, and Celeste stands. I see then that she's at the front, behind the driver. Of course she is – she's in charge. Her gloved hands move around the screen like a POV video-game character. I resist the urge to try and make her walk forward with the arrow keys. She gets off and takes in her surroundings.

The sun is starting to rise. The grainy orange glow from the streetlights makes on-screen visibility poor. On one side of the road, there is a redbrick smokestack, and opposite that a line of overgrown bushes bordered by a fence. Celeste helps the driver unload the gear from the baggage hold. The wind and rain hog the microphone, muffling anything that's being said. The video scans the group of activists as Celeste walks up and down the street to check that everyone is there. Then she gives a signal to the van driver and he leaves. Only then does it sink in that this is really happening.

My friends are about to break into a prison.

Celeste leads the activists to a covered walkway that ascends into the park. It's been cordoned off with chains and a no-trespassing sign, but Celeste's bolt cutters make light work of it. She leads the group up a shadowy tunnel, momentarily protecting them from the storm. I can hear their feet on the steps and their loaded breathing. I can hear thirty people preparing themselves for whatever lies on the other side of the tunnel. The light changes, and the camera refocuses to reveal an expansive field. We lean in even closer.

'That can't be Mudchute Park,' Irie says, putting her hand over her mouth. It's hard to believe that this was ever a playground where kids played football and families had picnics. Now it's little more than a construction site.

Celeste heads for a block of shipping containers in the middle distance. The ground has been churned up by heavy-duty machinery which is now sinking into the waterlogged mud. When she reaches the containers, she waits for the rest of the activists to regroup. She says something. I can't make it out. Behind the containers, floodlights white-wash a barbed-wire-clad fence that stretches across the horizon. On one side of the fence, there's an unfinished building with exposed joists and two cranes bent at an angle. On the other side, there's the detention centre.

Irie was right – it looks like an aircraft hangar, a colossal steel building with a corrugated roof and no windows. It's the last place I'd suspect people to be. Perhaps that's the point. The fence soars almost as high as the building, caging it like a high security prison. The closer Celeste gets, the less I can see over the steel parapet. How is it that no one has noticed this eyesore being built in a public space? What about the people who live nearby? What exactly has the government done to keep this quiet?

When they reach the fence, the activists pair off. Celeste's hands come into shot. She unclips an abseiling rope from her harness and starts tying knots, then takes the wire cutters out of her tool belt and, I think from the way her hand moves, puts them in her mouth. In front of her, Beth is setting up the ladder. It has telescopic poles which extend up and over the steel parapet. Celeste looks to her left. The activists are standing in pairs and evenly spaced along one side of the fence. Each ladder is up, each climber has their foot on the bottom rung and each spotter is standing by, ready to anchor it. They are all looking at Celeste. The camera rises and falls as she takes a deep breath.

'I love you,' Beth says, her voice barely audible above the din of the weather.

'I love you, too,' Celeste says.

Then she gives another signal. Beth throws the weight of her body against the ladder as Celeste slams the soles of her boots against the rungs, the storm threatening to throw her off if Beth doesn't bear down as hard as she can. Celeste clears the parapet in seconds. The compound comes into view. A cement yard wraps around the enormous building, empty except for the water that's already bubbling up from the drains. I look up at the television. The nine other gates are still functioning. If all of this water is from just one failed gate, I can't bring myself to imagine what will happen when the others go. Celeste looks up. The twenty feet to the top of the fence looks treacherous. Irie grabs my hand, wincing as a gust of wind throws the ladder – and Celeste – against the chain-link fence. She holds on. She keeps going. At the top, Celeste pauses to check that everyone else is up. They are, and they're waiting for her. She makes a fist, then the wire cutters reappear, and her hands are hacking at the barbed wire in front of her. The barbs snag and pull at her gloves. She creates a gap big enough to fit through. Then she attaches herself to the abseiling rope, fixes it to the fence and throws it over the other side. After a brief pause, she turns her body to face the rest of the climbers. They are all at the top of the fence, poised to make the descent.

'Ready, Fi?' Celeste says into the microphone.

I hover my finger over the mouse pad.

'Ready,' I say.

Celeste goes over the fence. They all do. I watch as the rope glides through her hands and her feet rappel off the links in the chain. When her boots hit the ground, I click Go Live. And although I can't see it, I know that the light on her body cam is flashing red.

31

Around the world, twenty thousand pairs of eyes are watching the rescue mission unfold in real time – a number that is climbing by the second.

Celeste crosses the compound. The shadows of the group stretch over the concrete as the floodlights expose their every move. There can't be security here or else the mission would have failed already. Celeste reaches a side door. She turns the handle. I guess there's no harm in trying. But how are they going to get in? That's when the credit card reappears from her front pocket. She holds it against an illuminated panel. It flashes green. Just like that, she's in.

'Where did she get that from?' I ask Irie shrilly.

'The whistleblower. She posted it to Banmora in a birthday card.'

'But it can't be that easy, surely?'

'It's just a staff key card. They can't access the control room. They can't open the gates.'

'So how–?'

'Just watch, Fi,' Irie urges without taking her eyes off the screen. I take a deep breath and do as she says. Celeste enters the building. There is a hallway lit by emergency lights. I was expecting a vast airplane hangar with metal cages and partitions – not fully fabricated halls and rooms that look like they belong in a hospital. Celeste turns back to the door to check in with the others.

'All good?' she says. There is a silent unison of nods. Then the activists split off and head down the corridor, disappearing behind different doors. I can hear their boots splashing off into the distance. The water is already inside the building. I look up at the news.

'Oh god, the second gate is down.'

Irie snaps her head up.

'Dear Lord, please protect them,' she prays, her hand reflexively touching a crucifix that is hanging on a chain around her neck.

Celeste goes through a door marked *Canteen*. I hold my breath, waiting for a security guard to step out and shoot her on sight. But the room is empty – of people *and* of furniture. Why aren't there any tables or chairs in here? Did they make them eat off the floor? I glance at the viewer count. It's well over fifty thousand. Then I drag my eyes away from the footage long enough to check the comments.

No context moment

That's not Fifi, is it?

Anyone else getting GoldenEye?

Came for the crazy, stayed for the dodgy vibes

I look back at the livestream. Celeste is in the dormitory. It's an open-plan space with bunk beds lined against the walls and down the centre of the room, providing no privacy to those detained. All of the beds have been stripped, leaving bare mattresses and a few personal items – the only indication that people have been here. Celeste picks up a family photo that is floating in the rising water.

'This makes no sense,' she says.

A viewer comments, You're telling me!

There are supposed to be six hundred people here. Where have they all gone? Unless Jenny got it wrong? Unless they did get evacuated? Or – more likely – unless the whistleblower was never on our side and this is some kind of elaborate trap?

Room after room is abandoned. Not only that, the whole place has been gutted. Celeste goes into an office, but there aren't any chairs. She goes into a bathroom, but there aren't any shower curtains. Where could everything have gone? They come to a steel staircase and wait for the other climbers. One of the activists touches his ear and points up. There is a bang followed by another one. It's coming from above them. Celeste's feet thrash up the stairs. She searches the second floor. A few of the climbers start shouting 'Hello?'

I wince. Surely it's not wise to draw attention to themselves like this? The police could be waiting to ambush them. Then there's the banging again. Celeste turns on her heels. There isn't a third floor, the stairs breaking out of the fabricated rooms and into the dead space of the hangar above. Celeste's hands fumble in her tool belt. She pulls out the knife. My heart pounds like a jackhammer. Irie takes my hand and squeezes so hard that I can feel her finger bones moving underneath her skin.

When Celeste reaches the top, there is a door. It says *Danger: Roof Access Only*. This time, she doesn't need to use her key card. The door is already open. It swings shut. The camera jerks. Celeste approaches the door and pushes it open with her foot. The wind bangs it shut. She checks the lock. It's been sawn off.

'It's too dangerous to go onto the roof!' I cry out. Irie digs her nails into my hand.

Celeste pushes the door open and walks out. The storm is viscous, and she is pushed back. She steadies herself and tries again. There is a safety railing. She grabs it and dips her head against the wind so that the camera is facing her feet. She makes her way along a metal grate. The corrugated roof is visible underneath her feet, rain rushing off it like a white-water ravine. There is the sound of metal straining. She looks back, taking in a rooftop view of the Greenwich Peninsula. I spot the iconic white dome of the O_2 on the bend of the river. The Thames Barrier is behind that dome. The camera lands on the others who are following close behind, their heads down, their shoulders hunched against the windblast. When Celeste turns to face ahead, the grate widens. A platform has been built on top of the roof to accommodate a helipad. As they walk out onto it, there are hundreds of people gathered there.

'They're here!' Celeste shouts loud enough for us to hear. She breaks into a jog. The people on the helipad see her approach. They duck behind some kind of haphazard barrier made of furniture:

that explains the empty rooms. Celeste's hands can be seen splayed out in a gesture of peace, the knife hidden back inside her tool belt. From the cowering crowd, a figure steps forward. She walks towards Celeste with one arm extended, a pipe held aloft like a sword. She has short hair, brown skin and fierce eyes.

'Dissident Uprising!' Celeste announces herself. 'We're Dissident Uprising!'

The pipe-wielding woman falters, then a member of Dissident Uprising breaks away from the group and runs in her direction. His arms are open as if for an embrace. It's the elderly man who arrived at Irie's with binoculars. A flash of recognition transforms the short-haired woman's face, and she drops the pipe. She starts running, too. They know each other. They are hugging. Celeste catches up with them. The woman is saying something inaudible. I try to lip-read. I think she's saying, 'You're here. You're here. You're really here.' The binoculars man is holding her face and nodding and trying to reassure her.

'We're Dissident Uprising,' Celeste shouts again. The woman smiles, then she turns and gives a thumbs up to the other prisoners. She appears to be in charge. The energy on the roof changes then. People move closer. They are all wearing dark grey tracksuits and resemble a collection of ancient standing stones. I scan the comments to see if anyone has figured out what's happening yet.

What is going on? Who are those people?

Where is this?

saw the millennium dome-they're in london

Did she say Dissident Uprising?

I'm so confused right now lol

'We have to get off this roof,' Celeste says to the woman. She goes over to the other prisoners. The haphazard barrier turns out to be a makeshift battering ram. The bed linen has been torn into strips and woven into rope, then benches and industrial-sized metal baskets have been tied to office chairs. Failing that, they've constructed ladders by tying the bed-linen rope onto splintered table legs. It's clearly not enough to escape, but the sight of their will to survive breaks me. I burst into tears, choking and spluttering so loudly that June wakes up. Irie isn't annoyed. She seems relieved to have something else to focus on.

The wind howls, and I can't hear what's being said. The binoculars man is explaining something to the short-haired woman. They look so similar that they must be father and daughter. Her hand is on the battering ram, ready to move it. He's shaking his head and pointing off the roof. He's trying to convince her to leave it behind. I read his lips. I think he says, 'You have to trust me.' She lets go. Then the other prisoners back away from it.

'Why did they build it on the roof?' I ask Irie between wheezing sobs.

'To get away from the flood. They had no way of knowing how quickly it would happen.' She looks up at the television. 'The third gate is down, Fi. They're running out of time.'

Celeste seems to sense it, because everything picks up pace. People begin moving off the helipad. Celeste and the other climbers are prioritising the prisoners, shepherding them through the door while they grip onto the safety railing.

'When we get down there,' I can hear Celeste saying to the woman, 'everyone needs to go to the left side of the building. You got it?'

The woman nods. Celeste pushes her inside, the gale bouncing off the building and threatening to send them all tumbling to the ground. The comments are racing up my screen now.

I'm from CNN. Can we set up an interview? Check your DMs.

Why have they all been left there???

wtf is going on I can't believe what i'm seeing

I can't watch

I can't watch, either. But I have to. Only once every last prisoner is off the roof do Celeste and the other climbers follow them. Then Celeste's boots are pounding down the stairs again, descending back into the darkness of the detention centre. In front of her, hundreds of people are spiralling towards the bottom, the cacophonous hangar now ringing with the sound of feet hitting metal. It's a relief in comparison to the feral wind. Then she stops.

'What's the holdup?' she shouts across the crowd of prisoners, who have come to an abrupt standstill. The word *flood* echoes back. I look up at the television. Four gates are down. Almost half. The flood will be in full swing now. After an agonising wait, the crowd starts to shuffle forward. When Celeste reaches the bottom, tears aren't enough to express my dismay. The first floor is flooded with four, maybe even five feet of water. A riot of terrified voices bounces down the hall and reverberates off the water like a swimming pool. Celeste takes off her tool belt and buckles it over the body cam, plunging the livestream into darkness.

Where did you go?

We're with you!

BBC correspondent here, can we get permission to use footage?

This is like that scene in the fucking titanic!

Then the hallway reappears.

'Sorry,' Celeste says, her voice strained. 'Forgot you were there.' She bends over. The water comes up to her waist. Up ahead, some people are wading through it, others are swimming. The emergency lights are flickering. It *is* like that scene in *Titanic*. My whole body is shaking now. I'm going to be sick. I stand up. When I look back at the screen, faint daylight can be seen filtering into the hallway through the open door. Celeste starts swimming. The water must be rising. At least we know now that the camera is waterproof. Bubbles cross the screen. Submerged boots and trainers and legs.

Hands grappling, holding, reaching. She reemerges above the water.

'Fuck,' Celeste splutters, spitting water. She is the last person out the door. Then she starts screaming, 'To the left! Go to the left of the building. Away from the construction site. Now!' People stumble and flail. I catch sight of the short-haired woman, her arms around her father's waist, pulling him across the surface. Water laps at the wall surrounding the detention centre. That's when I see it: this place is watertight. That's what the steel parapet is for – to contain at least ten feet of water. Celeste fumbles with the tool belt she's been holding above her head. She takes out the flare gun.

'Fire!' she yells, her voice disintegrating into the storm.

'Fire!' shouts another activist. A handful of voices join in.

'Fire! Fire! Fire!'

Celeste turns to look behind her. She can't be sure that everyone is with them. There's no way to be sure. I pace up and down the living room and chew my fingers to bleeding, my pulse punching against my veins. Celeste turns back to the crowd. She fires the flare above her head. It sounds like a gun. Like a real gun. The crowd ducks and shrieks, thinking it's security. Then more gunfire. Flares soar into the sky, sparks reflecting off the water and illuminating the yard with the glow of a New Year's fireworks display. The red smoke reminds me of The Final Strike, of the moments before I lost him.

Hooves smash against the windowpanes.

Red smoke emanates through the laptop speakers.

Not here. Not now. Please.

But I don't know how to stop them. I can't do what I did in the attic and scream at them to leave me alone, not with June here. But I can't risk falling to pieces and adding another casualty to the list. Then Vashti jumps up and licks my face. She paws at my chest, trying to get me to sit on the floor. When I do, she climbs onto my lap and rests her head on my shoulder. I feel the heat of her body against my skin, the gentle rise and fall of her breathing, her wet nose against my neck. Then my eyebrows stitch in fierce defiance. I exhale all of the sorrow and the horror and the fucking bitter disappointment from my lungs.

Not here.

Not now.

'Good girl,' I tell her, running my hand down her back.

The on-screen flares fade alongside the ones in the living room, their smoke trails lingering in the sky, and everyone looks around for the promised escape route. An eerie quiet descends. It is punctuated by splashing and soft cries of fear.

It's too late. Surely it's too late.

Then there is an explosion. A booming crash. A sound belonging to warfare, ricocheting off the parapet and sending shock waves across the water. Then another.

'What was that?' I wail at Irie, Vashti jumping off my lap in alarm. Irie just shakes her head and cries.

The water level is much higher now, engulfing the camera entirely. It churns as limbs thrash and tumble. It's impossible to make anything out. Then Celeste's fingers come into view. She is groping for the camera, trying to unclip it from the harness. Even now, with her life on the line, she's thinking about the livestream. She raises the camera out of the water and turns it. They have moved to the right side of the building. The side next to the construction site. It takes a second to process what I'm seeing.

If I'd had one hundred years to figure out what Operation Grus involved, I would never have guessed.

Two shipping containers have crushed the fence like a tin can. My first thought is that it's some kind of miracle – how else could two giant anvils have fallen out of the sky? Then Celeste angles the camera up. Two cranes are positioned above the shipping containers, their empty hooks swinging against the wind. In the cockpit of each crane, a person is leaning out of the window and waving a red flare. Jenny and Richard. Somehow, they've managed to hijack cranes from the construction site, lift shipping containers into the air and drop them on top of the fence. Celeste pans back down to the ground. The doors on either end of the containers are open, forming two corridors that remind me of flumes at a water park, water rushing through them and out of the compound.

People start cheering. Tentatively at first, then a growling thunder of relief. The water level drops as the flood disperses through the containers and out onto the open field. The climbers regroup, slapping each other on the back. Some of the prisoners drop to their knees.

That's one way to get out lol

You're all heroes!

this is the craziest shit i've ever seen man

Biggest news story in the world right now

But the mission isn't over. Not until the detention centre is miles behind them.

'Go through the containers! Get everyone out,' Celeste commands the short-haired woman. 'Go, carefully!'

The prisoners are soaked and wobbly with shock, tripping over the lip of the containers and putting their arms around each other for support. Celeste turns the camera around to face her. I check the viewer count. Five million people look back.

'The government left these people here to drown!' she bellows with a might that surpasses the weather, spit flying from her mouth. The camera is close enough to see the whites of her eyes. 'And why? For having the guts to fight back! Well, guess what? YOU CAN'T DROWN A MOVEMENT!' She screams the words with so much rage that they resonate down the microphone. 'We are Dissident Uprising. And we will win – BY ANY MEANS NECESSARY!'

The screen goes black. I catch my breath with the urgency of someone who's had their head held underwater. Irie and I look at each other, our faces drained, our minds unable to make sense of what's just happened.

Just then, a sound rumbles through the windows. It deafens the storm. I can feel it like the drums at The Final Strike. For a second, I think the horses have returned, Vashti's intervention no longer enough to stave them off. But instead of hooves hitting hot concrete, I hear people applauding. Thousands of people. Irie and I jump up. We laugh. And then we join in. We bang the walls with our fists. We send up the flares of our joy, and we let the sound rain down all around us. The streets of London roar. The country listens. And it joins in. And so the chorus grows, becoming stronger and more harmonious. Until soon, it can surely be heard from space.

It is the chorus of dissent.

And of hope, too.

32

When the fifth barrier fails, the River Thames bursts its banks, taking the city's network of canals and waterways down with it. Although Irie once told me that they'd have to float her out of her house in a coffin, she changes her mind. The River Lea is flooding the streets faster than she expected, and by the time we get the baby into Tracy's car, the water is creeping up the tires. We chase the flood through North London and towards Hertfordshire. The radio is comparing it to the North Sea storm surge of 1953, when three hundred and seven people died and thousands were made homeless. There are no reports of fatalities yet, but only half of the barrier is down. Who knows what will happen when the whole thing goes.

But it's not just the flood drawing us away from the city. When the celebrations subsided and we'd had the chance to compose ourselves, Irie said, 'Get your things' and started packing the car. We couldn't stay put while our friends recovered from a feat so heroic it forced the city of London to its feet. We had to be with them, at least to see for ourselves that it really happened and that everyone is safe.

June is asleep in her car seat beside Vashti, who is curled up like a croissant. I am sitting in the passenger's seat with Ed on my lap, letting Irie drive. In these apocalyptic conditions, insurance seems an entirely trivial concern.

I've brought him with me out of a sense of duty more than anything. He's been here since the start of this journey. He deserves to see how it ends. And I suppose I'm still clinging onto the conviction that, if I can just prove that I've made a difference, Ed will come back. But that relies on having actually *made* a difference. I didn't break into the detention centre or save any lives. I didn't join Dissident Uprising in the way that Ed was pushing me to. I just watched the whole thing from the comfort of Irie's living room.

Then I see something that makes me hesitate.

I see signs. Hundreds of handmade signs. Down street after street, in window after window, there are signs scrawled onto bed sheets, painted onto cereal boxes and typed onto printer paper. Some of them have been drawn by children with hearts and smiley faces. Some have the anarchic, jagged script of seasoned activists. Some have the wobbly cursive of the elderly. But they all say the same thing:

YOU CAN'T DROWN A MOVEMENT

There's the Dissident Uprising symbol, too, the shattered planet recreated in a thousand different colours and styles. Irie slows down and starts laughing, then she's holding back the tears. That's when I know.

I did *do something*. I did exactly what I set out to do. I seeded an idea that germinated the second it was planted. From it grew not only hope – that ephemeral thing that I have spent so many months recultivating – but resistance. And from that tree of resistance bloomed an unassailable truth: disobedience, when done in denial of cruelty, is a radical act of love. Because everyone with a sign in their window now risks arrest, yet they value their right to speak out more than their own freedom. And what are the authorities going to do? Arrest us all? Then who will teach their children and who will heal their wounds? And who will drive their trains and sail their boats and collect their rubbish? And who will stock their shelves and fix their plumbing and bake their bread? And who will brew them coffee and write their news and make their gardens grow? And who will be there to stand by their side when the earth finally calls it quits? Because I know that those cowardly few, those failed conquerors, won't want to be alone when their gilded towers come crashing down all around them.

I don't know if Ed is around to see this, but I hope that, wherever he is now, he knows how hard I have tried, how far I have come. And how I have grown to realise that I can *do something* on my own terms, not his.

We drive down a tunnel of trees and onto a dirt track. Irie skirts a few waterlogged potholes and swings through a farm gate, arriving in a field where a row of vans idle. There is a tractor spreading hay to stop them from getting stuck in the mud. Before we can get our bearings, a woman with a clipboard approaches.

'Welcome to Wellspring Farm,' she says from underneath an umbrella.

'We're with Jenny,' Irie says, the baby tucked inside her coat.

'That'll be the green tent,' the woman replies, pointing towards the field ahead. We trudge through the rain. When we pass the next farm gate, we look down on what can only be described as a festival nestled in a small valley. There's a cluster of enormous tents and rows of portaloos, with hand-painted signs directing people to a canteen, a first-aid station and a family meetup point.

Inside the green tent, a military operation is underway. Teams of people are attending to the rescued prisoners, swapping foil blankets for dry robes, taking their vitals, treating any injuries and then discharging them into another tent. I have no idea where Jenny managed to recruit all of these people, or how she financed this, but those are questions for another day.

We take off our raincoats and look around.

'Do you know where we can find Jenny?' Irie asks a first-aider.

'She's in the next tent over, I think.'

We pass through the green tent and into the adjacent one. It's a café, with two rows of mess-hall tables on one side and a counter on the other where people are queuing for food.

'Fi!' someone shouts across the tent. I look over to see Beth waving at me. She is sitting at the end of a table with Celeste and Jenny, all of whom are wearing dry robes and clutching coffee cups. Vashti barks and runs towards them. Jenny stands, her face brimming with anticipation at seeing June. Once Vashti has stopped jumping and I've managed to put Ed on the table, I squeeze each of them in turn. We become a jumble of hot, tired bodies all knotted together with love.

'I'm so proud,' I say into the crook of someone's neck, 'I'm so, so proud.'

Everyone is nodding and smiling and hugging compulsively. With the baby handed back to Jenny, Irie goes to get us something to eat, telling me to sit down and catch up with my sisters. I love her for saying that.

'Your speech!' I shout, throwing my hands in the air. 'Oh my god, Celeste, you've got no idea what you've started! On the way here, we saw so many signs in people's windows. They all said the same thing – *you can't drown a movement!*'

'No way!' Beth and Celeste squeal, their flailing hands grasping at each other.

'That was *you*,' Celeste says to me emphatically. 'The livestream was *your idea*, Fi. I told you it was genius. You've spread this thing far wider than any of us—'

'Shut up!' I cut over her. 'Look at what you guys just did! I've never seen such bravery in all my life. I've never felt so… just so many extremes all at once.'

Beth and Celeste cackle like hyenas. I think the shock is making them hysterical because they're acting like we've just bumped into each other at an actual festival and not an emergency-aid camp set up to treat political prisoners.

'Have you seen the news?' Jenny asks with her phone in hand, putting a brusque stop to the hysterics.

'No,' the three of us reply.

'It's all kicking off.' She turns the phone to reveal a news presenter. We lean in to watch. The headline reads *Breaking: Prison Escape Causes Political Turmoil*. In the top right-hand corner of the screen, there is a screengrab from the livestream – a still of Celeste's defiant, soaking-wet face contorted into a righteous scream.

'There are calls for the prime minister to resign today after hundreds of people escaped from a detention centre on the Isle of Dogs,' the presenter says. 'Members of the environmental activist group Dissident Uprising livestreamed the prison break on a well-known influencer's account, Foliage Fifi – the surviving girlfriend of late eco-activist Edward Galbraith. One as-yet unidentified Dissident Uprising member took to the camera to expose an alleged government plot to drown inmates. The Dissident Detention Centre is close to the Thames Barrier, a vital flood defence which failed to withstand a tidal surge this morning as Storm Enlil battered England. The government is reportedly holding an emergency COBRA meeting at an unspecified location, though officials have yet to comment on accusations of intent to harm. Meanwhile, there is growing civil unrest throughout the country, with millions signing a petition calling for the immediate dissolution of parliament.'

'Holy fucking shit,' Beth says.

'Right?' Jenny says.

'Oh my actual god,' Celeste says.

'What's going on?' Irie asks, returning with a tray of food. But her voice is snatched away by an immense whirring sound that shakes the canvas walls of the tent. We pass around puzzled faces and then, without a word, leave the table and go outside. The rain is still pelting in furious sheets, and the sky is one solid mass of storm clouds. But despite the conditions, a helicopter is hovering above us like a dragonfly.

My first thought is that it's some kind of SWAT team come to arrest us *at best*, but then I see a camera positioned at the window. The blades of the helicopter oscillate in the air like someone rolling their *R*s down a megaphone. As we watch on, it struggles against the wind, attempting to land in the field. When it finally does, a small cohort of journalists jump out holding microphones. Jenny pulls various people into a meeting to discuss Dissident Uprising's media response. Just as I'm about to join them, I feel like something's missing. Like I've lost my phone or misplaced my purse. I pat my wet body down, trying to figure out what it could be. I look at the mess-hall table where we were just sitting. Irie's tray of food is still there.

But Ed is not.

In all the excitement about the helicopter, I forgot to bring him with me. I walk up and down the tent, looking under tables and asking passersby if they've seen him. I go up to the food counter where a man with a nose ring is tidying up.

'Have you seen a plant?'

'No,' he says dismissively, stacking empty trays.

'Are you sure? It was in a plastic pot. It didn't have any leaves.'

'What, that dead old stick?' he asks, looking behind him.

'Yes, that dead old stick,' I snap back, following his eyeline.

'I thought it was rubbish. I put it out with the compost.'

'You're joking me!'

The look on his face tells me that he is not. I walk around the counter and into the ad hoc kitchen. I find Ed's pot on top of the fridge, the one Ian gave me the night that Tracy dropped him on the floor. But Ed isn't in the pot.

'Compost's by the sink,' the man tells me with irritating nonchalance. I go over to the sink and open the bin. It's full of half-eaten croissants, gluey porridge and coffee granules. Beneath a layer of food waste, I spot the broken legs of a stick insect. I reach my hands inside and lift him out. Ed's dry soil falls away. His ashes are lost to the half-eaten spoilage of liberated protesters. There should be some kind of poetic justice in that, but I'm too tired to make sense of it. I cradle his bare root ball close to my chest. His branches poke into my skin. Although I know I should be devastated, I feel nothing.

Because he's gone, hasn't he? I think he's been gone since the day I saw his toothless smile. I don't know. All I know is that this isn't how it was supposed to end. Ed, a dead old stick, and me, a nonbeliever. But how can I keep believing in something I have so vehemently evangelised when this dead old stick has been in a state of decline since Banmora? Because of *me*, because of what *I* did, people are calling for the dissolution of parliament. If that's not enough to make him come back to me, perhaps he was never really here.

I hold the plant over the bin and look down at the food waste. I take a deep breath.

It's time to let go.

This is where a dead old stick belongs. This is where a dead old stick decomposes and becomes compost for someone else's garden. There is poetic justice in that, I'm sure.

I loosen my fingers.

Then, as the plant falls, a flash of colour catches my eye. Among the beige effluence of breakfast, a speck of green. I fish the plant out and peer closer.

On the tip of a single stem, something is emerging.

It is a fingernail-sized pin cushion of pine needles.

It is a yew tree, fulfilling the myth.

EPILOGUE

One year after The Final Strike

We don't often have breakfast together, but this morning is different. Beth said we could hold some kind of ceremony or intimate gathering, something to mark the occasion, but I told them no, I want to do this on my own. Still, breakfast feels special, with pastries from the local coffee shop and Celeste's superfood smoothies. It's one of her habits that I've come to enjoy – not just the smoothies but the hum of the blender in the morning. It's a sign that she and Beth are awake. That they are both here.

Bruce jumps onto the kitchen table, and Irie screams blue murder, still adjusting to life with pets. Vashti, also adjusting, chases after him. Beth and Celeste shout, 'Leave Bruce alone!' – a phrase that is fast becoming a household motto – and apologise.

As landladies go, I wouldn't call Irie laid-back. She's become a stickler for cleanliness, rediscovering the house proudness she'd lost to despair – and demanding that we do the same. I enjoy the exasperated way she tells us to put our shoes away. I think she does, too. She would have loved to have had daughters, she told me.

After breakfast, I put the plant in the front basket of my bike and cycle to East Peace. The journey from Clapton to Dalston is pleasant enough, especially since the trees have returned to leaf, but it's hot. Too hot. Still, the floodwater is deep within the trees' root systems, giving them an electric display of green that feels so different from this time last year. As I cycle through Hackney Downs, I pass a wildflower meadow and stop for a photo. There are red poppies, white daisies, blue cornflowers and the occasional mauve foxglove. I kneel down to take a picture. When I post the photo to my stories, I spot a text from Dad.

DEAR FIONA, THINKING OF YOU TODAY. ED LIVES ON IN YOUR MEMORIES, AND OURS TOO. LOOKING FORWARD TO SEEING YOU IN JUNE – AS IS JUNE, HA HA! LOVE FROM DAD (JOHN).

He follows up with a photo of my baby sister. She is sitting on the floor of the chicken coop with an egg clutched in one hand and the other reaching for a reluctant chicken. It's good of him to remember. Tracy hasn't, of course. The last we spoke, she said she was liquidating her assets to invest in cryptocurrency and hurling insults at Ian's divorce lawyers. According to her, she called it quits because Ian had joined 'the sheeple' – though I have my doubts that it was *her* who left *him*. Ian was making his contentions known back when I'd stayed with them in Strathyre. He's a reasonable person. There's only so long a reasonable person can live with an unreasonable one before that turns into irreconcilable differences.

Now Tracy is alone. I feel sorry for her. I know the dangers of solitude. I've tried to impart that wisdom. I've tried telling her that self-imposed alienation is a vicious cycle, but she doesn't want to hear it. 'I have all the friends I need on Facebook,' she told me.

I pull up outside East Peace and lock my bike to the railing, then pause to admire my artwork. It's been months since I finished the mural, but I get a thrill every time I see it. I painted it shortly after Irie agreed to a joint social enterprise, turning East Peace into a community garden and Dissident Uprising HQ. The artwork stretches across one side of a building, depicting a vibrant group of gardeners and activists who, this time, actually represent the diversity of our community. Behind them, there is a wave that tumbles from the sky and breaks into a carpet of flowers – no white horses in sight. Written at the top of the mural in big, bold script are the words *You can't drown a movement*.

I take the plant out of my basket and unlock the East Peace gate. I head towards the workshop which Dad helped us build last autumn. It's similar to his place – a cob roundhouse with a self-supporting roof. By the front door there's a brass plaque that reads *Paid for by our generous donors*.

After Juniper, people started throwing money at us. It was overwhelming. We went from an underground activist group to a national cause overnight, and as the hundreds turned into thousands, we scrabbled to make Dissident Uprising a proper organisation with ambitions beyond liberating the detention centre. Once we'd built the workshop, there was enough left over to pay Beth, Celeste and me a humble salary for at least a year. I took the role of art director, Beth, project manager and Celeste, actions coordinator, with Jenny lending fundraising support from afar. We use the workshop for meetings, events, debriefs and the occasional party. Right now, the tables are littered with plans for our first major action against the new government. They've delayed their promise to fix the Thames Barrier for a second month in a row. We're ready to tell them what we think about that.

Once parliament was dissolved, the leader of the opposition was elected to take the old prime minister's place, the latter escaping to the Cayman Islands and staying there. The new PM claims to be passionately dedicated to achieving net zero, but a few months ago, she was exposed for accepting donations from a fossil fuel company.

The work is never done.

I walk through the garden, past rows of early vegetables, tepees covered in sweet peas and a display of white rhododendrons. A bench sits in the shade of a tree, a poem by Tennyson etched across its slats. I open the workshop and switch on the solar-powered lights. When Ananya, the short-haired woman who led the prisoners onto the roof of the detention centre, arrives with a few other volunteers, we chat through what needs to be done that day, and I leave them to it.

I take my bike and the plant onto the Overground to Whitechapel, then wait on the District line platform. The last time I made this journey, I was the only one on the carriage. Today, I have to wait for a few trains to pass before I can fit my bike in. The population of London came out of hiding once the floodwaters had receded, returning to find their homes waterlogged and their lives in need of much rebuilding. But humans were made to adapt. We survive. I live in hope that, one day, we'll be granted the means to thrive.

I get off at Kew Gardens and cycle down Lichfield Road. The supercars are back in their gated driveways. The London plane trees are green. I look at the plant in my basket. While, in the days and weeks after Juniper, that first speck of green extended to every branch, it hasn't flowered in almost nine months.

There is a queue outside the main gates to Kew Gardens. I cycle to the side gate – the one reserved for locals – and lock my bike outside. I take the plant out of the basket and head for the Woodland Walk. The garden looks much like I remember it before the heat wave – verdant with life and planted with pollinator-friendly flowers. As I approach Queen Charlotte's Cottage, I see a large group of people crowded around the entrance to the boardwalk. It's an unexpected sight. Most people only come here for the Palm House, leaving the farthest reaches of the three-hundred-acre estate as peaceful as woodlands are supposed to be. When I reach the crowd, I stand on my toes and crane my neck over the throng of heads. I consider turning around and coming back another day. But today is *the day*. Unless I wait another year, it's now or never.

'What's everyone queuing for?' I ask a woman beside me.

'To see the flowers,' she says.

'What flowers?'

She doesn't reply, turning away to chat with her friends. It's comforting to see that London's famously standoffish nature has returned along with its people. The queue shuffles forward. As we approach the corner, a mob of cameras blocks my view. Journalists are interviewing outdoorsy-looking people in Kew Gardens uniforms.

'In all my years as a botanist,' a member of staff is saying, 'I've never seen anything like this. It's absolutely thrilling. It changes everything.'

'This particular specimen has been here for centuries,' says another, 'but we have no record of this happening before. Our experts are in the lab as we speak, conducting plant-tissue analysis to understand what's causing this.'

'Do you have any hypotheses?' a journalist asks.

'It could be something to do with soil quality,' the botanist answers, scratching her head, 'or perhaps cross-pollination. It's a real mystery. Yew trees are gymnosperms. They don't flower. They never have.'

I step off the boardwalk and cut the queue, ignoring a surge of complaints. I stride towards the tree. It droops over the corner like a weeping willow, creating a tunnel of evergreen branches. Except they're not just green. They're decorated in clusters of lily white. A cameraperson tells me to get out of shot. I duck underneath the branches and into the canopy of the tree. There, hidden from the view of the media circus, I pick a flower. It has ruffled white petals, a checkered yellow centre and slender, pollen-tipped stamens. It reminds me of the rhododendrons at East Peace. When I twist it between my fingers, it glistens in the dappled light.

It *is* a real mystery. But I have long since surrendered logic in the face of such things. The earth is full of intrigue. It possesses inexplicable magic – the kind of magic that allows a houseplant to materialise on a doorstep, with no clue as to its origins. What's clear to me now is that it doesn't matter where it came from, just that it did.

I squeeze inside the outer trunk, through the split in the wood that Ed once called his front door. The ground is covered in little white petals, creating a feathery mattress underfoot. I kneel in front of the carving.

E + C WOZ ERE

I trace the lettering with my fingertip. I breathe deeply and focus my attention on the melodic birdsong, drowning out the babble of the nearby scrum. I clear a space on the ground below the carving, pushing aside petals with my bare hands until the fertile mulch of the forest floor is exposed. I take a trowel and a bottle of water out of my bag. I dig a hole. I remove the plant from the pot and place it inside the hole. I stop to admire its frilly branches. It kept on living, even after it died. I fill the hole with soil. I push the plant down with both palms. I water it in. I don't cry.

I sit back in front of the little yew tree, the dead heartwood surrounding it like a protective fortress. Here, in the centre of this ancient place, it will continue to grow. From the decay of an imperfect love story, from the shadows of unbearable loss, light will find the leaves of this remarkable tree and summon it skyward.

I look up at the chandelier of blooming boughs above me. A single flower spirals down from a branch that is heavy with blossom. It lands on my lap.

'Hello, you,' I say with a soft smile.

Hello, you, Ed replies.

AUTHOR'S NOTE

The River Thames last broke its banks in 1928. Almost three decades later, a deadly tidal surge killed hundreds. In 1984, the Thames Barrier was constructed, protecting London from tidal surges and safeguarding billions of pounds' worth of property. However, the barrier was not designed to withstand climate change. It was closed four times in the 1980s, 35 times in the 1990s, 75 times in the 2000s and 74 times in the 2010s. The Environment Agency reports that, without significant investment, sea-level rise and extreme weather could cause the Thames Barrier to fail. Critics say that efforts to address this risk lack the urgency and ambition required to climate-proof the barrier – as political action on climate change so often does. This storyline was informed by 'Before the Flood: How Much Longer Will the Thames Barrier Protect London?' by Karen McVeigh (The Guardian), 'The Thames Barrier' (Royal Geographical Society, 21st Century Challenges) and 'Risk and Uncertainty: Calculating the Thames Barrier's Future' (Carbon Brief).

The crackdown on protest rights in the UK is well-documented and, at the time of writing, an ongoing effort. In 2023, the UN High Commissioner for Human Rights, Volker Türk, urged the UK government to reverse the 'deeply troubling' Public Order Bill, calling it 'incompatible with the UK's international human rights obligations regarding people's rights to freedom of expression, peaceful assembly and association.' The speculative elements of this story might feel implausible, but in 2024, five Just Stop Oil activists received the longest ever sentences for non-violent direct action in British history. Not for taking action, but for merely *talking about it* on Zoom. Their demand? That the government end new oil and gas exploration in the North Sea – an energy policy which would bring the UK into long-overdue alignment with climate science.

The term 'social cohesion' is taken from *Heat Wave: A Social Autopsy of Disaster in Chicago* by Eric Klinenberg. This book was crucial in understanding the impact of a heat wave on a major city and the unjust effects of extreme weather on impoverished communities. *The Immortal Yew* by Tony Hall helped me better appreciate these exceptional trees and their connection to druid mythology. *The Origins of Totalitarianism* by political theorist Hannah Arendt laid the groundwork for my exploration of cynicism and how it can be manufactured to stifle movements for change. *Out of the Darkness: Greenham Voices 1981 – 2000* by Kate Kerrow and Rebecca Mordan informed Irie's background. There is an ongoing archival effort to ensure that Greenham Common Women's Peace Camp isn't forgotten by history. To this end, I recommend visiting greenhamwomeneverywhere.co.uk.

The island of Banmora is inspired by the remarkable, self-sufficient community on the Isle of Eigg, where I penned the first draft. Until the sixteenth century, Eigg was known in Gaelic as Eilean Nimban More, or the Island of the Powerful Women, due to local legend that warrior women once roamed the land. Banmora is named after Eigg's Loch Nam Ban Mora – the Loch of the Big Women – making it the ideal location to set an eco-feminist story. Thanks also to the team at Dalston Eastern Curve Garden, whose community work and impressive mural inspired East Peace.

The author Lora Mathis first coined the phrase *radical softness as a weapon*. At the time, this gave me permission to find not only peace with my vulnerability but power. I recognise that emotionality is not without risk for most people. To be soft, you need to be safe. I am committed to a world where everyone has equal access to the means that got me here.

ACKNOWLEDGEMENTS

Thank you to my agent, Hayley Steed, and the team at Janklow & Nesbit, for taking this novel from a dream to a reality. Thank you to my editors, Nicole Luongo and Annie Chagnot at Park Row Books and Jenna Gordon at VERVE Books. Although the ideas I've explored here aren't radical to me, I appreciate that they could be considered subversive. I am so grateful to have found editors who didn't shy away from that.

Thank you to my spouse, Alexander, for providing the emotional security I needed to make this happen, for taking care of housework and dog walks so that I could write, and for fourteen years of love from which to draw inspiration.

Thank you to my family. To my mum, Shaz, for nurturing my love of literature and for your fantastic ideas – so many of which made it to the page! To my dad, Neil, for your unwavering support. To my sisters, Hannah and Rebekah, for reading early drafts and loving me like only two magical sisters can – you make writing powerful women easy. To my brother, Dan, for celebrating my wins. To my nibling, Kobi, and my nieces, Eliza and Evelyn – baby June is inspired by many happy memories of being your Aunty Mimi. And thank you to Chloe Eversfield, my oldest and dearest friend. Wellspring Farm planted so many seeds for this story, as did our enduring sisterhood.

Thank you to my early readers: Indi Heath, Chloe Eversfield, Fiona Nicholls and Aimee Keeble. Special thanks to Fi for lending your name to my protagonist – I don't think there's higher praise of your character than that, my petal! To the members of my writing group, Hannah Martin, Julian Moorman, Laila Sumpton and Abby

Joy. To Flora Baker and Elizabeth Monaghan for proofreading. To Jack Ramm for your indispensable advice and moral support. To Henry Fry, Lex Croucher and Kate Davies for demystifying publishing. To Franziska Grobke for your climbing expertise. To Priya Oades for making me look much cooler than I am in photos. To Lee Quane for your remarkable generosity during the pandemic, without which I'd have had to give up writing. And to Maggie Ford (forever Miss Jones to me) for setting me on this path.

Thank you to activists everywhere. This book is a love letter to you. Whenever I'm struggling to feel hopeful, there you are, marching in the streets, occupying boardrooms and using your big, beautiful hearts to tell our story. And thanks to you, dear reader. I started writing as a child and never dared dream that one day, you would be holding this book in your hands. I feel so privileged that you chose to read it.

BOOK CLUB QUESTIONS

1. What do you think the author is trying to say about protest? What specific critiques are they making regarding the laws and attitudes surrounding protest rights in the UK?
2. What are your thoughts on collective action in the text and in reality? Despite its history of being effective, why do you think Fifi becomes disillusioned with collective action?
3. Do you think Ed's reasons for breaking up with Fifi were justified? Do you think they could have salvaged their relationship, or would he always have wanted her to put everything on the line for climate justice?
4. Why do you think Fifi's mother, Tracy, is the antithesis of her daughter and her ex-husband, John? Can you empathise with how Tracy might have fallen down the conspiracy pipeline? What do her views say about society as a whole?
5. What did this novel teach you about the history of organising and activism? Is there anything you weren't aware of in the UK's history, and if so, why do you think it was not part of our curriculum?
6. Fifi struggles to find her place among the activists, feeling throughout the novel that she is unable to contribute to Dissident Uprising's mission. How do you feel about her realisation that 'radical' acts of love and softness are just as important to the movement as direct action?
7. The author also highlights the experience of Black women activists, who are often subjected to complete erasure or targeted violence. What did you think about their stories? Does comparing these stories to Ed's sense of entitlement

and confidence in his own safety on the frontline affect your perception of him?

8. Throughout the text, it is difficult to tell if Ed was reincarnated as the plant, or if Fifi is simply imagining this due to her grief. Were there moments when you doubted her experience? Do you believe that Ed was communicating with her?

9. Which themes resonated with you the most from this novel? How do you think you can apply what you have learnt to the real world?

10. Were you shocked to find that a lot of this novel is rooted in fact, such as the government so far failing to climate-proof the Thames Barrier? How did you feel when realising that Fifi's reality is not so different from our own?

ABOUT THE AUTHOR

(Photo credit: Priya Oades)

EMILY BUCHANAN grew up on the Kent coast, where her first reader was her little sister, for whom she wrote bedtime stories. After studying English Literature at the University of East Anglia, she worked as a multidisciplinary creative for environmental NGOs, with a focus on climate and conservation campaigns. She lives in Norwich with her pianist spouse, a small herd of animals and more houseplants than she cares to admit. *Send Flowers* is her first novel.

emilybuchanan.co.uk
@emilyebuchanan

VERVE BOOKS

Launched in 2018, VERVE Books is an independent
publisher of page-turning, diverse and original
fiction from fresh and impactful voices.

Our books are connected by rich storytelling, vividly
imagined settings and unforgettable characters.
The list is tightly curated by a small team of
passionate booklovers whose hope is that
if you love one VERVE book, you'll love them all!

WANT TO JOIN THE CONVERSATION AND FIND OUT MORE ABOUT WHAT WE DO?

Catch us on social media or sign up to our newsletter
for all the latest news from VERVE HQ.

vervebooks.co.uk/signup

📷 f 🐦 ♪ **@VERVE_Books**